# About the Authors

*USA TODAY* bestselling author **Joanne Rock** credits her decision to write romance to a book she picked up during a flight delay that engrossed her so thoroughly, she didn't mind at all when her flight was delayed two more times. Giving her readers the chance to escape into another world has motivated her to write over ninety books for a variety of Mills & Boon series.

**Lara Lacombe** is a recovering research scientist turned college professor who now spends her days writing and wrangling a toddler. She lives in Texas with her family and two entitled cats, and loves chocolate and her Crock Pot. She uses Facebook to procrastinate—stop by Lara Lacombe Books if you'd like to chat!

**Brenda Jackson** is a *New York Times* bestselling author of more than one hundred romance titles. Brenda lives in Jacksonville, Florida, and divides her time between family, writing and travelling. Email Brenda at authorbrendajackson@gmail.com or visit her on her website at brendajackson.net

D1385918

# Irresistible Bachelors

# Irresistible Bachelors:
# Protecting her Honour

**JOANNE ROCK**

**LARA LACOMBE**

**BRENDA JACKSON**

MILLS & BOON

First Published in Great Britain 2021
by Mills & Boon, an imprint of HarperCollins*Publishers* Ltd,
1 London Bridge Street, London, SE1 9GF

www.harpercollins.co.uk

HarperCollins*Publishers*
1st Floor, Watermarque Building,
Ringsend Road, Dublin 4, Ireland

IRRESISTIBLE BACHELORS: PROTECTING HER HONOUR
© 2021 Harlequin Books S.A.

*The Rancher's Bargain* © 2018 Harlequin Books S.A.
*The Marine's Christmas Case* © 2017 Harlequin Books S.A.
*Bachelor Undone* © 2011 Brenda Streater Jackson

Special thanks and acknowledgement are given to Joanne Rock for her contribution to the *Texas Cattleman's Club: Bachelor Auction* series.

Special thanks and acknowledgement are given to Lara Lacombe for her contribution to *The Coltons of Shadow Creek* series.

ISBN 978-0-263-30295-0

**MIX**
Paper from
responsible sources
FSC™ C007454

# THE RANCHER'S BARGAIN

**JOANNE ROCK**

# One

*It is okay to say no to unnecessary crazy.*

Lydia Walker repeated it like a mantra while she read the digital headline from a story that had run in the Royal, Texas, newspaper earlier in the week while she'd been out of town.

*Local woman boosts charity bachelor auction with $100K bid!*

Seated at her tiny kitchen table with a cup of coffee grown cold, Lydia hovered her finger over the scroll button on her cell phone. She wished she could just swipe right and not worry about the "local woman" who happened to be her irresponsible sister Gail. The impulsive sibling who did *not* have $100,000 to her name. What had Gail been thinking?

In spite of herself, Lydia started reading the article again.

*Gail Walker, a local entrepreneur, made the surprise bid on Lloyd Richardson, a local rancher. Ms. Walker could not be reached for comment while she is out of town on a romantic getaway with her chosen bachelor, but the Great Bachelor Auction master of ceremonies, James Harris, said he's grateful for the generous donation that benefits the Pancreatic Cancer Research Foundation. "This is what the event is all about..."*

Closing her eyes, Lydia flipped the phone facedown on the table to stop herself from going over the story a third time.

*Definitely unnecessary crazy.*

She had just gotten back into town after a visit to her mother's home in Arkansas for Thanksgiving, a trip she'd been guilted into since she hadn't been home in almost two years. Her mom had used the time to corner Lydia about being in Fiona's upcoming wedding to a fourth husband, making the holiday a total disaster. Lydia had wanted her sister to make the long drive with her, but Gail had insisted she needed to stay in Royal and personally oversee her fledgling grocery delivery service. An excuse Lydia had accepted, proud of Gail for doing something fiscally responsible for a change.

Ha! Apparently, Gail just wanted to stay in town to bid on a sexy bachelor during the event at the swanky Texas Cattleman's Club. Had the word already gotten out around town that Gail didn't have the money? Lydia scanned the Royal paper for more news but found only stories about the auction's lone bachelorette, Tessa Noble, and her date with a local rancher. There was no follow-up article about Gail's date or her outrageous bid.

Yet.

Lydia's stomach knotted. How could Gail do something like that to a *charity*, for crying out loud? Furthermore, they shared the same last name. How did it look for the Walker women, both trying to start their own business, when they didn't pay their debts?

Anger flaring, she flipped her phone screen toward her again and dialed her sister's number. As the oldest of eight siblings, Lydia was used to high drama in the family. But for most of her life, the main perpetrator had been her mother, a woman who had parlayed her parenting experience into a successful homemaking blog, *House Rules*. Fiona Walker's online followers loved her "whimsical" approach to childrearing that Lydia viewed as flighty at best and, at times, downright dangerous. Lydia had hoped Royal, Texas, would be a fresh start for her and Gail once the youngest of their siblings was old enough to fend for himself with their mom.

But now, with the mortifying news of Gail's over-the-top bachelor auction bid, Lydia had to admit that her sister hadn't fallen far from the maternal tree.

"Lydia!" Her sister squealed her name as she answered her phone. "You'll never guess where I am!"

Frustration simmered.

"I certainly hope you're at the Pancreatic Cancer Research Foundation explaining how you're going to magically make one hundred thousand dollars appear," Lydia snapped, powerless to restrain herself. "Gail, what on earth are you doing?"

Anxious and irate, she paced around her half-finished kitchen in the house she'd been slowly renovating to one day open an in-home child care business. She nearly tripped on the flooring samples she'd carefully laid out by the sliding glass door leading to the backyard. The toe of her slipper sent Spanish cedar and mahogany samples flying over the ash and buckthorn pieces.

"I am having a romantic holiday with the man of my dreams," her sister retorted, her tone shifting from excited to petulant. "Is it too much to ask for you to be happy for me? For once?"

Lydia covered her eyes with one hand, remembering her mother had said those same words to her—almost verbatim—just last week when Lydia refused to be in her wedding. Now, her head throbbed while the morning sunlight poured in through the back door. "I'm happy that you're having a good time. But I'm very worried about how you're going to cover the bid you placed at the bachelor auction. Have you spoken with the cancer foundation?"

"I'll bet that's why my credit card didn't work yesterday at the spa," Gail mused. In the background, music that sounded like it came from a mariachi band was growing louder. "I forgot about the payment to the bachelor auction."

"What payment?" Lydia pressed, heading back to the kitchen table to clear her plate and cup. "You don't have the kind of money you bid."

She held the phone on her shoulder, pinning it to her cheek while she set the dishes in the sink.

"And I'll figure it out after vacation, okay, Ms. Worrywart?" Her sister raised her voice to be heard over the music. "Oh, and just FYI, I'm ignoring calls from anyone I don't know this week."

"Who has been calling you?" Apprehension spiked. "The charity people?"

"No, the guy who was in charge that night. John? James?" Gail sighed. "Just forget it, okay? Right now, I've got to get back to my margarita before the ice melts!"

"Gail, wait—"

But her screen already read, "Call Ended." And she knew her sister well. There wasn't a chance Gail would answer if she phoned again.

*It is okay to say no to unnecessary crazy.*

The words had helped Lydia survive her teen-age years. But right now, the mantra didn't roll off the tongue so well when she thought about how the local folks who had worked hard to raise money for charity were being misled. The Texas Cattleman's Club had hosted the event, and their members were a who's who list of the town's most influential people. Lydia wanted to put roots down in Royal. She'd already bought the fixer-upper property to start her child care business here. The last thing she needed was a mark against her family name because of Gail's impulsiveness.

Maybe she could at least explain the situation to someone before the news surfaced about Gail's lack of payment.

Scrolling back to the news piece, she found the name she was looking for. James Harris. The MC of the event must have been the one who'd tried contacting Gail. She'd missed seeing his photo in the margin of the story the first time, too dismayed by her sister's behavior to see beyond the text of the story. But now, Lydia's eyes lingered on the image of the man who was also the current president of the Texas Cattleman's Club.

Handsome didn't *begin* to describe him. The photo showed him in front of the organization's historic clubhouse building, a fawn-colored Stetson shielding his face from the Texas sun. Tall and well built, he wore a fitted gray jacket that skimmed im-

pressive muscles. Broad where a man should be.
Lean in the hips. An angular jaw with a great smile.
She couldn't see his eyes clearly because they were
shadowed by the brim of his hat, but his skin was
a warm, inviting brown.

She blinked fast to banish the image from her
brain since she could not afford to be sidelined by
the man's potent sex appeal. Lydia was not in the
market for romance. Her mother's active, dramatic
love life had given Lydia a front-row seat for the
way romance changed people. Fiona had metamor-
phosed into someone new for each guy she'd dated,
heedless of how her whims affected the whole family. Lydia wasn't looking for even mild flirtation,
*especially* not with someone her sister had bilked
out of a small fortune.

She knew better than to try to fix things that were
out of her control, but she could at least extend Mr.
Harris the common courtesy of explaining Gail's
situation. And, perhaps, learn possible options for
compromise on the bill so she could speak sensibly
to her sister upon her return. If she could still salvage some goodwill in the community in spite of
Gail's fake bid, it would be a minor miracle.

Lydia had an appointment to meet with the contractor who was supposed to work on her kitchen
at noon. But right after that, she'd stop by the Texas
Cattleman's Club.

And hope with all her heart that James Harris was an understanding man.

"Lydia Walker is here to see you," the disembodied voice announced through James Harris's office intercom system.

He straightened from where he'd been practicing his golf swing in his office at the clubhouse. Although he'd never been much of a golfer, he had a golf tournament on his calendar and his competitive streak bristled at the idea of bringing down his foursome. Besides, focusing on a sport during his lunch break helped distract him from the knot of stress at the base of his spine. He'd never guessed the amount of work that came with his new position in the TCC, duties that ate into his time running his own ranch every day. But to complicate matters immeasurably, he now had a toddler nephew to raise.

When his brother, Parker, and Parker's wife had died in a car accident three months ago, James had been devastated. But in addition to his own grief at losing a loved one he'd deeply respected, he had been struggling with the fact that Parker's will entrusted James with the care of his son, Teddy. The weight of that responsibility threatened to take his knees out from under him if he allowed himself to dwell on it too long.

"Walker?" James repeated. The stress knot in

his back tightened more at the mention of his visitor's name. Setting aside the putter, he walked closer to the intercom. "As in the woman who ran off without paying her bachelor bid last week?"

How could someone publicly bid money they didn't have? Or maybe she did have the money, but she just didn't care to give the $100,000 she promised to the Pancreatic Cancer Research Foundation. Unwilling to risk the bad publicity, especially for an event he'd supervised, he'd ended up covering the debt himself. Better to keep the club out of the papers.

That didn't mean the matter was settled.

"That was *Gail* Walker." The woman at the desk out front lowered her voice. "Maybe Lydia is a relative."

"Send her in." He kicked two golf balls under the couch near the window. Lately, he didn't mind extending his hours on-site at the clubhouse since there was a child care facility in the building and it seemed the one place his nephew was content. At home, Teddy was a handful. And then some.

James strode toward his office door to greet his guest. He hoped she was carrying a big fat check. Because while James hadn't begrudged spending his personal funds on a worthy cause, he couldn't help but resent a woman who felt no obligation to uphold a social contract.

Pulling open the office door, he could see he'd startled the woman on the other side.

Tall and slim, she had light brown hair and honey-colored skin that set off wide hazel eyes. She was dressed in khakis and a neat white blouse with a long pink sweater belted at her waist. She had one hand raised as if to knock while she nibbled at her lush lower lip. Her gaze darted anxiously to his.

A wholly unexpected attraction blindsided him.

He stared at her a beat too long.

"Lydia Walker?" He offered his hand belatedly, irritated with himself for the wayward thoughts. "I'm James Harris."

"Nice to meet you." Her handshake was cool and firm. Businesslike. "Thank you for seeing me, Mr. Harris."

"Please, call me James." Standing back, he waved her into the office, leaving the door open to the club-house behind her. He glanced over toward the double doors leading into the child care facility, half expecting to see Teddy banging on the window. Or a child care worker running for the hills. But all was quiet. Thankfully. Returning his attention to his guest, he said, "Have a seat."

James gestured to one of the leather chairs near the windows overlooking the garden and swimming pool. The TCC president's office had been remodeled along with the rest of the historic building. Larger windows and higher ceilings now let in more light, and there were brighter colors in the decor. But the dark hardwood floors and oversize leather furnishings retained the feel of a men's club from a bygone era. Historic photographs and artifacts from the club's storied past filled the walls.

For a few hours here each week, he could pretend his life was normal again. That he wasn't a stand-in father struggling to provide a home for an eighteen-month-old boy who surely felt the absence of his parents, yet was far too young to express himself. Dragging his fractured thoughts back to the appealing woman in his office, James focused on the here and now.

"Can I get you something to drink, Ms. Walker? Coffee or tea? A water?"

"No, thank you. And please call me Lydia." She set her simple leather handbag on the floor by her feet while he lowered himself into the chair beside hers. "I won't take up much of your time. I just came to see what I could to do in regard to my sister's debt. I've been out of town, and I only just read the news this morning."

"Ah." He nodded, admiring her frank approach. "I appreciate that, Lydia, but I'm not sure how much I'm at liberty to divulge regarding your sister's… finances."

He was no expert in the law, but he felt sure that if Gail Walker hadn't specifically asked her sister to intervene on her behalf, he shouldn't discuss the woman's bad debt with her sibling.

"I'm not asking for any information." Lydia sat forward in her seat, her expression serious. "I already know that Gail couldn't possibly pay what she promised the charity on the night of the auction. I'm sure she will contact you when she returns from her trip. But until then, I wondered about a potential compromise."

So much for his hope that Lydia Walker came bearing a check.

"A compromise?" Impatience flared. He wasn't interested in a nominal payment toward the balance. "This isn't a credit card debt where you can take out a consolidation loan and suddenly pay less than you owe."

Lips compressed in a flat line, she straightened in her seat. "And I'm aware of that. But she can't produce funds she doesn't have. So I had hoped to give Gail some ideas for what she could do instead. Perhaps donate her time volunteering for the charity in some way?"

Her hazel eyes turned greener as she bristled. The color intrigued him, even as he knew he shouldn't take any pleasure from her frustration. She'd meant well.

"I see." He nodded, thinking over her offer. She didn't know that the charity had already been paid, but he wasn't sure he wanted to share his own contribution. Instead, he found himself asking, "May I ask your interest in the matter? Why not just let your sister contact us when she returns home?"

She arched an eyebrow. "Do you have any siblings, James?"

The question cut straight through him, his grief still fresh. "Not as of three months ago."

The terse sound of the words didn't begin to convey the ache behind them.

Lydia paled. "I'm so sorry. I had no idea—"

"You couldn't possibly know." Stuffing down the rawness of the loss, James stood suddenly, needing to move. He headed toward the minifridge and retrieved two small bottles of water, more for something to do than anything else. Still, he brought one back to Lydia and then cracked open his own. "My brother and his wife died in a car crash this fall. Parker lived on the other side of the state, but we were still close."

He had no living relatives now except for his nephew. His own mother had died of breast cancer when he was very young, and his father had passed after a heart attack two years ago. The Grim Reaper had been kicking him in the teeth lately, taking those he loved.

Except for Teddy. And James would move heaven and earth to keep that little hellion happy and safe. Even if it meant giving up the boy to his maternal grandparents—an option he was investigating since his schedule didn't allow the time the boy needed.

"I can't imagine how difficult that has been." The concern in her voice, the empathy, was unmistakable. "Most of my brothers and sisters are still back home in Arkansas, but I check in with them often. Gail moved here with me to—start over. I can't help but feel somewhat responsible for her."

He wondered why. Lured by curiosity about this beautiful woman, he almost sat back down beside her to continue their conversation. But a noise outside the office—the cadence of urgent voices speaking in low tones—distracted him from replying. He glanced toward the door that opened onto the clubhouse and saw the building's administrative assistant speaking with one of the women who worked in the child care facility.

A feeling of foreboding grew. He knew it couldn't be the boy's tree nut allergy acting up or they would have notified him. But what if Teddy had overstayed his welcome in the child care facility? James hadn't been able to keep a nanny for more than two weeks with his nephew's swings from shy and withdrawn to uncontrollable bouts of temper. James had no plan B if the TCC child care couldn't take the toddler for at least part of the time. The boy's only grandparents lived five hours away—too far for babysitting help.

"Lydia, you needn't worry about the donation,"

he told his guest, the stress at the base of his spine ratcheting higher up his back. As compelling as he found his unexpected guest, he needed to end this meeting so he could see what was going on with the boy. "I've already taken care of the matter with the charity, and I'll speak to your sister about it when she returns to Royal."

He remained standing, hoping his response would satisfy Lydia and send her on her way. Bad enough he'd felt an immediate attraction to the woman. But he was too strapped emotionally and mentally this week to figure out a creative solution to help her sister work off a debt that James had already paid.

"Taken care of?" Lydia sounded wary. "What does that mean?"

Tension throbbed in his temples. He would have never guessed that concerns about one tiny kid could consume a person day and night. But that's exactly where he found himself right now, worrying about the boy around the clock, certain that his lack of consistent care was going to screw up the child Parker had been so proud of.

"I paid off the bid myself," James clarified while he watched the child care worker edge around the administrative assistant and bustle toward his office door.

Damn it.

"You can't go in there," the front desk secretary called after her, while James waited, tension vibrating through him.

From behind him, Lydia Walker's gasp was followed by the whispered words, "One hundred thousand dollars?"

Damn it again.

Pivoting toward Lydia, he already regretted his haste. But he needed to concentrate on whatever new crisis was developing.

"That information is confidential, and stays between the two of us. I only shared it so you won't worry about the bid anymore."

Standing, Lydia gaped at him. She shook her head, the warm streaks in her brown hair glinting in the sunlight streaming through the windows behind her. "I'll worry twice as much now. How can we ever hope to repay you?"

He didn't have time to answer before a childish cry filled the room.

His nephew, little Teddy Harris, came barreling toward him with big crocodile tears running down both cheeks, his wispy baby curls bouncing with each jarring step. The two women stepped out of the boy's way as he ran straight into James's leg. Crushing the wool gabardine in damp baby hands, the boy let out a wail that all of Royal must have heard.

With proof of his inadequacy as a stand-in parent clinging to his calf, James had never felt so powerless. Reaching down, he lifted his nephew in his arms to offer whatever comfort he could, knowing it wasn't going to be enough. The toddler thrashed in his arms, his back arching, kicking with sock-clad feet.

James had all he could do to hang on to the squirming kid let alone soothe him.

Until, miraculously, the child stilled. The two women lingering at the threshold of his office door were both smiling as they watched. James had to crane his neck to see the boy's expression since Teddy peered at something over his shoulder, tantrum forgotten.

For a split second, he wondered what on earth that could be. Until he remembered the enticing woman in the room with them.

He sensed her presence behind him in a hint of feminine fragrance and a soft footfall on the hardwood floor. It was James's only warning, before her voice whispered, "peekaboo!" in a way that tickled against his left ear.

Teddy erupted in giggles.

It was, without question, the best magic trick James had ever witnessed. And he knew immediately that there was a way Ms. Lydia Walker could repay him.

# Two

Once the child in James's arms had settled down, the Texas Cattleman's Club's handsome president set the boy on his feet while he went to speak in low tones to the two women who hovered near the entrance of his office.

Lydia did her best not to eavesdrop even though she was wildly curious about the identity of the toddler. The brief bio she'd read of James online hadn't mentioned a wife or family, and he didn't wear a wedding ring. Not that it was any of her business. But clearly, the child was his based on the way the toddler had flung chubby arms around James's leg like he was home base in a game of tag.

For that matter, they shared the same brown eyes flecked with gold, as well.

A gentle tug on the sleeve of her sweater made Lydia realize she'd gotten sidetracked during this round of "peekaboo." She glanced back to the sober little boy in front of her, his damp hand clutching the ribbed cuff of her sweater to help him keep balance. He looked sleepy and out of sorts as he wobbled on unsteady legs, but the game was still entertaining him. Obediently, she covered her face to hide again, remembering how much her youngest brother had loved playing.

"Thank you," James said to the woman from the front desk. "I'll take care of it."

Then he turned and walked back toward Lydia.

She watched him through her fingers as she hid her face from Teddy. Tall and lean, James Harris moved with the grace of an athlete even in jeans and boots. His button-down shirt looked custom fitted, the only giveaway to his position at the club. Without the Stetson he'd been wearing in the photo she'd seen of him online, she could now appreciate the golden color of his eyes. His dark hair was close cropped, the kind of cut that meant regular trips to the barber. Everything about him was neat. Well-groomed. Incredibly good-looking.

The sight of him was enough to make her throat dry right up in feminine appreciation. She might have forgotten all about the peekaboo game if

Teddy hadn't patted her knee. Belatedly, she slid her hands from her face and surprised the toddler again.

The boy giggled softly before resting his head on her knee, as though he was too tired to hold himself upright any longer. Poor little guy. She rubbed his back absently while the baby fidgeted with his feet.

"I think he'll be down for the count in another minute," she told James quietly. "He's an adorable child."

"He's normally a handful," James admitted, taking the seat across from her. "You're very good with him."

His charming smile made her breath hitch in her chest. James Harris's photo online hadn't fully prepared her for how devastatingly sexy he'd be in person, an attraction she had no business feeling for a man who had a family of his own. A man who'd bailed her sister out of a thorny financial mess that could have very well derailed both their careers. How could Lydia ever thank him?

"As the oldest of eight kids, I had a lot of first-hand experience," she admitted, accustomed to glossing over the hurtful aspects of feeling more like hired help than her mother's daughter. "I've worked as a nanny ever since and I hope to open my own child care business out of my home this year." It couldn't hurt to start spreading the word to people in the community with young families. "Do you have any other children?"

The question sounded benign enough, right? Not like she was fishing to find out more about whether or not this handsome man was married with a house full of adorable offspring waiting to greet him at the end of the day.

"No." A shadowed expression crossed his face. "Teddy is my brother's son. And up until Teddy's parents died three months ago, I was a bachelor spending every waking hour running a ranch or performing my duties here. My life has been turned upside down."

She couldn't deny the momentary relief that James was single. But just as quickly, she thought of the sadness and weariness in his voice and what that meant for Teddy. Her heart ached for all the little boy had lost. She stared down at him, his soft cheek still resting on her knee while he shifted his weight from one foot to the other, his light-up sneakers flashing back and forth at odd intervals while he rocked.

"I'm so sorry." She smoothed a palm across the back of the boy's gray dinosaur T-shirt. "For you both. I can't imagine how difficult that transition has been to deal with, especially when you're grieving such a tragic loss."

She glanced back at James to find him studying her.

His fixed attention rattled her, reminding her that he'd just admitted to being a single man. Warmth rose to her cheeks and she looked away, trying to remember the thread of the conversation.

"You could help us immeasurably." James's voice was pitched low in deference to the weary baby between them, but the tone made her think of pillow talk. Intimate conversations between two lovers who knew one another incredibly well.

Who would have guessed a whisper could be so seductive?

"I'm—um." She tried to think beyond murmured confidences and came up blank, her brain already supplying images of tangled sheets and limbs. "And how would that be?"

"You arrived at my door looking for a compromise on your sister's bid, and we've just found the perfect one." He pointed to Teddy, who had stopped moving, his eyes closed. Breathing even. "If you'll take the job of Teddy's nanny, you can consider Gail's debt paid in full."

His suggestion staggered her. Called her from her sensual daydreams.

"She bid *one hundred thousand dollars*," Lydia reminded him, wondering where she should lay Teddy down for a nap. "You'd be forgiving the cost of a home for the sake of child care. That's far too generous of you."

He shook his head, his jaw flexing. "I haven't

kept a nanny for more than two weeks because he's such a handful, between the tantrums and days of being withdrawn. We could have a trial period to see how it worked out." He seemed to warm to the idea quickly, laying out terms. "If you stayed for a trial period of two months, then I'd forgive half the debt. Stick around for a year, and we'll call it even."

"You can't be serious." She got distracted around him after a few minutes. How could she ever work in his home for a year?

"I'm running out of options and I can't afford this much time away from my ranching business. You have no idea what it would be worth to me to know my brother's boy is in good hands."

She couldn't miss the desperation in his eyes. In his voice. But as much as she felt called to help him, it wasn't her debt to pay. Gail was the one who should be providing free nanny services, not her. Still, another thought trickled through, making her realize things weren't quite so simple. No matter how strongly she felt that Gail needed to clean up her own messes, Lydia recognized that without James's clearing the debt with the charity, the Walker name might have become the kiss of death for a new business in a close-knit community like Royal. While she wrestled with what to do, she turned her attention to the sleeping baby between them.

"First things first, we should find a comfortable place for Teddy." She reached to lift him, but James moved closer.

"I can get him." He slipped his hands around the boy's waist to pick him up, his hand briefly brushing against her calf and causing a whole riot of sensations in her before he shifted the child to rest on his shoulder. "And you don't need to make a decision about my offer right now. If you're okay with continuing our meeting another time, I should be leaving for the day anyhow. I think he'll stay asleep if I put him in his car seat."

Lydia tried to ignore the residual tingling in her skin. She appreciated the opportunity he was giving her to think about his proposal. And distance from his striking good looks would give her the chance to think with a clearer head.

"You have someone to watch him today?" Lydia didn't mean to sound like she was questioning his arrangements for the child. She was just trying to keep the focus on Teddy and not the heady jolt of attraction she was feeling.

She stood to follow James toward the door.

"My foreman's daughter is home from college for the holidays, and she agreed to give me afternoon help two days a week for the next month. That's as much child care as I've got covered when I'm not here. Provided she doesn't give up on Teddy, too, when he has his next atomic meltdown." He sounded frustrated and she understood why.

James shouldered the leather diaper bag that the child care worker had set near the door to his office, then lifted his Stetson from the coat rack and dropped it into place. When she stepped out of the room, he locked the door behind them. She couldn't miss the way his large hands cradled the child so gently against his broad chest. The gesture called to her, reminding her of dreams she had for her own children one day.

Not that she was thinking of James in that way. She must be overtired and stressed to let her imagination wander like that. The sooner she made tracks out of here and away from James's tempting presence, the better.

As they left the clubhouse and strode out into the December sunlight, James tugged a blanket from an exterior pocket of the diaper bag and laid it over the sleeping boy. The day was mild, but with the holidays approaching, the temperatures had been dropping. Lydia tipped her face into the breeze, grateful for the cooler air on her too-warm skin.

"I researched the child care facilities in town when I got the idea to open a full-service business here, and I know there's a definite need." Royal was thriving, and the demographics for young families were a particular area of growth. "I've heard there are waiting lists at the most coveted places."

James nodded in response. "You've got that right. When I called one day care they said families reserve space when they're pregnant, even knowing they might not put a child into the system for a full year." He sighed wearily. "The last few months have been an education—from learning how to change a diaper to educating myself on how to avoid tree nuts for his allergy."

"He has allergies?" Lydia was accustomed to the dietary needs for children with the most common allergies. Her brother broke out in hives if he even got in the same room as a peanut.

"Just tree nuts. But I live in fear I'll leave the house without the EpiPen." He huffed out a long breath, clearly feeling the same stress that many new parents went through. "I hope you'll consider my offer, Lydia. Maybe you can work for me, and your sister can do something to repay you."

"I'd need to figure out a way to pay my bills in the meantime." It was true she was between nanny jobs right now, but she had hoped to devote the extra time toward working on her house, doing some of the simpler labor she didn't want to pay a contractor for.

James tucked the blanket more securely around the baby's feet, a gesture that touched her all the more now that she knew he wasn't the baby's father. He was simply a man trying to do his best taking care of a child he hadn't been ready for.

"And I can't put a price on what it would mean to me to have qualified help with Teddy." He nodded at a gray-haired cowboy walking into the club. Then, once the man had passed, James turned to Lydia again. "Forget about Gail and the charity money. The universe is smiling on me by having a nanny walk into my office at a time in my life when I'm hanging on by my fingernails. Consider this a job offer for whatever you usually charge. I would have sought you out before this if I'd known about you."

"I couldn't possibly—"

"Please." He cut her off, his tone laced with an urgency—a need—she hadn't anticipated. "Just think about it. Start with the trial period and sign on for two months. See how it goes. If things don't work out, I'll understand."

Swallowing her protests, she nodded. "It's a very generous offer and I will consider it."

He seemed to relax then, a tension sliding away from him as he exhaled. "Thank you. I'll be working from the main house at the Double H tomorrow. If you'd like to stop by, I can show you around. You could see what the job would entail and take a look at the nanny's quarters before you decide."

"The Double H is your ranch?" She knew the property. It was close to the Clayton family ranch, the Silver C. The portions of the Double H she could see from the main road were all beautifully manicured. The stables and ranch house were both painted crisp white with dark gray trim, and the window boxes were refreshed year-round with red flowers.

"It is." His smile was warm. "I never knew how easy ranch work was until I tried my hand at child care. I'm very ready to return to my cattle full-time."

The idea troubled her, given that his responsibility to his nephew wasn't going to end when he filled the nanny position. But she couldn't afford to feel any more empathy for this man than she already did. She had some tough decisions ahead of her where he was concerned.

"I'll stop by tomorrow. Does after lunch work for you?"

"That's perfect." He laid a protective hand on Teddy's back. "You can repeat the trick you did today of getting him to fall asleep for his nap."

She'd been given similar compliments many times from happy clients. She was good with children. Period. And yet, somehow the thought of putting the child to sleep with James Harris looking on filled her with a whole host of fluttery sensations.

"I'll see you then." Nodding, she backed away fast, needing refuge from the strong pull of desire. Retreating to her car, she forced her gaze away from James and shut the door behind her.

She locked the door for good measure. And then felt like an idiot if he'd heard her flick the locks. She wasn't trying to keep anyone out as much as she was trying to keep herself in check around the too-handsome rancher with golden-brown eyes.

Switching on the ignition, she pulled out of the parking lot fast, hating herself for thinking that if it wasn't for James's blatant sex appeal, she probably already would have accepted the job he'd offered.

That wasn't fair to him. And it definitely wasn't fair to the innocent boy who'd just lost both his parents.

She could help Teddy and James. And no matter what she told herself about not getting involved in her sister's mayhem, Lydia felt a responsibility to repay James in whatever way she could. By covering Gail's debt, he'd ensured both Walker women would be able to run their small businesses in Royal without censure from locals knowing that Gail had cheated the Pancreatic Cancer Research Foundation.

Lydia would just have to find a way to do the job while avoiding the hot rancher as much as possible.

Shouldering the pole pruner he'd been using to trim an apple tree, James squinted in the afternoon sunlight to check his watch at half-past noon.

Based on the number of times he'd glanced at the vintage Omega Seamaster timepiece that had belonged to his grandfather, James couldn't deny that he looked forward to a visit from Lydia Walker today. And as much as he wanted to credit his anticipation to the possibility he'd found a solution to his nanny problem, he knew that accounted for only part of it.

He wanted to see her again.

Taking his time to wipe down the blade on the pruner—an important step to prevent spreading disease—James needed to be sure Lydia agreed to his bargain. And frankly, that need was at odds with how fiercely he was attracted to her. She'd invaded his thoughts constantly since their last meeting. During the daytime, he shut down the visions as fast as possible. But during the night? His dreams about her had been wildly inappropriate and hot as hell.

Securing a nanny was his number one goal right now, and had been for the past three months. He couldn't afford to let an undeniable hunger for her confuse the issue that should be a simple business arrangement. Her sister's overbid aside, James needed Lydia. He'd spent time the night before researching her credentials and had been thoroughly impressed. Not only had she served as a nanny for two TCC members who spoke highly of her—he'd messaged them both to check—but Lydia also had an intriguing connection to the popular childrearing blog *House Rules*.

The blog was written by her mother, Fiona, but had often featured Lydia even as a teenager. There was a whole video library of Lydia, showing her mother's followers how to do everything from making organic baby food to refreshing vintage nursery furniture to meeting modern health codes. Simply put, she was incredibly qualified. But the most convincing fact for him was that he'd seen how quickly she could turn Teddy's stormy tantrums into full-fledged smiles.

That alone made her services necessary. And he'd be damned if he allowed his unbidden desire for the woman to get in the way. Besides, if his divorce had taught him anything, it was that chemistry between people could fade fast, and made shaky ground for any relationship.

Heading toward the potting shed to stow the garden tools, James heard the crunch of car tires on gravel. Turning, he recognized Lydia's vehicle from the day before. He made quick work of putting away the tools and washed his hands at the shed's utility sink before stepping outside again.

He had almost reached her car when she stepped from it. Her long legs were clad in tall boots and dark leggings. A gray sweater dress and long herringbone-patterned coat were simple, efficient pieces. Definitely nothing overtly sexy. And yet, he found his gaze wandering over the way the sweater dress hugged her curves. But it was her smile that drew him more than anything. From her light brown hair streaked with honey to the sun-warmed shade of her skin, she seemed to glow from within. Today, like yesterday, she wore little makeup that he could see. A long golden necklace glinted as she straightened, the charms jingling gently as they settled.

"Welcome to the Double H," he greeted her, arms spread wide. "Home of the Harris family since nineteen fifty-three."

He and his brother had been born here and he took immense pride in the place, the same as his father had before his death. His brother had planned to move back to Royal one day and help expand the ranching operation. A plan that would never happen now. Strange how many ways grief could find to stab him when he least expected it.

Still, James continued to think about expanding on his own, to give Teddy the future that his father had dreamed for him.

"Thank you." She let him close the car door behind her while she spun in a slow circle to view the closest buildings. "I've always thought this was a pretty property when I've driven past here."

He couldn't help the rueful grin. "I don't know how thrilled my grandfather would be to hear that I've turned the place 'pretty.' But I've toyed with the idea of expanding the horse sales side of the business after we've had some success with recent yearlings. And traditionally, horse farms have more curb appeal since potential clients often come through the barns."

"You've done a great job." Lydia walked toward the small grove where he'd been working. "Are these fruit trees?"

He nodded, pleased she'd noticed. "I've got a dozen apple trees, a few peaches and pears. Just enough to make the ranch hands grumble about the extra work at harvest time." Although no one complained about taking fresh fruit home at the end of the day. "I was pruning these before you arrived."

"I hope I didn't catch you at a bad time." She stopped her trek through the grove and peered back at him. "I know I'm a little early, but I wasn't sure how long the drive would take."

"I had just quit when you pulled in. Your timing is perfect." He waved her toward a side entrance to the main house. "Come on in. Can I get you something to drink?"

"No. Thank you." She waited while he opened the door, then stepped inside the mudroom. "Where's Teddy? I brought him a gift." She tugged at the sleeve of her coat and he moved behind her to help.

Her hair brushed the backs of his knuckles, the silk lining of her coat warm from her body. He tried to move quickly—to keep himself from lingering too long—but he wasn't fast enough to avoid a hint of her fragrance. Something vanilla with a trace of floral.

With effort, he turned away from her to hang the coat on one of the metal hooks from the rack.

"That's very kind of you. My housekeeper took Teddy for a couple of hours while he naps so I could get the trees sprayed and pruned. I've been falling behind on every conceivable chore." He led her deeper into the house, pausing outside the kitchen. "Besides, I wanted to give my sales pitch for the nanny gig without any distraction."

Shaking her head, she gave him a half smile. "But *he* is the job, James. Your best selling point."

Skeptical, he figured he'd hedge his bets on showing off the house first. "Your three predecessors didn't seem quite as charmed by their charge."

Lydia crossed her arms as she studied him. "They don't sound worthy of the task, then."

Her defensiveness on Teddy's behalf was a credit to her character, yes. But she'd been with the boy for only a few minutes. She hadn't seen the long crying jags or the stormy rages that had caught the other nannies off guard.

"That makes me all the more eager to sign you on," he told her honestly.

After taking her on a tour of the kitchen and great room, he took the main staircase up to the nursery where his housekeeper, Mrs. Davis, all but bolted from the room when she spotted them. Her greeting was brusque at best.

"Thank you, Mrs. Davis." James knew the house-

keeper wasn't happy with the added babysitting responsibilities, but he'd shown his gratitude in her
paycheck over the last two weeks. "This is Lydia
Walker. She's here to discuss the possibility of taking over child care duties full-time."

"In that case, I won't keep you." She gave an
abrupt nod and hurried on her way, her white tennis shoes squeaking on the hardwood in the hall
as she stalked off.

"The household staff is overburdened," he explained, hoping Lydia wouldn't be put off by the
woman's cool reception. "Mrs. Davis has helped
me out more than once, and I've also got temporary
help from my foreman's daughter. But the extra
work is taking a toll."

"Understandable," Lydia murmured softly while
she peered down into the crib at the sleeping baby.
"Caring for a child is a huge life adjustment. Expectant parents have nine months to prepare themselves, and most of them are still overwhelmed
by the transition." She smiled up at him. "You're
doing well."

No doubt she intended the words to be reassur-
ing, but the effect on him was anything but.

"You can't possibly know that," he told her flatly,
refusing to accept a comfort he didn't deserve. "I
can't help but think that my brother would have
been far more involved with his son's upbringing
than I can afford to be right now. I've reached out

to Teddy's maternal grandparents to try to involve them more." He'd written to them twice, in fact, and hadn't heard back. "Maybe their home will be a better place for my nephew."

Lydia chewed her lush lower lip, looking thoughtful. The gesture distracted him from the dark cloud of his own failed responsibilities, making him wish his relationship with this woman could be a whole lot less complicated.

"You're thinking about asking his grandparents to raise him?" She stepped away from the crib, her boots soundless on the thick carpeting as she moved.

His gaze tracked her movements, lingering on the way her sweater dress hugged her curves. But then, thinking about Lydia was a whole lot more enticing than remembering all the ways he'd fallen short in his sudden parental role.

He'd had the nursery assembled in a hurry. The room contained all the necessary furniture but hadn't been decorated with much that would appeal to a child.

"Definitely. I can't even keep a nanny for him, let alone be a meaningful part of his life right now." He wasn't sure any of this was helping his cause to convince her to take the job. But something about Lydia made it easy for him to talk to her.

A sensation he rarely experienced with anyone.

"But that doesn't mean you'll always be too

busy for him." Her hazel eyes took on a bluish cast in the baby's room with azure-colored walls. "And your brother and his wife must have trusted you a great deal if they named you as his guardian."

Frustration and guilt fired through him.

"I'm sure they never believed it would come to that." He couldn't bear the weight of failing Teddy. Failing his brother. Unwilling to argue the point, James gestured toward the door. "Come this way and I'll show you the nanny's quarters. Because no matter what happens with Teddy's future, I can't escape the fact that I need a solution for his care right now."

And that meant not letting his guard down around this beautiful, desirable woman.

# Three

"I can't accept these terms." Back in the ranch's great room, Lydia stared down at the neatly typed offer James had passed her inside a crisp manila folder.

After a tour of the Double H Ranch main house, with special attention to the nursery, nanny's quarters and a potential playroom she could equip as she saw fit, James had briefly outlined very generous compensation for retaining her services. Not only was room and board included—useful for her while her contractor outfitted her home for a child care facility—but James also offered a salary, health care benefits and a recommendation if she stayed in his employ for six months. Gail's debt would be partially forgiven after the two-month trial period, and fully after one whole year.

Furthermore, there were additional pages that spelled out potential budgets for renovating the playroom and nursery, as well as a spending allowance for toys, books, equipment, outings and anything else that she thought Teddy required.

"What do you mean?" James frowned, stepping closer to glance over her shoulder at the formalized offer he'd given her. "Are there things I'm overlooking? It's all up for negotiation."

Closing the folder, she passed it back to him as they stood in front of the huge stone hearth where a fire crackled. "You haven't overlooked a thing. This is far too generous."

She'd never heard of such a well-paid nanny. And it made her heart hurt to think he was so eager to give over the boy's care that he would pay someone such an inflated fee. Especially when he was debating relinquishing the child to Teddy's maternal grandparents.

"Honoring my brother's wishes means everything to me." His jaw flexed as raw emotion flashed in his eyes, but he folded his arms, as if defying her to argue that statement.

"I understand that." Truly, she did. "But the whole reason I came to see you yesterday was to discuss options for repaying your generosity toward my sister. I can't let you give us anything else."

He was shaking his head before she even finished speaking. "You can't sacrifice your own income for the sake of your sibling. I won't hear of it." Before she could argue, he continued, "I read about you online, Lydia. You're extremely qualified."

His words pleased her. Or maybe it was the knowledge that he'd spent time thinking of her, if only in a professional capacity. Warmth crawled over her that didn't have a thing to do with the fire.

"Thank you. I already have a health care plan, so I don't need that. But if you cut the salary in half, I would be amenable."

"Half?" He shook his head. "I couldn't look myself in the mirror if you took a nickel under three-quarters of that."

"Half," she insisted. "And I'll find a way to put my sister to work for me so she's making up the difference."

Gail needed to learn that there were consequences to her impulsive actions.

He scrubbed a hand through his close-cropped dark hair. "I don't know."

She suspected he would have continued to argue the figure if a wail from the nursery hadn't sounded at that precise moment. James's gaze went to the staircase.

"I could start immediately," she offered, sensing his weakening on the salary issue.

He extended his hand. "You've got yourself a deal."

Lydia slipped her small palm into his much larger one, seized with the memory of their brief contact the day before when he'd taken Teddy from her arms. Just like then, an electric current seemed to jump between them, hot to the point of melting. Her gaze met his, and she would swear he was aware of it, too.

She was grateful for the baby's next cry, since it gave her the perfect excuse to retract her fingers. She darted from the room to escape the temptation of her new boss—and the fear that she'd just made a huge mistake.

After a brief supper shared with her new charge in the nursery, Lydia debated the wisdom of starting her new job so quickly.

She'd jumped into the baby's routine with both feet, comfortable with knowing where most things were located since her new employer had given her a quick tour. She knew the protocol for Teddy's food allergies and where the EpiPens were kept. But she hadn't clarified how or when she would go about moving her things into her suite at the Double H, thinking she'd see her new boss at dinnertime.

But James still hadn't come in from his chores at eight o'clock after she put Teddy into his crib for the night. Lydia knew because she'd peered down the stairs a few times, and twice had checked in with the housekeeper.

On both occasions, Mrs. Davis had looked at her as though she might steal the house silver at any moment. And between the woman's terse answers and general lack of hospitality, Lydia had the distinct impression that her presence was not welcomed by the older housekeeper.

Not that she was too worried. Usually, her work spoke for itself. Maybe Mrs. Davis was simply tired from the strain of caring for a little one. Lydia was more concerned to think that James might not be accessible in the coming weeks. As Teddy's parental figure, James had an important role in the boy's life even if he hadn't fully committed himself to it yet.

Then again, maybe James's disappearing act had nothing to do with his nephew and everything to do with the blossoming attraction between them.

Figuring she'd never improve things around here if she stayed hidden in her room, Lydia stepped out of the sprawling nanny suite and hurried down the hall to the staircase. The natural wood banister was polished to a high sheen, and the house's log cabin elements mingled seamlessly with more contemporary touches, like the walls painted in shades of taupe and tan. Downstairs, the stone hearth rose to a high ceiling right through the upstairs gallery walkway. A rough wood mantel and steer horns decorated the fireplace, but the leather couches and cream-colored slipper chairs were sleekly styled and inviting. Agriculture books filled the shelves in the far corner of the room, the leather spines freshly dusted.

She peered around for any signs of Mrs. Davis but didn't see the housekeeper. Before Lydia could debate her next move, the side door opened and James stepped inside.

She stood far enough away that he didn't notice her at first. He took his time hanging his Stetson and shrugging out of a weatherproof duster. Belatedly, she felt a hint of cool air that must have entered the house with him. The temperature had dropped, and she knew a storm was predicted tonight. In the shadows of the mudroom, his features looked all the more sculpted. He had high cheekbones. A strong jaw. Well-muscled shoulders that would turn any woman's head.

And yes, she acknowledged, she liked looking at him.

"Do you always work so late?" she asked as a way to reveal her presence, feeling suddenly self-conscious.

He glanced up quickly, his expression more pleased than surprised.

"Hello, Lydia. I didn't expect to see you so late."

She glanced at the antique clock on the opposite wall. "It's not even nine."

"Right. And when I've been on duty with my nephew, I'm ready for bed before he is." He toed off his boots and lined them up on the far side of the welcome mat.

There was something oddly intimate about seeing him take off his shoes. Being in his home at this hour.

Which was a silly thing to think given that she'd been a nanny before. She'd seen parents moving around their living space while she helped out with children. Maybe it felt different with James because he was single.

And…smoking hot. Her gaze tracked him as he strode into the kitchen in sock feet. In a long-sleeved gray tee and dark jeans, he looked less like the polished Texas Cattleman's Club president and more like a ruggedly handsome rancher. He scrubbed his hands at the kitchen sink.

"Teddy went to bed fairly well for me." So far, she couldn't see any evidence of the toddler being more difficult than most children his age. "Beginner's luck, maybe."

"Or maybe you're just that good." He grinned at her while he dried off, her thoughts scrambling at the mild flirtation in the words. "Would you like to join me for dinner? I'm starving, but I'd appreciate hearing more about your day."

He moved toward the stainless steel refrigerator and tugged it open.

"No, thank you. Teddy and I ate dinner earlier." She couldn't risk spending too much time in her employer's presence based on her over-the-top physical reaction to just a handshake, for crying out loud. If she was going to reach at least the two-month mark on this trial period, she really shouldn't have late meals alone with him. "I just thought maybe now would be a good time for me to return to my house and pick up a few items to get me through the next week."

"I forgot you didn't move your things in today." He backed out of the refrigerator with a sandwich on a crusty French roll and proceeded to remove the clear plastic wrap. "There's a storm brewing that could turn nasty if the temperature drops any more."

"I'll be careful." She stepped closer to the kitchen but didn't enter it, remaining outside the granite-topped breakfast bar as she watched him retrieve a plate and glass. "I can be back in two hours."

He parted the curtain on the window over the kitchen sink, peering out into the night. "The roads are going to be dangerous if we get ice."

"As the oldest of eight in my family, I have to say it's a unique experience to have someone worry about my safety for a change." She couldn't help a rueful smile, since she was usually the one doing the worrying.

"What about your mom?" he asked, letting go of the sheer curtain to fill a water glass. "She didn't ever tell you not to go out into an ice storm?"

Even with the barrier of the counter between them, she felt the draw of his curiosity about her. She'd never experienced the pinprick of awareness all over her skin with anyone else and wondered why, of all the people Gail could have indebted herself to, it had to be a man whom Lydia found so potently sexy.

"My mother doesn't take much notice of potential dangers in the environment." To put it mildly. Lydia had saved her youngest sister from drowning in a neighbor's backyard pool while her mom led a workshop on fostering a love of Mother Earth in children. She'd been totally oblivious. "Fiona Walker truly believes that if you see hearts and flowers wherever you go, then the world must be a happy, safe place."

James's eyebrows lifted as he slid his sandwich into the microwave. "Sounds like you got to see a different side of the *House Rules* parenting approach."

She wasn't surprised he knew about the blog. Her mother's PR machine regularly spit out stats about how many lives the parenting website actively changed for the better—which was their highly embroidered way of reporting social media reach.

Choosing her words carefully, she replied, "Let's

just say that I hope you didn't hire me because you thought I'd be giving Teddy lessons in the power of positive thinking."

"Honestly, I was just happy to read that you have CPR certification along with good references and a clean driving record." He withdrew his meal from the microwave. "But how about you let me drive you to pick up your things and we'll talk about your first day on the way?"

"What about Teddy?"

"Mrs. Davis will hear him if he cries." He picked up a key ring from a dish on the granite countertop. "Besides, we'll be back before he wakes."

She needed to speak to him about that. It didn't make her comfortable to leave her young charge in the care of woman who seemed to resent having to watch over him. But chances were good—even if she insisted on driving herself—that James would let his housekeeper tend the child if Teddy woke anyhow.

Somehow, she had to help James feel more comfortable in a father role. And no matter that the close proximity of a car ride with her strikingly handsome boss might prove tempting, Lydia knew the sooner she discussed those issues with him, the better.

"Okay. Let me just get the nursery monitor set up for her." She had the baby monitor feed on her phone, but she knew the model in the nursery came with a physical receiver.

James nodded as he pulled out his phone. "Take your time. I'll finish up my meal while you do that." He scrolled through his screens. "Mrs. Davis's room is the first one on the left just downstairs. You can leave the monitor outside her door and I'll text her the plan. She doesn't go to sleep until after the late news anyhow."

Lydia walked upstairs to the nursery, hurrying in spite of James's assurance they could take their time. Teddy Harris had been through enough these last few months. The quicker they went, the sooner Lydia would be back here, minimizing the chance that the child would wake up to Mrs. Davis.

After retrieving the receiver, she paused near the baby's crib, gazing at his little face in the glow of a night-light. So angelic. His rosebud mouth slightly open, his fingers clutching a soft rattle in the shape of a blue puppy dog.

Tenderness filled her as she closed the door quietly behind her. Somehow, some way, she would get through at least the next two months. Not just for the way it would help Gail.

She knew she could make a difference in the baby's life. And, she hoped, in his uncle's, too.

Windshield wipers working double time, James focused on the road ahead as he navigated his pickup truck down the quiet county road that led to Lydia's place. He'd eaten enough dinner to take the edge off one hunger, but having his nephew's new nanny beside him stirred another.

He tried his damnedest not to think about that. But with her light vanilla fragrance teasing his nose when she leaned closer to switch the radio station away from some political news, he couldn't resist the urge to drag in a deep breath.

"There." She leaned back in the passenger seat once a steel guitar sounded through the surround-sound speakers. "I hope that's okay. I hate to shirk my civic duty, but some days I can't cope with even one more story about politics."

"Rainy nights and steel guitars go hand in hand." He glanced over at her profile in the reflected light of the dashboard. "But then, you're talking to a man with a lot of Texas in his blood."

"Is that right?"

He heard the smile in her voice, even with his eyes back on the road and the glare of another vehicle's bright lights.

"Yes, ma'am. My granddaddy was born on Galveston Island, but he moved here after the Korean War when an army buddy of his died and left him the care of his family farm."

"Your grandfather inherited the Double H?" She shifted her legs toward him, her knees not all that far from his.

For a moment, he cursed the size of his truck. If they'd taken her car, her leg would be brushing up against him right now. But then, he recalled that he was not supposed to be imagining his legs entwined with hers. He had no business thinking about an employee that way.

"The land wasn't really a ranch at that time. Just some farm acreage. His friend's widow was struggling to raise three kids and get the crops in, so Henry Harris Sr. moved into a trailer on the land and got to work." He'd heard the story from his father often enough, since his granddad had passed away when James was still a child.

"My house is up here on the left." She pointed to a turn ahead. "I'm sure your grandfather would be proud of how you're maintaining the property. It's a showplace."

Her words pleased him. He'd worked tirelessly for the last ten years to modernize.

"Thank you." He slowed the vehicle as he guided it into the horseshoe driveway in front of a single-story residence. Concrete-block built, the white house had what appeared to be building materials neatly stacked under tarps in the front yard. "Looks like you've got some improvements planned yourself."

"Not as quickly as I would like, but yes." She pointed toward a portico structure on the far side of the building. "If you want to park under there, we can get inside without getting too drenched."

Moments later, he followed her inside, the rain

battering hard on the portico roof as she jiggled her key in a stubborn lock. He noticed the overhang leaked in a few places, with rivulets of water streaming through the gaps.

Inside, she flipped on a light to reveal a home in transit. Plastic sheeting hung on one end of a functional kitchen, an attempt to keep dust at a minimum, he guessed. But the workable section of living space that he could see showed tidy counters and cabinets, a big worktable covered with flooring samples and countertop tiles.

Beyond that, there were small touches of the woman who lived here. A bright braided rug. Heart-shaped magnets on the refrigerator that pinned a child's crayon art in places of honor. A small wall shelf contained a collection of glass and ceramic birds.

"I'll just be a minute." She headed toward an overlapping section of the plastic sheeting that divided the living space. "I need to grab some clothes."

"Can I carry anything for you?" He studied her in the light of a wrought iron chandelier over the kitchen table. "There's plenty of room in the extended cab if you want to bring any furniture or personal items to make you feel more at home."

"I don't need much—" She hesitated. "Actually, I have a few toys that Teddy might like if you want to come with me."

She held the plastic sheeting open for him and he ducked through, passing close to her. Brushing her shoulder with his accidentally. Was it his imagination, or did she suck in a breath at the contact?

He stopped too close to her in the small space, but a temporary wall had been constructed of plywood, making the hallway narrow here.

"Sorry about the mess," she said, quickly stepping ahead of him. "I've been living in a construction zone. I hardly notice it anymore when it's just me here."

His gaze roved—without his permission—to the sultry curve of her hips in her khaki slacks as she strode ahead of him. She paused to flip a light switch on one wall, and then she turned into what looked like a storage area.

"I'm glad to help," he told her honestly, not wanting to admit how much he liked spending time with her. How content he would be to linger with her here.

"Do you want to pull down those two suitcases?" she asked, pivoting in her tennis shoes to face him.

He hoped he'd lifted his gaze to eye level fast enough.

Damn. What the hell was he thinking to ogle her?

"Sure thing." He skirted around a couple of box fans to the shelves that held the luggage, and pulled down the items she'd indicated.

While he did that, she dug in a big box filled

with plastic scooters, ride-on toys and trucks. He resisted the view of her tempting feminine form, concentrating on opening the first suitcase like his life depended on it.

He steeled himself for the inevitable draw of her proximity when he brought the bag over to her. In short order, she tossed in a farm set with clear plastic bags full of toy animals, fencing and tractors. She added a few other items he didn't recognize—baby gear of some sort.

"You know you can buy whatever you think he needs—"

"Babies outgrow things so quickly. It makes more sense to share." Their eyes met over the suitcase he held.

He studied her, forgetting what they'd been talking about as sparks singed between them. For a moment, they breathed in one another's air. And from the protracted pause, he knew she was as distracted by the sizzling connection as he was.

If she was any other woman, he would have set aside the suitcase and pulled her into his arms. Tested her lips to see if they were as petal soft as they looked. Wrapped his arms around her curves to see if she fit against him as perfectly as he imagined she would.

He could practically hear his own heartbeat. It rushed in time with her fast breathing in the otherwise silent room.

What he wouldn't give for just one taste…

"I'd better get my clothes," she said suddenly, pulling him out of his thoughts just in time for him to see her rush out the door and disappear down the hall.

Cursing himself up one side and down the other, James zipped the suitcase and carried it back out to the safety of the empty kitchen.

As he waited for Lydia to finish, he ground his teeth together and reminded himself that the luggage wasn't the only thing that needed to stay zipped.

# Four

As the holidays neared, Lydia put all her focus on setting up happy daily routines for Teddy Harris.

She was good at her job, after all, and she needed to have something in her life that was working in her favor when she felt like she was tempted by her boss every time she turned around. Not that either of them had acknowledged the almost-kiss that happened nearly two weeks ago on the night he'd driven her to her home.

He seemed as wary as she was to cross that line since she worked for him. Because James had a high standard of ethics? Or was he simply unwilling to jeopardize his child care arrangement? Maybe a

little of both. Either way, they'd been staying out
of one another's way, never spending much time in
each other's presence.

Now, decorating the playroom for Christmas,
Lydia hummed a carol while the toddler raced in
circles, tugging a Santa sleigh pull toy behind him.
She liked reading to him before he fell asleep, but
some nights he was simply too wound up to sit still.
He liked running, jumping and climbing stairs, although she was always careful to follow him up
each step, in case he fell. But he was agile and co-
ordinated, just very energetic.

She angled back to look at the snowflake cling-
on stickers she'd pressed to the playroom windows.

A quick knock sounded on the door before it
opened.

She turned in time to see James lean into the
room. It wasn't fair how quickly her belly filled
with butterflies when she was around him.

"May I come in?" he asked, still dressed in his
work clothes, jeans and a tee with the Double H
logo.

He must have left his boots and hat in the mudroom, but she guessed he'd been working on one
of the fences in a northern pasture. She'd seen him
repairing it earlier in the week, too, when she'd
taken Teddy out for a stroller ride along one of the
better dirt roads on the ranch. She'd hoped James
would take some time away from the chore to visit

with his nephew, but he'd barely given them a wave before returning to the task.

She'd noticed that he kept long hours, and sometimes he didn't return to the house until well past nightfall. Could he possibly be as wary of time alone with her as she was of the forbidden temptation of his presence? Or could that just be her imagination? The man might truly be just a workaholic.

"Please do. I'm sure Teddy misses you. I've been hoping you could spend some more time with him." Lydia waved James in as she climbed down the step stool. "I only had the door closed so he didn't run out of the room."

She'd placed baby safety covers in the interior door knobs in the nursery and playroom to ensure the boy didn't wander out without her knowing.

"I won't stay long," James assured her, his dark eyes lingering on her. "It must be nearing the little guy's bedtime, right?"

A shiver of awareness snaked up her spine, and she thought about how she looked with her hair falling out of its ponytail and juice stains on her shirt. She almost reached to smooth her hair, then stopped herself for making the telling motion. Instead, she pulled her gaze away from her boss's enticing stare, focusing on Teddy.

"I'm not sure there's any sense putting him in his crib just yet. Look at him." Now that she had a rhythm to the days with the little boy, she knew it was time to get James more involved with him.

To help him feel more comfortable in his new role as the boy's father figure. There was more to being a good nanny than feeding and caring for a child. Part of the job was enabling a thriving family. And so far, she hadn't seen much emotional commitment from James, let alone one-on-one time with the boy.

"He looks like he's ready to run a marathon," James observed, patting the child's fluffy dark curls as Teddy rushed past him on wobbly legs.

"Exactly." Lydia noticed Teddy had dropped the pull string to the sleigh, though, his pattern of circling more erratic now. "And I've noticed when I force the bedtime issue, he only protests loudly, whereas if I wait an extra half hour, he usually settles down faster on his own."

"Mrs. Davis says you're doing an excellent job." James stepped deeper into the room, glancing toward the bag full of holiday decorations.

Her pulse skittered faster as he approached her.

"Really?" Lydia frowned. "I find that a little hard to imagine after all the times your housekeeper has glowered at me in the past two weeks."

"I'm sorry if she's made you uncomfortable. I will speak to her," he offered, taking a seat on the cushioned bench in front of a rocking chair.

"No. I didn't mean to suggest—" She definitely

didn't want to stir up trouble in the household. "She hasn't done anything to make me uncomfortable. And I'm glad to know she thinks I'm doing a good job."

Regretting the unguarded comment, she busied herself by reaching into her shopping bag to retrieve a quilted advent calendar. Farm animals peered out of the stitched barn, a new animal revealed each day until Christmas when a baby in a manger appeared in the center. She hung it from one of the plastic hooks meant to display a child's artwork.

When she turned around from her task, James had a smile on his face as he pointed to the playroom floor. Her gaze followed where he pointed to see Teddy lying on his side, a soft puppy dog rattle in one hand. Absently, the boy rubbed his fingers over the pale blue terry cloth, stroking the toy puppy's ear.

"Someone's getting sleepy." James spoke quietly. "Would you like me to carry him to his crib?"

"That would be great." Because while it was no trouble to lift him herself, Lydia had been wanting to get James more involved in the baby's daily routine. She watched as the rugged rancher leaned down to scoop up the child and cradle him against one big, broad shoulder.

James's shadowed jaw rested briefly atop his nephew's dark curls and Lydia's heart melted a little. Or maybe it was the sight of such a strong man displaying infinite tenderness toward a baby. No matter what it was that made her all soft and swoony inside, she recognized that standing shoulder to shoulder with her attractive employer in a darkened room might not be wise.

Lydia backed up a step as James headed down the hallway. "I'll be in the nursery in a minute," she assured him before darting in the other direction.

Just for a second, so she could get a handle on herself.

Instead of finding some breathing room, however, she stepped right into Mrs. Davis.

"Oh!" Lydia reached to right herself, placing a steadying hand against the wall. "I'm so sorry."

The housekeeper scowled, shaking her head. Her gray hair was down for the night, instead of in the tight twist she wore most days. Lydia was surprised to see her upstairs since she was usually in her room for the night at this hour. She tried not to react to the woman's displeased expression, remembering what James had said about the compliment she'd paid Lydia.

"I thought I heard Mr. Harris's voice," Mrs. Davis said. "I hoped to speak with him about something." The woman still wore the gray dress and apron that were her work uniform even though it was long past dinnertime.

"He's tucking Teddy into bed for the night."

Nodding, the housekeeper started to move toward the stairs and then turned back to Lydia.

"He is still grieving his brother, you know," Mrs. Davis said haltingly as she glanced toward the door to the nursery.

It was the most the housekeeper had ever said to her apart from where their duties overlapped.

"I'm sure he is," Lydia agreed. "It's only been a few months."

"And before that, he was dealing with the loss of his wife." Mrs. Davis lowered her voice even more while Lydia tried to conceal her shock.

James had been *married*?

She wanted to ask about that, but Mrs. Davis continued in her low, confidential tone. "I'm not sure he could handle getting attached to this boy and then possibly lose his nephew to the boy's grandparents. That's why I lobbied for Teddy to live with his grandparents from the start. I'm not heartless, Ms. Walker. I just don't want to see Mr. Harris hurt again."

Lydia could scarcely process all that, still reeling from the news that James had lost his wife. Had something happened to her? Had they divorced?

Before she could ask, James emerged from the nursery. Seeing the two women there, he paused.

Lydia was still too surprised to speak. Mrs. Davis straightened, and informed him, "The outdoor chest freezer needs to be replaced as soon as possible."

The two of them spoke briefly about that before resolving it to the housekeeper's satisfaction. Lydia told herself to simply say good-night and retreat.

Her boss's private affairs weren't her concern. Except what if his wife's family could make some kind of claim on Teddy? She knew that was a stretch considering the boy was James's blood relative. But still, wouldn't that have some bearing on her job? Or was she justifying her curiosity?

Before she could debate the wisdom of it, she blurted, "I didn't know you'd been married."

James braced for the inevitable pain that came from any reminder of his failed marriage.

To his surprise, it didn't come. Some resentment lingered, but not to the same degree. Had he finally put some of his past to rest? Because instead of feeling the old flare of anger about Raelynn, James only felt a surge of male satisfaction that Lydia Walker wanted to know about his romantic history.

"I didn't think it was relevant," he told her honestly. "I believe you've been as careful as I have about not getting too…personal."

He'd been working ridiculously long hours lately, not just to catch up with chores around the ranch, but to keep his distance from Lydia and their undeniable attraction. To avoid the intimacy of time together after that rainy night when he'd driven her to her house.

"It's none of my business, of course," she agreed, picking at a loose thread on the ribbed cuff of her pale green sweater sleeve.

A shade that brought out the green in her beautiful hazel eyes.

"It *is* your business. You work with my nephew, and my family status is relative to Teddy's." He gestured toward the stairs. "Let's talk in the kitchen and we can grab something to drink."

She followed him into the expansive kitchen, sliding onto one of the back-less saddle-shaped stools that pulled up to a long limestone countertop on an island. He tugged open one of the double doors to the refrigerator and chose two bottles of sparkling water and an orange. He sliced it and served a section on the rim of her glass along with her bottle.

"Thank you." She twisted off the cap and poured her own glass while he assembled some cheeses on a serving platter with a fresh baguette he found in the bread drawer.

Sliding onto the stool near her—carefully leaving a seat empty between them—he poured his own drink. The small pendant lights over the bar were on the nighttime setting, low enough to see what they were doing, but dim enough to be relaxing. He liked taking his meals here at the end of a day.

"I don't talk about my ex-wife very often since the divorce is just over a year old, and until recently, it was a source of tremendous regret."

"You certainly don't owe me any explanations." She slid a single slice of bread onto the appetizer plate along with one slice of cheese. "I just wouldn't want to be caught off guard if she came to the house, or asked to see Teddy."

"That will never happen." For so many reasons. "Raelynn never wanted children, for one thing." He'd thought about that many times since bringing his nephew into his life. If his wife hadn't left him then, she sure as hell would have bolted when she found out James was the guardian to a pint-sized tornado. "But more importantly, she's moved out of state. With her new husband."

Lydia stared at him, wide-eyed. "I'm so sorry."

"I'm not. At least we're not forced to see each other around town." He'd been hurt at first when he'd discovered how quickly she found someone new, but even he'd been able to see that she was happier in her second marriage. "I knew we were having problems, but I didn't realize how much she disliked being a rancher's wife. We agreed on a settlement, and she left. End of story."

"That still must have been painful."

"Of course. But I learned a valuable lesson. Because while I don't plan to get hitched again, I do know that I'd take a more mercenary approach next time." He dragged the cutting board closer and cut the remainder of the orange he'd used for their drinks, adding the slices to the serving platter.

The sharp tang of citrus filled the air and Lydia helped herself to a segment.

"A mercenary approach to marriage?" She lifted an eyebrow. "That just sounds wrong."

"Think about how many more successful marriages there used to be when families helped arrange the match. A wedding was for practical purposes, yes. But when a partner shares your values and interests, love can grow out of that." His gaze snagged on the sheen of juice coating her lips, and he felt a new kind of thirst.

"You can't be serious." She shook her head, a smile tugging at the corners of her lips.

She mesmerized him so much it took him a moment to remember what they'd been talking about.

"I'm totally serious. I've given it a lot of thought, and I think maybe romance is overrated."

Picking up the slice of baguette on her plate, she tore it in half and pointed at him with the ripped half. "That much we can agree on."

"Oh really?" he asked while she took a bite. "I would hate to think that you're already a cynic when it comes to love, too." He was teasing her, but he felt sad to hear it. "I hope no one's trounced your heart, Lydia."

He'd seen her tenderness with Teddy, and it made him feel protective of her.

"No. But I know not everyone views marriage as a binding agreement." She slanted a glance his way. "My mother, for example, has taken a 'trial and error' approach to finding the right guy. She was married three times before I moved out of Arkansas, and she's contemplating husband number four even now."

"That couldn't have been easy for you or your siblings." He'd read about the family on the *House Rules* blog, but didn't remember anything about a father figure in the clan.

"We managed." There was a defensive note in her voice, a hint of defiant pride. "But it certainly gave me a skeptical view of matrimony."

He wondered if that meant she'd ruled it out for herself, but wasn't sure how much to push. He was curious, though.

"What about your dad?" he asked instead, wanting to know more about her. Because even though he'd been avoiding her for the last two weeks, that didn't mean he hadn't been thinking about her most waking hours. And fantasizing about her the second his head hit the pillow at night. "Did he remarry?"

"He did." She nodded, and then took a long sip

of her water. "My father is Brazilian, and he met my mother while he was a foreign exchange student. He went back home after things fell apart with my mother. I've only seen him once since then, and I've never met his second wife."

He wondered about her last name—Walker didn't strike him as Brazilian—but maybe she'd taken her mother's surname. When he didn't respond right away, Lydia smothered a laugh, stirring her orange around her glass with a cocktail straw.

"My family has some interesting dynamics, I realize."

"Every family is unique." He understood that. "My nephew will be faced with that challenge, too. Whether I keep him with me or his maternal grandparents raise him, his childhood will be very different from what it should have been."

Lydia was quiet for a long moment. "You're seriously considering...giving him up?"

"I'm hardly equipped to raise a child by myself." Frustration simmered, not that she'd raised the question, but because he hated the situation. Hated that his brother wasn't here to be the father he'd always dreamed of being. "I want what's best for the boy."

He reached for more food, filling his plate a second time. Busying himself to dodge a sense of crushing guilt.

"That's admirable to put his needs first," she said softly, reaching a hand over to touch his forearm. Distracting him from the mixture of unhappy emotions with that spike of awareness never far beneath the surface when she was near. "But if you really want what's best for Teddy, please don't rule yourself out yet. You might make a better father than you realize."

He knew the only reason he didn't discount the suggestion immediately was because of that gentle touch on his forearm. The cool brush of her skin along his. It made it impossible to think about anything else but her. His heart slugged hard against his ribs. His gaze dipped to her lips as they parted ever so slightly.

An invitation?

Or wishful imagining?

If she'd been closer, he would have kissed her. He couldn't decide, then, if it was good thing or a bad thing that there was a vacant seat between them, keeping them apart. Instead, he covered her hand with his, watching her all the while.

Her pupils widened a fraction. Even in the dim light of the kitchen, he could see that hint of reaction. A sign of shared desire.

She didn't pull away. At least, not at first.

After a moment, she blinked fast and then withdrew her fingers slowly.

"I'd better say good-night." She rose awkwardly

and backed toward the door before she turned away, her ponytail swishing as he watched her retreat.

He employed all his restraint not to follow her. Because he knew if he stood now, even just to extend their conversation, that kiss he wanted would somehow happen. It was so close he could almost taste her on his lips. And if this was what it was like between them after he'd deliberately avoided her for two weeks, what would happen if he spent more time with her and Teddy, the way she wanted him to?

He didn't have a plan for how to handle the magnetic attraction he felt for this woman, and he needed to come up with one. Fast. Because hiding out on the ranch, burying himself in physical labor, clearly wasn't working.

# Five

Rose Clayton peered out her bedroom window just after dawn, not surprised to see James Harris's truck in one of the few remaining fields around the Silver C that didn't border Lone Wolf Ranch property. The Double H owner was a hard worker, no doubt, but over the past two weeks Rose had noticed James's truck at all hours in that shared pasture. The man was putting a lot of time into his place.

But then, she'd heard that his brother had died this past fall. Maybe James needed the distraction of exhausting, physical labor. She understood all too well the way grief could consume a person.

She'd grieved for the love she'd lost with Gus when her father had forced her to wed Edward. She'd grieved for her mother to be married to a man who didn't care about her. Eventually, she'd even hurt for her children, who'd been raised by a hard, unforgiving man.

Rose understood the way hard work could make a person forget, for a little while at least.

Turning from the window, she took a moment to inhale the scent of bacon frying in her kitchen. For the forty years she'd been married, she'd never once awoken to the scent of breakfast being made in her kitchen. All those years wed to Ed, she'd been the one doing the cooking since he'd never managed the ranch well enough to afford much help. At least, not for her.

Pulling on a pair of old jeans and a T-shirt from a recent rodeo, Rose took her time brushing her teeth, liking the idea that she would walk into her kitchen to find Gus Slade making her breakfast.

After all they'd been through, all the ways they'd hurt each other over the years, who would have thought they could end up together? It almost seemed too good to be true. Like if she pinched herself she might roll over in her bed and find it had all been a dream. Heaven knew, she'd dreamed of Gus often enough while married to the man handpicked by her daddy when she was only eighteen years old.

Now, running a brush through her short brown hair going gray at the temples, Rose breathed in the scent of fresh coffee and headed toward the kitchen. She tugged a soft blue sweater off the back of the bathroom door and tucked her arms into the sleeves, then padded out to the kitchen in sock feet.

Her overnight guest stood in front of the farmhouse sink, sipping from a red stoneware mug while the dawn light spilled through the window onto his thick white hair. Augustus "Gus" Slade had celebrated his sixty-ninth birthday this year, but he was still well muscled, strong enough to work the hay wagon if he was so inclined. And still undeniably sexy.

"Good morning." She couldn't help the smile that came with the words, the unexpected joy filling her whole body. It might not be the first time he'd spent the night with her, but it still felt magical to wake up to him.

Gus turned from the sink. "Good morning, beautiful." He toasted her with his coffee mug before setting it on the countertop. "Your breakfast is ready if you want to take a seat."

"I can help," she started, stepping toward the refrigerator to get the juice and creamer.

Gus made a shooing motion with his hand, chasing her toward the table. "I won't hear of it. I'm in charge of breakfast, so have a seat and get used to being spoiled."

"I will never get used to being spoiled," she admitted, wondering—not for the first time—what her life might have been like with this bold man at her side.

Would it have been this blissful every day? Or would she have been too young to appreciate how truly fortunate she was to have such a man? They'd been so in love as teens, until Gus went off to make his way in the world, promising to come back and marry her one day. Four years later he'd returned after earning enough money on the rodeo circuit to purchase a little piece of land nearby. Only her daddy was a cruel man who didn't want his daughter to have anything to do with a "nobody" like Gus. Jedediah Clayton had considered himself—and his daughter—too good for a Slade, forcing Rose to marry a man of Jed's choosing, threatening to kick out Rose's ill mother if Rose didn't do as he commanded.

She'd resented her father all her life for that. But now that Ed was long gone and Gus's wife, Sarah, had died, too, Rose wondered if she would have been as good of a wife to Gus as he deserved. He was an amazing man.

Stubborn. Surly. And one hell of a ranching rival all those years that they'd been bitterly estranged, with Gus blaming Rose for marrying another man. But that was all in the past. Gus now

knew that Rose had married Ed only out of fear
for her mother.

"Then you underestimate me, Rose Clayton,"
Gus promised, stepping closer to her so he could
fold her hands in his. "Because you don't know
what great lengths I would go to in order to spoil
you."

That joy bubbled up inside her again, making
her feel like a giddy teenager falling in love with
him all over again.

"Gus, all of Royal thinks I'm the toughest old
bird in the county." She had spent a lifetime rein-
forcing the defenses around her heart and her life,
trying to focus on her family and the ranch instead
of all that she'd given up. "What will they say if
you turn me soft?"

Gus's piercing blue eyes seemed to peer right
into her soul. "They may say I'm one hell of a lucky
man to win over the hottest woman in town."

She laughed. "You're too much."

The look he gave her about melted her socks off,
before he kissed her tenderly on the cheek.

"Then have a seat, Rose, and let me get your
breakfast."

Before she could move away, a voice cleared on
the far side of the room. Rose tensed, her cheeks
heating to be "caught" by her grandson, Daniel,
the ranch manager of the Silver C.

Tall and well built, Daniel had turned into a formidable man who made Rose so proud. She'd gladly raised him from boyhood when her own daughter had been overwhelmed by single parenthood, turning to alcohol instead of her family for help. Rose blamed Ed for that, but she hadn't given up hope on Stephanie.

"Good morning, Daniel." She waved him over to the table. "Join us for some breakfast."

Daniel scowled. "I'll take something for the road," he muttered, stepping into the pantry before coming out with a few protein bars. "And Gran, have you thought about what you're doing, carrying on like this with this man?"

Flustered to have her own grandchild call her out, Rose was at a loss for words, her cheeks heating even though she had no cause to be embarrassed.

"Your grandmother does not 'carry on,' son," Gus told him mildly as he slid slices of bacon onto two plates. "Show her some respect."

Rose's gaze darted to Daniel's. The younger man looked as uncomfortable as she felt. Although she did appreciate Gus's easy defense of her.

"I meant no disrespect," Daniel insisted, scrubbing a hand through his dark hair. "But Gran is a well-respected member of the community. People will start to talk when they see your truck here every night."

Would people talk? She hadn't thought about

that, but Daniel probably had a point. People did love gossip.

"That's no one's business but ours." Gus smiled at her as he strode closer to the table, her plate in hand. He set it in front of her while she took a seat. "But if it will put your mind at ease, I love your grandmother very much, and soon I'm going to marry her, like I should have all those years ago."

*Is he serious?* she thought wildly, her heart racing faster.

Her gaze went to Gus's, seeing the calm self-assurance in his blue eyes. Of course he was serious.

Just when she thought she couldn't feel any more joy in this life…boom. She felt a deep sense of happiness, as if the world was suddenly tilted right again. But she tucked those thoughts away for now, in front of Daniel, knowing her grandson didn't share her joy.

Not when his own heart was so thoroughly broken. Worse? She feared it was all her fault.

Lydia wasn't surprised when she awoke the next day to discover that James had left town on a business trip. He'd sent her a text with his contact information for a hotel in Houston in case she needed anything.

She didn't know much more than that, so throughout the week, she'd tried to look at his absence as a good thing—a favor that made her job easier. Without him in the house, she didn't have to worry about the attraction leading to anything. Except, as she went through the motions of her job, bringing Teddy for a holiday shopping outing and to have his photo taken with Santa, Lydia couldn't deny that she missed seeing her boss.

And in some ways, that felt even more dangerous to her peace of mind than the ever-present awareness between them. When he wasn't around, she found her subconscious supplied plenty of fantasy scenarios starring him.

Late in the week, shortly past dinnertime, she was in the kitchen storing some toddler portions of veggies that she'd cooked in batches for Teddy. The little boy still sat in his high chair, chasing oat cereal around his tray, tired out from the day since they'd skipped naptime while they were out doing errands.

Midway through the cooking operation, Lydia realized she'd gravitated toward the chore out of habit, an old way of coping with stress from the days when she'd lived under her mother's roof. Back then, she'd always found comfort in the ritual of work when her mother's love life got too crazy. Or her mother was too busy being romanced by her latest "Mr. Right" that she forgot to film a podcast for her blog. Lydia appreciated the way work made her feel in control.

And today, while she and Teddy had been out shopping, her mother had texted to remind her that

Fiona expected a spa day before her bachelorette party—both of which were Lydia's job to organize as her maid of honor. Clearly, her mom had ignored the fact that Lydia refused to be in the wedding.

Here she was two hours later, chopping carrots and butternut squash like a madwoman, all because she hadn't found a way to make her mother listen.

Lydia heard the doorbell ring, and she assumed Mrs. Davis answered it when she heard the low rumble of voices in the front of the house. They had visitors.

And one of the voices—a woman's—she felt sure she recognized.

"Do you want to see who's here?" she asked Teddy, already unbuckling the straps on the high chair so she could lift him up.

"See here," he repeated in perfect imitation of her.

It was the first time she'd heard that combination of words, far more complicated than *bye-bye* or *coo-kie*, both of which he used well.

"Yes!" The sound of his clear words cheered her, reminding her that her work here was so much more than a job. More than a means to repay her sister's debt. In so many ways her involvement with children was a gift. "That's right, Teddy. We're going to see who is here."

She settled him on her hip and he laid his head

against her shoulder. She couldn't resist resting her cheek on his fluffy crop of curls for a moment while she breathed in the scent of baby shampoo.

Then, she headed into the living area so she had a clear view of the foyer. She recognized Tessa Noble, a woman she'd gotten to know through her sister Gail, standing beside the tall, handsome rancher who'd bid on Tessa at the same charity bachelor auction where Gail had bid on Lloyd Richardson. Lydia recognized him only from photos in the articles she'd read online about the auction.

"Hello, Tessa." She strode closer to greet the woman who'd been supportive of Gail's fledgling grocery delivery business. Now, in simple heeled boots and jeans with her blue hoodie and a bright orange scarf, Tessa wore her dark hair loose and curly, but there was something about her that just glowed. "I don't know if you remember me—"

"Of course I do, Lydia." Tessa gave her a wide smile, stepping deeper into the room, her light brown eyes darting over the child in Lydia's arms. "But I sure didn't expect to see you here."

Before Lydia could reply, Mrs. Davis excused herself to retreat downstairs for the evening, leaving the guests to her.

Lydia waved the couple into the room. "Would you like to have a seat? James is away on business, but you're more than welcome—"

"We won't stay." Tessa exchanged a quick look

with her tall, green-eyed companion. "This is Ryan Bateman, by the way. Ryan, Lydia Walker is Gail's older sister."

Lydia shook the man's hand and he gave her a warm smile.

"We just came by to thank James for encouraging Tessa to take part in the bachelor auction." He slid his arm around Tessa's waist, tucking her close as if he'd missed her in the brief moment they hadn't been side by side. "Tessa's been my best friend for a long time, but without the nudge of that night, I don't know how long it would have taken me to see that she was the right woman for me all along."

Tessa, who already glowed with happiness, brightened even more as she flashed a stunning ring on her left finger—chocolate and white diamonds set in a rose gold band. "I couldn't wait to tell James that we're getting married."

The new couple's love warmed the whole room. And while Lydia was thrilled for them, it was hard not to feel like a romantic failure by comparison.

"That's wonderful news! Tessa, your ring is gorgeous." She wished Gail was here to share her friend's engagement news. "I'm so happy for you and I know James will be thrilled for you, too." Unwilling to linger on the topic of the charity auction since she hadn't worked out what to say about her sister's exorbitant bid, Lydia steered the conversation away from the event. "I'm working here as Teddy's nanny, by the way, so I'm sure to see James as soon as he returns."

Not that she had any idea when that might be.

With Christmas just a few days away, she wondered if he would stay away for the holiday. What if her presence in the house was actually preventing him from bonding with his nephew? The thought made hear heart ache for the boy.

Tessa ducked to peer into Teddy's face. "He's almost asleep. He looks very comfortable with you, Lydia, but please let James know that I'd be happy to help out with the baby on your days off."

"That's very kind of you. Thank you." She'd thought about taking Teddy with her the next time she had a meeting with her contractor if James hadn't returned to town by then, but it was nice to know Tessa didn't mind the occasional babysitting gig. "James worries that Teddy can be a handful, but I think it's just because he's been through so much these last few months."

"Poor baby." Tessa stroked the boy's back for a moment, her face softening. "He needs his uncle now more than ever."

The woman's words were a powerful reminder of what Lydia had thought all along.

If she wanted to be a good nanny to Teddy, she needed to recommit to bringing James more firmly into the child's routine. A task that wasn't easy if James continued to keep his distance.

So while Lydia said good-night to the guests, waving at them while they headed out to Ryan's big black pickup truck in the driveway, Lydia was already formulating a plan to bring James home for good. No matter that his presence was an undeniable temptation for her. The sweet child in her arms deserved to know the comfort of a father figure.

James sat in a luxury hotel suite in Houston, working on taxes three days before Christmas.

He couldn't decide if he felt like Scrooge for working with figures when the rest of the world was preparing for the holiday, or if should feel proud of himself for starting the Double H's tax forms before the year ended. Either way, the kind of jump start was a first for him and he owed it all to the woman who'd dominated his thoughts all week.

Lydia.

The phone rang even as he thought her name, the screen showing her as the incoming call. Not really a coincidence given that he'd been thinking of her more often than not.

He checked the antique timepiece that had belonged to his grandfather. A trickle of anxiety made him wonder if everything was okay back home when he saw it was almost nine o'clock.

"Hello, Lydia." He wished he could see her face. Know her expression right now.

"Hi." She didn't sound upset. Somehow, through that one syllable, he could tell by her tone that there was nothing wrong with his nephew. "How's Houston?"

Relief kicked through him hard, making him realize how attached he was growing to the boy in spite of himself. Pushing away from the hotel room's small desk, he tipped back in the rolling chair to peer out his window at the city skyline.

"It's quiet. I've been taking meetings with some locals who are interested in expanding the Texas Cattleman's Club into Houston, but I could wrap things up anytime now." He needed to be back in Royal, in fact, and had extended the trip this long only to make sure he gave Lydia space to get comfortable in his home.

He didn't want to crowd her with the heat that seemed inevitable when they were in the same room.

"That's good," she said in a rush. "I was calling to see if you could spend some time with Teddy this weekend."

Frowning, he straightened in the leather desk chair.

"Do you need time off?" He hadn't thought about what to do if Lydia wanted some downtime.

But he recognized that her work made her on-call twenty-four hours a day.

"No. I'd be here, too," she clarified. "I just thought it would be nice for Teddy if you could spend some time with him." She seemed to hesitate a moment, before adding, "And he seems to be settling into a routine, which I think is helping with some of the behavior issues he might have had before. He's fun to be around."

James felt like a heel. Did she think that's why he'd been staying away? Because of a tantrum or two? Worse, what if she had a point? He'd been so quick to give over complete care of the child to her. And no matter what he thought about his brother's decision to appoint James as Teddy's legal guardian, he owed his brother better than paying lip service to Parker's wishes. Frustration simmered, and he rose to his feet, pacing the hotel suite.

Even if Teddy eventually went to live with his grandparents, James always wanted him to feel welcome at the Double H.

"I will be home tomorrow," he assured her, mentally making room in his schedule. "How do you suggest we spend the day?"

"Oh. Um…thank you." She sounded surprised. And pleased. "In that case, there's a holiday ice show that he might enjoy. Even if we only get to see a part of it, I think it would be fun for him."

"Of course. I'll take care of the tickets tonight.

Should we do anything else? Dinner afterward?" He couldn't deny that he was looking forward to spending time with Lydia.

"We might be pushing our luck with an active toddler," she mused aloud. "What if we bring him out to get a Christmas tree?"

"Even though we already have one?" He'd sent one of the ranch hands to the house last week to help Mrs. Davis take one out of storage.

There was a pause on the other end of the call.

"You don't like my Christmas tree?" he pressed, trying to remember what it looked like.

"It's beautiful." She seemed to be weighing her words. "But maybe we could cut down a little one for the playroom where Teddy and I could hang some homemade ornaments? You know, give him a little more buy-in?"

James couldn't help but laugh.

"By all means, a kid should have buy-in on his own Christmas." Yet even as he spoke the words, he realized there wasn't a damned thing funny about it. If anything, he found it sad to think of his nephew not being a part of a family Christmas.

The sudden punch of grief hit hard while Lydia suggested a playroom picnic afterward.

Only half listening, he was lost in his own thoughts for a moment as James recognized that he'd been screwing up his time with Teddy. He'd been so focused on providing the boy with better care than he could offer him personally, he'd ended up having very little to do with the child. His last remaining relative.

And he had Lydia to thank for helping him to see that before Teddy's grandparents got involved. He still had time to make memories with the boy. Ensure that he felt at home in the house where his father was raised.

"That all sounds good," James told her before she signed off for the night. "I've been trying to give you space. To make things easier for you while you get settled at the ranch." He hesitated. Did he need to spell out his reasons? He was pretty sure she knew all about the crackle of awareness between them. "But I'm definitely ready to spend more time with you and Teddy."

"I know Teddy will be happy to have you back home," she admitted softly, as careful as ever with her words.

His last question remained unspoken.

Would *she* be happy to have him back in the house with her every day? Every *night*?

This would be the last time he backed off that question, however. Tomorrow, they were going to face their simmering mutual attraction head-on and see what happened. No more letting it keep him from his nephew. Decision made, he felt a surge of anticipation.

"Good," he said simply. "I'm looking forward to

seeing him, and *you*, too. Very much." He let the words hover there for a moment, wanting them to linger in her mind long after the call disconnected. "Sleep well, Lydia."

Morning couldn't come soon enough.

# Six

Seated beside James in a black BMW sedan the next day, Lydia reminded herself not to think about his phone call the night before. The one where he'd said how much he was looking forward to seeing her.

After all, she'd already lost sleep thinking about what he'd meant. She didn't dare lose focus on her job now that he was back in Royal, bringing her and Teddy on the special outing she'd requested.

Still, as the sleek luxury car sped toward the civic center for the holiday ice show, she couldn't help thinking how much the trip felt like a date. Especially with Teddy quietly taking in the scen-

ery from his car seat. There was no need to entertain the baby with silly songs or toys passed over
her shoulder. There was only the scent of leather
seats and a hint of spicy aftershave. The sound of
steel guitars muted from the speakers. And the too-
rapid beat of her heart as she smoothed the belted
trench coat over her knees to cover the hem of her
red sweater dress.

She was hyperaware of the compelling man behind the wheel. He wore black pants and a dark
polo shirt with a camel-colored blazer and suede
boots. Well dressed but not overdressed for an ice
show meant for families. The tailored jacket accen-
tuated his lean, muscular physique. No doubt she
was gawking a little as he navigated easily through
midday traffic for the matinee show.

Searching for a topic to distract her, she remembered the visitors from the night before.

"I'm not sure if Mrs. Davis mentioned it, but
Tessa Noble and Ryan Bateman stopped in yesterday evening to thank you for encouraging Tessa to
go on the auction block at the Pancreatic Cancer
Research Foundation event." She remembered how
starry-eyed they both looked. How glowing with
happiness. "They are engaged to be married, and
very much in love."

"Is that right?" James grinned as he glanced
over at her. "And Tessa was always his best friend

before." The deep timbre of his voice hummed right through her.

"Ryan said the auction was the nudge he needed to see her in a different light."

"I couldn't be happier for them." He frowned. "Although the last I knew, Rose Clayton was angling for her grandson, Daniel, to date Tessa."

Lydia recalled the matriarch of the Silver C only from the occasional sightings around Royal and the woman's charitable efforts in town. Everyone seemed to know about the enmity between the Claytons and the Slades, Royal's answer to the Hatfields and McCoys. As a newcomer to town, Lydia had heard only bits of gossip about old battles over property lines and water rights. The feud might be dying down now that Rose Clayton's husband was long gone and Gus Slade's wife, Sarah, had passed away. The Great Royal Bachelor Auction had been dedicated to the memory of Sarah Slade, in fact.

"Well, Tessa is most definitely taken," Lydia observed. "Rose will have to turn her matchmaking efforts elsewhere."

"After the press coverage Daniel received following the auction, he shouldn't have any trouble finding his own dates. The story calling him the 'Most Eligible Bachelor in Texas' was picked up all over the place." James pulled off the interstate onto the ramp that led toward the civic center.

Colorful billboards hung outside the arena with ads for upcoming shows, including one for the holiday ice show.

"Look, Teddy." Lydia pointed to the characters twirling on skates. "Do you see the polar bear?"

He clapped his hands once, his brown eyes wide with childish wonder. She adored this little boy.

"Bear," he said.

Clear as a bell. She couldn't help a swell of pride in him.

"Wow. Did you teach him that?" James sounded as awed as his nephew.

She flushed with pleasure, even if she couldn't take credit.

"No. Kids his age are little sponges, soaking it all in. He surprised me yesterday by repeating a phrase really clearly."

"That's incredible." He drummed his thumbs on the steering wheel while he waited for a parking space. The lot was already busy. While he waited, he glanced over at her, his gaze lingering. "And it's easy to see you've been a good influence on him. He seems calmer."

She knew the praise shouldn't feel any different from the approval she'd received from other satisfied parents in the past. Yet somehow, coming from this handsome, charismatic man, it meant more. Or maybe she just wanted more with him. The realization—that it wasn't just physical attraction between them but maybe something deeper—rattled her.

She was growing attached to James and his sweet nephew.

"Thank you," she said thickly, dragging her gaze away from his. "We've had fun together." Then, in a rush, she added, "Teddy and I."

Her cheeks felt warm. All of her felt warm from his attention. His praise. This damned awareness.

"And I appreciate you helping me to be a part of that," he said smoothly as he parked the sedan and switched off the ignition. In the quiet aftermath, he slid his hand over hers where it rested on the console. "No matter what else happens between us, Lydia, with your job or our agreement, please know that I am deeply grateful to you for stepping in to help me with my nephew. I realized last night that I was screwing up the one thing my brother asked of me."

Behind them in the backseat, Teddy made cooing sounds as he kicked the base of his car seat with one sneaker. The boy was content.

And she was completely caught off guard by James's sincerity. Not to mention his touch. She wondered if her racing heart was obvious where his finger lay along her forearm. Her breath caught as she went to answer.

"I'm glad I could help." She told herself if he

moved his hand away now, then the touch was just an indication of simple human gratitude.

His hand remained.

"The last thing I want to do is complicate matters between us when you're so good for Teddy." His thumb shifted along her inner arm. Just a fraction of an inch. A tiny stroke of her wrist. Back and forth. "But I can't be with you and pretend that I don't feel drawn to you. Because I do, Lydia. That's the reason I spent this past week in Houston. And why I worked all the long hours on the ranch before I left. I tried my best to stay away."

She was spellbound by his touch. Gentle, but sure. She had no doubt he would remove his hand instantly if she asked him to. She met his eyes again, shifting toward him to meet his gaze head-on, his words sinking in.

"Because of me," she clarified, surprised that he would admit it so plainly.

There would be no taking back these words. No pretending this conversation hadn't happened. And where did that leave them, now that their mutual attraction was out there in the open? A tangible thing they couldn't hide from, especially while living under the same roof.

"Because I didn't want you to feel uncomfortable." He slid his hand under hers and then laid his other palm on top, capturing her fingers between his. "But I realized last night when you called that staying away from you wasn't good for Teddy. And I'm not interested in staying apart from you either, even if it means that we have to revisit our arrangement."

"But we only just worked out the details of how I can help Gail repay you." She opted to focus on that last part of what he'd said—about revisiting their arrangement—since she wasn't ready to think about why he wanted to renegotiate the agreement. "I don't know if I trust Gail to make an honest effort to repay you in some way, and I can't just let it go either."

"I don't want you to quit, Lydia. Just the opposite, in fact. But I guess, right now, all I really want to know is this." He stared down at the place where their hands were joined, studying the knot of fingers like a complex problem before he looked up at her again. "Could we not worry about our professional relationship so that, just for today, I could kiss you the way I've wanted to for weeks?"

They were already so close. That kiss was just a breath away, but indulging in it meant admitting that she wanted it, too. And while James had clearly already come to terms with confronting this desire, Lydia hadn't wrapped her brain around all the ways a relationship could complicate things.

Desire tightened inside her, the need for him turning into an ache.

"I wish it was that simple." She whispered her thoughts aloud, unable to move away from him.

"Do you?" He raked his gaze over her and she felt the heat of his longing as thoroughly as her own.

Her skin tingled, and it was all she could do to nod. Yes. She craved that kiss.

"Then that will have to be enough. For now." Sliding his hands away from hers, he lifted a finger to skim along her cheek. Then dragged his thumb along her lower lip in a way that did something sweetly erotic to her insides. "Knowing that you're thinking about that kiss, too…" He let the thought trail off along with his touch before he leaned back in his seat. "That's more than I had at the beginning of this day. And that's a start."

He was out of the vehicle and around to her side of the car, opening the door for her before she caught her breath. With a stern warning to herself to rein it in, Lydia redoubled her focus on Teddy. On making this a memorable day for the little boy who deserved a happy Christmas outing.

But she'd be lying if she said she wasn't thinking about kissing James, too. Every. Single. Moment.

That evening, after the holiday ice show and the trip to cut down a small Christmas tree for the playroom, James sat with legs sprawled on the red-and-green tartan picnic blanket. It was only eight o'clock, but time spent with a toddler made it feel later. Teddy had been well behaved all day. His exclamations at the ice show were no louder than the majority of the crowd made up of almost 50 percent kids. The toddler had grown weary of sitting in the seat after about forty-five minutes, so they'd slipped out during a change of scenery and brought him out on a sleigh to hike around the ranch and choose a little three-foot tree that was perfect for the play area.

They'd decorated it with only a couple of snowflakes that Lydia had made ahead of time, but she'd said they would add to it in the coming days. Besides, Teddy had set some of his toys on the branches. The rubber balls hadn't worked out as ornaments, but a couple of his stuffed toys and a few blocks still rested on the boughs. No surprise that Lydia had been correct about the boy needing a more hands-on tree. Teddy still sat on the floor beside it, now dressed in his pajamas while Lydia read a story to him from a plastic-coated book.

She glanced toward James as she read, and any sense of contentment with the day fled like smoke from a fire. Just that one shared look and his mind rewound to the intriguing conversation they'd had in the parking lot before the ice show.

When he'd been a moment away from kissing her.

He studied her now, as her attention returned to

the baby and his book. With her boots off, he could see her polka-dot Christmas socks. Gold hoop earrings shone in the lamplight with her light brown hair twisted into a low braid.

Realizing how close they were to Teddy's bedtime, and the hour he would finally have Lydia all to himself, James made quick work of the picnic remains. He packed the few containers of leftover fruit and cheeses back into the straw basket that the cook had delivered earlier in the day. Then, he rolled up the blanket carefully and tucked it under the basket's handle.

"How about I tuck him in?" he offered, wanting to show Lydia he'd heard her concerns about spending more time with his nephew.

He wanted the boy to always feel welcome here, even if Teddy's maternal grandparents decided they were ready to raise him.

"That would be great. Thank you." She closed the book and rose. "I'll bring the picnic hamper to the kitchen."

He lifted Teddy in his arms.

"The maid will get it." He had a cleaning service twice a week to help Mrs. Davis. "Why don't you head to the library and I'll meet you down there? I have a surprise for you."

"A surprise?" She leaned closer so she could ruffle Teddy's hair.

The soft vanilla scent of her lingered after she eased away. Hunger for her stirred.

"It will only take a minute. I know you've had a full day with this guy." He lifted Teddy slightly and the boy giggled. "I'll see you in a few."

Turning on his heel, he went to lay Teddy in his crib. It had gone well enough the last time he'd done it that he felt more sure of himself this time. Besides, the kid had to be tired after how busy they'd kept him all day long.

Flicking on the night-light and the nursery monitor, James made sure the crib was clear of extra toys. He was old enough for a light blanket and a stuffed rattle, but the baby seemed content to poke one foot through the slats of the crib, making babbling sounds.

Right up until he said, "Night-night."

The words clutched at James's heart, making him glad again that he'd come back to Royal today. He might not be ready for kids of his own, but he didn't want to screw up this window of time with his nephew. Not when Parker had entrusted him to care for the boy.

"Good night, Teddy," he called back to him, before shutting the door.

He carried the receiver for the baby monitor downstairs with him, his thoughts turning to the alluring woman who waited for him in his library. He hadn't dated anyone seriously since his divorce, going out a few times just to prove to himself he could.

Now? Lydia dominated his thoughts, and not just because she was good with Teddy.

She was honorable, for one thing. She hadn't needed to seek him out after her sister fled town without paying for her bachelor. But here Lydia was, trying to salvage the integrity of her family name. Doing what she thought was right.

She worked hard, for another, taking her job seriously. The difference she'd already made with Teddy was all the proof he needed.

And, as he stepped through the open library doors to see her silhouetted by moonlight streaming through the windows of an otherwise darkened room, James was reminded how incredibly sexy she was, too. The sweater dress hugged her curves, her face tipped upward. She'd slipped into the leather boots she'd worn earlier in the day, the heels making her almost as tall as him.

"You should see the moon," she said softly. "It's so huge above the tree line, it looks like a movie set. Or a honky-tonk bar."

He sucked in a breath, steeling himself for the inevitable draw of her nearness. Knowing the next move had to be hers after he'd made his intentions clear this afternoon.

"One of the benefits of living out here," he admitted. "No city lights or buildings to get in the way of the view."

He stopped short of her, since touching her again was out of the question. Without the barrier of the baby around, he had only his own restraint to rely on. And he sure as hell wasn't going to test it for a second time today.

He leaned against the windowsill the same way she did, leaving two feet between them.

"Thank you for today." She folded her arms, one shoulder tipping against the glass pane. "For coming home and being a part of everything I had planned."

"I know you did it for Teddy." She'd been very clear about her motives. Very careful to draw boundaries. "But I had fun, too."

"So did I." Her hazel eyes locked on his.

Desire for her flared hotter. His hands itched to reach for her. To pull her against him and keep her there while he tested the softness of her lips. Tasted his fill.

Instead, he eased away from the window, needing more space from her if he was going to maintain this facade of a professional relationship. "Are you ready to see your surprise?"

Her eyebrow arched. Straightening, she nodded. "Absolutely."

"Then follow me." He headed toward the back wall of the library, to a door almost hidden by bookshelves. The room was designed that way, giving this added space an intimate ambiance. "I have a secret retreat that I thought you might enjoy some evenings after Teddy goes to bed."

He slid open the door with the antique brass handle and hit the switch for the floor lights. Inside, tiny white bulbs glowed on either side of the aisle down the center of his media room. Big leather chairs flanked the aisle in pairs, for sixteen seats in all. The screen ahead was dark for a moment until he hit a command on his phone and cued up the opening credits of a nature documentary. On the screen, the sun rose on an African savannah while birds dipped and called. He hit the mute button but let the video run.

"All this time you've been hiding a home movie theater in here?" Her fingers smoothed along the leather seat rest of a chair. "What a great space."

"I didn't show it to you that first day because I had a few clients in to look at film of one of our horses in training and there was still some electronic equipment out." He rolled aside one of the screens on some built-in shelving to show her a sample of the technology not in use at the moment. "This isn't always a good spot for a toddler. But I thought you might enjoy unwinding here sometimes."

"I will. May I?" At his nod, she lowered herself into one of the chairs as if to test it out. "This is so comfortable. Do you ever fall asleep watching movies?"

He sat in the chair beside her, only an armrest separating them in the dim room while the film showed a family of lions on the move. "Never. Believe it or not, I've only used the room for previewing racing footage or rodeo competitions since our training program involves a lot of animal analysis."

Lydia made a face, wrinkling her nose. "You remember what they say about all work and no play?"

"Guilty." He couldn't deny it. Although being around this woman made him want to be someone different. Someone more inclined to have fun. "But my life has been anything but dull these last few weeks."

Leaning deeper into the seat back, she turned to look at him. She appeared comfortable. More relaxed than he'd ever seen her. Was she more at ease now that Teddy was sleeping? Or maybe she was simply worn out from a long day of caregiving.

"Mine, too." A smile hitched at her lips. "James, I haven't forgotten what we talked about in the car today."

Anticipation fired through him, but he didn't shift closer. Didn't touch her. He'd put the ball in her court for making the next move and he intended to be patient while she grappled with the hunger he'd wrestled since they first met. "It's been on my mind all day, too."

"I'm afraid I still don't have any more answers than I did earlier." Frowning, she nibbled at her lip for a moment as she turned her eyes toward the viewing screen where little lion cubs tackled each other. Then, she glanced back at him. "Although, I will say it's easier to contemplate a kiss when I'm not working."

The words reverberated through him like a bell, the hum of it remaining in his body long after she finished speaking. Every nerve ending acutely attuned to her.

He slid his hand under the armrest between them and tilted it up and out of the way. Removing the only physical barrier between them, but not crossing it.

"Then, solely in the interest of refreshing your memory, I'd like to remind you of my proposition."

Her shoulder angled a fraction closer to him. "Please do."

Her words were a throaty rasp of air as her fingers landed lightly on his chest.

She had to feel the rapid thrum of his heart. Wanting more.

"I thought we should shove aside all the things keeping us apart and just test run that kiss." He liked her hand on him, not just because it felt so damn good to have her touch him, but also because it freed him to touch her back.

He cradled her jaw in one hand, testing the softness of her lower lip with his thumb.

"See if it's worthwhile?" she asked.

The play of her mouth against his skin mesmerized him as she arched closer still.

"Something like that." He watched up until the last moment when her lips brushed his.

A tentative exploration. A minty breath. The tender grip of her fist twisting his shirt placket.

And then, confident he'd let her make the first move, he wrapped his arms around her, dragging her against him. She was so soft and sweetly scented, her hair fraying loose from its confining braid and her sweater dress teasing his skin.

He molded her curves to the hard planes of his body, liking the way she fit against him. Needing more, but knowing it wasn't time yet.

Knowing he'd negotiated for only a kiss. A taste.

He focused on just that—the feel of her lips and the damp stroke of her tongue. He gave and took in equal measures, exploring what she liked, breathing her in. Her hands were restless on him, gliding up his arms and down his chest.

Her touch made it impossible to pull away. She felt so damned good in his arms. So right. He adjusted the angle, deepening the kiss, telling himself it was just for a moment. She gripped his shoulders tightly, dragging him closer. Her breasts brushed his chest, and the contact made everything hotter, threatening his control.

He kissed her until his restraint stretched as thin as he dared.

Only then did he ease away carefully. Slowly.

Lydia's eyes fluttered open, her lips still parted. Damp.

With an effort, he closed his eyes. Let go of her completely.

"I should—um. Go." She sounded rattled. Or maybe she was simply as revved up as him.

But he couldn't have stopped her. Not without falling into that kiss all over again. So he just nodded tightly, remaining in his seat while she rose to her feet.

On the screen behind her, he saw night had fallen on the savannah. As for the test run of a kiss, he wasn't sure if he'd call it a success or a failure since it turned out to be the most combustible kiss he'd ever experienced.

One thing he knew for sure, though. He wouldn't try that again unless they were both prepared for it to lead to a whole lot more.

# Seven

With Christmas just days away, Rose Clayton suspected she should have been prepared for the crowds of people at the Courtyard Shops just west of Royal's downtown area. This was the town's most popular shopping district, the property a reclaimed old farm where the big red barn was now an antiques store and the main house sheltered local artisans. But it had been so long since Rose had shopped for something in person—as opposed to online or through one of her ranch's administrative assistants—that she'd forgotten how much of a crush the holiday shopping outing could be. It seemed like she'd seen half the townspeople here in the last hour, from local rancher Caleb Mackenzie and his fiancée, Shelby Arthur, to the newly engaged Ryan Bateman and Tessa Noble.

Then again, maybe Rose's eye was simply drawn to all the happy couples in town. She wanted that kind of happiness for her grandson, Daniel.

And for herself.

Taking a moment to rest in front of the live pine tree decorated with lights and oversize ornaments just outside the antiques shop, Rose soaked in the atmosphere. From the local children's choir singing carols to the scent of hot pretzels and roasted chestnuts, the outdoor venue oozed holiday cheer. Or maybe it was her who was filled with so much goodwill in the days following Gus's declaration that he was going to marry her.

Had he meant it?

Or had he just told Daniel that in an effort to keep the peace? She hadn't wanted to quiz Gus about it, unwilling to ripple the waters in this tenuous new joyful place in her life. Besides, daydreaming about a future with him made her feel like a teenager again.

Except this time, she began to think their story could have a happy ending.

"Hello, Rose." The deep timbre of a male voice sounded nearby, and she turned to see her neighbor, James Harris.

Dressed in dark jeans and a coffee-colored

suede jacket, he looked more relaxed than the last time she'd seen him—working tirelessly to restring fencing near her property line.

"Nice to see you, James." She hadn't attended his brother's funeral halfway across the state, but she'd sent flowers with her condolences. The Harris family had been good to her over the years and she was sorry to see James lose a brother at such a young age. "I've been wondering how you're doing with a toddler in the house."

"Hanging in there." He grinned as he tipped up his Stetson a fraction, juggling his shopping bags over to one hand. "I found a nanny who has really been making a difference with Teddy. Her name is Lydia Walker and I'm sure you'll see her around the ranch sooner or later."

"Mrs. Davis mentioned her to me when she came over to store some things in our extra freezer." Rose gathered the older woman wasn't thrilled with the new hire, but then Bernadette Davis had always been protective of the Harris boys. She'd been livid that James's first wife had been more interested in the Harris family fortune than her husband.

"Thank you for letting us use the freezer, by the way. I appreciated that."

The children's choir gave way to a handbell group, the ringing chimes filling the air as Rose waved off James's thanks, unwilling to accept praise for something so small.

"Your granddaddy was one of the kindest men I've ever met." Henry Harris had been one of the few people in Royal who had seen right through her act when she'd rebuffed her friends during those awful years after she'd married Edward. She couldn't bear for any of her former friends to know how Edward treated her, so she'd been cruel in the way she'd alienated everyone. But James's grandfather, a shrewd military veteran, had never bought the act. He'd kept right on being good to Rose. "You know if you ever need anything, you only have to ask. And what did you say the nanny's name was?"

She'd thought it sounded familiar.

"Lydia Walker." He lifted a hand in greeting to someone behind her as he said it. "Here she is now, in fact. She's helping me finish my holiday shopping today."

Rose turned, curious to see the woman who made James smile that way. There was a blatant male interest there that was hard to miss. And wasn't it interesting that James was out with the nanny—but no child in sight?

"Hello." The younger woman greeted her, extending her hand as she tucked a small shopping bag under her arm. Tall and slim, she wore a long skirt with boots and shawl-collar sweater, fashionable but down-to-earth. "I'm Lydia Walker, Mrs. Clayton. I recognize you from volunteering with the Family Fun Run you organized for the children's club last summer."

"Walker." Rose repeated it without meaning to, a trick that sometimes worked to jog a memory. She snapped her fingers as it came to her. "Wasn't that the name of the big bidder at the bachelor auction?" She had been stunned—along with the rest of the crowd—at the bid from the young woman. "What a tremendously generous donation to the charity."

Uh-oh. Apparently she'd stepped in it, based on the wary looks the two of them exchanged. As the awkward silence hovered, the scent of roasted chestnuts intensified with a vendor walking past with a silver concession cart. Fragrant smoke billowed to either side.

"Gail Walker is my sister," Lydia confirmed as she dodged a pair of little girls playing tag. "She definitely surprised us all with her bid."

Lydia's smile looked strained while James added, "But thanks to your grandson, Rose, the press coverage after the event really helped bring in more donations. The Pancreatic Cancer Research Foundation couldn't have asked for a better spokesperson than Daniel."

Rose was glad to hear it. But had the added donations been worth alienating her own grandson?

"Daniel isn't thrilled about being the 'Most Eligible Bachelor in Texas,' but he's been a good sport."

Rose traded a few more words with the two of them before they left to finish their holiday shopping. Her gaze followed James and Lydia, curious about the relationship that struck her as more than just professional. It was in the way they looked at one another. The way they stood close without touching.

The way they'd gone on a shopping outing without Teddy.

Not that it was any of her business. But Rose had learned a thing or two about the ways romance could grow between unsuspecting people over the years. Maybe she had an eye for matchmaking. She'd gained a keen eye for romance since it had been decidedly absent in her own life for so long.

But now, she had Gus.

Which reminded her, she needed to finish up her shopping, too.

She was about to enter Priceless, the antiques store in the big red barn that anchored the Courtyard Shops, when her phone vibrated. She pulled it from her jacket pocket to see a text from her grandson.

I'm getting more messages and deliveries every day from nutcases who want to meet me because of that damned article. From now on, I'm forwarding everything to the main house for you since this is what you wanted. I'm done.

Knowing how frustrated Daniel was sure didn't lift Rose's spirits. She'd only meant well by having the reporter write an article about Daniel. But he seemed more miserable than ever since she and Gus had orchestrated the breakup between him and Gus's granddaughter, Alexis Slade. At the time, they'd been so sure their feud would last forever, and their grandkids didn't belong together.

But she'd gone and fallen for Gus again in spite of herself. So what right did she have to keep Daniel and Alexis apart?

Maybe she didn't have such a good eye for matchmaking after all. One way or another, she and Gus needed to make this right for their grandchildren.

Listening to James on the phone with Teddy's babysitter, Lydia walked with him to his car parked near the Courtyard Shops.

"Just make sure you have the nursery monitor with you when you go downstairs," he explained to the young woman, his ranch foreman's daughter, who was home from college for the holidays. "I'm sure Mrs. Davis left some snacks for you on the counter."

Lydia smiled to hear him, thinking he was getting the hang of caring for his nephew. Ever since she'd started at the Harris house, she could see more ease in his interactions with the boy. But would his increased comfort level with his role prompt him to raise Teddy as his own?

Clearly, that had been his brother's preference.

Weaving between parked cars, she allowed her eyes to linger on James as they neared his vehicle. Memories of their kiss still made her breathless, sparking a fresh longing in her as she admired his athletic grace and powerfully built body. She'd agreed to the shopping outing when he had urged her to take some downtime away from the ranch, and she'd thought that was a good idea. Since she had some of her own Christmas shopping to do, she'd thought it could be fun to help him purchase gifts for Teddy while they had a sitter for the boy.

And it had been.

But she hadn't been prepared to field questions about Gail's bid from Rose Clayton. Not that Rose had questioned her, per se. Lydia had simply felt uncomfortable accepting any kind of "thanks" on Gail's behalf since her sister hadn't made the donation in the first place.

James had.

He finished up his call with the babysitter a moment later and pocketed his phone.

"The sitter is set for a few hours and I've got the feed from the nursery monitor on my phone." He opened the passenger door of the black BMW sedan. He'd already loaded the shopping bags in the backseat while she'd been preoccupied. "I had hoped I could talk you into dinner."

She hadn't expected the shopping outing to lead to more. And dinner definitely sounded like *more*. But after that kiss in his home theater, she'd been thinking about him all the time.

Imagining what might have happened if she hadn't retreated to her room that night.

"Dinner?" She met his gaze.

"The timing is perfect," he told her reasonably. Before he leaned fractionally closer, his voice lowering. "And I have been forthright about wanting to know you better."

A clear invitation.

Her heart beat faster.

"You have." She appreciated that. It made things easier with their working relationship that he'd put the ball in her court about how things would advance. Or not. "Can we just commit to that much? A get-to-know-you dinner?"

"Dinner only." He nodded as she slid into the passenger seat. "Dessert optional. I'm game. I'd like to spend a couple of hours learning more about what makes Lydia Walker tick."

His words circled around her mind as he walked to the driver's side door and started the car.

"You're serious about that?" She thought of all the men her mother had dated—and there had been many. She wondered if any of them had ever taken the time to really understand the real Fiona Walker.

She couldn't help but admire James for going to the effort.

"Of course. We should play a round of twenty questions or something. Make it fun."

The idea appealed to her, especially since she knew that James had been dealing with a lot recently. Not just the death of his sibling, but adjusting to a child in his life and the demands on his time from his relatively new position as Texas Cattleman's Club president.

Her own frustrations—mainly with Gail, but also with her mom—seemed small by comparison. Gail would come back to Royal sooner or later and Lydia would help her find a way to repay James if only in child care help. As for their mom, Lydia had to make Fiona understand she wasn't going to be a part of her wedding.

"I like it. Who goes first?" She didn't ask where they were going to dinner, although she was a little curious. It had been a long time since she'd been on a date.

And there was no denying it now that the shopping outing had turned to dinner—this *was* a date.

"Lydia, you wound me. Ladies first, of course."

"Sorry." She grinned as she shifted in her seat to see him better. "My usual male companions are in the one- to ten-year-old demographic, and they don't always have the manners you do. But if I'm going first, I want to know what you do for fun."

"For fun?"

"Yes. I've seen you work on the ranch and at the club. But even a busy man like you needs to unwind. And I know you don't take in a movie in the home theater since you've only used that for work."

He took his time thinking. "I used to do saddle bronc riding," he said finally. "I quit once I took on full responsibilities as the head of Double H, but I always enjoyed it."

There was a wistfulness in his voice that made her wonder how long it had been since responsibilities had consumed all his time. She wanted to learn so much more about him.

"You deserve a new hobby," she settled for saying instead.

"Inspire me, then. What do you do for fun?" He turned her question back on her as they drove under streetlights draped with wreaths and holiday lights.

"I'm a nanny. I play all the time."

"If you needed to unwind, I guarantee you peek-aboo isn't your first choice for entertainment."

She smiled. "Point taken. I like hiking. I don't get to go often anymore, but growing up I liked taking my siblings onto the trails in the Ozarks."

"Sounds nice. Although you have to admit, you

might need to update your hobbies, too, if your best memories of hiking are from when you were growing up." He turned off the main road and it took her a moment to see the sign for The Bellamy.

"We can't have dinner here." She'd never been to the five-star resort inspired by George Vanderbilt's iconic French Renaissance chateau in North Carolina, but she'd seen photos and knew the place epitomized luxury.

"Of course we can. You like to visit the farmers market on Saturdays at the Courtyard Shops, right?"

She'd told him as much during their shopping outing today.

"Yes. And the farmers market is more my speed for a meal." Even at night, she could see the gorgeous, castle-like building looming ahead and all lit up. The stone turrets had huge holiday wreaths adorned with red bows, while white lights illuminated a massive poinsettia tree out front. So romantic. Anticipation heated through her.

"The Bellamy has a great farm-to-table restaurant, the Glass House. You'll love it." He was already pulling up to the valet stand.

"I'm not sure I'm dressed appropriately," she told him before he could lower the window.

"It's not overly glitzy, I promise." With the car in Park, he took her hand in his, his clasp firm and gentle all at once. "The emphasis is on great food, not decor. And you look beautiful."

She warmed at his words. She'd never been the glamorous type, but she appreciated that he saw beyond the superficial, that he saw *her*.

And wanted her.

"In that case, thank you," she said, her heart beating faster. "And based on our first round of questions, it seems like we owe it to ourselves to have some fun, don't we?"

"I'm on a mission tonight." He lifted her hand in his, kissing the back of it. "We're going to unwind and have fun."

Her skin tingled where his lips had touched her, leaving her breathless. For a moment, she forgot all about dinner, her brain stuck on the feel of his mouth on her. She'd signed on for this. Dinner. Getting to know him. A date.

And if a little shiver of nerves scuttled through her to think about what that meant—getting into a relationship with her boss—she chose to ignore it. She had worked hard. Like James, she'd taken on a lot of responsibilities at a young age. She'd always been the one to deny herself what she wanted to help out her family, while her mother and her sister certainly never thought twice about indulging themselves. Why couldn't she have a chance to do something a little wild? A little reckless?

If tonight presented her with a chance to simply

enjoy herself on the arm of a handsome man intent on charming her, Lydia wasn't going to refuse.

In fact, given how much she wanted him, she might be the one to suggest they go for dessert after all.

# Eight

"This is amazing." Lydia closed her eyes after a bite of the wood-roasted mushrooms midway through their dinner, clearly savoring the experience.

James hadn't eaten at the Glass House before, but he had to admit he was impressed, too. The farm-to-table restaurant had a tasting menu and he'd talked her into trying it with him so they could see what they liked best. So far, there hadn't been a bad dish in the lot, each new plate boasting locally farmed fruits and vegetables, plus cheeses made on-site and wines from an extensive cellar. Lydia professed a special love of the mushroom dish, though, even after their waiter had delivered tasting plates of smoked trout, grilled guinea hen and roasted duck.

They sat at a quiet table in the back that overlooked The Bellamy grounds, including an ornamental garden decorated with white lights for the holidays. Inside, a pianist played in the front of the restaurant, the sound pleasantly dulled for conversing thanks to the live plants and potted trees that served as the main decor. Even inside, the Glass House was full of greenery.

"It's good to see you enjoying yourself since we now know that we both work too hard." He'd been surprised to realize how long it had been since he'd taken any time for fun when she'd asked him about it earlier.

Lydia sipped her wine, a pinot noir the sommelier had paired for this course.

"I'm very fulfilled by my work," she said as she replaced her glass on the table near a tray full of white votive candles and interspersed with white poinsettia blooms. "So I'm not sure that I necessarily devote too much time to it. But I could probably balance the job with more fun outlets."

"And yet your job with the child care facility will be different from what you've been doing, right?" he asked, liking the way she'd let her guard down tonight. "Why the change?"

"I thought it would be rewarding to oversee more children. To potentially touch more kids' lives than I could as a nanny." She pushed back from the table slightly, crossing her legs in a way that had her calf brush against his for a moment.

Her gaze darted to his, awareness from that touch pinging back and forth between them. Heat rising from even that brief contact. Was she finding it as tough to refrain from more as him? That kiss they'd shared was never far from his mind.

"Yet you've been taking care of kids your whole life. Or so it seemed to me when I read your mother's blog."

That flash of heat he'd seen in her eyes faded a bit, and he partially regretted bringing it up. But hadn't they said they were going to get to know each other?

"The *House Rules* empire is built on a whitewashed version of my family. The truth bears little resemblance to the fiction she posts online." She stopped speaking when their waiter neared to clear the plates from the meal and bring them the next round of the tasting menu, a selection of desserts.

The restaurant had grown more crowded since they'd started their meal, the muffled conversations of other diners rising though their corner of the room remained private.

Once the waiter left, Lydia dipped her spoon in the ginger ice cream while James wondered how to get their conversation back on track. He wanted Lydia first and foremost. But until she was ready for things to move forward between them, he would at least make sure he understood her more. Find out what made her tick.

"So you weren't involved with raising your siblings?" he asked, wondering how she could have faked all that knowledge she'd seemed to have in the videos online where she gave mini-lessons to parents on making homemade baby food or how to swaddle an infant.

"I was very involved," she clarified while he scooped some of the strawberry sorbet onto his plate. "But we weren't the carefree family my mother tried to pretend when she wrote blogs about our outings to the mountains or a day at the lake. While she was making daisy chain crowns with one kid for a good photo op, I was chasing six others to keep them from drowning or falling off a cliff."

He waited a beat to see if there was a follow-up to that story. An indication that she'd been exaggerating. But she simply swirled her spoon through the ice cream and took another bite.

"Didn't anyone else from your mother's business notice? Or get involved to help?"

"For years, there was no one else in the business. It wasn't until my late teens that the YouTube videos took off and started driving traffic to her blog, expanding her reach to what it is today." She set aside her spoon and leaned back in her seat while the pianist switched to a holiday tune on the far side of the restaurant.

Lydia's hazel eyes met his, and she swept a lock of her light brown hair away from her face. She wore a long skirt and a creamy-colored sweater belted at her waist, the shawl collar parting enough to show a hint of the pink tank she wore beneath it. A long gold necklace full of tiny charms nestled at the V of the sweater's opening, her initial glinting in tiny amber-colored stones on one of the pendants that dangled between her breasts.

"In that case, your mother owes a great deal to you for her success." He nudged a plate of green apple cobbler toward her to tempt her. "Not just for watching your siblings while she worked, but also for creating all those videos."

She arched an eyebrow at him. "Please don't tell me you watched any of my videos. I sound like the world's most pompous seventeen-year-old."

"I'm not going to lie. I was too curious about how to swaddle a baby to pass that one up. But I thought you sounded like a very knowledgeable young lady."

Shaking her head, she gave a wry laugh. "I made those videos after I argued with my mother. I told her she was doing her visitors a disservice by emphasizing child-centered learning to the point where her kids were no longer being parented. I thought she should provide more practical advice."

"So she let you do the work for her, and you made the videos." From what he'd seen when he visited the blog, Lydia's videos were the biggest draw.

"It was her way of putting my experience in my own hands," she said drily. "She would say that she gave me all the resources I needed to have a meaningful childhood. And she did give me a percentage of the advertising dollars that those videos made. But I always resented not being able to attend college full-time because I was scared to leave the younger kids unattended."

How different their childhood years had been. Lydia had been raised by a woman whom many people looked up to as a role model for motherhood, surrounded by siblings. James and his brother had been raised by nannies once their mother died, their father too involved with the ranch to spend time with his kids.

"And yet you went into a profession centered on children. You must look forward to having a family of your own one day."

The observation was automatic, and maybe too personal. But he was curious.

"One day," she acknowledged, a hint of wariness in her expression.

He wanted to know more about her, to ask more about her family, but she leaned closer to him then, her fingers sliding onto his wrist where his hand rested on the table. The contact robbed him of whatever he'd been about to say while her light fragrance teased him, stirring a different hunger.

"You're getting way ahead of me on the questions," she announced, her hair sliding forward as she tipped her forehead closer to his. "It must be my turn by now."

He wanted to kiss her. Would have kissed her if they were alone. Maybe it was just as well they'd spent the day together out in public. Because without Teddy around, he couldn't help but see Lydia as a desirable woman and not as his nephew's nanny.

"By all means." His voice lowered since she was so close to him. "Ask me anything."

She stared back at him, her hazel eyes reflecting the candlelight's glow. He lifted his free hand to smooth her silky hair away from her face so he could see her better. Or maybe he simply needed to touch her in some way.

When he tucked the strands behind her ear, he skimmed his fingertips down the side of her neck. Felt the wild race of her pulse just beneath her ear. Once they were alone, he promised himself he would kiss her right there, for a long, lingering taste.

Her eyelids fluttered even now, as if she could feel the burning imprint of his lips on her skin.

"I hope you mean that." She eased back a bit, nibbling on her lower lip as her hand slid away from his wrist. "Because I've been wondering where things stand with Teddy's grandparents. You said you'd reached out to them. Have they expressed an interest in taking him in?"

The question was a far cry from what he'd expected. But he'd been honest about wanting to know more about her. So he needed to let her understand him better, too. He'd made a mistake with his wife not to give her a clearer idea of what life would be like on the Double H. It would have benefited them both to discuss their expectations.

"I get the impression they're still grieving deeply for their daughter." He hadn't wanted to push them, but their lack of response the first time had made him send a follow-up letter. "They were still struggling with the loss, even though from what Parker told me, they were unhappy with her for marrying him in the first place and hadn't spoken to their daughter after the wedding."

Lydia shook her head, her expression showing dismay while the waiter cleared plates and refreshed their water.

"James, isn't that all the more reason for you to raise Teddy instead of them? You can't let that sweet baby go to a cold and unforgiving household who will have nothing positive to say about Teddy's father."

He didn't miss the hint of accusation in her voice. In her eyes.

"Parker always thought they'd come around."

James had trusted his brother's judgment of his in-laws. "They didn't necessarily dislike Parker, but they had planned for their daughter to marry the rancher with land neighboring theirs. Her marriage to my brother caused them to lose some of their acreage to the neighbor."

James hadn't remembered all the details since he'd been knee-deep in expanding the Double H at the time and marrying Raelynn. His focus had been on his own bride.

"That hardly seems like grounds for not speaking to your own daughter." Lydia toyed with the petal of one of the white poinsettias on the table, her pink manicured fingernail tracing the outline. "What if they cut Teddy off that way? Decide to stop speaking to him?"

James reached over to squeeze her hand, needing to reassure her. "I promise I would never let my nephew go into a home unless I was certain he would be raised with love."

He owed Parker that, and more.

Her eyes searched his. And whatever she saw there must have eased her concerns somewhat because some of the tension slid from her shoulders.

"Thank you." She nodded. Accepting. "Can I ask one more thing? Since you were ahead of me in the question game?"

"Is this one going to be as dicey as the last one?" He signed the tab the waiter had left on the table, and then sat back, wanting Lydia to feel comfortable talking to him.

He wasn't going to reach the level of intimacy he craved with her if she couldn't speak freely to him. And he wanted her more with each passing minute.

"Possibly." She recrossed her legs, her calf nudging his for a second time. "Can I still ask?"

Awareness flared from the contact. Hotter this time. His thoughts about what he wanted from this night threatened to derail his focus.

"Of course." He couldn't stop himself from threading his fingers through hers.

She stared at him in the candlelight, the loveliest woman he could imagine. Not just because of her looks, but because of her giving nature. Her warm heart. He wanted to lose himself in all that beautiful inner radiance.

But before she could ask him her next question, a feminine voice trilled from behind them.

"James Harris, you gorgeous man! Where've you been hiding?"

He recognized the voice of Cady Lawson, an outrageous flirt and an old friend. He knew exactly when Lydia spotted her because her luscious lips turned into a quick frown before an unreadable mask settled over her expression. She tugged her hand from his. Folded her arms across her chest.

Standing to introduce the women, James wondered how fast he could send Cady on her way so he could get this night back on track.

If Lydia had been the jealous type, she guessed the arrival of James's lady friend could have ruffled her feathers. Dressed in sleek white leather pants and a designer white silk blouse, the woman was beautiful enough to have walked out of the pages of a magazine. Glossy dark curls spilled over her shoulders, her natural beauty not needing any adornment as she flung her arms around James.

But as Lydia listened to James's introduction to Cady Lawson, a friend from his college days, Lydia could think only how grateful she was for the woman's timing. Lydia had been about to quiz James about the fact that he'd married a woman who hadn't wanted children—a significant detail she'd caught in that first conversation she'd had with him about his ex. But with all the heated awareness between them, and his tempting touches, she'd found herself wanting to back off a question that was probably—at this stage of their relationship—none of her business.

She'd used the twenty questions game to find out enough to know she cared about him, and that she appreciated his willingness to be forthright with her. Was it really necessary to have her every curiosity about him answered before she indulged in the attraction? No doubt her mother's haste to rush into relationships had made Lydia overly cautious.

At least, she hoped it had. She never wanted to be the kind of woman who catapulted into romance.

So even though James wore a wary expression as he conducted his conversation with the absurdly beautiful—and overtly flirtatious—Cady, Lydia found herself thankful for the reprieve from a dicey conversation. Apparently Cady was from Royal but lived in Dallas now, and had met a few friends at the Glass House for dinner.

"Well, I hope you know I would have attended that bachelor auction fundraiser if you'd been on the slate," Cady teased James, winking at Lydia. "I heard it through the grapevine that's why you took the Texas Cattleman's Club job as president. To keep yourself off the auction block."

Lydia found herself smiling. That sounded like the man who preferred to work over having fun.

They spoke for another moment before one of Cady's friends waved her back to their table.

"I really should go." She made a point of squeezing Lydia's shoulder in a friendly gesture. "It was nice meeting you, Lydia. Take care of him. He's a keeper."

The woman wouldn't have heard even if Lydia had tried to reply since she hurried away on metallic silver pumps that looked worthy of Cinderella herself. Instead, she glanced up at James, who could only shake his head.

"I'm sorry about that—"

Lydia cut him off and rose to her feet. "No need to apologize for having glamorous friends. I'm ready to go home, if you are."

"Of course. I hope you didn't feel rushed."

"Not at all." She slid her arm through the crook of his elbow, grateful for the chance to redirect the evening. "I was ready to leave."

"What about your question?" He readjusted her hand on his arm, covering it with his. Tucking her closer. "You were just about to throw me back in the hot seat."

She caught a hint of his aftershave as she glanced up at him, eye level with his jaw.

"I changed my question," she confided as he opened the door for her and passed the valet his ticket.

The cool night air made her step even closer to him and he wrapped his arm around her waist, his hand an inviting warmth on her hip.

"You did?" The question was a deep vibration of sound against her ear as he kissed her hair there.

Pleasurable shivers raced up and down her spine, his voice enticing her. She half wished the valet wouldn't return with the vehicle so they could stand this way longer.

Then again, the sooner the car came, the sooner

they'd be back at his home with the night ahead of them.

"Yes." She knew what she wanted, and she didn't want to be cautious about it anymore. "I just want to ask you, how fast can you get us home so we can be alone?"

As it happened, James had gotten them home very quickly.

Lydia hadn't realized that The Bellamy was so close to the Double H since they'd made a stop at the shops before dinner. A fire flamed hot inside her on the ride home, her body tense from holding back now that she'd decided to move forward with this out-of-control attraction. But before she knew it, James was steering the luxury sedan into the third bay of the ranch's main garage. The overhead door closed silently behind them.

"I just need to pay the sitter." He switched off the engine and exited the car, opening her door a moment later to offer his hand. "I'll meet you upstairs?"

She touched him only briefly, just enough to let him help her from the vehicle. If her hands lingered on him now, she feared she might not be able to pry herself away again.

As it was, his eyes dipped to her legs where her coat parted, the gaze smoking over her skin like a caress.

"Okay." She nodded, breathless from the contact. From thoughts of where tonight was going to lead. "I'll check on Teddy."

She hurried ahead of him when he let her inside the house, rushing up the stairs before she ran into one of the household staff or the sitter. She had used up all her restraint where this man was concerned, and she didn't want to risk any more delays.

Stopping by her room to shed her coat and her shoes, Lydia wondered if this was how her mother felt when she fell for a new man. Padding barefoot into her bathroom to run a brush through her windblown hair, Lydia recalled that it seemed like Fiona was in a mental fog when she met someone new. Her mom's starry-eyed attempts to get any work done were hampered by an inability to focus, an almost giddy preoccupation with the new man. Lydia had thought it looked more like a sickness than romance. But for the first time, as she stared into the mirror and her own bright eyes, she had an inkling of that sweetly off-balance feeling, a sensation no other man had ever stirred.

She hoped it was just because she'd ignored the attraction for so long. Surely that's why it felt so over the top.

Setting the hairbrush on the sleek white quartz counter beneath the rustic wood-framed mirror, Lydia left the bathroom to check on Teddy for the night.

The nursery door was slightly open, making it easy to slip into the boy's room. The new airplane night-light she'd bought for him glowed blue on the far side of the room, giving her enough light to see his face. Eyes closed, his arms rested on either side of his head, his green cotton sleeper snapped up to his neck. Lydia leaned over the crib to tug a lightweight blanket over his legs.

Turning on her heel, she almost ran into a solid wall of muscle and man.

James.

He steadied her shoulders, his hands an inviting warmth as they slid down her arms. She realized he'd taken off his shoes, too. No wonder she hadn't heard him on the plush carpet behind her.

"Sorry." He breathed the word into her ear before he glanced into the crib to see Teddy for himself. "Looks like he's down for the count."

Her heart beat too fast. James still held her hand, his fingers interlacing with hers.

"Is the sitter gone?" she asked, breathless and hoping that it sounded like she whispered on purpose.

"She is." He drew her out the door and into the hall with him before tugging her toward the master bedroom.

She hadn't seen that room on her tour of the house.

The arched double doors at the end of the corridor had been a source of intrigue for her other times during the past weeks. Now, as he turned the handle and opened them, she stepped over the threshold into his private retreat for the first time.

He let go of her hand to twist the lock, sealing them in the sitting area of the suite. Heavy linen curtains were drawn across one wall that she knew must be the bank of windows overlooking the front grounds. A stone fireplace held a stack of wood logs, and a steel-gray sectional sofa filled a corner near built-in bookshelves full of dark leather volumes. Framed paintings of stylized rodeo horses hung in a cluster above the mantel.

And, on the far side of the room, a massive four-poster bed.

James reached in the pocket of his jacket and withdrew the nursery monitor receiver. He set it on the wooden chest that served as a coffee table before returning to stand before her.

He made a point of checking his watch before he spoke.

"So, to answer your question from back at the restaurant, it seems I could have you home—and alone—in nineteen minutes." He relaxed his arms at his sides. Stepped fractionally closer. "I have to admit I'm curious where you wanted things to go from here."

Her heart beat so loudly now she could feel the

rush of blood in her ears, a vibration that drowned out everything else.

"Would you like me to be explicit?" She didn't know where she found that surge of boldness, but she smoothed the lapel of his jacket between her thumb and fingers, gliding up the fabric. "Or shall I just show you?"

She saw the flare of his nostrils. The way his pupils dilated so his eyes were almost black. She liked knowing she had that effect on him, too.

"I think I've gone past the point where I can handle anything explicit." He traced the line of her jaw with his knuckle, a teasing caress when she needed so much more. "I'll take the hands-on demonstration."

Heat tickled its way up her spine. And back down. Desire tantalizing her as her breathing grew ragged.

Arching up on her toes, she twined her arms around his neck, pressed herself to him and kissed him the way she'd been dying to for weeks.

# Nine

Her kiss felt like he'd reached the oasis after a long slog through the dessert.

James let the sensations roll over him as he anchored her against him. Her vanilla-and-floral fragrance, the silky sweep of her hair feathering along his shoulders, the soft, feminine curves molding to the hard planes of his body. All of it was so damned scintillating.

And that kiss.

Her lips moved with a ravenous hunger he'd only guessed at in the weeks leading up to this moment. For so long, she'd been the consummate professional. So careful to present her capable, efficient side to the world, that seeing this facet of her reminded him that she'd trusted him with something special.

He refused to waste a second of it. Easing back to look at her, he placed a kiss on her cheek. Each of her closed eyes.

"Come with me." Releasing his hold on her, he took her hand and led her toward the bed.

She paused a second before following him, and he realized she was reaching for the nursery monitor. Would he have forgotten? Maybe. But surely they would have heard him even from the other side of the large suite.

She'd slipped off her boots earlier, and her feet were soundless on the floor behind him. Her long skirt swished against his calf, a teasing caress as they reached the edge of the mattress. He hit the remote by the bed to dim the lights except for the two sconces flanking the fireplace.

He waited while she set the nursery monitor beside the remote on the nightstand, reminding himself not to rush this. To savor every moment of having her here with him.

But Lydia wasn't waiting. Because her fingers were already unfastening the top button of his shirt, her lips pressing a kiss to the skin she bared. Propelling him to a new tier of craving for her.

Heat flared over his skin. He skimmed a touch down her shoulders, tugging at the belted sweater, parting the shawl collar until he could see more of the silky tank she wore beneath. He bent to kiss her neck, liking the way she arched into him. He felt her heartbeat race in the soft hollow below her ear. Lingered there until he nipped her earlobe and peeled her sweater the rest of the way down.

Her soft moan coincided with her fingers' speeding up on his shirt buttons. Her hips sidled against him, a sign of the same restless ache he was feeling. An ache that had become second nature to him in the last week. The trip to Houston hadn't helped him douse it. If anything, time apart had only made him want her more.

With a fierceness he'd never felt for any woman.

Maybe that's why he was so careful not to let that hunger rule him now. Being with Lydia felt like uncharted terrain for him. An all-new experience.

"More naked," she demanded against his ear, her voice a breathless whisper he couldn't ignore.

He tugged her sweater off. Skimmed the silky tank up over her head, leaving her in the long skirt and a band of sheer lace around her breasts. The rosy peaks of her nipples tempted him, but Lydia was already sliding his shirt off.

"I meant you," she clarified, twisting to unfasten a hook on the side of her skirt that sent the pleated wool to the floor almost at the same time as his shirt joined it. "It's you who needs to be more naked."

She moved quickly now that she'd made up her mind to go through with this night, but James had been waiting so long to touch her he wanted to savor everything about her.

Sheer gray lace hugged her hips at the juncture of long, slender legs. The sight of her made him realize that taking his time wasn't going to work. Not when she trembled that way, her fingers jittery with anticipation and need.

He reeled her closer, wrapping her in his arms. Kissing her until some of that tension turned hot. Molten. She gripped his shoulders and he lifted her up, clamping an arm around her waist. He reached behind them to rake back the covers before he laid her down, her hair spilling over the pillowcase.

Lying down beside her, he kissed and touched her, finding the places she liked best. A kiss under her ear. A touch on the curve of her hip. Skimming across her belly. Cupping the lace between her legs.

The soft, whimpering sounds she made while he caressed her fueled his restraint, every throaty sigh steeling his resolve to wait. To bring her pleasure first. Ignoring the heated ache for her, he shifted all his focus on Lydia.

Ever so slowly, he rolled away the thin lace barrier over her breasts so he could tease one nipple with his tongue. She wrapped a hand around his back, palm splayed, holding him close. Drawing on the taut peak harder, he slid aside the lace between her legs, stroking her there.

Her breathing grew harsh, her short nails grazing his skin. Her back arched, her hips pushing against his hand until the tension broke in lush spasms that racked her whole body. A beautiful release that filled him with as much satisfaction as any of his own. He kissed her neck in the aftermath, holding her close until her heartbeat slowed a little.

Still a little dazed by the sweet shimmer of every nerve ending, Lydia had almost caught her breath when he slid out of bed. Before she could protest, she watched as his hands moved to his belt.

Just like that, the heat inside her flared again. That fast, her body reminded her of a new ache. The hunger for him returning. Wriggling out of her twisted lace underthings, she shed her clothes while he tossed aside the rest of his and returned to the mattress beside her.

He placed a condom on the nightstand. Gauntlet dropped.

She wrapped herself around him, arms twining behind his neck while he rolled her on top. She could feel how ready he was for her and it sent another shiver through her. Anticipation mingling with breathless desire.

When he kissed her this time, there was no holding back. No careful wait while she found release. This kiss was hungrier, a little less controlled. And she loved it.

She explored his body with her hands and mouth, reveling in the perfectly formed muscle, the taut strength evident with every flex and movement. When she kissed lower, though, tempted to give him the same kind of pleasure he'd shown her, he rolled her to her back. Pinning her briefly to the bed before he knelt up to find the condom on the nightstand.

She arched against him, hurrying him with frenzied movements of her hips. Her hands. She couldn't wait another moment.

And then, finally, he made room for himself between her legs. Entered her with a slow, perfect slide of their bodies together. The sensation stole her breath, her body slowly accommodating him while ribbons of pleasure trickled through her. She closed her eyes, savoring it, wanting to hold on to it for as long as she could.

But he started moving, and the magic of that only took her higher. Hotter. She was mindless again, all caution shredded and burnt to ashes as she clung to him, chanting her pleasure against his ear while they drove each other wild.

By the time he took her hands in his, holding

them over her head while he kissed her, she was lost to everything but this moment and the man. He reared back to look at her, his dark eyes locking on her for a long moment before he lowered his head to suckle her breast.

Sending her catapulting over the edge, release sweeping through her in one exquisite wave after another.

She wasn't sure if the squeeze of her body was what spurred his release or if he'd been that close already, but their voices mingled in a hoarse song of fulfillment. His a throaty shout, hers a high cry of perfect bliss.

He rolled to her side afterward, tucking her against him while she breathed in the scent of his skin. His jaw rested on her hair, the slight bristle of whiskers catching on her hair. She nuzzled deeper into the crook of his neck, more content than she had a right to be.

But she refused to think about that now. Not when everything inside her glowed with pleasure. She planned to hold on to this feeling for as long as she could. To simply be.

As their breathing slowed and Lydia thought she might doze off, a wail erupted from the speaker on the baby monitor.

A real-world reminder that this night hadn't changed anything and that she still had a job to do.

Nothing could have brought home faster the fact that she'd just slept with her boss.

But even as she righted herself to find her clothes, James gently pressed her shoulders back to the mattress.

"I'll get him." He brushed a caress over her hair. Kissed her forehead. "Don't go anywhere."

She thought about protesting, since she really didn't mind. She had missed Teddy today while he'd been with the sitter and she found herself looking forward to seeing him, if only to comfort him for a few minutes before putting him back to bed. But her nanny training told her it would be better for James to do that. To build the bond between the toddler and the man Lydia hoped would become his father.

"Okay." She smiled as James stepped into his boxers and shrugged his way into a T-shirt. "Thank you."

But as she watched him scoop up his phone and leave the room, she couldn't help but think it strange that her professional life had dictated her actions now instead of her personal preferences. Even though this evening had been the furthest thing from professional.

Tucking the covers higher under her chin, Lydia hoped she could figure out a way to balance the two sides sooner rather than later. Because she'd just experienced only her first taste of behaving with a little reckless abandon. She couldn't bear to return to her careful, cautious self just yet.

James paced around the nursery with his nephew asleep on his shoulder half an hour later, not ready to put him back in his crib quite yet.

Part of the reason was because he guessed Lydia would have dozed off by now, too, so no need to rush. But the other reason that had him still pacing? He knew that bringing Lydia to his bed tonight would have repercussions. She wasn't a woman to get involved lightly. He knew that in his bones. Yet here he was, risking losing a nanny he desperately needed just to be with her.

He tipped his cheek to his nephew's curls, stroking the baby's back while he stared at the stuffed felt figures that Lydia had strung along one wall. A bunny in a Santa hat. A couple of cats dressed like elves, one hammering a toy train and the other sewing a doll. She was so good at her job. Compassionate. Warmhearted.

She had come into James's life for Teddy's sake, but she'd brought a whole lot of happiness for both of them. Was it fair to Teddy to deprive the boy of Lydia if he went to live with his maternal grandparents? Thinking about parting with the child was getting tougher every day, but James had to do what was best for him.

Settling the baby back into the crib, James stepped

out of the nursery and into the hall to check his phone. He'd seen a message from Teddy's grandmother while they'd been out shopping, but he hadn't responded to her yet. He reread it now.

We gratefully accept your invitation to spend the new year with our grandson, Samantha Mason had written in a short email. We will be arriving in midafternoon on New Year's Eve and can watch Teddy for you that evening and the next day. Thank you for opening your home to us so we can get to know our grandson.

There was nothing in the note about taking Teddy full-time. But James understood they wanted to meet the boy first. Still, it shouldn't be like a job interview where Teddy had to perform well in order for his grandparents to want to raise him.

Either they wanted the child or not.

Still, this was a step in the right direction, he hoped. Teddy needed a more stable family than what James could provide. Plus, he deserved the tender touch of a mother figure in his life.

Opening an email screen for a response to Mrs. Mason, James tapped out a quick reply, confirming the details of their trip to Royal. The annual Texas Cattleman's Club New Year's Eve Ball was that night, and this way, Lydia would be available to accompany him.

James clicked the button to send the email and then strode back to the bedroom. He knew Lydia wanted to attend the New Year's Eve Ball for networking purposes, to find potential clients for the day care business she would open next fall. But he hoped she would be pleased to attend as his guest so they could share more incredible nights like this one.

He looked forward to thinking about how to invite her. Maybe with an extravagant Christmas present as a hint—earrings or a necklace, something beautiful to wear—could be his segue to asking her.

They had a lot of fun ahead of them. Together.

But first things first, he planned to slide back into his bed beside her. Kiss her. Touch her. Wake her slowly, in the most seductive way imaginable.

# Ten

Christmas Eve day passed in a whirl of holiday preparations, and Lydia had so much fun with James and Teddy that she felt a twinge of guilt by the time the evening rolled around. She hadn't phoned her mother. Hadn't tried calling Gail.

But as she watched Teddy and James lying side by side in the living room, making "snow" angels in giant piles of cotton balls, she couldn't muster much regret about her family. They hadn't phoned her either. A fact that made her wonder why she always had to be the one to give. Was it so wrong to soak up the fun with the Harris males? One, a giggling, overtired toddler patting the cotton ball snow onto his head. The other, an exceedingly attractive rancher who had hurdled all her defenses and inspired her to start thinking about her own wants for a change.

Maybe it was high time she did just that.

Seeing how much fun her two companions were having while they played at least reassured her she'd done one thing right in helping James to be more comfortable in his father role. There was no denying he was good at this.

"Mrs. Davis is going to wonder what happened when she gets home from her holiday with family and finds cotton everywhere for the next two weeks," James observed as he sat up. Fluffy white balls rolled off his shoulders, disappearing under the sofa.

For her part, Lydia was happy to have the house to themselves for three whole days. The cook, the housekeeper and the extra part-time staffers were all on vacation for Christmas. At least now she didn't have to pretend there was nothing going on between her and her sexy employer.

"I'll vacuum it up," she assured him, her gaze wandering over him appreciatively. "It was my idea."

"You're not allowed to clean." Something heated glinted in his eyes as he leaned closer to her, kissing her hands where they rested on her knees. "I'm pulling rank on you with that one. Besides, we can turn the cotton into a tree skirt, right?" He shoved a pile closer to the fifteen-foot Fraser fir near the windows. "It will look like it snowed in here."

"What should we do with the tired little boy in the middle of the floor?" She smiled to see Teddy carefully pulling apart a cotton ball, his fingers picking at the fluffy strands before he waved a hand impatiently to remove the tufts.

James was already on his feet, scooping Teddy up in his big, strong arms. "I'll only put him in bed if I can trust you not to clean anything while I'm gone."

Lydia rose, following him so she could wipe the remnants from the baby. "It's a deal, but let me make sure he doesn't have any extra pieces on him." She picked off a few bits clinging to his sleeper, making Teddy giggle. Then she carefully examined his hands. "My little sister got a strand of hair wrapped around her toe once inside her footie pajamas, and we had to take her to the ER to have the hair removed."

"You went to the ER for a strand of hair?"

"When it winds tightly enough, it can cut off circulation." She stepped back. "But he looks good to me."

James shook his head as he spoke to Teddy. "Champ, it looks like we're going to have to change your sleeper and examine all your toes now." He glanced back at Lydia before he started up the stairs. "And I've got an early present for *you* when I'm done. Don't go anywhere."

Something about the tone of his voice sent a shiver of awareness through her. Waking up in his arms this morning had felt incredibly decadent. Making love in the shower while Teddy napped had been even more self-indulgent. Still…

She could get used to it.

Not that she'd have the chance since this window of time with James was only temporary. Soon enough, the holidays would end, her sister would return and Lydia would convince Gail to step up and take over the nanny duties with Teddy. After all, it was still Gail who owed the debt to James, and Lydia had faith her sister would do what she could to pay him back for generously covering her donation. But could Lydia maintain a relationship with James if she was no longer working for him?

The idea tempted her.

Being with James had made her take more chances, and so far, she had reaped wonderful rewards from her gambles. Continuing to see him, to date, would be an even bigger risk. She'd never wanted to turn into a woman like her mother, falling head over heels at the drop of a hat. Yet what Lydia had with James seemed so much different from that. So much more special.

Sure, she may have felt like she'd rushed into an intimate relationship. But in comparison with how fast her mom normally moved from dating to the altar, Lydia had practically proceeded at a snail's pace.

She corralled a few rogue snowballs under the tree, liking the idea of a snowy tree skirt. Teddy had so much fun playing with the fake snow anyway, he would enjoy it tomorrow, too.

James's deep voice behind her sent a thrill through her. "Remember what I said about no cleaning?"

His arms went around her a moment later and she forgot everything but being with him. About falling for him. Maybe it would be simpler if it was just about the heated connection they shared. But that didn't begin to account for her growing feelings for this incredible man. The tenderness she experienced when she watched him play with his nephew. The respect she had for his generosity and his work ethic.

She couldn't pretend what she felt was simply attraction.

"I don't think you can boss me around when I'm not technically working now," she teased. Tipping her head back to his chest, she rubbed her cheek against all that hard strength. "And I think we'll have more fun tonight if I remain off-duty, don't you?"

"Yes." He spun her in his arms so she faced him. His eyes probed hers, his expression more serious than she'd expected. "I've been looking forward to tonight all day."

His hand cupped her cheek, cradling her face. Her heart stuttered a jerky rhythm. Had Gail felt anything close to this when she ran off on a weeks-long vacation with her bachelor?

If so, maybe Lydia owed her the tiniest bit of slack. Because right now, she could almost imagine turning her back on everything to be with him.

"Me, too," she told him honestly. As much fun as she'd had preparing for Christmas and playing with Teddy today, she'd be lying if she said she wasn't looking forward to a repeat of the night before.

The chance to be in James's arms.

"But first…" He let go of her to lead her toward the Christmas tree. "…presents."

He guided her toward the big leather sofa closest to the pine branches and waited while she took a seat. She tucked the skirt of her burgundy-colored sweater dress closer to her while she watched him retrieve a small box from the back of the tree.

Wrapped in gold foil painted with white snow-flakes, the paper was elegant, the package itself curiously shaped. He handed it to her, and she could feel a flat square on one side, and a heavier square against it. Almost like he'd wrapped a card.

"I only have one gift for you," she protested, wondering if she should retrieve it. "Shouldn't I wait to open this until tomorrow?"

He lowered himself onto the sofa beside her, his hand sliding around her waist. "No. This is a bonus present for tonight. Something I wanted you to have sooner rather than later."

How quickly she'd grown used to his touch. She leaned into it now while she slid a finger into the wrapping, not wanting to tear it needlessly. Inside, there was a card with her name on it along with a smaller box. But why had he wrapped the card?

She glanced over at him, but his expression gave nothing away as he waited. Opening the envelope, she saw it wasn't a greeting card, but an invitation.

"The Texas Cattleman's Club New Year's Eve Ball?" She read the embossed letters aloud. It was one of the most anticipated and prestigious events in Royal. "Really?"

"I want you to be my date," he added. "It should be fun, and I think it would really help you meet potential clients for the child care facility."

"That's very generous of you." She was touched that he'd thought of the business that meant so much to her. "I would be honored to be there."

She didn't know what the date said about their new relationship, but he must realize that taking his nanny to the New Year's Eve Ball would be a very public way to acknowledge their relationship. Surely that implied the same level of seriousness she felt about him?

"Good." He kissed her temple and squeezed her

waist a little tighter, hugging her. "Then open the next part of the gift."

Excited, she opened the foil paper carefully, then lifted the lid on a yellow-and-red box. Inside, nestled on a velvet cushion, rested an old-fashioned hair comb in art deco style, with crystals outlining three tiny skyscraper buildings.

"James, it's beautiful," she breathed, already imagining how she could wear her hair to show off the piece.

"It belonged to my mother. I have a photo of her and my father on New Year's Eve with that comb in her hair, and I would like you to have it."

Overwhelmed from the magnitude of the gesture, she shook her head. "I couldn't possibly accept a family heirloom—"

"Please." He laid his hand on her forearm. "She had an extensive collection of jewelry, and I think your kindness to her grandson warrants a thank-you. I know she would be as grateful to you as I am for all you've done to help Teddy."

Blinking away the sudden moisture in her eyes, she smiled. "In that case, thank you. I will treasure it."

She felt something shift inside her. A tender place in her heart that was just for this man. Or maybe it was the last of her defenses crumbling in the face of his warmth and generosity. No one had ever put her first the way he did.

Maybe that's why it was so easy to lose herself

in his kiss when he captured her chin in one strong hand. Because giving in to the heated attraction, and the simplicity of that connection, was easier than trusting the feelings for him multiplying with every moment they spent together.

James didn't waste a second coaxing Lydia up the stairs when he wanted her right here. Right Now.

The front door was locked. He had the nursery monitor feed on his phone. So he dragged the cashmere blanket from the arm of a nearby chair and spread it out on the leather sofa behind her before he gently lowered her there.

They'd been together on multiple occasions since that first electric encounter. But far from quenching his hunger for her, each time only made him want her more.

Lydia's frenzied touches were as desperate as his own, as if not touching for hours all day long drove them to this frantic shedding of clothes. His shirt. Her shoes. He didn't even bother removing her sweater dress. Between her wriggling and his greedy hands, they had the fabric up around her waist in no time.

"Condom?" she rasped against his lips, not even bothering to open her eyes while they kissed.

"Mmm." He reached in his pocket to put the packet in her hand since he didn't feel like breaking that kiss either.

He'd waited all day to have her mouth on him.

She must have set the packet aside, because her hands wandered over his fly, stroking and seeking, speeding his pulse to a drumroll. He helped her only to save himself from the zipper, but he appreciated her desire that echoed his own. The way she touched him threatened his control.

Together, they made quick work of his pants. Her panties. And, for expediency's sake, he ended up with her straddling his lap while he rolled the condom into place.

Her hands laced behind his neck, thighs bracketing his hips as he slid inside her. She tipped her forehead to his, holding herself very still for a long moment. He waited, need for her burning through him. But when she started to move, the sweetness of it made him want to give her free rein with him. She kissed her way up his neck. His jaw. All the while moving with a hypnotic grace that had him seeing stars.

It was too soon.

He'd hardly even touched her yet. But she seemed intent on her course, pinning his hands to the sofa cushion with the light press of her fingers. Her breath was a sweet brush of air along his earlobe when she told him how good it felt.

He closed his eyes, scavenging for the control he'd exercised the night before. But between her soft words, the gentle glide of her hips and the way her fingers circled his wrists, he was burning from the inside out. He kissed her deeply, then trailed his lips down her neck to her breast. He captured the peak with his mouth, feeling the answering shiver that coursed through her right before her release hit her.

He focused on the feel of it, her body throbbing all around him, drawing him deeper. Squeezing. He couldn't have held out another second, his own completion surging hard.

He banded his arms around her, anchoring her to him while the passion burned white hot. Leaving him spent and sagging into her. Strands of her hair clung to his skin as she laid her head on his shoulder. He kissed the top of her head, wanting to carry her to his bed. To wrap her in his arms and his blankets.

"That was just a warm-up," he assured her, drawing the cashmere throw up to her shoulders.

She gave a soft laugh as she disentangled herself from him and dressed. "In that case, I'm not sure I'd survive the main event. Besides, we have Christmas presents to bring downstairs. I know Teddy is young, but he will be excited to see all the packages in the morning."

James admired her commitment to making the day special for the boy. "You're a pretty great nanny." He slid on his boxers and pants. "The women who looked after Parker and me never gave much thought to our holidays."

She regarded him silently, as if waiting for

more. Making him realize how self-pitying that had sounded.

Damn.

"We had great holidays thanks to my dad." It was sort of true. Christmas was one of the few days their father didn't work. "I only pointed it out to let you know you're very generous with your time and attention."

"Every child deserves happy holiday memories." She folded her arms around herself. "And Teddy is all the more special to me because he's your family."

Her words chased around his head long after they went upstairs to bring down the presents they'd wrapped from their shopping outing, distracting him. He tried picking them apart, to figure out what it was about her statement that troubled him.

It was good she cared about his nephew.

And yes, James was grateful that she cared about him, too.

But if she was already this attached to the boy, would Lydia understand if James followed through on his resolution to let Teddy's grandparents raise him?

He had a week before the New Year's Eve Ball when the Masons arrived in town to watch Teddy for the night. He hoped it would be enough time for him to find a way to tell her that if things went well with the Masons, he wouldn't need a nanny anymore.

# Eleven

Christmas Day got off to a fitful start.

Lydia hoped Teddy was just teething, but he remained grumpy and unimpressed by the holidays. He'd made grouchy sounds off and on while he played with a toy train, gripping it tightly in his hand as he pushed it around and around the floor.

She hoped it was just the toddler's irritability that made the day feel awkward. At noontime, over brunch fare in the large, eat-in kitchen, she traced an idle finger over the natural wood grain in the Texas ebony slab polished into a tabletop. Yet she returned her gaze to James again and again, wondering if something had shifted between them the day before.

James had participated fully in the cooking and preparations for the meal, but as she halfheartedly nibbled a bite of her French toast, she tried to pinpoint when things had begun to feel strained. His words about his own Christmases—that his nannies hadn't participated in the holidays—had made her wonder if she'd overstepped his expectations for her role here.

She'd always been very involved with her charges, imagining a child would thrive with that warmth of connection to a caregiver. She'd received a degree in early childhood development, patching together enough online coursework for her bachelor's over the years. But her real source of knowledge about child care came from her years in Arkansas, helping to raise her brothers and sisters. But had she brought too much of her own experience with her siblings into her nannying? Too much familiarity?

Then again, maybe James's own background skewed his perception of her role here. He'd lost his mother early and hadn't been close with his caregivers. He had loved and married a woman who hadn't wanted children, after all. A fact she'd never asked him about.

Maybe it was past time she did. Because she adored children and had crafted a profession around them. One day, she dreamed of a family of her own.

Shoving aside her half-eaten plate, she sipped

her sparkling water with orange and debated how to be tactful.

The doorbell's resonant chime interrupted her thoughts.

James frowned, setting down his fork. "I wasn't expecting anyone."

Teddy piped up from his high chair where he spun the wheels on his toy train. "Hel-lo?" he asked, his brown eyes turning to Lydia. "Hello?" He opened and closed his hand in a baby wave.

Her heart melted to see him make that connection, his eyes wide with curiosity as he watched James leave the room to answer the door. The small moment made her more certain of herself and the way she did her job. Forming a bond with children she cared for was only natural. Even if she didn't have strong feelings for James, his nephew would hold a piece of her heart.

"Do you want to say hello?" she asked him, getting to her feet. "We can go see who's here."

"Who. Here." He banged his train on the tray of the high chair. "Here. Here. Here."

Lydia unbuckled Teddy's safety belt and lifted him. He hadn't eaten anything besides a few pieces of dry cereal, so he was clean enough. She settled him on her hip, straightening his navy blue reindeer sweater before striding toward the living area.

"Merry Christmas!" a feminine voice trilled

from the front room as James opened the door for their guest.

Lydia's sister Gail breezed right into the house, dressed in a poinsettia-printed skirt and fuzzy red sweater. Tanned and sporting fresh caramel-colored highlights in her dark brown hair, Gail wore leather boots that appeared brand-new. Worst of all? The woman who owed a hundred thousand dollars to James came with her arms full of lavishly wrapped Christmas presents.

James appeared too surprised to return her greeting. Then again, maybe he didn't even remember what she looked like since the bachelor auction had been a month ago.

"James." Lydia cleared her throat and hurried closer, mortified that her sister would think it was okay to come by unannounced on Christmas, waltzing into James's house like a conquering hero, when she'd ignored his calls and the messages from the Pancreatic Cancer Research Foundation. "You remember my sister Gail?"

"Of course." Stepping forward, he recovered himself quickly. "Let me help you with those."

"Thank you!" Gail gushed, handing over the stack of boxes and a shopping bag to James. "I don't think we had the chance to speak at the charity event. You were a wonderful MC for the auction."

Gail's hazel eyes were bright and clear, her gaze direct as she strode deeper into the living area. As if she had absolutely no conscience about what she'd done. In that moment, with her sunny smile and perfectly primped brown curls, she bore a striking resemblance to their mother. Even her voice, relentlessly upbeat as if she could deliver a House Rules podcast at any moment, reminded Lydia of Fiona Walker.

Or maybe it was simply that, no matter how much Lydia had tried to teach her siblings about hard work and practical values, Gail preferred the laissez-faire approach to life. Both Fiona and Gail were determined that things would "work themselves out." Even astronomical bids for bachelors with money you didn't have.

Incensed, Lydia couldn't seem to make her feet move from where she stood in Gail's way, blocking her from the living area where James was putting the packages under the Christmas tree.

"He wasn't just the MC, Gail." Lydia hadn't planned to confront her sister. But the realization that Gail had turned out exactly like their mother rattled Lydia to her core. Why did she keep trying to fix her family's messes when they let her down time and time again? "As the president of the Texas Cattleman's Club, James was also the main liaison for the charity when they hosted the bachelor auction."

"Is that right?" Gail stopped her forward momentum, her smile faltering only for a moment.

"How nice. Mom told me you were working here now, so I hoped we could spend some family time together. It *is* Christmas."

Teddy bounced in Lydia's arms, ready to be put down.

James moved closer, reaching for his nephew. "I can take him so you two can visit."

She handed over the child, anger at her sister building as she kept her focus on Gail. "Do you know *why* I'm working here now?"

James palmed her lower back, speaking to her quietly. "Lydia, there's no need to go into that just yet."

She disagreed. Because if Gail was audacious enough to stride in here and play the benevolent sister while Lydia worked to repay Gail's debt, a conversation was warranted.

Gail's expression shifted to something that looked like concern. "I've always known how much you enjoy children, Lydia. You have since we were little girls playing with baby dolls."

"Ba-by?" Teddy asked, bouncing excitedly in James's arms.

Lydia tensed, realizing her sister's view of their shared past was too far from her own to ever be reconciled.

"No, Gail." She dragged in a deep breath to cool down the fiery frustration. "I'm working here to help repay James, who covered your outrageous bid at the bachelor auction."

"Ba-by! Ba-by!" Teddy shouted, wriggling so hard that James had to let him down to run around the Christmas tree, his light-up sneakers flashing red and blue.

She guessed James was probably glad for the chance to escape the confrontation as he chased Teddy. Lydia hadn't meant to put him in the middle of this. Then again, she hadn't expected her sister to arrive on Christmas Day, pretending nothing had happened.

"Why would you do that?" Gail studied her, shaking her head. She spared a glance for James, who'd moved to the far side of the room where Teddy had tried to hide behind a chair.

*"Why?"* Exasperated, Lydia paced in a circle. "Because it's the right thing to do. Because I don't want our name attached to bad debts while we're trying to get new businesses off the ground. This is a small town. Word gets around."

"But I didn't ask for help. And I told you I'd figure things out after vacation." Gail squeezed her arm. "I can tell this is a bad time. I should have known you don't like spontaneous visits."

An old dig. Her mother had always thought that the reason Lydia didn't like impulsive family outings was because she couldn't be "spontaneous." When the truth was she simply preferred to have sunscreen packed so the kids didn't end up with third-degree burns from a day at the beach. Or she liked having swimming vests for the little ones since there were too many of them to keep an eye on in the water.

But Fiona—and apparently Gail—preferred to think Lydia was just no fun. Overly cautious. Turning on the heel of her new leather boots, Gail headed for the door. The movement shook Lydia from her thoughts.

"So you're leaving again? Without figuring out anything?" Lydia followed her sister toward the foyer, feeling as frustrated as Teddy had this morning. It was a good thing she wasn't carrying around a toy train or she would have been tempted to throw it the way the toddler had during the gift-opening.

What was it about family that could catapult a person right back to childhood dynamics?

"Why should I try to figure it out?" Gail asked over her shoulder, her hand on the big brass handle. "You'd only do a better job of it than I would anyhow." She lifted a hand to her mouth as she called back to the living area, "Merry Christmas, James!"

Lydia felt the steam hiss slowly from her ears. "Gail, we need to talk."

"You should ask James to take you to the New Year's Eve Ball at the Texas Cattleman's Club. Lloyd and I will be there." Gail grinned again, her happiness irrepressible in the face of everything. "I'm over the moon about him."

And then Gail was gone. Sauntering off to her compact car decorated with a wreath on the grill.

Something about the vehicle, her sister's joy, even her "spontaneity," made Lydia feel like Scrooge by comparison.

"Are you all right?" James's voice over her shoulder made her realize she'd been standing at the closed door for too long.

She hadn't even heard him approach.

Pivoting to face him while he held Teddy, Lydia felt her chest squeeze with a mixture of fierce attraction and soul-deep affection. She'd come to care for him so much. So fast.

*I'm over the moon about him.*

Gail's comment circled around Lydia's brain, the only words her sister had spoken today that Lydia could identify with. She knew the feeling all too well. Because she felt it for the generous, hardworking man standing in front of her.

She was over the moon for James Harris. And just as quickly as Gail had plunged into her own whirlwind relationship.

The idea of sharing something in common with her impulsive sister triggered a flicker of anxiety in her chest.

"I'm—not sure." She wanted to step into the warmth and comfort of his arms. But given that she'd known James for an even shorter length of time than Gail had known Lloyd Richardson, did that make Lydia's feeling imprudent? Unwise? "I mean, I'm upset. Obviously."

She'd never had a panic attack before, but she wondered if this was how it started. She felt unsettled. Nervous. Fidgety. She swallowed fast and tried to catch her breath.

"Why don't you come sit?" James juggled Teddy in his arms and gestured in the direction of the kitchen. "We can finish our brunch. Talk."

That sounded reasonable. Because James was a reasonable, rational person, like her. She clung to the idea with both hands as she followed him toward the kitchen. At least she hadn't bid money she didn't have to win a date with him.

No, she only started an affair with her employer. Which, for all of her mother's hasty relationships, even Fiona had never done.

"Do you think we jumped into things too quickly?" Lydia asked as James carefully settled Teddy in his high chair.

"I think *quickly* is subjective." He seemed to choose the words carefully.

"You're right." She appreciated his thoughtful response.

Some of the worry in her chest eased. James was a good man, and just because she'd developed strong feelings for him didn't mean she was turning into her mother.

She hoped.

"Can I warm up your plate?" he asked, his hand resting on her shoulder for a moment. "Or get you something else to eat?"

His touch settled her and stirred her at the same time. But she resisted the urge to tip her head against his forearm and soak in the comfort of his presence.

"No, thank you." She returned to her seat at the long table, hoping they could address some of the things that had troubled her earlier. "I'll just have some fruit."

She appreciated the distraction of Teddy banging his train on the high chair tray while she spooned a few pieces of fruit into a serving bowl.

"I thought I heard your sister mention the New Year's Eve Ball." James helped himself to more orange juice from a glass pitcher.

"She'll be attending with Lloyd," she confirmed, wishing they could rewind time. Somehow find more even footing again. "I hope that's not too awkward."

"Of course not." He sounded sincere. "Lydia, I made the donation because handling it that way was easiest for me. I'm not worried about anyone repaying the debt."

He'd told her that before. All along, he'd been willing to forgive the debt and simply pay her to be Teddy's nanny.

"That's very generous of you."

"It also served my best interests since I was drowning in my grief and obligations, feeling like I was failing on all fronts." He took her hand in his. Stroked his thumb along her knuckles. "I am so grateful to you for getting me through these last few weeks, Lydia. But it's still my hope that Teddy's maternal grandparents will welcome him into their home and be able to give him all the time and attention he needs."

The gentle caress of his thumb was at odds with the discordant crash of his words through her.

"You still plan to give him up?" She couldn't have possibly heard him correctly.

"The Masons are driving down from Amarillo to watch Teddy on New Year's Eve so we can attend the ball," he explained. "If things go well that night, we can start discussing how to make the transition—"

"You don't want him." She wrenched her hand from his as the harsh truth smashed through her romantic hopes and the tender feelings she'd developed for James. "You never wanted children in the first place."

"That's not true." He sat back in his chair, the space between them feeling five times bigger than the physical distance. "I will keep Teddy if things don't work out with the Masons."

"Even though your brother wanted you to raise him, you're still considering giving him up?" Hurt and anger propelled the question from her even though it was a low blow. That she wasn't being fair.

But how was he being fair to Teddy, who'd so clearly bonded with James? The child had already suffered a devastating loss with the death of his parents. How would he cope with more feelings of abandonment?

James held himself very still. Calm and controlled in the face of her anger. "You of all people should understand that our siblings don't always know what's best."

Begrudgingly, she nodded, acknowledging the point even if she didn't like it. "You're right. But I'd like to ask you one more thing. Just so I understand you better."

She had to put a lid on her feelings for him. To stop them from evolving even further. Because she had been starting to love this man.

That was the only explanation for how she could be hurting so much right now.

"I'm listening." He studied her, but his gaze was shuttered, revealing nothing of his own feelings.

Making her realize how much he'd let her in over the last weeks. How much he'd shared with her. It made losing that emotional intimacy hurt even more.

But there was no going back now. No ignoring this question that she kept returning to about him.

"When we spoke about your ex-wife," she began, twisting a cloth napkin in her lap, the linen hopelessly crumpled, "you said she didn't want children." The question was highly personal, and no doubt it revealed too much about what she felt for him. But it burned in her throat and she had to ask. "Did that mean—you didn't want children either?"

His mouth flattened into a thin line. An answer all its own even before he spoke.

"I hadn't given it much thought before Raelynn. And when she told me her wishes before the wedding…it wasn't a deal breaker for me."

She nodded awkwardly, her whole body feeling clumsy and strange. Maybe it was just because she didn't know where to put the hurt she was feeling. For her. For him. For those stupid romantic hopes that weren't ever going to amount to anything.

Because even if they were just in the early stages of a relationship, she couldn't spend her time with someone who didn't have the same kind of dreams she did for a future that would always include kids.

"I see." She stood from the table, needing to escape the table. The man. "I'll put Teddy down for his nap now."

"Lydia." James said her name with a tenderness she couldn't bear, but he didn't reach for her. Didn't touch her. "I think we should talk about this more."

"I can't." She'd been so judgmental of her mother

and her sister. But their foolishness couldn't compare to hers. "I'm—sorry."

She had built her life around children. Her family. Her job. Her future. Of course she had fallen for a man who didn't want them, at least not in the way she did. There was a kind of cosmic humor in it. Maybe she'd even laugh about it one day. Fifty years from now.

She fumbled with the safety belt on the high chair, her fingers not quite working. Or maybe it was because her vision was slightly blurred from tears she wouldn't let James see.

"Lydia, please." James pushed back his chair and came to help her. "I can put him down for his nap."

Ideally, she would have been able to be a professional. To still do the job she shouldn't have taken in the first place.

But right now, she couldn't even manage that.

"Thank you," she managed, before she retreated with as much dignity as possible.

She needed the quiet of her room for a few hours. To regroup. To figure out a way out of this impossible situation that wouldn't leave Teddy without a caregiver.

But one thing was certain. Now that she understood how wrong she'd been about James and the feelings she thought they shared, she couldn't possibly remain under the same roof even one more night.

# Twelve

Three days before the new year, James sat in his office at the Texas Cattleman's Club and wondered if he should call Lydia. The days after their conversation had been painful, and he felt like they still didn't have any resolution yet on where things were headed between them.

Was she really ready to call it quits between them without delving deeper into what was upsetting for her? He understood why she was upset about the plans he'd made for Teddy without telling her. Because he had a different sort of life mapped out from the one she had planned for herself. Did that mean they couldn't compromise?

He feared the answer was yes. But that didn't mean they couldn't talk about it to be sure.

James hadn't wanted Lydia to leave when Teddy was clearly so attached to her, so he'd offered to work out of his office at the Texas Cattleman's Club for a few days. He had plenty to do with preparations for the New Year's Eve Ball, and the rest of the staff came in so sporadically between the holidays that no one noticed he was sleeping on his office couch.

Or, more accurately, *trying* to sleep on the office couch. Night after night, he couldn't stop dreaming about Lydia, and then he'd wake up feeling empty and alone, remembering the hurt in her eyes when he'd told her about the Masons.

Now, with the day of the ball closing in, he wondered if she even planned to follow through on their date. Checking the antique clock on the wall, he realized it was a quarter after nine. Past Teddy's bedtime, but not past Lydia's. Pulling in a deep breath, he punched the number for her cell into his phone. Waited while it rang once.

Twice.

"Hello?" Her voice sounded wary.

Even so, he was damned glad to hear it. He'd missed the sound of her, along with so many other things. Her scent. Her touch. The sweet way she cared for his nephew.

"Lydia." He hadn't thought beyond getting in

touch with her. Hadn't planned for how to wade through the awkwardness. "How are things at home?"

"Good," she answered quickly. "Fine. We're both—fine."

Right.

"I will need to meet Teddy's grandparents at the house midafternoon on New Year's Eve to welcome them. I wanted some time to speak with them and review Teddy's schedule."

"Of course. It's your home." Her words were clipped, her tone distant in a way that made him think of how her joy in the past had moved him. He felt the loss all the more deeply. "And I understood from our last conversation that I'm only here until your new arrangements are in place."

He ground his teeth, unwilling to tackle a complex conversation over the phone. Especially not when she was clearly still unhappy with him.

"I had hoped we could discuss that at the New Year's Eve Ball." He had been drawn to her practicality and sense of honor from their first meeting. He'd been banking on those qualities in her to ensure she showed up for their date. "Assuming you still plan to attend with me?"

She hesitated for a moment. "Do you really think it's wise for us to spend that time together when it's become obvious that..." She cleared her throat. Began again. "When it's clear now that our hopes for the future are so far apart?"

He thought it wise to at least have a discussion about what they wanted instead of assuming the worst about each other. But he clamped his tongue on that response. Besides, he wanted to be with Lydia. Being without her this week had made him realize how just how deep his feelings ran for her.

He loved her. But was he ready to risk his heart again on another woman who wasn't in it for the long haul? Regardless of the answer to that, he couldn't share how he felt about her. Not over the phone.

"I need a date for this event." He spelled it out in the only way he thought might convince her to attend. "And you could use an introduction to people who need your child care services. So the plan is practical, if nothing else."

"I recently learned there's such a thing as being too practical for your own good," she said drily. "But since I'll be unemployed again very shortly, I can't afford to turn down a good opportunity for my business. I will attend the ball with you as planned, James."

A possibility he hadn't considered hit him, something he should have thought of for Teddy's sake. What if she planned to quit even if the Masons didn't decide to take in their grandson? But he wasn't going to push for any more during an already difficult conversation. Hopefully he wouldn't need the answer to that at all. He confirmed the time for their date before he disconnected the call.

And wondered how on earth he could win back a woman hell-bent on ending things between them.

New Year's Eve was packed with Cinderella potential.

The Texas Cattleman's Club had been transformed into a shimmering silver-and-white haven. Long chains of white gladiolas were strung from the rafters, the delicate petals rimmed with hints of metallic glitter that made them shine in the candlelight. Tall candelabra draped with silver tulle and white ribbons stood atop every table in the room. A twelve-piece orchestra played along the back of the dining area, filling the room with lilting waltzes.

Lydia had splurged on a new dress for the event. Formfitting down to a little kick hem around her knees, the gown was pale green silk organza. Pairing it with an older pair of silver strappy heels, she felt as glamorous as she possibly could. Which wasn't to say she was the most beautiful woman in the room. But she looked like she belonged for at least one night. It hurt to think she'd never be a real part of this community that meant so much to James. Tomorrow, she'd return to her old life.

Alone.

Beside her, James Harris was the man everyone wanted to speak to, his job as esteemed president of the club underscoring how well liked he was. How respected. He was genuine and charming with everyone who greeted him. But despite the fairy-tale trappings of the evening all around her, Lydia had no illusions about how the night would end.

When midnight chimed, she wasn't just going back to her old life on the other side of town. She was also losing the man she'd fallen in love with, the sweet child she'd come to adore and all her illusions about herself.

She could never return to the old Lydia who used to feel good about her smart choices, her practical approach to relationships and her professionalism. Now she had to at least admit that love could rock anyone's world, skewing their perspective and making them behave in a way they normally wouldn't. She wasn't any less susceptible to that than any other woman. While she wouldn't ever get so swept away by love that she'd forget to supervise a child the way her mother had, Lydia also realized she'd been deluding herself into thinking she wasn't vulnerable to making other mistakes.

"Would you like to dance?" James bent closer to ask after he finished up a lengthy talk about yearling prospects with another rancher.

She couldn't help the shiver that tripped down her spine as he spoke close to her ear. The attraction that had been so apparent between them from day one hadn't magically faded when she'd discovered he had no intention of keeping his nephew.

"Yes. Thank you." She nodded, knowing everything she said to him sounded stilted. But she feared if she didn't carefully monitor her words, she would say something far too revealing.

So for now, she let him lead her to the dance floor and sweep her into his strong arms. His tuxedo was custom tailored, the black wool gabardine tapering to his narrow waist. There was a hint of sheen in the lapels of the jacket on either side of the crisp white pleats of his shirt. She wondered how he could appear equally at home in a Stetson and jeans as much as Hugo Boss, but some people simply seemed extraordinarily comfortable in their own skin.

"I've been wondering what you thought of the Masons," he asked as he spun her out of an easy turn, her silk organza gown flaring slightly.

As if she hadn't already been reminding herself that she was no Cinderella, the topic of conversation gave her another dose of cold reality.

Teddy's grandparents had been younger than Lydia imagined. They'd been in their early fifties, but could have passed for a decade younger. Physically fit and well dressed, they had been polite and kind. And yet…she couldn't shake the feeling that they were all wrong to raise Teddy.

"It matters more what you think," she reminded him, making the mistake of looking into his eyes. Holding his gaze made her think of more intimate moments with him. Of the ways he'd touched and kissed her. "I may be biased since I pictured something different for Teddy."

His brows pulled together. "I wish they would have responded to me sooner when I invited them to meet their grandson in the first place." He shook his head, a hint of frustration in his voice. "I realize their relationship with their daughter had been strained after she married Parker, but wouldn't you think that would be all the more reason for them to be eager to meet Teddy?"

"Yes." She couldn't stand the idea of that little boy enduring any more upheaval in his young life. "Unequivocally, yes."

"But in their defense, everyone processes grief in their own way. They might have needed that time to mourn before they came here." His grip shifted on her waist, his palm absently stroking for the briefest moment until he seemed to catch himself and still the movement.

"Perhaps." She couldn't say anything more, her senses too overloaded by that touch. By all that she would miss when she walked away from him.

She'd probably been foolish to show up tonight, to follow through with this doomed date. But she really did need the networking opportunity that it offered. Especially since she would be without a job soon.

"The comb is pretty in your hair," he said in a low, husky tone as the dance came to an end. "I'm glad you wore it tonight."

The crowd applauded for the orchestra as they took a break in their set. Lydia clapped, too, though her chest ached at the memory of James giving her the hair comb. Of how special Christmas Eve had been when they were together just one week ago. Or the long, breathless night she'd spent in his arms afterward.

Before she could respond, the microphone in front of the orchestra rang with a harsh sound. Turning, she spotted a dashing older man at the podium. He had a full head of white hair and piercing blue eyes, his skin deeply tanned. He tugged the microphone out of its stand so he could hold it in one hand, then he strode out from behind to podium to speak. The crowd quieted to listen.

James bent closer to whisper to her, "That's Gus Slade. He's a past president of the Texas Cattleman's Club."

She recognized the rancher from around town, the feud between the Slades and the Clayton family one of the bits of Royal history she'd picked up through local gossip. She welcomed the distraction for a moment to gather her defenses against leaning into the temping man beside her.

"Sorry for the feedback, folks." Gus Slade spoke into the microphone as he strode into the center of the raised platform near the orchestra. "We'll get back to the music in a minute. But first, I hope you'll indulge me. I have an announcement to make, and I want you all to be my witnesses."

The crowd settled into an even deeper silence. They all seemed to collectively hold their breath. Lydia peered over at James to see if his face gave any indication he knew what was about to happen since he'd helped put together the event. James must have felt her gaze since he glanced her way and shrugged.

"The new year is a time for a fresh start," Gus said, his voice strong and certain. "And more than anything, I want a chance to begin again, with the woman I love at my side." He paused for a moment, before someone turned a house spotlight on. The white-and-blue light fell around Rose Clayton seated at a table in the back. "Rose, would you do me the honor of becoming my wife?"

*Rose and Gus?*

The rest of the crowd seemed as stunned as Lydia felt, a shocked murmur reverberating through the well-heeled guests while Rose covered her surprised gasp with one hand, her eyes getting teary before she nodded quickly.

"Yes!" she called out across the room, standing up in her sparkly silver dress. "I will marry you, Gus Slade."

The microphone shrieked as Gus dropped it, forgotten, on the platform. He charged toward Rose with his arms open. The crowd clapped and there were a few cheers, although everyone still seemed taken aback by the proposal.

Behind her, Lydia heard a man say, "But I thought they were sworn enemies?"

Moved by the romantic gesture, Lydia felt her heart in her throat. The orchestra played a refrain from a popular country love song while someone turned off the microphone and the party got back under way. James guided Lydia from the dance floor, the romantic moment reminding her of all that was missing in their relationship.

It took her a moment to realize that she was following James out of the building into the garden, her thoughts still on the couple inside and all the love shining in their eyes. The night air was warm for December, but still a refreshing break from the crowded party rooms. It was quiet out here, where a few landscape lights gave the bushes and ornamental trees a silvery glow. More white lights outlined the walkways of smooth, decorative stone.

Here, there wouldn't be any networking opportunities for her child care business. Under the moonlight with James, there was only the two of them. Why would he bring her out here? And more important, how would she hold strong against his powerful allure?

He turned to her, his expression serious. "Seeing Gus and Rose in there made me all the more determined to speak to you about what's happening between us, Lydia."

"There's nothing else to say," she reminded him, unwilling to hurt any more than she already did. It would already be tough enough living in the same town with him. "I can't be with someone who doesn't want to have children in his life."

"But it's not that I don't ever want them," he clarified. "I'm just not ready right now. Today."

A whisper of hope swirled through her. And just as quickly, she tamped it down.

"I understand that's the right decision for you." She wondered what had made him so certain he wasn't ready to welcome a child into his life. "But in the meantime, a confused little boy who already lost one father is going to lose another man he's grown attached to."

"A child deserves to have a family in place. A family that's going to stay together." He spoke with passionate conviction. "The Masons have that, Lydia. I don't."

"You have me." She had thought that meant something to him.

"And look at how ready you are to walk out at the first sign of trouble." He shoved his hands in his pockets, his shoulders tense. "As soon as I brought up the idea of bringing the Masons to town, you shut down the discussion."

Surprise stole any response she might have made. Is that how he saw it? Perhaps she hadn't understood how deeply wary his failed marriage had made him. For that matter, maybe he hadn't known how incredibly gun-shy her past made her either.

"I'm sorry, James." She didn't know what else to say. The knowledge that he was hurting, too, didn't make the breakup any easier. If anything, it only increased the ache in her chest. She hadn't wanted things to end this way.

The vibration of a cell phone cut through the awkward silence, the soft hum emanating from James's breast pocket.

"I'd better see if it's the Masons," he muttered, reaching into his jacket. Stabbing at the screen. "Hello?"

He must have hit the speakerphone button because Samantha Mason's panicked voice cut through the quiet.

"Teddy's having an allergic reaction," the woman sobbed in a rush of words. "We're on the way to Royal Memorial Hospital, James. Please hurry."

# Thirteen

James wasn't surprised when Lydia insisted on riding with him to the hospital. She might be done with him, but her attachment to Teddy was undeniable. Whatever her reason to be in the passenger seat with him, and then rushing into the emergency room with him fifteen minutes later, James was grateful as hell to have her at his side.

"I told them where the EpiPen was." James knew he'd said it more than once on the way to the hospital.

But the thought kept circling around in his brain after he'd hung up from Samantha Mason's frantic first call.

"You did. You showed it to them," Lydia reminded him again as they wound through the triage area to the desk. "Maybe the shot didn't help. Maybe they weren't able to give it to him fast enough."

He hadn't asked what happened when he got the call. He'd been too shaken up, too terrified. What if something happened to his brother's son, when protecting Teddy had been the only thing Parker had asked of him?

"We're here for Teddy Harris." He willed the nurse at the counter to give him good news. Tell him his nephew was okay. "I'm his legal guardian."

"He's in room three." She pointed to a door behind the nurse's station. "The doctor is in with him now."

James was already moving. Lydia's high heels tapped a quick beat to his longer strides and he slowed a fraction to give her his arm. His movements felt wooden, his body on autopilot.

She accepted his help in silence, her expression mirroring the fear that chilled his insides.

"He's going to be okay." He told himself as much as her. Needing it to be true.

The hospital room was quiet, after all. Surely there would be all sorts of noise and staff in motion if the worst was happening.

Still, dread filled him as he pushed the door open. Teddy's grandparents stood on either side of the toddler. Between them, Teddy lay in a hospital crib. Around him, monitors beeped quietly and an IV bag hung by the bed, giving some kind of fluids into the boy's tiny arm. An oxygen mask covered the lower half of his face. His eyes were closed, but James wasn't sure if that was because he was sleeping or because of the swelling around his eyes.

His skin was pink and splotchy.

James didn't know how he remained standing upright. But he thought it helped that Lydia squeezed his arm hard for a moment before she hurried to the baby's side. Her hands fell to his little knee through the white blanket that partially covered him.

"Is he—" James felt his throat close up tight.

Death had stolen everyone from him. *Everyone.* He could not lose Teddy.

His eyes burned.

"He'll be fine, Mr. Harris." A shorter man in a white lab coat stepped between James and the crib, offering his hand. "I'm Dr. Voss."

"He's okay?" James shook the man's hand, though half his attention was still on the other side of the room where Lydia leaned over the crib wall to stroke Teddy's dark curls.

A swell of love for her filled his chest, easing some of the fear. He turned back to the doctor, needing the rest of the story before he could believe Teddy would make a full recovery.

"He's stable now. The EMT crew faced the worst of it on the way over here." Behind Dr. Voss, Mrs. Mason released a quiet sob, a ball of tissues wadded up in one hand.

Teddy's grandfather moved around to the other side of the bed to be by his wife, sliding an arm around her shoulders.

The doctor continued, "We're still giving him some cortisone and antihistamines intravenously, and we wanted to keep him on supplemental oxygen for a little while. But we're monitoring him carefully just in case he exhibits any more signs of distress."

"What about his face?" Lydia asked from the bedside. "He's so swollen."

"We'll get some ice on that," the doctor assured her, backing toward the door. "I'll ask a nurse to come in and remove the oxygen in about thirty minutes, and we'll start some ice for the swelling. But it should go down on its own in time."

"He already looks better than—" Teddy's grandfather, George, interjected "—before."

"Don't be too hard on yourselves, folks." The doctor paused with the door half open. "You did the right thing coming in. Even if you had administered his EpiPen, we would have wanted to see him after that kind of a reaction."

Samantha Mason let out another sob behind her tissue as she sat down.

Relief flooded through James. "He's going to be okay."

"James, I'm so sorry." Samantha straightened from where she'd been slumped in a metal chair near the bed. "George had a snack pack of cereal that he eats sometimes when his sugar is low. We'd never give Teddy anything like that after what you said about the nut allergy, but we think he must have eaten a piece that fell on the floor. Right?" She turned to her husband for confirmation.

George shrugged. "I don't remember dropping any, but maybe I did. I was feeling a little shaky. But the next thing we knew, Teddy was wheezing."

James understood mistakes happened. It could have been him who'd dropped a piece of food that Teddy ate. Or Lydia. Still, he couldn't help a spike of frustration. "So what happened with the EpiPen?"

The couple exchanged looks before George answered, "When you showed it to us, I thought you took it from the top kitchen drawer in the island."

James shook his head. "I keep it in the diaper bag."

He knew the bag had been sitting on top of the island when he'd shown it to them. But it didn't matter now. He'd make sure the hospital sent them home with another. While he spoke with the Masons, Lydia rose and let herself out of the room.

His gaze followed her. Was she leaving for good? Or just getting a nurse? Maybe she simply didn't want to hear all the ways the Masons had endangered

Teddy. Truth was, he found it tough to hear the story, too. Especially since their babysitting had ended with Teddy in an oxygen mask, hooked up to an IV.

Guilt swamped him. He should've done so much better by his brother's child. Teddy was the only family James had left, and he hadn't taken that responsibility seriously enough.

Was this some kind of cosmic payback for almost giving up custody of the boy? He'd been a fool to ever consider it.

Samantha shivered, rubbing her arms as tears welled in her eyes again. "I was pulling out all the drawers in the island. I just kept thinking how we'd already lost Mandy, and now we were going to lose her little boy, too."

"I called 911 right away," George offered, shaking his balding head. "It all happened so fast."

James had heard enough. He really wanted to be with his nephew. "Anyone would have been scared to see that happen," he reassured them since there was nothing to be gained in arguing with them. "You must be exhausted after going through that. If you want to go back to the hotel, I can call you if there's any change in his condition."

He also really hoped Lydia hadn't left. But Samantha Mason was still visibly upset as she continued telling him about her daughter, Parker's wife. Between tears, she said, "And we never did see Mandy again. Never had a chance to heal our differences. Little Teddy is all we have left of our beautiful daughter now."

Something about the way she'd phrased it made James uncomfortable. Did they really see Teddy as a replacement for their dead daughter? James tried to offer some comforting words if only to speed the Masons out the door.

Teddy wasn't a replacement for anyone. He was an innocent boy who'd lost too much in his young life, and he deserved the best that James had to offer.

From now on, he needed to focus on his family.

That meant Teddy. He saw that all too clearly now. Teddy was his, now and always.

And, if he could find her, he wanted to tell Lydia that he finally understood what she'd been trying to tell him all along. That Teddy was his family. But the part that Lydia hadn't figured out yet was that she was his family, too. Because he was ready to claim Teddy as his son, and he wanted Lydia to be at his side when he did.

Lydia couldn't sleep when she got back to the house.

She put the kitchen back in order so Mrs. Davis wouldn't return from her New Year's holiday to find spoons and papers on the tile floor, but after that she went upstairs to pack her things.

Seeing Teddy in the hospital bed had been devastating. Rationally, she knew his exposure to tree nuts could have happened to any babysitter. Yet it upset her to think the Masons not only let the substance into the house where their grandson had a serious allergy, but then they hadn't even been able to locate the medicine that could have slowed the reaction and possibly prevented anaphylaxis. Every second would have counted for that first responder team when they arrived on the scene.

They could have lost Teddy.

Although as much as she'd grown to love the little boy and his uncle, Lydia knew she had no claim on them. They weren't hers to love. So she had phoned her sister in the predawn hours, asking Gail to act as a babysitter if Teddy needed one when James returned from the hospital with him.

Gail might be financially irresponsible, but Lydia trusted her to watch a child. Even a severely allergic child. That certainty in her gut made Lydia realize she needed to make peace with Gail. Because they were still family, and Gail had never asked her to cover for her with the bachelor auction bid.

Lydia had involved herself in that situation on her own. She was a caretaker. A fixer. And she could tell herself that it was okay to say no to unnecessary crazy as many times as she wanted, but she kept jumping in to help. She'd realized in this last painful week without James that she needed to take ownership of her own life.

She had changed for the better because of knowing him. Lydia had a newfound acceptance of her family—and the pieces of herself that had been shaped by them. She would have to appreciate those changes, since they would be all she had left of her time with James. She understood herself too well to try to accept the path he chose, a path without Teddy.

When she heard the low hum of a car engine outside, she hurried to the front door, expecting to see her sister. She twisted the knob, tugging the double panels open, and was shocked to find James's black sedan rolling to a stop in the driveway.

A lump rose to her throat. The tug of emotions in her belly was nothing new around him, but it hurt far more now that she couldn't act on those feelings. Now that she had to find a way to forget about him.

The thought twisted sharply inside her, reminding her that wouldn't ever happen.

James stepped from the driver's side door, his gaze locking on her. "I'm glad you're here."

Opening the rear door, he leaned into the vehicle to unfasten the restraint on the car seat.

Lydia moved closer, wanting to see Teddy even though she knew every moment she spent with him only made it harder to leave. She needed to know he was okay.

"My sister's coming over," she told James while he lifted the baby in his strong arms, his shoulders blocking her view of Teddy. She closed the door behind them, then heard another car turning into the driveway. "That might be her now, in fact."

She reminded herself it was for the best to turn over her nanny duties to Gail for however long James still needed help with Teddy. Lydia didn't want to be in the house when they packed his things to send him to Amarillo with the Masons.

"I know. I spoke to Lloyd a few minutes ago."

"Lloyd?" Lydia followed James as he strode toward the house, trying to peek around his shoulder to see Teddy's face.

She'd changed into jeans and a sweater, but James still wore his tuxedo from the New Year's Eve Ball. The bow tie hung around his neck, the top button of his shirt undone. He still looked too handsome for his own good.

Too handsome for hers, at least.

James paused on the front mat, glancing down at her. "The bachelor she fell head over heels for, remember?"

"Right." She found it hard to think about her sister's drama with too much of her own crowding her thoughts and breaking her heart. "Of course."

Glancing back at new vehicle in the driveway,

she realized it wasn't Gail's compact. There was a man in the driver's seat of an exotic-looking sports car, but from the passenger side, Gail gave Lydia a wave.

Confused, Lydia waved back, then hurried after James as he stepped inside the house.

"Lloyd wants to give me a check to cover your sister's bid. I told him it was not necessary, but he was so insistent, we agreed he'd donate the money to the Pancreatic Research Cancer Foundation."

"Really? That's amazing." She couldn't fully process that news and the implications it might have when she really just wanted to see Teddy's face first. Distracted by worries about the baby, she stepped closer to James again. "May I just see him? Is he really okay?"

"He's still a little groggy." James dipped his shoulder so Lydia could have a better view of the boy. "The doctor said to just let him rest for a few hours and the last of the swelling should dissipate by evening."

"Thank goodness." Relief rushed through her, so strong it made her weak in the knees. She couldn't resist a final, gentle squeeze of Teddy's arm. A stroke of his fluffy dark curls. "I'm so glad he's okay."

"Me, too." James's gaze held hers for a moment, making her aware of how close they stood.

Heat grazed her skin, the pull of attraction so

strong in spite of everything. Stepping away from him was downright painful.

"Hello!" Gail called through the front door, knocking gently before cracking it open a sliver. "Can we come in?"

"Please do." James invited them inside. Gail and a tall, blond-haired man with a square jaw and aviator sunglasses.

Gail had the same "in love" glow that Tessa Noble had when she'd stopped by with Ryan earlier in the month. Gail introduced Lydia to Lloyd while James excused himself to put Teddy in his crib.

"Nice to meet you," Lydia said automatically as she shook Lloyd's hand, although her eyes followed James's progress up the main staircase.

"You, too," Lloyd said, tugging off his shades. "And we're going to stay out of your hair. We're only here for babysitting duty." He grinned. "You get two for the price of one with us."

Lydia tried to smile, charmed in spite of herself by Gail's new boyfriend. But it was hard to make small talk when her heart ached.

Once Gail and Lloyd went to watch over Teddy, there was nothing to keep Lydia here. Her gaze fell on the suitcases she'd already packed and set near the front door.

"There's a playroom near the nursery," she told them, thinking of all the hours she'd spent there in the last weeks, delighting in Teddy's accomplishments as he lost himself in playtime and forgot to be the confused, fractious little boy she'd met that first day at the Texas Cattleman's Club. "It has a sitting area—"

"We'll be fine," Gail assured her while Lloyd tugged her toward the stairs by the hand. Behind him, she mouthed silently to Lydia, "He's so hot!"

If there'd been any doubt what she was saying, Gail fanned herself before she had to focus on the steps.

"But—" She had hoped to speak with her sister longer. At very least, to apologize for intruding in Gail's business when clearly she had addressed the situation herself.

The couple holding hands were too far up the stairs now, however. They passed James, who pointed out the door to the nursery and the play-room on his way down.

Toward her.

Her throat closed right up at the thought of say-ing goodbye to him.

"Lydia, wait." He'd taken the time to change into dark jeans and a long-sleeved white T-shirt. He tugged one of the ribbed cuffs higher on his forearm as he strode into the living area. "Can we talk?"

"I was just—" She pointed to her suitcases, not sure what else there was to say. "I called my sister to take over for me until the Masons—"

"There will be no Masons." He took her hands in his, surprising her with his touch as much as his words. She looked up into his light brown eyes flecked with gold, and, as always, warmth tripped down her spine at the mere sight of him.

Sunlight spilled over her shoulders through the big windows, the holiday decorations casting rainbow reflections around the room.

"I don't understand." Unless…a horrible thought occurred to her. "Did they decide not to take him because of what happened? Is he too much trouble?"

"No." He shook his head. "Nothing like that. They love Teddy and feel terrible about triggering the allergy."

She relaxed slightly as the maternal defensiveness eased. "Then what do you mean?"

He squeezed her hands tighter, his thumbs stroking the insides of her wrists. "I can't describe the fear I felt last night when we walked into that emergency room. Not just a fear that I'd messed up my brother's one wish for me that I keep his son safe." He hauled in a long breath. "I knew I'd be devastated to lose him, too. Because I love that child, and I'm not going to ever let him go."

"Oh, James, that's wonderful." She was thrilled for him. For Teddy. "You'll make such an amazing father."

She was overwhelmed with the urge to hug him,

so she did. Even though it hurt to feel so much love for him, to feel so close to him, and not be able to share in the future he painted.

Because even though it was almost everything she could have wished for, the picture he painted hadn't included her.

The reality of that brought her back to earth in a thud of awkwardness over how she'd thrown herself into his strong arms to hug him. She tried to ease back.

Only he kept on holding her tight, burying his head in her hair.

"Lydia. I've missed you so much," he spoke into her hair, the scruff on his jaw snagging the strands.

Her heart pounded harder. She hardly dared to hope…

"I'm—" She'd already told him how she felt. So she clamped down on the thought now as she pulled away. "I know Teddy will be so happy to grow up here. Where he belongs."

Her eyes stung a little. Happy tears, she told herself.

"You belong here, too, Lydia. With me." His voice hit that deep note that rumbled right through her, even though it was softly spoken.

"I—" Blinking, she tried to focus on what he was saying. She couldn't afford to misunderstand when she was already holding together the pieces of herself from the heartbreak of the past week. "I can't be his nanny anymore, though. Not when—"

"Not as a nanny." He drew her closer again, curling a finger under her chin to look into her eyes. "As my wife." He let the words sink in. Holding her gaze with his. Canting closer to speak softly against her cheek. "Marry me, Lydia Walker. I can't get through another day without you in my life. I love you too much."

Happiness stole her breath, filling her with a shiny new hope that made her feel lighter. So light she might float right away with it.

"Really?" She closed her eyes, swaying into him, needing to hear it again.

"Every day without you has been painful. But I knew it was wrong to ask you to come back when I wasn't sure about Teddy. I think I was still grieving for Parker. Still feeling like I'd never have enough to offer a child of my own." He cupped her face in both hands, his gaze steady, certain. "But I've got everything he needs, because I love him."

"That's true." She arched up to brush her mouth along his, knowing she could help the Harris males find happiness. But more than that, she was going to love them, too.

"And it felt so right when I figured that out." He kissed her eyelids. Her cheeks. "But then, it got even better when I realized that I might still be able to win you back. Because it's not a family without you."

"Consider me won." She wrapped her arms around his waist, fitting against him like she was made for him. "I love you, too, James."

His expression lit up at her words. "I don't have a ring yet." He stroked her shoulders and peered down at her. "And I'm not going to rob you of a special proposal—"

"I'm not worried about that." She wasn't the kind of woman who needed a splashy display. It was enough to have her "over the moon" love.

"I can't let Gus Slade outdo me in the romance department." He arched a teasing eyebrow at her. "I want to give you the fairy tale, Lydia. You deserve that."

"I just need you." She smoothed her hands over his chest, feeling all that delicious male strength. Feeling the steady beat of his heart. "Everything else is a bonus."

"It's a new year today." He kissed her lips. A slow, thorough kiss that promised so much more, a lifetime of more. "A new start. And I can't imagine a happier way to begin it than having the woman I love in my arms."

She wasn't ever going to get tired of hearing him say that. A shiver of pleasure tickled her neck. Anticipation hummed through her.

She stepped away from him so she could lace her fingers in his. Leading him toward the staircase.

"Actually, I can think of one way that might add to our happiness." She felt breathless with new love. New hope. And a whole lot of desire. "Especially since we have babysitting help."

"I've heard that new parents need to make the most of their alone time." He caught her up in his arms, kissing her again until they were both breathless.

They stared at each other for a heated moment before their feet were moving again. Up the stairs, straight for the master suite.

Sometimes, no other words were needed.

# Epilogue

*Four weeks later*

Rose Clayton Slade could have danced all night.

She and Gus had invited half of Royal to the wedding ceremony and reception held in one of the restored barns at the Silver C. They'd brought in patio heaters and obtained special permission from the local fire commissioner so they could celebrate their night in a place close to their hearts. She twirled under her groom's arm as he spun her in a country waltz they both knew all too well. Gus had hummed the same tune to her many, many years ago when he'd asked her to dance with him in this very barn.

She'd never forgotten the steps. And she wanted to repeat them with him a thousand more times at least.

When the music shifted to a more upbeat piece, Rose relinquished her new husband to one of his daughter's friends who wanted to claim a dance.

"I want a two-step when I come back," Rose whispered in Gus's ear before he kissed her on the cheek.

"I want that and a whole lot more," he told her with a wink.

How was it he could make her feel like a girl again, all blushing and flirtatious, when they'd argued like cats and dogs for so many years? Rose tried not to question it. She wanted to just be. To let this beautiful wedding reception unfurl all around her like an endless summer day. They'd paid the fiddler and his band to play as long as there were guests still in the barn, since all their friends from the Texas Cattleman's Club came out in force to celebrate.

It did her heart good to see all the couples together having fun, even outside the barn in the cooler night air where you could still hear the music. They'd put up a canopy strung with white lights, decked with more greenery and patio heaters. She was surprised so many people had made use of it in the cool evening. But James Harris and his new fiancée, Lydia, were so wrapped up in each other as she strode past them, she was sure they didn't even hear her say hello.

Which was the lovely thing about a wedding. Everyone could celebrate their love. If only her grandson had that in his life.

Ducking behind a rose-covered archway they walked through earlier, Rose breathed deep and looked up at the moon, savoring a peaceful moment alone before she went back inside. She was about to return to the barn when a familiar voice on the other side of the flower-covered arch stopped her.

It sounded like Gus's granddaughter, Alexis, was speaking in hushed tones to someone.

"No, I'm not worried," the woman was saying. "I'm pregnant, not helpless! I'll manage. It will be fine."

Rose nearly fell over straining to hear more, but the voice outside must have moved farther away. Not even remotely concerned about eavesdropping, Rose rushed outside to see if it really had been Alexis.

Pregnant?

It couldn't possibly be.

Except there, walking fast toward the front lawn of the main house, she caught a glimpse of Alexis Slade clutching a cell phone to her ear. Her back was to Rose, but the pink floral lace dress was unmistakable in the outdoor lights.

Rose felt faint.

She walked as fast as she dared in her tiered white wedding dress and turquoise-colored cowboy boots. She was not surprised to see her grandson, Daniel, charging toward Alexis, too, a look of determination on his chiseled features.

Not many women would have dared stop him with that look on his face. But those rules did not apply to grandmothers.

"Daniel." She double-timed her step to intercept him, tugging his arm.

His gaze stayed on Alexis for a long moment before he focused on her. "Yes?"

"Daniel, is it true?" She kept her voice low, mindful of guests even though they weren't close to anyone here by a stack of hay bales left out in case anyone needed an impromptu seat. "Is Alexis pregnant?"

His jaw jutted. "How did you find out?"

Her heart sank. She didn't need to ask if he was the father. She remembered seeing them together before. The spark between them was impossible to miss. Breaking them up had brought her and Gus together, and now Rose felt sick about it.

"Daniel, you have to—"

"I have." His dark brown eyes flashed fire. "I asked her to marry me, and she said it was too late. That I was only asking because of the baby."

"Were you?" She couldn't help but ask. But, seeing his expression and his patience worn thin, she changed tactics. "I'm sorry, Daniel. I—"

"Gran, you know I'd do anything for you. And I'm happy for you today. But I really need to go."

She nodded, seeing the way his shoulders bunched. His hands flexing into fists at his sides. She understood the way feelings could drive you to dark, unhappy places. She'd feuded with Gus for most of her adult life because she loved him and couldn't be with him.

It hurt to see him walk away. Not toward where Alexis had been, but toward his truck, parked close to the main house.

"Where's my bride?" Gus's voice called her from her worries.

She watched him stride toward her across the grass, so handsome and vital. A wave of love steadied her despite the ache in her chest.

"Sweetheart, what's wrong?" he asked as he came closer, pulling her into his arms. "You don't look like the happy bride who promised to meet me on the dance floor."

"I know." She nodded, gripping his hand. Needing his strength. "I just overheard that Alexis is pregnant."

Gus lifted a weathered hand to his face, covering whatever he might have said. She could see the shock in his eyes.

"The baby is Daniel's," she continued, wishing

she'd found a gentler way to break the news to him. She leaned into him, wrapping her arms around his waist. "I asked him about it, and he said he asked her to marry him, but she won't because he's only proposing for the baby's sake."

Gus stroked her back, hugging her closer. Until that moment, she hadn't realized how chilled she'd grown outside. She was shivering.

"What a mess we made," Gus said gruffly, tucking her against him.

"It was hard enough seeing them so unhappy. And now this?" She heard the music pause inside and she worried it might be time to cut the cake. "Gus, we need to go back. But promise me we'll figure out a way to get them together?"

She would gladly delay the honeymoon so they could put their heads together and figure something out.

Gus nodded. He took her hand and squeezed. "I've got an idea. So don't you worry about it for even another instant, Rose. I'm going to fix things this time. For good."

And at the strength of the conviction in his voice, a strength she wished she'd trusted in decades ago, she believed him. She tucked her fingers into the crook of his arm and started walking back toward the barn where their guests, their community, their future waited.

\* \* \* \* \*

# THE MARINE'S
# CHRISTMAS CASE

## LARA LACOMBE

**For O. Can't wait to meet you!**

# *Chapter 1*

It was a nice party…for an engagement celebration.

Dario Ortega stood in the corner, nursing his beer as he watched the group. The ranch house was packed, the walls practically bulging as friends, family and well-wishers crowded in alongside the usual menagerie of dogs and cats that always seemed to find his parents. The two veterinarians had soft hearts and never had been able to say no to an animal in need. He and his brother, Emiliano, had practically grown up in a zoo, and as he watched one of the members of his family's current pack nose the guests in a hopeful manner, he couldn't help but smile. Some things never changed…

All the bodies made the house warm, but Dario didn't mind. He enjoyed being around his family; he traveled a lot thanks to his freelance tech work, so it was nice to stay in one place for a bit and spend some time with his parents and brother.

He'd never seen Emiliano so happy before. His brother was normally serious and reserved, but Dario didn't think he had stopped smiling in days. And it was all thanks to the woman by his side.

Marie Meyers was a beautiful lady, made even more pretty by the love shining in her eyes as she looked up at her fiancé, laughing at something he said. Emiliano had his arm around her, and it was clear from the way their bodies were angled toward each other that they were sharing a private moment despite standing in the middle of the crowd. Dario was happy for his brother and the love he'd found, but he had to admit he didn't understand Emiliano's desire to get married.

Dario didn't have anything against relationships, per se. He loved women—their smell, their laugh, the way they moved and talked. He enjoyed hearing their thoughts and figuring out what made them tick. And he didn't mind having an exclusive relationship with one at a time. In fact, he preferred it that way.

But there was something about the whole till-death-do-us-part-forever-and-ever-amen aspect of marriage that made him tense up. Maybe he was just cynical, but Dario liked going into a relationship knowing that he had an escape option if things went south. And while divorce was a possibility, it was often a messy, drawn-out process. Besides, what kind of a pessimist thought about divorce as they were getting married?

"There he is!" Emiliano's voice boomed over the din of conversation. "Get over here, best man!"

Dario smiled and pushed off the wall, threading through the crowd until he reached his brother's side. "You rang?" he said drily. He nodded at Marie, who smiled at him.

Emiliano clapped him on the back. "I did. Why are you skulking in the corner? This is a party! You need to mix and mingle."

"I'm sorry," Dario replied. "I didn't realize I was being so evasive." He truly hadn't meant to put a damper on the party, but perhaps his thoughts about marriage had affected his mood.

"You weren't," Marie said. "He just doesn't want to be the only one in the thick of things."

"She's right," Emiliano admitted, sounding a little sheepish. He glanced around, his eyes widening a bit as he took in the size of the gathering. "I didn't realize we actually knew this many people. And having them all in one place is a bit claustrophobic."

"Just wait until the wedding," Dario said. He grinned, taking a perverse pleasure in his brother's discomfort. "Mom has a list of guests as long as your arm."

Emiliano and Marie exchanged a loaded glance. "Uh, we were kind of hoping for a small, quiet affair," she said.

"Yeah," Emiliano put in. "We figured if we let her go nuts for the engagement party, she'd be more likely to back off on the guest-list demands."

Dario nodded and bit his lip to hide a smile. "I'll keep my fingers crossed for you."

His brother was right to look so worried. Natalia Ortega was a force of nature—as a petite woman who worked with huge horses all day, her job practically demanded it. Dario didn't envy Emiliano's predicament, and he chuckled to himself. *One more reason to stay single...*

As if summoned by their conversation, their mother walked over. She slipped her arm around Dario's waist and pulled him close, and he leaned down to kiss the top of her head. "I'm so glad you're home," she said. "Having both my boys home for Christmas is the best gift I could ask for."

Dario smiled. "I'm glad I was able to take a break. It's good to be here." Even though he lived in Houston, only a few hours away, he'd been working steadily over the past year, moving from job to job without pause. But his next project didn't start until January, giving him a few weeks to catch up with everyone and get to know Marie a little better before she officially joined the family.

His father walked over and joined them. "Is this an impromptu family meeting?"

"Something like that," Emiliano replied, angling his body to make room for Aurelio Ortega to step into the circle.

"Are you two enjoying yourselves?" Aurelio asked Emiliano and Marie.

"Very much," Marie said. "It's a wonderful party—thank you again for hosting it."

"Our pleasure," Natalia said, her smile stretching from ear to ear. She practically vibrated with joy, and Dario's heart warmed to see his mother so happy.

"We can't wait to officially welcome you into the family," Aurelio said. He glanced at Emiliano and Dario. "But for now, we need to mingle so our guests don't feel neglected."

Dario and his brother nodded. "I'm on it," Dario said, raising his glass in salute. He scanned the crowd as his parents slipped away, seeking out a friendly face. Maybe he could find an old family friend to chat with for a minute, to ease himself into being social.

Jade and Claudia Colton had found Marie, and the three women were talking and laughing by the Christmas tree. While he watched, his mother joined the group—she had long been the vet for Jade's horses, and Jade hugged her in greeting.

Dario's father caught his eye and nodded meaningfully at the crowd. Dario lifted his glass in acknowledgment. Message received.

He spied Mrs. Jenkins by the refreshment table. She'd been their neighbor for years, and she was always nice to talk to. Dario took a step in her direction but a flash of red caught his eye and made him turn.

She was standing by the window, sipping from a glass of white wine. She was limned by the glow of the Christmas lights lining the roof of the house, giving her an ethereal look. How had he missed seeing her before? With her long brown hair, full lips and delicately arched eyebrows, she was exactly the kind of beautiful woman he usually appreciated.

"Who's that?" he asked his brother, keeping his gaze locked on her lest she disappear.

"That's Felicity Grant. She just came back to Shadow Creek and is now working for Adeline Kincaid's PI agency."

"Excellent," he murmured. He started forward, but a hand on his shoulder stopped him.

"I don't think she's going to be interested, little brother." Emiliano nodded in her direction. "She looks like she wants to be left alone right now."

"We'll see," Dario said, shrugging off Emiliano's hand. "I'm sure I can put her at ease."

He heard his brother's soft chuckle. "This ought to be good," Emiliano muttered. But Dario ignored him, focusing instead on the beauty across the room.

He started toward her, taking his time so he didn't seem too eager. He wasn't exactly looking for a relationship right now, but he couldn't pass up an opportunity to get to know such a lovely woman better. And if she wanted to have a little fun while he was home? Well, that was just fine by him…

Her eyes landed on him as he approached. He offered her a suggestive smile designed to melt feminine resistance. In his experience, women usually blushed and giggled after such attention. But she didn't.

One eyebrow arched slightly, but her expression didn't otherwise change. His confidence faltered; perhaps Emiliano had been right, after all? But he'd come too far to stop now, and he was aware of his brother's eyes on his back. If he veered away at this point, he'd never hear the end of it.

So Dario took a deep breath and pressed forward. One conversation—they could both get through something as simple as that. Maybe he could even coax a smile out of her. The thought stiffened his spine and filled him with determination. He had yet to meet a woman who was immune to his charms.

And he loved a good challenge.

*He's coming this way!*

Felicity's stomach twisted as the handsome cowboy drew near. She'd spied him the minute she'd walked into the party, and not just because of his shiny boots and bolo tie. He was a difficult man to ignore. He was tall and broad-shouldered, and his dark hair had a mussed look that made her want to run her hands through the strands. She couldn't tell the color of his eyes from this distance, but it didn't matter. His gaze was intense, landing on her like a touch.

The smile he aimed at her was full of sensual promise, and she knew without a doubt he could deliver on his offer. Heat suffused her limbs at the thought of those full lips on her body, and she shivered as she imagined the rasp of his beard stubble scraping across her skin. For a brief, thrilling second, she allowed herself to indulge in a vivid fantasy involving an empty bathroom, the sexy cowboy and a locked door. It would be so easy to slip away and discover if he felt as hot as he looked.

She shook herself free of the enticing thought. The idea was appealing, but she wasn't interested in a fling. She'd come back to Shadow Creek to start a second career after leaving the Marines. Whoever he was, the man approaching her was a distraction she simply didn't need.

"Hello." His voice was deep and soft, the tone better suited to whispering sweet nothings rather than making polite conversation.

"Hi." She nodded once in acknowledgment, hoping he wouldn't take the gesture as an invitation.

He did.

"I don't believe we've met before." He stuck out his right hand. "I'm Dario Ortega. Emiliano is my brother."

Felicity considered not touching him, but she didn't want to appear rude. "Felicity Grant," she replied, slipping her hand into his.

Instead of shaking her hand, he smoothly turned it over and brought it to his lips. His kiss was featherlight, the barest whisper of a touch, and the warmth of his breath on her skin sent sparks of sensation arcing up her arm.

She gritted her teeth, determined to ignore her body's response. But if a casual touch had this much of an effect on her, how would she respond if he really kissed her?

*Doesn't matter*, she told herself sternly. *I'm not going to find out.*

"Nice to meet you, Felicity," he said, releasing her hand. His eyes were a warm hazel, a swirl of blue and green and gold that was mesmerizing. If she wasn't careful, Felicity could get lost in his gaze.

"I heard through the grapevine you've come back to Shadow Creek. Why haven't I met you before?"

She shrugged and his eyes traced the curve of her shoulder before landing back on her face. His blatant appreciation of her body was a little unsettling; it had been years since a man had so openly stared at her. When she'd first joined the Marines, she'd dealt with her fair share of catcalling and crude remarks. But once she'd proved to the men she was just as good as the rest of them, they'd stopped treating her like a woman and had embraced her as one of the guys. Their acceptance had made her feel proud, but she was no longer used to a man's romantic attention.

"I'm, uh, not sure why we would have known each other." She definitely would have remembered him—he was just the type her young heart would have pined over during high school.

"You didn't go to school here." It wasn't a question. "I would have seen you."

"I think I was a few years ahead of you."

He winked at her.

She lifted a brow. "Well, that explains it."

"I've always liked older women," he said. "Especially when they're as pretty as you."

It was an obvious attempt at flattery, but Felicity's stomach fluttered nonetheless. Ignoring her body's response, she rolled her eyes. "Does that line usually work for you?"

He grinned and twin dimples appeared on his cheeks, giving him a boyish appeal. "Yes."

His honesty was unexpected and she couldn't help but laugh. "Sorry to break your record."

"That's okay. I have other lines." He lifted a brow suggestively and Felicity shook her head.

"I'm immune." Better to stop this now, before he wore down her resistance and she forgot her resolve to stay focused on her new job.

"So you say." Dario studied her thoughtfully as he took a sip of his beer. "But I bet I could find one that works on you. I'm very talented."

*That's what I'm afraid of.*

He took a step closer and Felicity's breath caught. His cologne was subtle and smelled expensive. "Have dinner with me tomorrow."

She straightened her spine. "No."

Surprise flared in the depths of his eyes. "No?"

"You heard me."

"Are you sure? We should really get to know each other before I take you to my brother's wedding."

Felicity shook her head at his audacious assumption. "I don't remember agreeing to accompany you."

"Not yet." Dario tilted his head to the side. "But you will."

A loud voice broke into their conversation, saving her from needing to reply to his arrogant statement. "Felicity Grant? Is that you?"

She turned to find a middle-aged man staring at her, a look of surprise on his face. "Mr. Perkins. What a nice surprise."

Her high school history teacher smiled and took a step closer. Dario shifted to include the man, and the tension in Felicity's muscles eased as she got some of her personal space back.

"I thought that was you!" Mr. Perkins said. He ignored Dario, focusing intently on her face. "Are you back in town on holiday leave?"

Felicity felt Dario's interest sharpen at the question and she mentally sighed. She hadn't really wanted to talk about her past with him, but it seemed there was no help for it.

"No, sir," she replied. "I retired from the Marines a few months ago."

"The Marines?" Dario interjected. He sounded a little astonished, and Felicity could tell that was the last thing he'd expected to hear.

"That's right, son," Mr. Perkins said proudly. "Felicity here joined the Corps after she graduated high school. She was the only one in her class to enlist." He turned back to Felicity. "Every time I ran into your father around town, I asked about you. He told me about your promotion to corporal, and when you shipped out to Afghanistan with the Third Battalion." His eyes shone with respect. "I was in the Third Battalion, too, you know. K Company."

A lump formed in Felicity's throat, and she blinked hard to clear her eyes. "I didn't know that, sir. I was in L Company, myself."

Mr. Perkins nodded. "Desert Storm. We were there for months but never lost a man—can you believe it?"

Felicity smiled sadly. "I wish we could say the same."

Afghanistan had been unlike anything she'd experienced before, and she'd seen her fair share of intense fighting. While her unit hadn't suffered many casualties, she'd personally known each marine who'd been wounded. And when one of their own had died—in a freak drowning accident, of all things—they'd grieved for months.

A faraway look entered Mr. Perkins's eyes, and Felicity knew he was recalling his days in the desert. "It was a different war for us," he said softly. "We didn't have to deal with insurgents and terrorists hunting us down."

"War is never easy, sir," she said. As far as Felicity was concerned, anyone who put on the uniform and served their country was deserving of respect. Some people liked to argue about which branch of the service had it worst, or which assignment had been the toughest, but she considered that to be counterproductive. Friendly banter between units was one thing, but she would never demean the experiences of another service member simply because they didn't match her own.

"Ooh-rah," he said softly. He shook his head, visibly casting off his memories. "It's good to have you back. Will you be staying long?"

"I hope so, sir," she replied. "I just took a job as a private investigator."

"That's wonderful." He smiled, appearing genuinely happy to hear it. "You let me know if you need any help settling in. That's an order."

"Yes, sir," Felicity said. She was touched by his offer, especially since she hadn't seen him in a dozen years. But that was the magic of the Corps—young or old, active duty or retired, the title of "Marine" lasted a lifetime.

Mr. Perkins stuck out his hand, and Felicity was happy to shake it. "Semper Fi," he said.

"Semper Fi," she repeated.

He melted back into the crowd, leaving Felicity alone

with Dario once again. She turned to face him and could tell by the look on his face he was brimming with questions. Felicity braced herself to rebuff him. It was one thing to talk about her combat experiences with a fellow veteran, but she didn't want to share those memories with a man she'd only just met.

"The Marines, huh?" he said simply. "That's pretty hard-core." He looked her up and down as if evaluating her in a new light. Then he stuck out his hand. "Thank you for your service."

"You're welcome." She slipped her hand into his again, and this time he didn't flirt with her.

"Dario!"

They both glanced over to see Emiliano beckoning his brother with a wave. Dario nodded and waved in acknowledgment. Then he turned back to her, one hand dipping into his jacket and reappearing with a business card.

He juggled his drink as he hastily scrawled something on the back of the card before offering it to her. Felicity took it, frowning slightly. "What's this for?"

"That's so you can reach me once you've decided where you'd like to have dinner." He grinned impishly. "Call me anytime."

Before she could explain she had no intention of contacting him, he winked at her and strode away, heading for Emiliano and Marie. Felicity watched him go, a mixture of relief and disappointment swirling in her chest.

Dario Ortega was a charming man, and she had to admit that knowing he found her attractive was a boost to her self-esteem. If circumstances were different, maybe they could have gotten to know each other better.

But now was not the time. Felicity had worked hard in the Corps and had earned her share of accolades and awards. But she was a civilian again, trying to start a new career. That didn't leave much time for romance, especially not with a charmer like Dario, who probably had a different woman in every city. She needed to focus on her cases and show Adeline that hiring her had not been a mistake. She didn't want to let her friend down, but more than that, Felicity's pride demanded she do her very best.

She had no other choice.

# *Chapter 2*

The next morning was cold and clear, with a sharp chill in the air that made Felicity's lungs burn a little. She clutched her travel mug of coffee in one hand, holding it close to her face so the thin column of steam that escaped through the lid could warm her nose. Thanks to the Christmas shopping crowds, she'd had to park several blocks away and had spent the last few minutes working her way back to the office. Only a few more steps before she was inside and could thaw out by the space heater near her desk.

She had just stepped onto the sidewalk when a loud bang broke the stillness of the morning. In the next instant, Felicity found herself on the ground, kneeling in a puddle of rapidly cooling coffee, groping for a weapon she no longer carried.

Her heart thundered in her ears and she gasped for breath, her eyes scanning the area as she instinctively searched for threats. After a few seconds her rational mind caught up with things and she realized Shadow Creek was not, in fact, under a mortar attack.

She stood, surveying the sidewalk with a frown. Her travel mug was ruined, the pieces scattered across the cement. The coffee had soaked into her pants, and the fabric clung to her knees in a chilly embrace that made her shiver. She glanced at her watch—there wasn't enough time to dash home to change them. *At least they're dark gray*, she thought wryly. Once everything dried, the stains wouldn't be too obvious. And there were worse things in life than going through the day smelling like coffee…

"Felicity?"

She turned to find Mr. Perkins approaching. He carried a bag in one hand, and it was clear he was getting an early start on shopping.

"Good morning," she said, trying to sound normal.

His gaze took in the coffee stain on the sidewalk, the remnants of her mug and the damp spots on her pants. His features softened. "It was a dropped crate."

"I'm sorry?"

He jerked his head toward the small market at the end of the block. "They were unloading some crates from a truck, and one of them fell off the tailgate. That's where the noise came from."

"Oh." She felt her face heat, a little embarrassed to learn she'd overreacted in such a dramatic fashion to such a simple event.

"Don't beat yourself up over it. It took me a few months before I stopped jumping at every little noise."

"I don't even know how it happened," she confessed. "One minute I was walking along, minding my own business. The next thing I know, I'm on the ground."

He nodded, as if this made perfect sense. "Gotta love those battlefield reflexes."

She shrugged, acutely aware of the mess she'd made. She knelt and began picking up the pieces of her mug, and Mr. Perkins joined her.

"For what it's worth, it gets better," he said kindly. "When I first got back, I freaked out every time a door so much as slammed shut. But I'm living proof that doesn't last forever."

"That's good to know," she said. While she realized on an intellectual level she would eventually adjust to the normal rhythms of civilian life again, it was hard not to feel like a failure for spooking so easily. She'd been evaluated for PTSD as part of her retirement health screen. Fortunately, she had shown no signs of the illness, which made her reaction all the more puzzling. But hearing Mr. Perkins talk about his experiences made her feel less alone, less self-conscious. She'd spent the last twelve years living a very different lifestyle from the people around her, and she felt like a bit of an outsider. It was nice to hear from a fellow marine that wouldn't always be the case.

They tossed the broken shards of pottery into a nearby trash can. "Thanks for your help, Mr. Perkins."

"Anytime." He smiled at her. "And I think under the circumstances, you should call me Henry. I'm not your teacher anymore."

It was a nice offer, but she couldn't bring herself to do it. "Yes, sir."

He laughed. "All right, Corporal. Fair enough. Have a good day."

"Thanks. You, too."

Felicity took a moment to smooth her hair back and run a hand down the front of her blouse. Feeling marginally more put together, she walked the rest of the way to the office and stepped inside the warm lobby.

"Felicity? Is that you?" Adeline's voice floated out of her office, and Felicity winced. She was late, and apparently her friend—*No, my boss,* she reminded herself—had been expecting her.

She headed down the hall, unwinding her scarf as she walked. "Sorry I wasn't here earlier," she said. "I had a bit of an accid—" The words died in her throat as she poked her head into Adeline's office and saw that she had a visitor.

But not just any visitor.

Dario Ortega sat across from Adeline's desk, sipping

a cup of coffee. He winked at her, plainly enjoying her reaction.

"Oh," she said, unable to hide her displeasure. "It's you."

It wasn't the most gracious remark, but Felicity still felt frazzled from her earlier mishap. The last thing she needed right now was a visit from a smooth-talking, good-looking distraction.

If her reaction bothered him, he didn't show it. He smiled broadly. "In the flesh. Nice to see you again, Felicity."

"You two know each other?" Adeline looked from Dario to Felicity, curiosity in her eyes.

"No," Felicity said, just as Dario replied, "Yes."

Adeline raised one eyebrow, a smile tugging at the corner of her mouth. "I see."

"We met last night, at Emiliano's engagement party," Felicity explained. "That's all." She didn't want Adeline to get the wrong idea, and if the look on Dario's face was anything to go by, he wasn't about to correct any misunderstandings as to the nature of their relationship.

"I didn't get a chance to ask you—how do you know my brother?"

"I, uh, don't. Not really." She had read some of Emiliano's reports on the Colton, Incorporated, hacking case, but she hadn't had a chance to meet him in person until last night. Dario frowned slightly, and Felicity felt her face heat.

Adeline came to her rescue. "She went in my stead. Jeremy's company holiday party was last night, and the boss couldn't very well skip the event. I asked Felicity to go and represent the agency. I thought it might be a good opportunity for her to meet some new people and get reacquainted with a few familiar faces." She looked at Felicity, her head tilted to the side. "I take it my plan was a success?"

"Looks that way." Felicity offered her a tight smile. "I'd better get started on my day." She nodded at Dario. "Nice to see you again." She heard the note of forced cheer in her voice, but couldn't muster the energy to care. She'd made it very clear last night that she had no interest in seeing Dario Ortega in any kind of social capacity. If he couldn't take a hint, that wasn't her fault.

"Always a pleasure, Ms. Grant." His voice was deep and sonorous, and Felicity clenched her jaw as goose bumps stippled her arms. Her body was responding as if he'd touched her rather than simply spoken a few words.

*Enough of that*, she told her traitorous flesh. She nodded once, then turned and marched down the hall to her office.

She tried to ignore the world on the other side of her desk, but no matter how hard she focused on booting up her computer and stowing her coat and purse, she heard every word coming out of Adeline's office.

"I won't keep you any longer," Dario said. "It was nice talking with you."

"Likewise," Adeline said, genuine warmth in her voice. "You know you're always welcome here."

"I appreciate that. You'll definitely be at Emiliano's wedding, right? Jeremy didn't schedule any work functions that conflict with the nuptials, I hope."

Adeline laughed. "No, I made sure our schedules are clear. We'll be there—we're both looking forward to it."

"Excellent." Dario sounded pleased. "See if you can talk Felicity into coming as well, will you?"

Felicity rolled her eyes and shook her head. Would the man ever stop?

"I'll see what I can do," Adeline replied. "That's nice of you to want to include her." There was a speculative note in her voice, and Felicity knew her friend was probing for information.

Dario didn't miss a beat. "Just don't want to see anyone left out. I know my family would agree."

Oh, he was slick. Felicity could almost admire his easy confidence and suave determination. She'd never met anyone with such an abundance of charm, and Dario knew exactly how to wield that particular weapon. She imagined he had women eating out of his hand everywhere he went.

All the more reason for her to bolster her resolve. She had no desire to be Dario Ortega's girl of the moment. And it was likely her very refusal to succumb to his flirtations that made him so determined to get through to her. It was the thrill of the chase that motivated him now, not any genuine interest in getting to know her.

Felicity pushed thoughts of Dario aside and turned to her computer. She needed to focus on her case, not worry about the actions of Shadow Creek's local playboy.

Adeline had assigned her the Colton, Incorporated, computer hacking case, and Felicity's main priority was tracking down Sulla, the infamous leader of the Cohort, which was the group that had claimed responsibility for the hack. It was a high-profile case; the FBI was leading the criminal investigation, but the Colton family had hired Adeline's agency to conduct their own investigation, in the hopes of bringing the matter to a swift end. It was a measure of Adeline's faith in Felicity that she'd turned over the reins of the investigation once she had joined her agency.

As if summoned by her thoughts, Adeline rapped on the open door of Felicity's office. "Got a minute?"

"Of course."

Adeline stepped inside and sat, then steepled her fingers in front of her chin. "What do you know about Dario Ortega?"

"I know he won't take no for an answer," Felicity muttered before she could think better of it. She shook her head. "Sorry. I know he's your friend."

Adeline tilted her head to the side. "Oh, I wouldn't nec-essarily say that. We're friendly, but he's not someone I consider a friend like you." She dropped her hands and leaned forward. "I take it he's been hitting on you?"

"And how." Felicity smiled ruefully. "He's very deter-mined."

"That sounds like Dario," Adeline confirmed. "He's got a bit of a reputation for being footloose and fancy-free. But I must say, I've never heard talk that any of his rela-tionships end badly. I think he's careful to make sure the women he dates know the score before they get involved."

"How kind of him," Felicity said drily.

Adeline shrugged. "I'm just saying, if you're looking to have a little fun, he's a good choice. I know it's probably been a while since you've had any romantic involvement."

Felicity's shoulders stiffened. "What makes you say that?" It was true, but did she wear the evidence of her dry spell like a shirt for everyone to see?

"I thought the Marines had rules about fraternization. Or are you telling me you ignored them?" Adeline's tone was equal parts teasing and hopeful, as if she had her fin-gers crossed that Felicity had flouted regulations in the interest of love.

Or lust, as it were.

Felicity shook her head. "Sorry to disappoint you, but I did not break the rules."

Adeline sighed. "I figured as much. You always were so proper."

"It's served me well so far."

"I know. But I worry about you. It might be good for you to let your hair down and have a little fun."

Felicity considered the idea for a split second, then shook her head. "I have no interest in being the next notch on Dario's bedpost."

Adeline leaned back. "Fair enough. But I think you're

looking at this the wrong way." She smiled wickedly. "He'd make a great notch on yours."

"Adeline!"

Her friend laughed. "Couldn't resist. Teasing you is too much fun. But that's not why I actually came in here."

"Oh?"

"Believe it or not, Dario is a top-notch computer expert. He's a genius with all things cyber related."

"Is that right?" Felicity couldn't keep a note of skepticism out of her voice. The handsome playboy actually had practical skills?

Adeline nodded. "Yeah. I know it's hard to believe, but he has an impeccable professional reputation. He's even more skilled than Emiliano in some respects."

"Wow." That *was* impressive. Emiliano was a respected agent on the FBI's National Cyber Investigative Joint Task Force. The men and women on that team were experts in every aspect of computers, so Adeline's words were high praise indeed.

"Dario came to visit me this morning because he's currently between cases, and he offered to assist in the Colton, Incorporated, hacking investigation while he's in town."

"What did you tell him?"

Adeline shrugged. "I thanked him for his offer and said we'd consider it. I didn't want to bring him on board until I'd talked to you."

"I appreciate that," Felicity said, touched at her friend's thoughtfulness. Adeline ran the PI agency, so as her boss, she had every right to accept help from whomever she chose. But it was nice of her to ask for Felicity's input first.

"This is your case, Felicity. I'm not going to tell you how to run it. But I do think it would be a mistake to turn down Dario's offer. His help might be just what you need to break this thing wide open. And for what it's worth, I think he'd be professional about it."

Felicity nodded slowly. "Can I take some time to think things over?"

"Of course." Adeline stood and smiled. "Like I said, this is your case and I trust your judgment. I know whatever you decide, you'll get the job done."

"Thanks, Addy," Felicity said. "I appreciate it."

Adeline made it to the door, but then stopped and turned back. "Oh, I almost forgot! You were saying something about an accident when you walked into my office this morning. Are you okay?" Her blue-gray eyes searched Felicity's face and her brows drew together in concern.

Felicity waved her off. "I'm fine." She didn't want to get into her earlier scare. Adeline was her friend, but Felicity still felt a little embarrassed over her reaction. She knew Mr. Perkins was right and that her jumpiness would fade with time, but until it did, she didn't want people to think she'd come back from the war broken. "I just dropped my coffee on the walk in."

"Bummer," Adeline said. "I put on a pot when I arrived this morning. It should still be pretty fresh."

"I'll grab some in a minute," Felicity said. "Thanks."

Adeline left and Felicity turned back to her computer, her mind whirring. The Colton hacking case was proving to be difficult, and she was under a lot of pressure to discover the identity of Sulla. Zane Colton, the head of security for Colton, Incorporated, had emailed her practically every day over the past two weeks asking for updates, and she'd even gotten messages from T. C. Colton, the executive vice president, and Fowler Colton, the president of the company. The corporate bigwigs were very interested in the case, and they were likely feeling a little paranoid since one of their own had recently been surrounded by scandal. Hugh Barrington, the family attorney, had schemed to take control of Colton, Inc., and he'd very nearly been successful. The cyberattack couldn't have come at a worse time for the company.

Felicity had worked as an intelligence specialist in the Corps, so she was used to compiling and sifting through data, looking for patterns or other nuggets of information that she could piece together to form a bigger picture. She knew her way around a computer, but she recognized her skills were nowhere near Emiliano's level.

Or Dario's, apparently.

If the talk about his talent was true, it would be nice to have someone of Dario's caliber join the investigation. Curious, Felicity did a quick internet search, looking for independent confirmation of Dario's computer prowess.

A few minutes later, she sat back, satisfied he was probably as good as he said. Could they really work together, though? Would he be willing to cool his flirtations and focus on the case?

Even if Dario agreed to stay on his best behavior, he would still be a distraction. Felicity would have to muster every scrap of self-discipline to ignore the temptation of his mouth and the knowing glint in his hazel eyes. Just the thought of being on guard all the time made her feel mentally and emotionally exhausted.

But did she have another choice?

A quiet chime sounded, and she glanced at her monitor to see the email icon blinking. She clicked on it, and a message from Zane Colton popped up: Any progress?

"If that isn't a sign from the universe, I don't know what is," she muttered to herself.

With a reluctant sigh, Felicity dug Dario's card out of her purse. She'd slipped it in the bag last night when she hadn't been able to find a trash can. She'd never intended to actually use it, but now she was glad she hadn't managed to throw it away.

She stared at the numbers he'd scrawled on the back,

imagining all too easily his triumphant smile when he answered the phone and realized she'd called him. Under any other circumstances, her pride would have kept her from asking for his help. But this was no ordinary case, and if she had to dance with the devil to make progress on it, then that was what she'd do.

She picked up the phone and began to dial, before she changed her mind.

# *Chapter 3*

Dario leaned back in his chair, trying to look casual. He didn't want Felicity to see how pleased he was to be meeting her. Something told him if she thought he was gloating, she'd turn around and walk out of the restaurant before he even got the chance to say a word. So he forced himself to relax and managed to keep a grin off his face while he waited for her.

Inside, though, he practically fizzed with anticipation.

Her call had been unexpected. When he'd offered his services to Adeline this morning, he hadn't known she'd assigned the case to Felicity. As soon as he'd learned that, he'd figured there was no chance Felicity would want to work with him. She was so very determined to keep him at arm's length, and he found her reluctance intriguing. Usually, he had no problem getting a woman to go out with him. Why was Felicity playing so hard to get? The question had dominated his thoughts ever since he'd met her, and maybe now he would get an opportunity to learn the answer.

The door opened with a gust of cold air, and Felicity stepped inside, her hand clutching the lapels of her coat tight against the frigid wind. He waved to get her attention, and she nodded in acknowledgment.

Dario stood as she approached the table. She eyed him warily and began to shed her coat and scarf, draping them both over the back of her chair. Once she sat, he did the same.

"I'm glad you called," he said.

"Before we get started, I want to make one thing inescapably clear." Felicity placed her hands on the table and leaned forward, holding his gaze. Her green eyes glinted with challenge, as if she was daring him to argue with what she was about to say. "I called you because of your reputation as a cyber expert. You offered to help investigate the Colton hacker case, and I'm willing to give you a chance to do that. But this is not personal in any way, shape or form. Our interactions will be limited to the professional, nothing more. No flirting, no teasing, no accidental touches. Treat me like you would your brother's fiancée."

*Where's the fun in that?* Dario merely nodded, though, knowing that if he did otherwise, Felicity would leave without a backward glance.

In truth, he was glad to be consulting on her case. It gave him something to do while he was in Shadow Creek, and it would help keep his skills sharp. The fact that he was going to spend more time with Felicity was simply the icing on the cake. She talked tough now, but he was confident that eventually she'd relax her guard and let him get to know her better.

Apparently satisfied with his response, Felicity relaxed into her chair. "Okay. Great."

The waitress chose that moment to saunter up to the table. "What can I get you, hon?"

"Uh…" Felicity hastily glanced at the menu, scanning the options with a slight frown.

"I can come back," the woman offered.

"No, it's fine," Felicity said quickly. "I'd like a cup of the tomato soup and a grilled cheese sandwich. Water for the drink, please."

The waitress nodded, scribbling on her pad. "And you?" She turned to Dario with an expectant look.

"Cheeseburger and fries for me. Iced tea to drink."

"Coming right up." The woman collected their menus and left.

Dario studied Felicity a moment as she unwrapped her silverware and placed the napkin in her lap. "Have you eaten here before?"

She shook her head. "No. But I did like to come here back when it was a pizza parlor." She glanced around at the café's cozy tables and soft green walls. "It looks a bit different now."

"If it's any consolation, the food is good. Emiliano and I ate here last week after I got back into town."

Felicity nodded but didn't otherwise respond.

Dario searched for something to say to break the ice between them. "I imagine a lot of things changed in the years you've been gone," he offered.

She lifted one shoulder in a shrug that was strangely elegant. "I suppose."

The waitress returned with their drinks, and Felicity offered her a smile of thanks. After the woman left again, she leaned forward. "Can you tell me what you already know about the case? I don't want to waste time."

He nodded. "Emiliano filled me in on the basic facts. Colton, Incorporated, was hacked by a group calling itself the Cohort, and the personal information of the company's employees was released to the general public. Emiliano posed as a digital freedom fighter and tried to infiltrate the group, but things unraveled before he really gained entry into the Cohort."

Felicity nodded. "That's one way of putting it," she said, referring to the shocking betrayal by Finn Townsend, one of Emiliano's FBI colleagues, who had secretly been working for the Cohort. "I heard he was shot."

Dario nodded. "But don't feel too bad for him. He did get a fiancée out of the deal."

Felicity shook her head, but smiled faintly at his joke.

"Did the FBI get any useful intelligence out of Emiliano's former partner?"

"Not that I know of," Dario replied. "To be honest, I'm not sure the man knows that much to begin with. I get the impression he was only told what he needed to know to play his part. I don't think he was privy to any of the bigger-picture stuff."

"Figures," she muttered.

"Adeline told me you're tasked with tracking down Sulla, the Cohort's leader."

"That's right." Her lips pressed together in a thin line, and he got the distinct impression she didn't want to say more. After a second, she sighed. "I hate to say it, but I haven't made as much progress on unmasking Sulla as I'd hoped."

Dario recognized how much the admission had cost her, so he said nothing. It was obvious Felicity was a proud woman and took her job seriously. Her failure to make headway on the case had to be frustrating, and it probably pained her to admit it out loud, especially to him.

It was a sentiment he understood all too well. He was a perfectionist, and he set very high standards for himself, especially in the professional realm. It wasn't uncommon for him to spend days working on a project, often to the exclusion of other aspects of his life. He saw that same drive in Felicity and knew that while she had currently hit a wall in her investigation, it wouldn't be long before she found a way around it.

"Let's go back to the beginning," he suggested. "What do we actually know about Sulla?" Maybe it would help her to talk over the evidence one more time, and his fresh perspective certainly couldn't hurt.

"Not much," she said. She paused as the waitress deposited their food on the table and blew out a breath, her lips pursing slightly in a manner that was entirely too appealing. In another time and place, he'd have interpreted the expression as an invitation. But Felicity had made no secret of the fact she wanted to keep their relationship on an impersonal footing, and she didn't seem like the type of woman to act the tease. She likely had no idea how sexy he found her, and for a fleeting instant, he regretted volunteering to help with the case. It had seemed like a good idea at the time, but now that he was faced with resisting her unconscious charms for the next several weeks, he wasn't so sure.

*Cold showers*, he decided grimly, tearing his gaze away from her mouth. *That's my only hope.*

"So far, Sulla has claimed responsibility for the hack. But I don't know why Colton, Incorporated, was on Sulla's radar. Furthermore, I don't know if there are other strikes planned."

Dario nodded, redirecting his thoughts to the case. "I think it's safe to assume the initial hack might not be the only attack. The Cohort probably has more trouble planned for Colton, Inc."

"Yes, but why?" Felicity took a bite of her sandwich and chewed thoughtfully. "Of all the companies out there, why target Colton, Incorporated? The Cohort said it was against the collection of personal information, but there are lots of corporations nowadays that create extensive digital profiles of their customers. It seems odd to target one company for doing something so common."

Dario dipped a fry in ketchup. "Maybe the privacy story is just a smoke screen to conceal the group's true motives."

Felicity's eyes brightened with interest. "What are you thinking?"

Dario took a sip of his tea. "It's no secret the Colton family has a lot of enemies. Do you suppose the company was targeted as a way of doing more damage to the family and the Colton name?"

"That's an interesting possibility," Felicity said. She sounded a little surprised, and Dario hid a smile in his napkin, pleased that he'd shown her he could be useful to her investigation.

"That would mean Sulla probably has a personal connection to the family," she continued.

"Most likely," he agreed.

She thought for a moment. "That doesn't exactly narrow the field," she said wryly. "There's no shortage of people who hate the Coltons."

"We should probably talk to the Coltons themselves. They might be able to come up with a list of names to check out."

Felicity nodded. "That's going to be a big job. There are six Colton siblings alone living in Shadow Creek."

"Which means if we each pick three, it will take half the time to interview them."

"You'd do that?" She arched one eyebrow, plainly surprised.

Dario tilted his head to the side. "I did volunteer to help you," he pointed out.

"Sure, but I figured you'd just want to stick to the computer stuff. I didn't realize you intended to actually embrace all aspects of the investigative process."

Dario leaned back and clapped his hand over his heart. "You wound me," he said, affecting his best Southern drawl. "I'm not a dilettante."

Felicity laughed, a light, bright sound that made her seem almost girlish. "Forgive me," she said. "I certainly didn't mean to impugn your honor."

"The truth is, it'll be fun to talk to the Coltons. I usually do my work in front of a computer and don't really get to participate in other aspects of a case."

"It's not like you see on TV," Felicity cautioned. "This

job isn't always exciting. Most of the time, it can be down-right boring."

"That's okay," Dario said. "I'm just happy to help." Hopefully, Felicity would appreciate his efforts and relax around him.

She was silent a moment, then said, "Thank you."

Dario swallowed a bite of his burger and felt a surge of warmth at her words. It seemed she was softening toward him already.

"So which siblings do you want to interview?" he asked. "I know River was in the Marines, so maybe you should talk to him. He'd probably be happy to chat with a fellow vet."

"Sounds good. I'll talk to Jade and Claudia, as well. Can you interview Knox, Thorne and Leonor?"

Dario nodded. "No problem. Can you give me your phone number?" He kept his voice casual. "In case I need to reach you?"

Felicity hesitated only a second before reaching into her bag. She pulled out a business card and wrote her cell number on the back, then slid it across the table toward him. "The main office line is on there as well, in case you need Adeline."

"Great." He quickly memorized her number, then put the card into his wallet. "Now, what about my badge?"

"Your badge?" Felicity frowned, her confusion plain.

Dario couldn't contain his grin. "Don't you need to deputize me or something?"

She nodded thoughtfully. "Of course. How could I forget?" She stood abruptly and grabbed her purse, then walked away from the table.

Dario sat there in shock, unsure of what was happening. He'd only meant to tease her; had he somehow overstepped his bounds and offended her? Was she headed back to the office to explain to Adeline how she couldn't work with him?

He needn't have worried. Felicity returned a moment later and tossed him something. "Here you go."

He caught it reflexively, then examined the object. It was a shiny gold plastic star stamped with the word *sheriff*. She must have gotten it out of the coin-operated toy dispensers located by the entrance to the café. Dario stared at it for a second, hardly believing his eyes. The gesture was so unexpected he wasn't sure how to respond, but after a second his laughter took over. It seemed the straitlaced former marine had a sense of humor, after all...

"I trust that's sufficient?" There was a spark of mischief in her eyes he'd never seen before, and Dario felt an answering flare of heat in his belly. He liked seeing this side of Felicity.

He sniffed, pretending to consider it. "I think I can work with this."

"I'm glad to hear it." She studied him over the top of her water glass. "Do you think you can get in touch with your group of Colton siblings today?"

He nodded, appreciating her sense of urgency. This was a big case, and the sooner they made progress, the better. "I'll start calling after we're done here."

"Excellent." Felicity glanced around and gestured to the waitress for their check. Apparently, she didn't want to linger. He shoved the last bite of his cheeseburger into his mouth and lifted his hip to pull out his wallet. It seemed their lunch was over.

Time to get to work.

One hour later, Dario parked in the driveway of Thorne Colton's home and killed the ignition. The house was a pretty ranch-style rambler with lots of exposed wood and a large front porch. Rocking chairs and a porch swing swayed gently in the breeze, adding to the picture of domesticity.

He climbed out of the car, his boots crunching on the crushed gravel of the driveway. He heard the distant sound of horses neighing, the noise carrying easily in the cold winter air. He knew from the drive in that Thorne's house was tucked away from the barn and other ranch structures, but he spied a paddock about fifty yards away where a beautiful palomino horse grazed peacefully as a smaller bay horse frolicked around. *Mother and foal?* he wondered as he climbed the porch stairs.

Dario pressed the doorbell, and a loud squeal sounded from inside the house. *What the—?*

A series of loud thumps sounded, accompanied by the murmur of a deep voice. After a few seconds, the door opened to reveal a tall, dark-haired man and a small, bright-eyed baby sporting a onesie that read Mommy's Little Cowboy.

"You must be Dario Ortega."

"That's me. Nice to meet you." He extended his hand, and Thorne reached for him.

The baby, sensing his father's distraction, chose that moment to make a break for the freedom of the outside world. He lunged forward, arching his back and angling his body away from his father's chest. Thorne made a grab for the child, but the little one was slippery, and his eyes filled with horror as he lost his grip on the baby...

Without stopping to think, Dario stepped forward and scooped up the child before he wriggled free of his father's arms. "Hey there, little man," he said calmly.

The child blinked at him, apparently stunned at this sudden change of circumstances. He studied Dario warily, glancing to his father for reassurance. Not wanting to scare the little boy, Dario stepped inside the house and handed him over to Thorne.

"Thanks," Thorne said. He looked at the boy in his arms. "Way to knock a few years off my life, Joseph."

The baby cooed, grinning at this pronouncement. He wriggled his legs, and Thorne tightened his grip on his offspring. "Come on in," Thorne called over his shoulder as he carried the baby down the hall, headed for the warm glow of the room beyond.

Dario followed at a slightly slower pace, feeling a little self-conscious. The house was warm and cozy, and the hallway was lined with what appeared to be pictures of family: he recognized the sheriff Knox Colton in a few of them, along with Thorne and his wife. He stepped into the living room to find Thorne sitting on the floor, stacking blocks with his little boy.

"Have a seat," Thorne said. "Sorry it's a little chaotic here today. Maggie's gone to the grocery store, and Joseph just woke up from his nap, so he's got a ton of energy to burn."

"It's no problem." Dario lowered himself to the couch and watched the two of them play, trying to reconcile what he knew about Thorne with the man sitting in front of him. Thorne Colton had a reputation as a quiet, reserved man, and yet here he was, laughing and playing with his son as if he didn't have a care in the world.

"You're Natalia Ortega's son, right?" Thorne glanced at him curiously. "The equine vet?"

Dario nodded. "That's my mom," he confirmed.

"She's taken care of some of our animals before. Excellent vet. You have her eyes."

"Thanks," he said. It wasn't the kind of observation he'd expected Thorne Colton to make, but he was pleased to know the man was impressed with his mother's skills.

Thorne must have recognized his surprise. "Sorry. Before Joseph came along, I never would have commented on your resemblance. Lack of sleep has removed my normal filter." He shook his head, then reached out to muss the little boy's hair. "A lot has changed."

"I imagine so." And that was the biggest reason Dario didn't want to settle down and have kids. Life after children was never the same, and he liked things the way they were now. He had the freedom to do what he wanted, when he wanted, with no one to answer to or consider. It was nice to be able to pick up at a moment's notice, and a wife and kids just seemed like an anchor that would hold him down.

Thorne seemed to be enjoying fatherhood, but despite the cozy picture he and his son made, Dario wasn't convinced this was the life for him.

"Are you sure this is a good time to talk?" Joseph had scrunched up his face and was emitting a soft whine.

Thorne picked him up and set him down a few steps away, next to a pile of picture books. "I'd hate for you to waste a trip," Thorne said, grabbing one off the stack and holding it open. Joseph began to pat the thick cardboard pages with his chubby hand, jabbering happily as Thorne flipped through the book.

"Well, as I said on the phone, I'm helping Felicity Grant investigate the Colton, Incorporated, hacking case. We're trying to unmask the leader of the group, and there's a very good chance it's someone known to the Colton family. Probably someone who harbors ill will toward your family, maybe feels like they've been wronged in some way and is looking to exact revenge. Can you think of anyone who fits that description?"

Thorne snorted, and his breath ruffled his son's fine brown hair. Joseph shivered, and Dario couldn't help but smile. He really was a cute kid, even though he never seemed to stop moving for very long.

"You know who my mother is, don't you?" Thorne's tone was heavy with sarcasm, and Dario nodded, smiling ruefully.

"I'm familiar with her reputation," he said carefully. He didn't want to start off on the wrong foot by offending Thorne. Livia Colton was a bona fide psychopath, and it sounded like there was no love lost between them. But she was still Thorne's mother, and that wasn't a bond that was easily broken.

"It would take days to tell you about all the people she hurt. Not only the victims of her crimes, but her former business partners who have an ax to grind."

"I take it she cheated them?"

Joseph waved his hands, grabbing a rattle his father held. He shoved it into his mouth and began to chew enthusiastically. Thorne smiled absently at his son.

"Livia is a user. She preys on people, identifying their weak spots and taking advantage of them. She has no conscience, no remorse at all. And no sense of loyalty. She gets what she wants from someone and then cuts them loose, no matter the cost."

"It sounds like she has a lot of enemies."

"That's putting it mildly," Thorne said.

Joseph squealed as if in punctuation, and even Dario had to smile at the child's evident joy.

"Can you think of anyone in particular whose anger toward Livia might extend beyond her? Someone who might choose to target the Colton family since Livia is now in hiding?"

Thorne's expression turned thoughtful. "I might be able to give you some names," he said after a moment. "But to be honest, I didn't really stay up to date on all of Livia's dirty laundry." He shook his head. "I tried to keep her out of my life as much as possible."

A low rumble sounded through the room. Joseph's eyes widened. Thorne stood and picked up the baby. "My wife is home," he called, heading for the other room. "Come on back and we can keep talking."

Dario followed the man and boy into the kitchen to find the baby staring at the door that presumably led to the garage. After a moment, the door opened to admit a pretty blonde woman, her arms laden with bags.

Joseph let out a squeal and lurched forward, clearly seeking his mother's arms. Thorne walked over and handed her the baby before giving her a smacking kiss, collecting the bags from her in one smooth motion. "Welcome back," he said.

The little boy pressed his face to his mother's cheek, clearly thrilled to be with her again.

Something flipped inside Dario's chest at the sight of this little family, so in love with one another. They were obviously a team, and he had no doubt that whatever life brought them, they would all face it together. Perhaps there was something to be said for that...

"Oh! Hello. I didn't see you." Thorne's wife offered Dario a smile. If she was bothered to see a stranger in her kitchen, she didn't show it.

Thorne made the introductions. "Maggie, this is Dario Ortega. He's working on the Colton hacking case. Dario, this is my wife, Maggie."

She balanced Joseph on her hip and extended her hand, which Dario shook. "Nice to meet you," he said.

"Likewise."

Thorne placed the bags on the kitchen counter and began unpacking them. Dario watched as he pulled out box after box of what looked like sugar cookies. "Um, babe?" Thorne frowned in confusion. "What's all this?"

"Cookies," she said, her tone making it clear that this should be perfectly obvious.

"I can see that," Thorne said. "But why did you buy all these?"

"For the cookie decorating tomorrow," she explained. She rifled one-handed through another bag, withdrawing tubes of icing and containers of brightly colored sugar sprinkles.

"I thought you were going to bake them," Thorne said.

Dario inwardly cringed, immediately recognizing Thorne's mistake. *Oh boy...*

Maggie leveled a stare at her husband, and to his credit, Thorne blushed.

"Sweetheart," she began, her tone saccharine sweet. "Do I look like I have time to bake six dozen sugar cookies?"

Thorne immediately shook his head. "Of course not. This is perfect. I only asked because I was looking forward to the house smelling so good."

Maggie reached into another bag and plunked a candle on the counter. Dario smiled to himself as he read the label: Sugar Cookie Wonderland.

"Knock yourself out, honey."

Thorne laughed and leaned over to kiss her cheek. "I see you thought of everything. As always."

Maggie shook her head, smiling wryly. "Flatterer." She glanced at Dario. "So you're working on the Colton, Incorporated, case? Are you with the police?"

"No. I'm consulting with Adeline Kincaid—one of her investigators is trying to track down the leader of the hacking group, and since I have some computer forensics expertise I volunteered to assist while I'm in town."

"Have you found any leads yet?" Maggie extracted her necklace from Joseph's chubby grip and grabbed a bottle from the fridge.

Surprising himself, Dario reached out and took the bottle from Maggie's hand. He quickly stuck it in the microwave, then aimed a questioning look at Maggie. She told him the correct time, and he punched the buttons for her. "Thanks," she said.

"No problem."

The microwave dinged, and Dario retrieved the bottle. Maggie tested the formula, then began to feed the baby. Dario watched them for a moment, then returned his attention to Maggie's question. "It's a tough case," he said. "My brother, Emiliano, is an agent on the FBI's cyber-crime team. They're working on it as well, but so far, there haven't been any credible leads. That's why I'm here— I was hoping your husband might know of anyone who would want to hurt the family."

"How much time do you have?" Maggie said sarcastically.

"That's what I told him," Thorne said, folding the empty paper bags flat.

"I'm beginning to think this avenue isn't going to be as helpful as I'd hoped," Dario admitted. He'd thought the Colton siblings could help narrow down the search for Sulla, but if the family really had that many enemies, it would take forever to comb through all the potential suspects.

"Have you talked to anyone else?"

Dario shook his head. "Not yet. I'm supposed to interview Knox and Leonor, and my partner is going to talk to River, Jade and Claudia. I was hoping to get in touch with Knox this afternoon."

"Why don't you just come over tomorrow for the cookie decorating?" Maggie suggested. "Everyone will be here— it's a Colton holiday tradition. Bring your partner, too. What's his name?"

"Her name is Felicity. And are you sure about this? I don't want to intrude on a family event." He glanced at Thorne, but the other man nodded.

"Absolutely," Thorne said. "It'll save you from having to track everyone down one by one. And it'll give me more time to come up with a list of names for you, as well."

"That would be great," Dario said. "If you really don't mind us crashing the party."

"Not at all," Maggie assured him. "The more, the merrier."

"I'll talk to my brothers and sisters and let them know what kind of information you're looking for," Thorne said. "That way, they can be thinking about it before tomorrow's event."

"I really appreciate that," Dario said. "It's a huge help."

Joseph wriggled his legs, and Maggie shifted the baby in her arms, readjusting the angle of the bottle as she moved.

"I'll get out of your way now," Dario said. "Can we bring anything to tomorrow's gathering?"

"Just yourselves," Maggie said. "Thorne is going to grill some burgers and hot dogs, and we'll spend a few hours eating and decorating cookies."

"You're going to grill?" Dario couldn't keep the surprise out of his voice. "I thought we have a chance of snow tomorrow."

"We do," Maggie confirmed. "And to any sane person, that would be reason enough to cook inside."

Thorne scoffed. "I'm not going to let a few snowflakes keep me away from Bessie."

Dario shot Maggie a questioning look. "He named his grill," she said, her expression one of long-suffering patience.

"Of course I did," Thorne said. "It's only right. We spend so much time together."

Maggie grinned and rolled her eyes, and Dario chuckled. "Sounds fair to me," he said. "What time should we come tomorrow?"

"The gang will start getting here around noon," Maggie said. "Food should be ready between twelve thirty and one. Come by around then so you can eat before we start working on the cookies."

"Yes, ma'am." Recognizing an order when he heard it, Dario nodded. "Looking forward to it."

# Chapter 4

"I can't believe we're doing this."

Dario glanced at Felicity before returning his focus to the road. "What's the matter?"

Felicity shifted in the passenger seat, struggling to find the words to explain her discomfort. "It seems wrong to intrude on their family event. Especially since we don't really know any of them on a personal level." She'd spoken to River and his wife, Edith, yesterday, and she'd liked them. River was also a veteran of the Marine Corps, and even though they had served in different units, they still had quite a bit in common. It had been nice to talk to a veteran her own age; she knew Mr. Perkins had offered to lend an ear if she needed it, but she had a hard time thinking of him as anything other than her high school teacher. River appeared to be adjusting to civilian life well, despite the loss of one eye. Perhaps once this investigation was over, she could talk to him about her worries and learn how he had dealt with his own...

"For what it's worth, I tried to refuse the invitation," Dario said. "But Thorne and Maggie insisted we come. If the rest of the family is anything like them, I think they'll be quite friendly and welcoming."

Felicity frowned. "I just hate to interrupt their celebrations with questions about the case. I'm sure the last thing they want to talk about is Livia Colton's enemies."

"It'll be fine," he said. "They don't seem like the type to stay gloomy for long."

Felicity envied his confidence. Hopefully, he was right. She'd feel terrible if they ruined the Coltons' holiday celebration.

Silence descended in the car. Felicity searched for something to say, wanting to make conversation. It would be easier to work on the case with Dario if she knew a bit more about him. But she had to be careful—she'd made it very clear she wasn't interested in any romantic involvement, and she didn't want to give him the wrong idea.

"How are your cookie decorating skills?"

He chuckled. "Rusty. I haven't decorated a cookie since I was a kid. I'm really good at eating them, though."

"Something tells me that won't be a problem," Felicity said.

"Probably not," he replied. "What about you? Did your family have any Christmas traditions?"

"We had a baking day," she said. "The second Saturday of December, my mom and I would spend the whole day baking cookies and breads. We'd box them all up and deliver them to the neighbors, and my dad would take some to his coworkers."

"That sounds like fun."

"It was." She hadn't thought about baking day in a while, and the memories made her smile. The tradition had fallen off after she'd joined the Marines. She hadn't always been able to get leave over the Christmas holidays, and when she had been home, she'd been more interested in sleeping and catching up with friends than baking. A pang of sadness speared her chest at the thought of the missed time with her mother. Maybe they could bake a few things together this year and recapture some of that holiday magic. It was exactly the kind of tradition she'd like to pass on to her own children someday.

Felicity made a mental note to call her parents later. "Your turn," she said, resuming the conversation. "Tell me about the Ortega family Christmas."

Dario glanced at her, a glint of surprise in his eyes as if he hadn't expected her to show interest in his life. "Well, we didn't have anything quite so formal. My parents often had to work over the holidays, since sick animals don't care about what day it is. When my brother and I were really small, one of my parents would make sure to stay home if the other had a call. But once Emiliano and I got a bit older, the whole family would go. I remember a few Christmases spent in a barn while my mom treated a sick horse or helped a mare foal. Once that was done, we'd return home and pick up the celebrations where we'd left off."

"Sounds like you guys made the best of things," Felicity said.

He nodded. "We did. All I can say is thank God for the microwave—it saved us from a cold dinner more times than I can count."

"I can imagine."

He pulled up in front of a nice-looking ranch house and angled the car onto a strip of the gravel drive. A handful of other cars were already parked, which meant the party was likely already under way.

Dario glanced at her, one eyebrow lifted in inquiry. "Ready?"

Felicity took a deep breath and nodded. Her heart was already pounding at the thought of being in a crowd, but she pushed back against her mounting anxiety. There were no insurgents hiding in this family gathering. Just like at the engagement party, these people were gathered to celebrate, and there was no traitor hell-bent on destruction in their midst.

Dario waited for her by the car, and he placed his hand on her lower back to escort her up the stairs onto the porch.

His touch was light, more a sign of good manners than anything else. Still, Felicity had to admit she liked having his hand on her. It gave her something to focus on, a distraction from her irrational fears. She leaned back a little as they waited for someone to answer the door, subtly increasing the contact between them. She glanced at Dario's face, expecting to see a flash of smug satisfaction in his eyes. But if Dario noticed what she was doing, he didn't show it.

She could hear the din of conversation and laughter even through the closed door, and she relaxed a tiny bit. *This is what normal life is like*, she reminded herself. It was something she had taken for granted once. Not anymore.

The door opened, and a pretty, curvy blonde woman smiled at them. "Dario! So glad you could make it!" She stepped forward and lightly kissed his cheek, then turned to Felicity. "And you must be Felicity. I'm Maggie Colton. Please come inside."

"Thank you for including us today," Felicity said, stepping across the threshold. The house was warm and smelled deliciously of cookies. Felicity was immediately transported back to the kitchen with her mother, the pair of them laughing and talking as they worked. "It smells amazing in here," she said. "Have you been baking all morning?"

Maggie's blue eyes sparkled. "Yes," she said with a nod. "Something like that." She winked at Dario, who smiled and ducked his head at what was clearly a private joke.

*Interesting*, Felicity thought. It seemed her initial assessment of Dario was correct; the man was a born charmer, and apparently even married women weren't immune to his charisma.

Oddly enough, this realization made her soften toward him. When she'd first met him, she'd assumed Dario's carefree, flirtatious attitude had been an act designed to manipulate people into giving him what he wanted. Now she saw that wasn't the case. He had the type of personality that drew people in, made them want to get closer. It was an effect she'd been fighting for the past few days, and for the first time, she began to wonder if her resistance was worth the effort.

"The gang's all here," Maggie said. "Thorne is just about to put the burgers and hot dogs on the grill."

"He's grilling in this weather?" Felicity said, incredulous. "Doesn't he know it's snowing?" The flurries had started on the drive in, and the week had been cold enough that the flakes were probably going to stick. It made for picture-perfect holiday weather, but it wasn't ideal for cooking outdoors.

Maggie rolled her eyes and smiled. "He sees the snow as a challenge rather than a sign to stay inside. I've given up trying to talk sense into him—I figure if he wants to freeze, then who am I to stop him?"

Felicity and Dario both laughed and Maggie led them down the entry hall into a large living room. All the Colton siblings were there; Felicity recognized River and his wife, Edith, and Knox, the sheriff of Shadow Creek. She spied Jade in the corner talking with a tall, striking redhead and a petite blonde woman. *Those must be her sisters*, she thought.

Maggie waved to get the group's attention. "Hey, everyone! Our guests have arrived!" She made the introductions and Felicity committed the names of the Colton siblings and their spouses to memory as she was guided around the room. She'd been right; the tall redhead was Leonor, and the other blonde woman was Claudia Colton. A moment later, Thorne popped his head into the room and waved.

"Good to see you again," he said to Dario, passing a baby off to Maggie. "And nice to meet you, Felicity."

Everyone was welcoming and Felicity soon found herself holding a mug of hot cider. Dario was pulled aside by Josh Howard, Leonor's husband, and Felicity drifted into the corner where she could watch the group. A young boy streaked through the room.

"Cody!" Both Knox and his wife, Allison, called out at the same time. "No running in the house," continued Knox.

The boy stopped, but Felicity could tell by the way his frame practically vibrated with energy that it wouldn't be long before he needed another reminder.

"Dad, it's snowing! Can I go outside and play?"

Knox and Allison exchanged a look, and Knox made to stand. "It's my turn," he said to his wife. "You stay warm."

"Both of you stay warm," Thorne instructed. He carried a plate of hamburger patties and hot dogs in one hand and a set of tools in the other. "I'll keep an eye on him."

Cody darted after his uncle. "Put your coat on," Allison called after him.

The baby Maggie was holding spied Dario, and his little face lit up. He stretched his arms out, clearly seeking Dario's hold.

Dario glanced down and grinned. "Hey there, Joseph." To Felicity's shock, he picked up the boy, settling him easily on his hip.

Maggie laughed. "Oh my. You made quite the impression yesterday," she said.

Dario laughed. "It's always good to have a friend."

"It's time for his bottle. Would you mind feeding him?" Maggie asked.

"I'd be happy to," Dario said easily.

Maggie stepped into the kitchen and returned a moment later with a bottle. "Let me know when you get tired of him," she said.

"No worries," Dario said. "Joseph and I will be just fine." He found a seat and settled the baby in his arms, then set about feeding him.

Felicity couldn't tear her gaze away from the sight. Dario hadn't struck her as the type of man to be interested in kids, but he looked like a natural sitting there with a squirming infant in his arms.

Something shifted inside her chest as she watched him interact with the baby. Dario patiently watched Joseph as he ate. The baby gulped audibly as he drank from the bottle and he hummed, clearly enjoying his meal. Dario smiled down at him, his expression one of genuine affection. Who was this man? He certainly didn't look like a carefree playboy now. Clearly, there was more to him than met the eye, and Felicity felt a pang of guilt at her assumption he was a one-dimensional flirt who was only interested in the next good time.

"Good to see you again." The quiet words interrupted her thoughts, and Felicity reluctantly looked away from Dario to find River Colton standing next to her.

She quickly took a sip of her cider, hoping to cover her interest in Dario. "It was so nice of your family to invite us," she said.

River glanced around the room at his siblings and their partners. The soft buzz of conversation filled the air, punctuated by the occasional laugh. It was a cozy, familial sound, the kind of noise Felicity wanted in her own home one day. "It's nice to have friends around, too," River said.

He turned back to study her, and Felicity tried not to fidget under his gaze. "You're doing really well," he said softly.

"I'm not so sure," she murmured.

"No, you are," he insisted. "It took me a long time to adjust to standing in a group of people. I got nervous being around my own family, it was that bad. You look great, though."

Felicity laughed softly. "Looks can be deceiving. I feel pretty wobbly inside."

"That will pass," he said confidently. "I know it doesn't feel that way now, but you will adjust." He lifted his arm as Edith walked over, and she snugged against his side. Felicity smiled, hoping it hid the weight of envy that settled on her shoulders as she saw the love shared by River and his wife. She wanted that someday—the closeness with someone, the sense of safety and belonging. Of feeling understood and accepted, flaws and all. She thought she'd had that once, but she'd been wrong and the memory of it still stung.

Edith gently poked River in the ribs. "Babe, would you mind getting me a cup of cider?"

"Not at all," he said, releasing her at once. He headed into the kitchen and Edith leaned closer to Felicity. "Are you okay?" Her brown eyes were full of compassion and understanding, as if she knew exactly what Felicity was feeling right now. And she probably did, since she'd had a front-row seat as River had adjusted to civilian life.

"I'm good, thanks."

Edith nodded. "Yeah, I've heard that line before." Felicity knew the other woman had seen through her social lie, but there was no accusation in Edith's tone. Just a matter-of-fact acknowledgment that Felicity appreciated. She got the sense that if she wanted to talk, Edith would listen.

"He's lucky to have you," she said.

Edith laughed and shook her head. "I'm lucky to have him," she corrected. "Or I guess you could say it's a good thing we found each other."

"I'm sure you helped him adjust to life after the war," Felicity said.

Edith tilted her head to the side, her expression turning thoughtful. "Yes. We've been good for each other." She glanced at Felicity's face and added, "You'll find that, too. The right man is out there."

"I'm not so sure," Felicity admitted. "I thought I'd found him once, but that wasn't the case."

"What happened?"

"We were high school sweethearts. We had big plans—marriage, kids, the whole nine yards. But then I joined the Marines, and he couldn't handle it. He had his reasons and didn't want to talk about it. So he dumped me the night before I shipped off to basic training." Felicity shook her head at the memory. Even twelve years later, the pain of his rejection still made her heart ache.

"I'm so sorry," Edith said. She gently touched Felicity's arm in sympathy.

Felicity shrugged. "It is what it is. Probably better things turned out the way they did. If our relationship wasn't strong enough to withstand my service, he wasn't the right guy, after all."

"That's true, but I'm sure that thought was cold comfort to you at the time."

"Yeah. It took me a while, but I've moved on."

"That's good," Edith said. "Are you seeing anyone now?"

"Ah, no," Felicity replied. She took a sip of cider, her eyes darting back to Dario. He still held Joseph, and now he was reading the boy a book. Her heart fluttered in her chest and she felt her resistance to him melt even more.

Did he know the effect he was having on her? Surely not. He couldn't be that calculating—he didn't seem like the kind of man to use a child as a prop to get into a woman's good graces. He looked far too genuinely interested in the boy for that.

"Something tells me you could be dating someone if you wanted," Edith said cryptically.

Felicity returned her focus to the other woman. "What do you mean?"

Edith's lips curved in a knowing smile. "You two

haven't stopped watching each other since you walked in here. Dario's doing well with Joesph, but he's been sneaking glances over at you when you've been distracted. And you've been doing the same to him. It's clear you're interested in him, and he returns it."

"Really?" Felicity felt equal parts dismay over being so transparent and giddy at the thought of Dario wanting her. When he'd approached her at Emiliano's engagement party, she'd figured he was just looking to flirt with a pretty face. But if his interest ran deeper than that, if he truly wanted to get to know her…the possibility made her feel warm inside.

"All I'm saying is that if you're feeling lonely, I don't think you need to stay that way. Unless that's what you truly want."

Felicity glanced at Dario again, her mind whirring as she considered Edith's point. Would it be so bad to go out with him once or twice? Adeline had said none of Dario's girlfriends had a bad word to say about him. Maybe he would be a good choice to reintroduce her to the dating scene, help her get her feet wet again. After years of being single, didn't she deserve to have a little fun?

At that moment, Thorne walked in the back door on a gust of cold wind, Cody hot on his heels. They both had snow in their hair and sported broad grins, and it was clear they'd had fun playing outside. "Food's up," Thorne called, carrying a plate of steaming hamburger patties and hot dogs into the kitchen. People began to drift into the other room, headed for the promise of warm food.

At the sound of his father's voice, little Joseph began to wriggle in earnest. Maggie retrieved her son with a smile, and Dario watched them go, then walked over to Edith and Felicity.

"Looks like you've been forgotten," Felicity said, her heart rate jumping at his nearness.

"That's okay," Dario said. "I think he was getting bored with me anyway."

"Kids can be rather fickle," Edith said. "But you made a great babysitter."

"Thanks." Dario grinned and glanced at Joseph again. The boy was now in Thorne's arms, his head against his father's chest. "He's an easy kid to get along with."

River joined them then and handed Edith a cup of cider. "Sorry it took me so long," he said. "I got caught up talking to Maggie in the kitchen."

"It's okay," Edith said. She turned to Felicity and Dario. "Are you guys hungry? We should get in there before it's gone."

River put his arm around Edith's shoulders, and the pair of them started for the kitchen.

Dario glanced at Felicity and tilted his head. "After you," he said gallantly. He gestured for her to precede him and fell in about a half step behind her. As they walked, his hand came to rest on the small of her back, and Felicity smiled.

He really needed to stop watching her.

Dario forced his gaze off Felicity and back onto the sugar cookies on the plate in front of him. Maggie had distributed the cookies after everyone had finished lunch, and Thorne had set up tubes of icing, bowls of sprinkles and dishes of small, pressed sugar pieces for use in decorating the treats. The entire Colton clan were gathered around the large farmhouse table, chatting over the soft din of Christmas carols drifting in from the stereo in the living room.

Fat snowflakes dropped lazily from the gray sky, completing the festive scene. It was exactly the kind of cozy, domestic setting that normally had him searching for the nearest exit, but today Dario found himself relaxing and enjoying the company.

It didn't hurt that Felicity sat across from him, her cheeks flushed from the warmth of the room and her hot apple cider. When they'd first arrived she had seemed a bit nervous. He'd meant to stay by her side until she felt more comfortable, but Joseph had claimed his attention and he'd had to leave her. Fortunately, River and his wife, Edith, had picked up the slack, and it hadn't taken long for Felicity to start smiling and chatting with the Coltons.

She sat between River and Edith now, and Dario was happy to see she appeared to be enjoying herself. She'd taken an instant liking to River Colton, a fact that had triggered a quick burst of irrational jealousy in his chest. Dario had squashed it immediately, knowing he was being ridiculous. It was only natural Felicity would feel comfortable around River, since they were both Marine Corps veterans who had been to war. They had the bond of shared experiences, something Dario would never be able to understand. The realization left him feeling a bit bereft in a way he couldn't fully explain. He had no desire to go to war, but there was a part of him that was sad to know he'd never be able to fully connect with Felicity on some levels. It was as if a piece of her was locked away, and he'd never be able to find the key.

Dario shook his head, dismissing the maudlin thoughts. It didn't matter anyway—Felicity had made it clear she had no interest in seeing him outside of a professional setting, so he had no reason to worry about how his lack of military experience would affect his ability to understand her.

But despite knowing they didn't have a future, Dario couldn't stop looking at Felicity.

Heaven help him, but he enjoyed watching her smile and the graceful movements of her hands as she worked to decorate her set of cookies. She was so beautiful, with a few tendrils of dark brown hair framing her face. She leaned forward, absorbed in her task, and he saw a flash of white as she gently bit her bottom lip in concentration. The sight hit him like a punch to the gut, and his stomach flip-flopped as he wondered if she'd apply that same focus to other, more pleasurable pursuits.

He slammed the door on the burgeoning fantasy and shoved back from the table a bit more forcefully than he'd intended. Everyone turned to look at him, and he felt his face heat. "Ah, I was just going to grab a glass of water. Can I bring anything back?"

There was a chorus of "No, thanks" and "Not right now." Dario nodded and walked into the kitchen, putting some much-needed space between him and Felicity.

He leaned against the counter and took a deep breath, then glanced around at the cupboards, trying to decide which one might hold glasses.

"Upper left," said Thorne as he walked into the room.

Dario followed his directions and retrieved a glass. "Thanks," he said, crossing to the sink to turn on the tap.

"No problem." Thorne leaned a hip against the counter and studied Dario as he took a sip of water. "Everything okay?"

Dario nodded. "Yep. Just got thirsty."

"Does she know?"

Dario glanced down, pretending not to understand. "Does who know what?"

Thorne merely tilted his head to the side and Dario sighed. "She knows I'm interested. She's not."

"I'm sorry, man. That's rough."

Dario shrugged. "It's not the first time I've been turned down." But for some reason, Felicity's rejection had stung. When other women had brushed off his attentions, Dario had moved on without a second thought. But Felicity's appeal went beyond the physical, and her refusal to give him a chance made him feel like he was missing out on something special.

"Is that why you volunteered to help with the case? Are you hoping to change her mind?"

"That's not the only reason," Dario said, sounding defensive even to his own ears.

Thorne held up a hand. "No judgment here. I might have something to help you get into her good graces." He stuck his hand in his pocket and withdrew a folded piece of paper. "I asked everyone to think of people who might have a grudge against us because someone in our family somehow did them wrong. Here's what we came up with." He passed the paper over and Dario unfolded it, surprised at the number of names on the list.

"I can't promise your guy is on there," Thorne said. "But for what it's worth, I hope this helps."

"This is fantastic," Dario said, scanning the paper before folding it and tucking it into his own pocket. His fingers tingled with the urge to touch a keyboard, and he couldn't wait to get back to his computer so he could start digging into the collection of potential suspects. If one of these people was Sulla, it wouldn't take him long to make the connection.

"I'm glad to hear that." Thorne clapped him on the shoulder as he walked past. "Now that you got what you came here for, are you going to leave right away, or can I convince you to stay and finish decorating your set of cookies? You know how hard Maggie worked baking everything."

Dario laughed and nodded. "I wouldn't want to upset the lady of the house."

"Smart man," Thorne commented. "With an attitude like that, I'd say you're ready for marriage."

"I don't know about that," Dario said. The thought of binding himself to one woman for the rest of his life usually triggered an automatic rejection in Dario's mind, but not this time. Having seen how happy Thorne was with his wife and child, and witnessing the other Coltons with their spouses, Dario had to admit the idea of marriage might not be as bad as he'd previously assumed. None of the Coltons appeared unsatisfied or unfulfilled. In fact, it was just the opposite. They all seemed quite happy. Just like his parents. Or Emiliano and Marie, for that matter.

He followed Thorne back into the dining room and sat across from Felicity once more. She glanced up and smiled at him, her eyebrows drawn together slightly in a silent question. Dario nodded, and her shoulders relaxed.

"That's a nice snowman you've got there," he said, indicating the cookie she was working on.

His comment drew the attention of the rest of the family, and a chorus of "oohs" and "'aahs" broke out as everyone caught a glimpse of the finely detailed winter scene Felicity had created.

She blushed, but he could tell by the look in her eyes she was pleased people liked her work. "Thanks," she said quietly.

Cody craned his neck to see what all the fuss was about. "That's so cool!" He climbed out of his chair and walked over to stand next to Felicity for a better look. "You're really good at this. Can you draw an octopus and a shark on one for me?"

Felicity looked a bit taken aback by the boy's request and Knox chuckled softly. "That's a lot to fit on one cookie," he said to his son. He turned to Felicity and said, "He's really into all things oceanic right now."

Felicity nodded. "There's a lot of cool things in the ocean. How about I put an octopus on one cookie and a shark on the other?"

"Okay!"

"Here, buddy." River stood and gestured to his chair. "Take my seat so you can watch the master work without crowding her."

"Thanks, Uncle River." Cody climbed onto the chair

and leaned forward, elbows on the table, getting as close to Felicity as he could without actually crawling into her lap. She reached out to grab a fresh cookie, and Dario's chest tightened as he watched the two of them—woman and boy, one dark head and one light close together, the pair of them talking quietly to each other. Cody was rattling off facts about his favorite ocean creatures, and Felicity was asking him questions as she worked. It was clear she liked children, and for a brief, fantastical moment, Dario imagined what life would be like if he and Felicity had a baby together. What holiday traditions would they celebrate? Would their son be fascinated with the ocean like Cody, or would he be more interested in trains and cars? Either way, Dario knew Felicity would be a great mother. She seemed genuinely interested in what Cody had to say, and she tolerated his frequent interruptions with good grace and humor.

After a few seconds, Dario shook himself free of the spell he was under. It didn't matter that Felicity was good with kids, or that she had all the makings of a great mother. He didn't want to get tied down in a relationship, and children weren't in his master plan. He was all about enjoying life and the variety of beautiful women in the world. He needed to stop fixating on Felicity and start looking for someone else to have fun with. Someone who wouldn't make him question his choices and wonder about things that had no chance of happening.

No matter how intriguing they seemed…

# *Chapter 5*

Felicity stared at her computer screen, reading the same sentence for the tenth time. It was hard to compose a response to Zane Colton's request for an update when her mind was occupied with thoughts of Dario.

He'd been strangely pensive on the drive back from the Coltons' yesterday. He'd seemed preoccupied, even, as if he'd been trying to work through a particularly knotty problem. After all her attempts at small talk had fizzled out, Felicity had stopped trying to make conversation and had embraced the silence. His lack of engagement hadn't bothered her—she understood the need for quiet while trying to think.

Had he been distracted by the case, or by something else? It was a question that still dogged her today and made her wonder just what was going on in his handsome head. The Colton siblings had given them a list of names yesterday, so now they had some leads to pursue. But was there something else bothering Dario?

She'd watched him yesterday, enjoying the sight of him with little Joseph. Dario had seemed to really like playing with the baby, but she hadn't missed the glint of surprise in his eyes every time Joseph turned to him or sought his attention. Was he currently rethinking his professed desire to remain footloose and fancy-free forever?

*Doubt it*, she thought with a snort. One afternoon with a cute infant probably wasn't enough to make Dario reconsider his enjoyment of serial monogamy. And why should it? Children were a huge responsibility, and while Felicity knew she'd like to have kids of her own someday, she wasn't ready to take that leap yet.

A rap on her office door broke through her musings, and Felicity looked up to find Edith Colton standing in the doorway.

Felicity rose from her chair. "Hi, Edith. What brings you in today?"

"I was in the area finishing up my holiday shopping, and I thought I'd stop in and say hello. Is this a bad time?"

"Not at all." Felicity waved her inside and gestured to the chair in front of her desk. "Please, sit down."

"Thanks." Edith plopped down and set her bags on the floor. "Every year I think I'm going to be more organized and get all the gifts bought early, and yet here I am on Christmas Eve, doing last-minute shopping."

Felicity laughed. "I can relate. I still need to find something for my parents." *And what about Dario?* The question popped into her head and Felicity froze. She had bought a little present for Adeline, but the two of them were more than just coworkers; they were friends. Still, she couldn't very well give Adeline something and not Dario. It seemed rude to ignore the fact that she and Dario had been spending so much time together lately, and she didn't want to exclude him from the office gift exchange later in the afternoon. She made a mental note to sneak out on her lunch break and search for a small token he might like. But what should she look for? She didn't have a lot of experience buying things for men, and Dario seemed like he already had everything.

"You okay?" Edith asked. "You have a funny look on your face."

Felicity swallowed. "I just realized Adeline and I are doing our gift exchange this afternoon before she leaves for the holiday. I didn't get anything for Dario, and I don't want him to feel left out."

"That's sweet of you," Edith said.

"Do you have any ideas? He always looks so polished and put together. I can't imagine there's anything he wants."

Edith considered the question for a moment. "I wouldn't try to get a personal gift, especially since you two don't know each other that well yet. There's a gourmet chocolate shop down the block. Why don't you get him some truffles? Everyone loves chocolate."

"That's a good idea," Felicity said. "I haven't seen him eat many sweets, though. He does drink a lot of coffee. He always seems to have a cup in his hand…"

"I was just in The French Press, that new coffee shop, and they have a lot of gifts on display," Edith said. "You'll probably find something there that will work."

"Perfect," Felicity said. "Thanks—you've saved me a lot of stress."

"No problem." Edith leaned forward, a spark of curiosity in her eyes. "Does this mean you're going to give him a shot?"

Felicity leaned back in her chair, wondering why everyone was suddenly so curious about her dating life. "I'm not sure yet. Why do you ask?"

"I think it would be a good distraction for you." Edith searched Felicity's face, her expression kind. "I hope you don't mind, but River told me some of the things you've been dealing with since you retired from the Corps. For what it's worth, he went through a lot of the same issues, too. It might be good for you to try something new, to take your mind off your worries."

"You might be right," Felicity murmured. She'd been thinking along those lines herself, and Edith's encouragement made her think it was probably the right thing to do.

At the very least, dating Dario would help her get out of her head and force her to interact with the world, rather than retreating to her lonely apartment every night.

Then another thought occurred to her, and Felicity's stomach twisted. "Say I do decide to go for it," she said. "How exactly do I approach him? I haven't been in a position to date anyone in years—I have no idea what to say!"

Edith shrugged. "In my experience, the direct approach is usually the most effective. And from what I know of you, I think it's probably your best option. You could invite him to a private holiday dinner or plan some other date. I don't think you'll have to worry about him saying no."

Felicity nodded, her mind whirring with possible activities. "Should I tell him right away that I just want to keep things casual?" Based on what he'd said to her before, she didn't think Dario was interested in anything serious or long-term. But would it kill the mood if she made it clear she felt the same way?

"It probably wouldn't hurt," Edith said. "But I wouldn't dwell on that. Kinda puts a damper on things, you know?" She winked mischievously, and Felicity had to laugh.

"Fair enough. Now I just have to work up my courage for the big ask."

Edith leaned forward. "That shouldn't be a problem. You're a marine. You have courage coming out your ears." She stood and gathered up her bags. "I've taken up enough of your time. I just want to say that I'm here for you if you ever want to talk. I know you and River have a connection, but if there's ever any girl stuff you don't want to say to him, I've got your back."

"Thank you." Felicity blinked against the sudden sting of tears. She stood and quickly rounded her desk, pulling Edith into a hug. "I really appreciate that. And I'm going to take you up on your offer."

"I hope so," Edith replied. "You've got to let me know

how it goes with Dario. I've got my fingers crossed for the two of you!"

Felicity smiled. "I think I'll have an update for you soon," she promised.

Edith left with a wave, and Felicity stayed in the middle of her office, considering her options. She glanced back at her computer, but she had no desire to finish composing her reply to Zane Colton at the moment. With her thoughts so centered on Dario, it was probably better for her to duck out and get his gift now. Once that was taken care of, she'd be able to focus on the case again.

Or so she hoped.

Dario tiptoed down the hall and retreated back into the relative safety of the temporary office Adeline had set up in the storage room just off the lobby. He'd accidentally overheard Felicity's conversation with Edith, and now his head was spinning. He needed quiet and privacy to think, and he didn't want Felicity to find him and think he'd been deliberately eavesdropping.

She liked him.

He'd suspected as much all along, but the confirmation made him smile. It was always gratifying to know a beautiful woman was interested in him, especially one as appealing as Felicity.

And he had to admit, he was pleased to know she also wanted to keep things casual. He'd done a lot of thinking after the Coltons' holiday gathering yesterday, and while he was no longer quite so against the idea of marriage and children, he knew those were milestones for a future time in his life.

From what he'd overheard, it sounded like Felicity was looking to ease back into the dating world. She must have had a bad experience, and for a brief second his heart ached for her. Her former boyfriend must have been a real jerk to turn her off of dating like that. Dario always took pains to make sure his relationships ended well, and he felt a spurt of disgust toward Felicity's unknown ex for not being as considerate.

Depending on how badly her former lover had hurt her, it might be quite a challenge to show Felicity that relationships didn't always mean emotional pain and regret. But Dario knew he was equal to the task. In fact, he relished the thought of being the man to show her how much fun dating could be.

He'd have to take things slow; that much was certain. Felicity was skittish, and he felt responsible for making sure they had a good time together. So as much as he wanted to walk into her office, gather her into his arms and kiss her soundly, he knew it was important to wait. To let her come to him.

And a little more than an hour later, she did.

"Have you got a minute?"

Dario glanced up and nodded. "Sure. Come on in."

Felicity stepped inside and sat down. She was still wearing her coat and scarf, and her cheeks were pink from the cold. "What's on your mind?" he asked.

"I was wondering if you'd made any progress on your half of the list of names the Coltons gave us." She began to unwind her scarf as she spoke, revealing the pale, slender column of her neck. Dario swallowed hard, his mind suddenly flooded with questions: Was the skin of her throat as soft as it looked? How would she respond if he kissed her just under the corner of her jaw?

She shrugged off her coat and his blood warmed. Even though there was nothing suggestive about her actions, Dario couldn't help but imagine her continuing to strip. He pictured her unbuttoning her jeans and peeling the fabric down those long legs. Lifting the hem of her sweater, exposing the skin of her belly, the curve of her ribs and the cups of her bra. And just what color was her bra? he wondered. A sensible white, or something more exciting, like red lace or black satin?

"Dario?" Her voice cut through his fantasy and he blinked, tuning back in to the conversation.

"Yes?"

She tilted her head to the side, her expression amused. "Are you okay? You seem a bit distracted."

There was a knowing glint in her eyes, and Dario realized his thoughts must have been more transparent than he'd realized. He felt his face heat and cleared his throat. "I'm fine. What was it you were saying?"

"I was asking if you'd made progress with your half of the names. I haven't been able to turn up much of anything. A couple of the people are dead, several have moved out of state and appear to have forgotten about the Coltons, and the rest don't seem to have the type of knowledge required to coordinate such a sophisticated cyberattack."

"They could always hire someone," he pointed out.

Felicity acknowledged his point with a nod. "True. I'm looking into what records I can, but so far I haven't found a smoking gun. Please tell me you've had more success."

"Maybe." Her expression brightened and he hastily amended, "I don't know for sure yet, but I've been hanging out on this forum that a lot of hackers frequent."

"Like an online coffee shop?"

"Something like that."

Felicity snorted. "I can't believe they'd be so brazen about discussing their actions. Sounds like a good way to get caught."

"Not exactly. The forum isn't on the regular web. It's part of the dark web, so most people don't even know it exists."

"The dark web?" Felicity sounded thoughtful. "Those sites are all heavily encrypted, right? And everyone uses throwaway names, so it's nearly impossible to connect a poster with a real person."

"Basically, yeah," Dario said, impressed at her knowledge. "That's why these guys aren't afraid to talk about what they've done. They feel protected by all the different layers of security set up, so they're a bit freer with their words."

"That makes sense. Do you think any of them are Principes?" she asked, referring to the term used for Cohort members.

"Almost certainly, but no one has admitted it yet."

"Have any of them bragged about participating in the Colton hack?" She sounded hopeful, and Dario wished he could say yes.

"No. At least, no one that I've found. I've been poking around a bit, asking the community if they know who was involved."

"Do you really think they'd tell you?" She wrinkled her nose. "These people are hyperparanoid about protecting their identities. I'd think they'd be suspicious of anyone asking questions like that."

"You'd be surprised," Dario replied. "Like you said, the users are very concerned with privacy. But mostly their own privacy. Most of them have no problem outing another user. It's a bit like the Wild West. And you're right—questions do tend to raise suspicions. But I'm a regular poster, and these people know me. I told them I'm interested in the details of the hack because I might have some work for whoever was responsible."

"Smart."

He smiled. "I'm glad you think so. Anyway, no one has responded to me on the message boards. But not too long ago, I received an email." He turned back to his computer monitor and, with a few quick keystrokes, pulled up the relevant message.

Felicity rose and moved to stand by his desk. She bent down to get a better look at the screen, and her breasts grazed the top of his shoulder. Dario caught his breath at the contact, wondering if she'd noticed. He risked a glance at her face, but she was so absorbed in reading his email she didn't seem to register the quick brush of her curves against him. Even though they weren't touching, he felt the warmth from her body and her scent filled his nose. She smelled faintly of coffee, and he fought the urge to lean over and bury his nose in her hair.

"Hmm." The sound she made was almost a purr, and he closed his eyes, letting it wash over him. It was exactly the kind of noise he enjoyed coaxing from women, and he wanted to hear it again under slightly different circumstances.

"What do you make of this?" Felicity straightened, putting distance between their bodies. Dario tried not to let his disappointment show. He glanced at the message, which was short and to the point: Look for ColtonQueen.

"To be honest, I think ColtonQueen is Livia Colton."

Felicity nodded slowly, her eyebrows drawn together. "Could be. Everyone knows she survived that accident. She's probably holed up somewhere, plotting revenge."

"If that's really the case, it makes sense she'd target Colton, Incorporated. What better way to get back at her family than to harm the company that bears their name?"

"Have you been able to find ColtonQueen user on your hacker forums?"

He shook his head. "Not yet. That's going to take a little more digging. Not everyone who is a member of the forum posts publicly."

"So it's possible ColtonQueen has seen your posts, and now she knows you're trying to find out more about her." Felicity looked down at him, her eyes bright with worry. "Have you just made yourself a target?"

"I don't think so." Dario stood and touched her arm in re-assurance. "It's possible, but if Livia really is ColtonQueen, I'm betting she'll be flattered by my interest rather than angry. People like her have huge egos, and if she thinks I'm impressed by what she's done, she might contact me so she can brag about it."

"I hope you're right." Felicity still looked worried, and her concern set off a warm tingle in the center of his chest.

"Let's say it really is Livia Colton hiding behind a computer screen, or maybe someone working for her. What's the worst she could do to me?" He tried to sound casual, but he could tell by the look in Felicity's eyes she wasn't buying it.

"Lots," she said grimly. "You might want to do a quick search and get up to speed on her list of crimes. That woman is a true sociopath, and she won't hesitate to act if she feels threatened by you."

Dario studied her for a moment, surprised by the note of fear in her voice. Felicity didn't seem like the type of person to let her emotions rule her actions. "What are you saying? Do you think we should stop investigating this lead because of what Livia Colton might do? She might not even be aware of my inquiries in the first place."

"Of course I don't want you to stop," Felicity said, straightening her spine.

*There she is*, he thought with a mental smile. The Felicity he knew was back.

"I just want you to be aware of the potential dangers that you might face. Don't be careless, okay?"

Dario nodded, letting his smile show on his face. "I'll take every precaution," he said, stepping closer.

Felicity's eyes widened. "Good. That's, um, good to hear."

"It's sweet of you to worry about me." He reached up and tucked a stray strand of hair behind her ear.

Felicity swallowed hard, and Dario had the sudden urge to trace the line of her throat with the tip of his tongue. "You're doing me a huge favor by helping with the investigation," she stammered. "I'd hate to see you get hurt."

"Is that the only reason you care?" he murmured. His gaze zeroed in on her mouth, and he was rewarded by the sight of her tongue darting out to slick across her lips.

"Well, no," she admitted. "It's not the only reason."

That was all the invitation he needed. Dario dipped his head and captured her mouth with his own. Felicity gasped, and for a split second, he thought she was going to pull away.

But she didn't. She lifted her arms and threaded her hands through his hair, stepping closer to press her body against his. Her breasts flattened against his chest and he choked back a groan as his blood raced south.

He'd thought this would be a simple kiss, a getting-to-know-you gesture. A way for him to show her how good things could be between them. He'd meant to blow her mind and leave her wanting more.

But it was his world that got rocked. Felicity kissed him with a raw intensity that sent him reeling and left him aching for more. She burned hot and hungry, and he was only too happy to match her fervor.

Her hands left his hair, sliding down his back and then lower, anchoring their hips together. He slipped one hand between them, finding her breast. She moaned as he cupped her, her body rocking forward in wordless encouragement.

Dario's thoughts began to fragment as the intensity of his arousal grew. Flat surface. He needed to find something flat so they could get horizontal and then—

The jangle of bells and the slam of a door sliced through the moment, and Dario and Felicity both jumped at the unexpected racket.

"Adeline must be back from lunch," Felicity whispered. She began to hastily rearrange her clothes, and Dario didn't have the heart to tell her not to bother. Her lips were swollen and shiny and her skin flushed. She looked like a woman who had been thoroughly kissed, and no amount of smoothing and tucking was going to change that.

He ran his hands through his hair, feeling equal parts relieved and sorry that the kiss was over. The interruption had come just in time—a moment later, and they would have been on the floor, past the point of distraction. "Have dinner with me tonight."

Felicity glanced over, regret shining in her eyes. "I can't. My parents are flying out tonight for a Christmas cruise. I'm eating with them before I take them to the airport."

"What about tomorrow?" he pressed. He had to see her again, the sooner the better.

"I don't think anything will be open tomorrow. It's Christmas," she pointed out.

"Then come over for brunch at the Ortegas'."

Felicity shook her head. "Oh no. I can't possibly crash your family holiday gathering."

"I insist," he said gently. "You wouldn't be crashing. You'd be saving me from feeling like a fifth wheel." He grinned. "Besides, you can't be alone on Christmas."

"Do you really think it would be okay with your family?" she said doubtfully. "I don't want to impose."

"They'll be happy to have you join us."

She was quiet a moment, then nodded. "That sounds nice. Thank you." She turned and gathered up her coat, scarf and bag. "I'll, uh, I'll see you at the gift exchange later?"

"Sounds good."

Felicity nodded and stepped toward the door. "Hey," he

said. She paused and glanced back. Dario smiled at her. "I'm looking forward to seeing you again."

She smiled back, and his heart flipped over in his chest. "Me, too."

# *Chapter 6*

Felicity rang the doorbell and ran her hand over her hair, then licked her lips as she waited for someone to answer the door. Her stomach churned with nervous excitement— she'd dreamed about Dario all night, and now she was going to see him again.

Yesterday's kiss had been...well, she was still searching for the words to describe it. *Amazing* didn't do it justice. Even now, just the thought of Dario's lips on hers sent zings of sensation through her limbs. She'd never experienced anything like it before, and the intensity of her reaction scared her a bit.

She hadn't expected Dario to kiss her yesterday. And she definitely hadn't expected her body to light up like a Christmas tree in response. But it was as if he'd unlocked the barrier she'd built to protect her heart, and twelve years of need and frustration had erupted inside her in a torrent that was impossible to ignore.

Truth be told, parts of yesterday's encounter were still a little fuzzy in her mind. As soon as Dario's mouth had met hers, her brain had short-circuited and lust had taken over, hijacking her body and taking control over her actions. She didn't know how long the kiss had lasted, or what, if anything, they'd said to each other. But she did know that if they hadn't been interrupted, that simple kiss would have turned into so much more.

It was a realization that both thrilled and scared her.

Her outsize response to Dario made it clear she was ready to connect with a man again. But they hadn't known each other for very long, and she was worried about moving too far, too fast. It had been a long time since she'd slept with anyone, and she worried about her ability to keep her heart protected.

The door swung open, and Dario himself stood on the threshold. He grinned widely, his hazel eyes glowing with warmth as he ran his gaze up and down her body. Felicity shivered, but it wasn't from the cold air.

"Merry Christmas." He reached out and laid his hand on her arm, tugging her forward and into the house.

"Merry Christmas," she replied. Dario leaned over and kissed her softly, a tame, polite version of what they'd shared in the office yesterday. But it didn't matter. Sensation arced through her, and just like that, she found herself wishing they were alone together so they could follow the kiss to its natural conclusion.

Dario reached for her bags and set them gently on the floor and then his hands were on her, unwinding her scarf, skimming across her shoulders and down her arms as he helped her out of her coat. His touch was light and probably looked impersonal to an outside observer, but Felicity felt as though he'd stripped her bare in preparation for a passionate encounter. Her nerve endings tingled, and she closed her eyes and took a deep breath, savoring the sensation and wishing it would never end.

Dario chuckled softly, and she opened her eyes to see him watching her. His knowing smile made it clear he knew exactly how his actions had affected her and he was enjoying her response.

*Two can play at that game*, she thought to herself. She stepped closer and laid her hand flat on his chest, then leaned in and nuzzled the curve of his jaw with the tip of her nose. Dario sucked in a breath, and she felt his heart start to pound against her palm. She hid her grin in the slope of his neck, pleased to know she had power over him, as well.

"Dario!" A woman's voice drifted in from the room beyond. "Did Felicity arrive?"

She drew back and smiled up at him, and he traced his fingertip across her lips. "Yes, Mom," he called loudly. "I'm just taking her coat." He leaned forward, his breath hot on her mouth. "We'll pick this up again later," he murmured. His voice was full of sensuous promise, and Felicity's stomach fluttered.

"Did your parents have a good flight?" he asked in a normal tone of voice. He grabbed her bags with one hand and placed his other hand on the small of her back as he led her toward the living room.

"They did, thanks," she responded.

"Do they go on a trip every Christmas?"

"Usually, yes. They started doing it after I joined the Marines. My mom said she couldn't bear to sit by the tree without me, so she talked my dad into starting a new tradition. They'd already made all the arrangements for this year's trip when they found out I would be here, and I told them to go and enjoy themselves one last time before we settled into our old routine again."

"That was nice of you," he remarked, leading her through the living room. A large tree sat in the far corner, the branches covered in twinkling white lights. Packages lay strewn on the red plaid tree skirt, and the homey sight triggered a sudden pang of loneliness. She was glad her parents were on their trip, but she missed them and the holiday traditions her family had built over the years. She hadn't even bothered to put a tree up this season, knowing no one would be around to celebrate with her.

Except, it seemed, Dario and his family.

He led her into the kitchen, where everyone was chatting and laughing. "Look who wandered in from the cold," he boomed, raising his voice to be heard over the din.

Everyone turned to look at her, and a chorus of voices rang out in welcome. A small corgi yipped in greeting, running over to sniff at Felicity's shoes and pants with great enthusiasm, while a larger dog continued to snooze in the corner.

"That's just Scrabble," Emiliano said, smiling. "She just needs to check you out, and then she'll leave you alone."

"Fine by me," Felicity said, bending down to scratch behind the dog's ears.

"I'm so glad you're here!" said Marie, stepping forward. She hugged Felicity. "I'm sorry I didn't get a chance to talk to you at the engagement party the other day."

"Don't worry about it," Felicity responded. "You guys were a little busy. I appreciate you including me now."

Dario's parents came over next, and his mother, Natalia, embraced her with a smile. "Welcome—it's always nice to meet one of Dario's friends." There was genuine warmth in her voice, and Felicity felt herself relax.

Emiliano handed her a cup of coffee. "Thanks for babysitting him for us," he said with a grin. "It's nice of you to let him play detective. We appreciate you keeping him out of trouble while he's in town."

"No problem," Felicity said. "Believe it or not, he's actually proved to be kind of useful." She winked at Dario, who pinned Emiliano with a mock scowl.

"Wow," Emiliano said. He punched Dario lightly in the arm. "I'll alert the media."

"Very funny," Dario said drily. He reached out and ruffled Emiliano's hair, and the two of them began to playfully wrestle in the middle of the kitchen. Scrabble danced around them, barking with excitement.

"Boys," said their father, Aurelio, his tone one of long-suffering patience. "How many times do I have to tell you? No roughhousing inside."

Their mother shook her head and aimed an apologetic glance at Marie and Felicity. "I'm sorry. I tried to civilize them. I really did."

"It's okay," Marie assured her. "There's only so much you can do when you're dealing with that much testosterone."

Felicity laughed. "Believe me, I've seen worse. The guys in the Corps were ten times as bad, and that was on a good day."

"I can imagine," Marie said. "Was it tough being surrounded by men all the time?" She wrinkled her nose. "Don't get me wrong—I like men. But there are times you just need to hang out with your girlfriends."

Felicity shrugged. "It was hard at first, but eventually I got used to it. Most of the time, they were professional." She didn't mention the occasions when the guys would turn off the self-censorship and really let loose. The things she'd heard and seen weren't the kind of topics people discussed in polite company. Still, there was a part of her that missed the camaraderie and that sense of belonging, even though as the lone woman in her squad she'd always been something of an outsider. The line separating her from her fellow marines had been bright at first, but as they had gone through training and then fought together, the men had viewed her as less of a curiosity and had grown to accept her as an equal. That, more than any medal or commendation, was the highest honor she could have received.

"And now you're working as a PI?" Aurelio asked.

"Yes. Trying to crack the Colton hacking case."

"I hope you're having better luck than I did," Emiliano said, smoothing the wrinkles out of his shirt. He and Dario had stopped their brotherly tussle and were now rejoining the conversation.

"Well, so far neither one of us has gotten shot, so I'd say we're ahead of you on that score," Dario teased.

"Boys, really." Natalia tsked softly.

"Ha ha," Emiliano said. He rolled his shoulder and winced a little, as if still pained by the injury.

The brothers continued their friendly banter as everyone settled around the table. Felicity enjoyed watching them tease each other, and their parents and Marie even poked fun at them a few times. It was so different from her experiences with her own family. She didn't have any siblings, and her holiday gatherings were a lot more subdued. They all loved each other, to be sure, but they didn't show it by joking back and forth like Dario's clan.

After a few minutes, Felicity began to join in the conversation. She was rewarded with a warm smile from Dario, and soon she felt like she'd been a part of the group for years.

Time seemed to fly by, and soon they were out of food. Marie stood and lifted her mimosa. "Time for presents!"

Everyone rose, and Dario took Felicity's arm. "Now the fun really begins," he whispered conspiratorially.

"I should go," she said, feeling out of place again.

"Not at all," he replied. They stopped before walking into the living room, letting everyone else go ahead of them. "I'd like you to stay, if you don't mind."

He sounded so hopeful she couldn't bear to disappoint him. "Okay. I did bring a few little things for your family, just as a token of appreciation for having me today."

Surprise flickered in his eyes. "That was sweet of you."

She shrugged. "I couldn't very well show up empty-handed. I even have something for you."

He grinned, his face lighting up with anticipation. "You have a present for me?"

"I meant to give it to you yesterday afternoon, but since

Adeline left early and we canceled the gift exchange, I brought it with me now."

He leaned closer, his breath warm on her neck. "I feel like you already gave me a present yesterday." His voice was low and intimate, for her ears only. She swayed toward him, unconsciously seeking his touch.

"I—I hadn't planned for that to happen," she said, feeling her cheeks heat at the reminder of the way she'd lost control. And in the middle of her office, no less!

"I know. That's what made it so great." He ran his hand lightly down her arm and a line of goose bumps sprang up in response.

"I'm glad you enjoyed it."

"Are you trying to pretend you didn't?" he teased.

She was saved from having to reply by the calls of his family. "Come on, slowpokes!" Marie called out. "We're sorting all the gifts!"

Felicity winked at Dario and walked into the living room to join them. He followed her and sat on the sofa while she retrieved her bag and withdrew the gifts she'd brought for Dario and his family. Once she was done, Dario gestured for her to sit next to him. She dropped onto the cushion, then sprang up again as her pocket began to vibrate.

She dug her phone out and offered an apologetic smile to his family. "Please excuse me for a moment. My parents are out of town, so I should take this in case something's gone wrong with their trip."

"Of course," Natalia said, waving her off.

Felicity retreated to the dining room and glanced at the phone, surprised to see Adeline's number flashing on the screen. "Hello?"

"Oh, thank God." Adeline sounded harried, and Felicity's stomach twisted.

"What's wrong?"

"Someone broke into the office," Adeline said. "The alarm company just called me. Can you meet the sheriff there? I'm really sorry to ask—you know I'd go if I was in town."

"Don't worry about it," Felicity assured her. "I'll take care of it."

"Thank you," Adeline said. She sounded relieved, as if Felicity had just taken the weight of the world off her shoulders. "I owe you big-time."

"It's not a problem. Just enjoy the holiday with your family."

"I'll try. Thank you again."

Felicity tucked her phone back into her pocket and returned to the living room. Dario turned to look at her as she walked in. "Everything all right?" he asked.

Felicity shook her head. "I'm afraid not. That was Adeline. There's been a break-in at the office, and she asked me to meet the police there." She began to circle the room, shaking hands with Dario's family as she said her goodbyes. "Thank you so much for including me today—I'm sorry to have to leave early."

Natalia and then Marie hugged her. "I hope everything is okay at your office," Marie said, frowning slightly. "I can't imagine why anyone would want to cause trouble like that on Christmas."

"I can," Emiliano said darkly. He tilted his head to the side. "I don't mean to question your abilities, but do you really think you should go by yourself?"

"She's not."

Felicity turned to find Dario standing in the doorway, holding her coat and scarf. He'd already donned his jacket, and he looked ready to head out. "I'm going with you."

She immediately rejected the idea, even as his offer made her heart lift. "No, Dario. I appreciate it, but you need to stay and celebrate with your family."

Dario opened his mouth to reply, but his mother beat him to it. "Nonsense," Natalia replied. "You shouldn't have to take care of this by yourself. Dario will help you."

"But your gifts—"

Aurelio smiled kindly. "This won't be the first time we've had to pause our holiday activities. We're used to it. You two go check things out, and we'll find something to do to occupy the time until you get back."

It was clear both Dario and his family were determined he should accompany her to the office. Recognizing defeat, Felicity nodded. "Thank you," she said simply.

Emiliano walked Felicity and Dario to the front door. "Be careful," he cautioned. "Please wait for the police to arrive before you go into the office. We don't need any heroes today." He aimed a meaningful look at Dario, who waved off his brother's concern.

"We'll be fine," he said. "There's no need to worry."

"I'll keep an eye on him," Felicity said with a smile.

Emiliano nodded. "Thanks. Good luck."

They stepped outside and a gust of cold wind stripped away the lingering warmth of the house. Felicity shivered, her nerves starting to jangle as she turned her thoughts to the office and what they might find there. A break-in sounded self-explanatory, but if her work in intelligence had taught her anything, it was that things were seldom as simple as they appeared.

She glanced over at Dario, grateful he'd insisted on joining her. She didn't think she'd have any trouble dealing with the sheriff and his men, but it was nice to know Dario was there if she needed him.

Still, she shouldn't get used to him being around. He'd made no secret of the fact he was only in town for his brother's wedding. And while Felicity wasn't opposed to spending time with Dario now, she had to make sure she didn't let him into her heart.

\* \* \*

It didn't take long to arrive at the office—thanks to the holiday, there was no traffic. Dario parked in front of the entrance and shook his head at the sight of the door. Even from this distance, it was clear the lock had been badly mangled, and someone had tried to smash the glass panel that ran the length of the door. A million cracks ran through the glass, but by some miracle, it hadn't fallen out of the frame.

"Oh man," Felicity said softly. "What a mess." She unbuckled her seat belt, clearly intending to get out and conduct a closer inspection.

Dario placed his hand on her thigh and she stilled. "Not yet," he said. "I know you want to check things out, but let's be safe and wait for the police to arrive."

She nodded. "You're right. I just got caught up in the moment." She bit her bottom lip as she studied the scene. "Do you think whoever did this made it inside?"

"I hate to say it, but yes. It looks like the door is at a strange angle. I think it was wrenched open and now it can't close properly."

"Maybe we'll get lucky and whoever did this is still inside," Felicity said darkly.

"Don't get your hopes up," Dario warned.

A black-and-white cruiser drove up and parked a few spots away, its siren lights flashing. Dario squinted against the bright red and blue pulses that strobed the interior of the car. "Ready?" he asked Felicity.

She nodded, and the two of them climbed out of the car. No sooner had Dario shut his door than one of the responding deputies turned around and frowned. "Get back in your vehicle, please."

"We're here on behalf of Adeline Kincaid. She's the owner of this business," Felicity explained.

"Wonderful," said the man. "Now please get back in your car while we check out the place."

It was clear that any further conversation would only complicate matters, so Dario gestured for Felicity to return to her seat. She did, but as the minutes ticked by, it was clear her impatience was mounting.

"At least it's warmer in here than it is outside," he said, trying to improve her mood.

"Yeah." She was quiet a moment, then spoke again. "What do you think is taking them so long? The place isn't that big." There was a thread of worry in her voice and Dario had to admit, he was starting to get nervous, too.

Dario shrugged, trying to seem unconcerned. "I'm not sure. There's probably some kind of protocol the sheriff's department have to follow when they respond to a call like this."

"I suppose," she muttered. "I know it won't change anything, but I really want to get inside and determine if anything was stolen."

"Do you have a list of items?"

"No, but I'll be able to tell if the more expensive stuff is gone—the computers, the copier, the printers."

Dario glanced at the sidewalk in front of the office, and the road beyond. A light dusting of snow covered both surfaces, but unfortunately, there were so many tracks it was impossible to follow any trail the burglars might have made. "I think the copier is probably safe," he said, giving her shoulder a nudge. "That thing is as big as an old VW Bug. Not the kind of thing someone could simply waltz away with unseen."

"Fair enough," Felicity admitted with a small smile. "But I am worried about the laptops."

"That's a valid concern," he said. "If I had to guess, I'd say whoever did this was after the computers. Otherwise, why target a PI office? It's not like there's cash or other valuables stored inside."

"Do you think this is connected to the Colton case?"

Dario mulled over her question. "It's certainly a possibility," he said. "Hopefully we'll know more once we can go inside."

A moment later, the two deputies returned to the door and stepped outside. One gestured for Dario and Felicity to join them.

"Your names, please?"

Dario and Felicity responded. "We work for Adeline Kincaid. She called me earlier after being notified by the alarm company about the break-in. She's out of town for the holiday, so she asked me to meet you here and make sure the office is secure," Felicity said.

The deputy nodded. "Okay. There's no one inside, and the place looks undisturbed. But why don't you both come in and see if you notice anything missing?" The other deputy headed for the car, the radio on his belt squawking to life as he walked.

Dario and Felicity followed the man inside. He was shocked to find the officer was right—everything looked fine, without so much as a scrap of paper out of place.

"I don't understand," Felicity said as they walked from room to room. "Why would someone break in if they didn't intend to take anything?"

The deputy shrugged. "Who knows? Maybe whoever did this wasn't intending to rob the place—they just broke the glass and wrenched open the door as part of a stupid prank. Or maybe the culprits made it inside and realized they didn't have time to take anything and still get away."

Dario frowned, not buying it. It was the work of a moment to grab a laptop and run. If someone was motivated enough to force their way into the office, he didn't think they'd be deterred from taking what they wanted once inside.

Felicity didn't look convinced, either, but she didn't argue the point.

"Is there anything missing?" the man asked.

"As far as I can tell, no," she said slowly. "But it's possible Adeline will notice something when she gets back to work."

The deputy scribbled something on his notepad. "That's fine. Just give us a call if you find something later. We'll do what we can to find the people who did this, but without witnesses, it'll be tough. I don't suppose there are any security cameras set up in the office?" He didn't sound especially hopeful.

Felicity shook her head. "No. Just the security system. There might be some cameras on one of the nearby stores monitoring the street."

"Okay." The man made another note, then flipped the little book closed. "Like I said, feel free to call if anything comes up." He pulled out business cards and passed one each to Felicity and Dario. "We're here if you need us."

"Thank you," Dario said. Felicity echoed his gratitude. "We appreciate you coming out today."

"That's what we do," the deputy replied. "Merry Christmas." He walked out, leaving Dario and Felicity alone in the office.

She turned to face him, her features twisted in confusion. "Does this seem odd to you?"

"Yeah." Together, they walked through the rooms again, their pace slower. But just as before, everything looked normal. The laptops were safely docked in their stations on Adeline's, Felicity's and Dario's desks. The printers hadn't been moved, and even the contents of the desk drawers were undisturbed. It was as if someone had come inside, looked around and then left without touching anything.

They stopped in Felicity's office, and she began to thoroughly search her desk for any evidence of tampering. "What are we going to do about the door?"

Dario's chest warmed at her use of the word *we*. "I have some duct tape in my trunk," he said. "I'll tape a few strips onto the glass to stabilize it until we can get it replaced. If you're okay in here, I'll take care of that now."

Felicity nodded, and Dario stepped out into the cold to retrieve the tape. He found an old bicycle lock in the trunk as well and figured they could slip it through the outer door's handles to secure the entrance.

It only took a few minutes to apply the tape to the glass. Dario stepped back and studied the door with a critical eye. The hasty repair wouldn't last long, but hopefully it would buy them enough time to get it fixed properly.

That job done, Dario headed back to Felicity's office. Had she discovered anything missing?

"How's it going in here?" he called out, strolling into the room.

Felicity sat in her desk chair, examining what looked like a piece of fabric. Her posture was normal enough, but the look on her face made Dario tense. "Felicity? What's wrong?"

She glanced up, her face so pale he thought she might faint. "I found something," she said dully. Her hand jerked, and the fabric she held dangling on the tip of a pen fluttered.

"What is it?" He stepped closer, trying to get a better look.

"I think it might be a message." She extended her hand and he realized he was looking at a pink handkerchief. He took it from her, frowning.

"A message? What makes you say that?"

"She's known for her pink handkerchiefs," Felicity said, her tone stark.

"She?" Dario repeated. But he needn't have asked. The answer came to him as soon as the word had left his mouth.

Livia Colton.

## *Chapter 7*

The next morning was cloudy and gray, the perfect complement to Felicity's mood. She stood in the small break room, staring impatiently at the world's slowest coffee maker as it sputtered and hissed.

"Come on," she muttered. She'd already had one cup this morning, slurping it down as she'd showered and dressed. But it wasn't enough. She'd barely slept the night before, and her body ached with fatigue.

*When did I get so old?* she wondered. Once upon a time, staying up all night would have triggered a few extra yawns the next day, nothing more. Now? She'd be lucky to keep her eyes open past lunch.

At long last, the coffee finished brewing. Felicity considered taking the whole pot back to her office, but decided the walk to refill her cup would help keep her awake.

Elixir in hand, she settled into her chair and booted up her computer. There was a message from Adeline, thanking her again for handling the situation yesterday and letting her know workmen would be stopping by today to replace the front doors. Felicity wasn't sure how her friend had managed to line up repairs so quickly given yesterday's holiday, but she felt better knowing the office would be made secure again.

She sighed as she clicked on her next message. The big man himself, Fowler Colton, had written for an update. She shook her head. "Don't you people talk to each other?" She was in regular contact with Zane; technically, it was Zane's job to keep the corporate bigwigs in the loop, but maybe Fowler thought he'd go straight to the horse's mouth this time.

Felicity leaned back in her chair, debating how much to tell the man. She and Dario had made good progress on the case, and thanks to his investigations on the dark web, they had a few more leads to pursue. She quickly typed up a response, then paused. Should she tell Fowler about the office break-in and their suspicions about Livia?

She opened her desk drawer and withdrew the plastic bag containing the pink handkerchief, studying it again in the vain hope of finding answers in the folds of the fabric. The *LC* monogrammed in one corner could have stood for a dozen names, but Felicity knew in her gut this was one of Livia Colton's handkerchiefs. The only question was, had she dropped it by accident, or had she deliberately left it behind to send a message?

A chill skittered through her and Felicity shoved the fabric back into her desk drawer. She'd called the sheriff's office yesterday after finding the pink square, but the deputies who had helped them earlier were busy.

*We'll come by and pick it up tomorrow afternoon*, he'd said. He had sounded unimpressed with her discovery, and Felicity suspected he didn't consider a handkerchief to be an important piece of evidence, despite Felicity's suspicions it was connected to Livia Colton.

Her thoughts were interrupted by a perfunctory rap on the door. "You're here early." Dario walked into her office, coffee in hand.

"Couldn't sleep," she admitted.

He nodded. "I had trouble, too."

Felicity eyed him up and down, taking in his pressed shirt and clean-shaven cheeks. He looked entirely too polished for a man who hadn't slept well, and Felicity felt even more rumpled in comparison.

"I just keep wondering why someone would go to the trouble of breaking in but then not steal anything," he continued. "And the handkerchief under your desk—do you think that was an accident?"

It was the same question she had pondered most of the night. "I don't know. But I'm beginning to wonder if the whole thing is some kind of message. Maybe Livia or one of her goons is trying to intimidate us, or scare Adeline into dropping the case."

"Like a warning?" Dario said. "Back off, or next time we'll do more than break your door?"

Felicity nodded. "Exactly."

"That makes sense." He was quiet a moment, then said, "How do you plan to respond?"

"If you're asking me if I'm going to stop digging, the answer is no," Felicity said. "But if you want to walk away, I won't think less of you. It's possible the next message will be more…personal, and that's a risk you didn't sign up for when you volunteered to help me."

Dario straightened and squared his shoulders, as if preparing to do battle. "Do you honestly believe I'd walk away and leave you to deal with this by yourself?"

"I'm not exactly alone," she pointed out. "Adeline can help me."

"No," he said flatly. "I'm sticking around. You can't get rid of me that easily." He winked, and a tendril of heat unfurled in her chest and spread through her limbs. Even though Felicity was confident she could take care of herself, it was nice to know Dario wasn't going anywhere.

"Hello?"

A new voice sounded from the lobby area, hesitant and a bit uncertain.

Felicity frowned and glanced at Dario. "Are you expecting anyone?" It was too early to be the deputies come to pick up the handkerchief, and she didn't have any appointments scheduled for today.

He shook his head. "Maybe it's a new client?"

They walked into the lobby, where they found Thorne Colton eyeing the door with a look of concern, his phone in hand. His face lightened with relief when he saw them.

"Oh good. I was just about to call Knox and tell him you guys were being robbed or something."

"Nothing so exciting," Felicity said.

"Someone smashed the glass and wrenched the door open yesterday," Dario explained.

"Oh man." Thorne shook his head. "Did they steal anything?"

"Not that we've noticed," Felicity said. "But Adeline will get back the day after tomorrow, and she might notice something's gone."

"That's a crappy thing to have to deal with on Christmas."

"Yeah." Dario nodded in agreement. "It wasn't the most festive way to spend the afternoon."

"Does Knox have any leads?"

"Not really." Felicity narrowed her eyes as an idea popped into her head. "But whoever did this left something behind. Would you mind taking a look at it?"

Thorne gave her a baffled look, but nodded. "Sure. If you think I can help."

Felicity quickly walked back to her office and grabbed the handkerchief, then retraced her steps. She held the bag out, trying to give it to Thorne. But he wouldn't touch it.

His eyes locked on to the pink handkerchief, and the color drained from his face. "Oh my God," he whispered hoarsely.

"Is this Livia's?" His reaction told her everything she needed to know, but she still had to ask the question.

He swallowed, his Adam's apple bobbing in his throat. He pressed his lips together and nodded. "It's hers." Thorne swore softly. "I thought she might be back. She's like a bad penny, always turning up where she's not wanted."

"What made you think she's come back to Shadow Creek?" Dario said. "The last I heard, she'd escaped. There's been rumors about her current location, but nothing concrete."

"That's actually why I came to talk to you both," Thorne said. "Is there someplace we can sit?"

"Of course." Felicity led them back to her office and they all settled into chairs.

"I don't have a lot of evidence," Thorne said. "But after seeing that—" he nodded at the handkerchief Felicity had placed on the desk "—I'm almost certain Livia is in town."

He leaned back and ran a hand over his hair. "You both know my sister Jade?" At their nods, he continued. "She's looking to expand her ranch, and before the holiday she put in an offer on some acres adjacent to her property. She called the Realtor this morning to check on the status of the paperwork, and the Realtor told her the land had already been sold—her offer never made it into the seller's hands."

Felicity frowned. "That's odd, but hardly reason to suspect Livia is back in Shadow Creek."

"No, you don't understand. The Realtor couldn't locate any evidence of Jade's offer. No paperwork, no emails, nothing. The woman remembers reading the messages from Jade before the holiday, but now it's as if everything has simply disappeared."

"Were any of her other files affected?" Felicity asked.

"No. That's what's so strange about it. Only Jade's communications and paperwork were gone."

"That sounds like a targeted hack," Dario said.

"That's kind of what I thought," Thorne said. "And since Livia hates Jade more than the rest of us, I started to wonder if Livia was targeting her, trying to make things difficult for her as a way of getting some revenge for turning over Livia's passwords to the FBI all those years ago. Jade's actions helped them crack the case wide open and allowed them to gather the evidence they needed to prosecute Livia."

"Is that possible, though?" Felicity asked. "To wipe out only a certain set of files without leaving any other trace of the hack?"

"Oh yeah." Dario sounded so casual about the possibility it made Felicity wonder just how often that kind of thing happened.

"Let's say the Realtor's computer was hacked," Felicity said. "Do you think the Cohort is responsible?"

Thorne nodded. "I do. I know you suspect Livia is the leader of the hackers, since they targeted Colton, Incorporated. I think since the cyberattack worked so well, she decided to use that strategy again. But this time, she went after Jade."

"Okay." Felicity nodded, willing to entertain his suspicions. "But that doesn't necessarily mean Livia is physically around. She could be anywhere that has an internet connection."

"That's what I thought, too," Thorne said. "Until you showed me her handkerchief."

"If it really is hers," Dario pointed out. "Maybe someone is trying to frame Livia."

"I suppose anything is possible," Thorne said. "But I think Livia is behind it all. The Colton, Inc., hack and Jade's missing files." He nodded at the handkerchief. "Have you told Knox you found that?"

"Yes," Felicity responded. "The deputies who came to investigate yesterday said they'd be back this afternoon to collect it."

Thorne frowned. "I'm going to call Knox, if you don't mind."

"Go ahead."

Thorne rose and pulled out his phone, then paced a few steps away to speak to his brother. Dario leaned forward, and Felicity did the same.

"What do you think?" he asked softly.

She shook her head. "I'm not sure. I'd like to talk to the Realtor and see if she'll give us access to her system. If she really was hacked, maybe we can find a digital signature or some trace of the person responsible."

"Good idea," Dario said. "I've been studying the method the Cohort used to hack into the Colton, Incorporated, system. If I can look at her computer, I can determine if her system has the same back doors and vulnerabilities to exploit. It won't be a smoking gun, but it might help advance the case."

"We might get lucky," Felicity said. "If the Cohort really is responsible for sabotaging Jade's bid, maybe they made a mistake that will help us catch them."

Thorne rejoined them with a sigh. "Knox is sending some deputies over now to pick up the handkerchief," he said. "He's also going to increase patrols in this area, and tell everyone to keep an eye out for anyone matching Livia's description." He aimed a direct look at Felicity. "I hope you won't be offended by what I'm about to say, but I think you shouldn't be in the office alone."

Felicity's first instinct was to roll her eyes, but she resisted the urge. There was no chauvinism in Thorne's tone or expression; he seemed genuinely worried about her safety.

To her surprise, Dario came to her defense. "She's hardly helpless," he said. "I'm sure the Marines taught her a few things."

"I'm sure they did," Thorne agreed. "But Livia is dangerous. Don't give her an opportunity to cause more trouble."

"We won't," Felicity said, touched by his concern. It was sweet of him to care, especially since they didn't know each other all that well. But from what she'd heard and seen lately, Thorne Colton was one of the good guys.

Thorne took a pen and the notepad from her desk and scribbled something, then handed the paper back to her. "This is Knox's personal cell number. If you get so much as a funny feeling, call him right away."

"I doubt he'd appreciate that," Felicity said jokingly, but Thorne's expression was serious.

"He won't mind. Trust me. He'd rather respond to a hundred false alarms than miss the one opportunity to catch Livia."

"Thanks."

Thorne nodded and let out a quiet sigh. "I'll let you both get to it, then."

Felicity and Dario both stood. "Please tell Jade we'll be in touch," she said.

"I will. And good luck. I have a feeling you're going to need it."

As Felicity watched the cowboy walk out of her office, she couldn't help but feel he was right.

Dario leaned back in his chair and stretched his arms above his head, trying to loosen his muscles. He and Felicity had been working steadily for the past couple of hours, and he was ready for a break.

He glanced over at Felicity. If she was growing tired, she didn't show it. Her back was ramrod straight as she concentrated on her laptop monitor, typing away with military precision.

She'd surprised him when she'd asked if he wanted to share her office. He'd immediately taken her up on the offer, and it hadn't taken long to drag his desk in from the supply room. He'd spent the first ten minutes or so distracted by her presence, sneaking covert glances and enjoying the subtle scent of her perfume that seemed to linger in the air. But fortunately, he'd soon lost himself in his work, and the sound of her breathing no longer sent his imagination running wild.

"Want some coffee?" It was about time for a midmorning refuel to top off his caffeine stores.

"Hmm?" she said absently.

"Coffee," he said, raising his voice a bit to break through her focus.

She blinked at him, and he saw her awareness return as she shifted her attention back to him and her surroundings. "Oh. Yes. That would be nice." She reached for her empty cup and stood, stretching a bit.

The movement pulled the fabric of her shirt taut across her curves, and Dario swallowed hard at the unexpected reminder of the beauty of her body. It had been two days since their mind-blowing kiss, and his palm tingled as he recalled the weight of her breasts in his hand. In the aftermath of the break-in, he'd pushed his attraction to Felicity aside so they could deal with the immediate issues, like talking to the deputies and securing the office. But now his libido came roaring back to life, and he suddenly wasn't interested in coffee anymore.

"Dario?" Felicity's voice broke into his thoughts, and from the look on her face, this wasn't the first time she'd said his name.

"Yeah?" He shook his head, trying to remember what they'd been talking about before the sight of her stretching had short-circuited his brain.

"Coffee?"

"Yes. Right. I could use a refill."

Felicity nodded and gestured for him to walk with her.

"Have you found any more posts about the Cohort on your hacker forum?"

"Campus Martius? Not really," he said. "There have been veiled references, but nothing obvious and nothing that appears to be helpful to the case."

"Figures," she muttered. She added coffee to his cup and then her own. "I hope the Realtor will let us access her computer so you can look for evidence of a hack."

"Did she give you any idea of when her boss would make a decision?"

Felicity shrugged. "She wasn't sure. I think if it were up to her, she'd agree immediately. But she has to clear things with her boss first, since they'd be giving us access to their system. I guess there are some privacy concerns, and in light of the recent troubles Colton, Incorporated, experienced, I think they're trying to be more diligent about protecting their clients' information."

"Can't really blame them for that," Dario said, taking a sip of his coffee.

"I know. I understand their reasoning, but it's a little hard to be patient when their system might hold the clue we need to find Livia Colton."

"Or it could be another dead end," he said. He didn't want to be overly negative, but he also didn't want Felicity to get her hopes up. There were limits on what they could do, and even if he found evidence Livia was behind the hack of the Realtor's system, there was no guarantee he'd be able to lead the authorities to her hiding place.

Felicity was quiet for a moment, studying him over the rim of her coffee cup. "That sounds a little defeatist. What happened to the brash, confident guy I met a few days ago?"

"I'm still confident," he said, sounding a little defensive even to his own ears. "I just think we need to manage our expectations a little. So far, nothing about this case has been easy." It was true, but there was more to it than that. It suddenly occurred to him that the reason he was trying to downplay his skills was because he didn't want to disappoint Felicity.

The realization made his stomach flip-flop. Normally, he didn't worry about failure—most of the time, the thought didn't even enter his mind while he was working. And on the odd occasion he ran up against a difficult problem that he couldn't solve? No big deal. He simply found a work-around or informed the client what they had asked for was impossible. He didn't lose any sleep over it or stress about letting anyone down. It was all a part of doing business, a risk that people understood before they hired him.

But things were different with Felicity. She definitely wasn't a normal client; in fact, he didn't think of her like that at all. He'd volunteered to help Adeline, yes, but not because he needed the work or because he was especially interested in the Colton case. It had just seemed like a good way to pass the time. But when he'd learned Felicity was in charge of the investigation, that had been an added bonus. He'd wanted to get to know her. And as he'd learned more about her, his feelings toward her had gone from the shallow hormonal surge of lust to a deeper, more complicated pool of emotion that had him second-guessing everything he thought he knew about what he wanted in his life. It was enough to drive a man crazy.

"That's true. But I have a feeling our luck is about to change."

He snorted quietly. "You don't strike me as the superstitious type."

Her cheeks flushed pink and she glanced down. "I'm not, really. But the guys I served with were. It kind of rubbed off on me."

"Oh yeah? How?" Dario found Felicity's stories about her time in the Marine Corps fascinating. It was a topic she didn't discuss all that often, so when she gave him an opening he jumped on it.

She leaned against the counter of the break room, getting comfortable. "Well, you have to understand all branches of the military have their own little superstitions. It's considered bad luck in the Navy to wash a coffee cup, for instance."

Dario glanced at his mug and winced. "Really?"

Felicity nodded, smiling. "Really. I once heard of a sailor being written up for scrubbing a superior officer's coffee cup clean during a fit of anger."

He laughed. "Please tell me you wash your mugs."

"Oh yeah. But I won't eat the candy out of an MRE. And I won't eat apricots, either."

"Wait—what?" Dario leaned forward, enchanted by this side of Felicity. "What have you got against candy and apricots?"

"A lot of the Meals, Ready to Eat have Charms candy as a dessert," she explained. "They're these fruit-flavored hard candies. And everyone knows that if you eat them, it will rain. Big-time. The green ones are the worst."

"I see," he said, nodding. "And the apricots?"

She tilted her head to the side, considering his question. "I'm not really sure how that one got started," she said. "I never bothered to ask. It was just part of the culture."

"And you still won't eat them even though you're no longer a marine?"

She gave him an affronted look and drew herself up. "I beg your pardon. I may no longer be on active duty, but I'm still a marine."

Dario held up his hand, palm out. "My bad. I apologize."

She settled back against the counter with a nod and a sly smile. "That's fine. You didn't know."

"It really is an identity, isn't it? Being a marine."

"Well," she said thoughtfully. "Yes. It's a brotherhood—

that's the best word I have for it, even though more and more women are joining the ranks."

"No wonder your high school teacher was so excited to see you at Emiliano's party."

"We have a common bond," she confirmed. "Doesn't matter if you never served together—when you find a fellow marine, you feel a connection to them."

Her words triggered a burst of irrational jealousy. *He* wanted to bond with Felicity and have her feel a connection to him. But did he even stand a chance?

"We should probably get back to work," he said abruptly. He straightened, wanting to retreat to the safety of the office where he could focus on work and not think about all the ways he and Felicia weren't right for each other.

If Felicia was surprised by his abrupt change of subject, she didn't show it. "Good idea." She pushed off the counter and together they walked down the hall. "I have a question for you," she said. "Can you show me how you'd trace the methods the hackers used to gain access to the Realtor's computer system? I'd like to learn more about forensic computing methods."

"No problem." He appreciated her question, and he felt himself relax as he turned his thoughts to teaching her the process he used during these types of investigations. "It's a lot easier than you'd think." He sat and pulled his laptop closer and gestured for Felicia to do the same. She pulled her chair next to him and leaned forward, clearly eager to learn.

"So I usually start by looking for any weak spots in their security software," he said, typing as he spoke. "Take this, for instance." He highlighted a line of code, but the computer didn't respond. "That's odd," he muttered. He clicked again, but nothing happened.

"Did it freeze up?" she asked.

"Maybe," he said, frowning. He reached for the keyboard, intending to reboot the machine. But before he could press the appropriate keys, the display on his screen changed.

"What's going on?" Felicity asked.

"I—I don't know." He watched in confusion as the text appeared to melt down the screen. "Maybe the computer has been infected with some kind of virus." He punched at the keyboard, but it was no use. He watched in horror as file after file opened and disintegrated in front of his eyes. All his most recent work on the Colton case, gone in seconds.

Felicity shoved out of her chair and grabbed her laptop, dragging it over to face them. "Oh my God, mine is doing the same thing." There was a note of fear in her voice, and Dario felt a swell of helplessness rise in his chest. She was looking to him to fix this, and there was nothing he could do.

It was over in a matter of minutes. The last files dissolved from their screens, leaving them both in a state of shock.

Dario exhaled. "Well, that was—"

An image suddenly appeared on the screens. It started out small, but quickly grew in size to fill each monitor.

"Is that—?" Felicity said.

"Yeah," Dario confirmed. "It is."

Livia Colton stared at them from their computer screens, a crooked crown on her head and a chilling smile on her face.

# *Chapter 8*

Felicity stared at the picture of Livia Colton, revulsion and anger filling her as the image of the woman responsible for destroying her computer flashed tauntingly on the screen. Suddenly, Livia's face disappeared behind a wall of red letters.

Stop digging, or people will start dying.

The message sent a shiver down Felicity's spine and she reached out to slam her laptop shut. Dario cursed softly, then reached out to close his own computer.

Felicity turned to look at him, her heart pounding. "What do we do now?"

He shook his head. "I'm not sure." He sounded like he was in a daze.

That wasn't the answer she was hoping to hear. Given his expertise in computers, Felicity had been counting on Dario to know how to fix this new problem.

"Should we call the sheriff?"

"Probably," he said. He shook his head again as if breaking free of a trance. "I'll call Emiliano as well—the FBI can probably do more to help us than the local sheriff's department." He pulled his phone free and called his brother, and Felicity dialed Knox Colton.

It didn't take long to explain the situation to Knox, and he promised to come over right away. Satisfied she'd done what she could, Felicity hung up and waited for Dario to finish his call.

"Emiliano is going to meet us here," he said. "He's going to confiscate the laptops as evidence."

"Do you think there's any way of recovering the files?" It was a long shot, but maybe they would get lucky.

"Probably not," he confirmed. "But I'm sure the FBI team will try. As long as the digital storage system is intact, we should be okay."

"How do you think she was able to hack into our system?"

Dario frowned. "That's a good question. Adeline has the latest and greatest in firewall and antivirus software. I'm surprised Livia was able to find an opening in the security."

Felicity eyed her laptop, wondering if she'd accidentally done something to compromise the system. "Maybe she used a website as a Trojan horse, to sneak past the defenses."

"That's possible," he mused. He eyed the laptops, as if he could unlock their secrets by sheer force of will. "I think I can discover how she did it if I can spend some time dissecting the computers."

Livia's warning flashed in her mind again, and Felicity's anxiety spiked. Livia Colton wasn't known for making idle threats. If Dario pursued the investigation, he was risking his life.

"I don't know if that's such a good idea," she said. She knew Dario was itching to discover how Livia had managed to pull this off, but Felicity would rather he let the FBI take over. The agents were trained to defend themselves if necessary, and they could call for backup if Livia tried to threaten them. Dario didn't have that luxury.

He glanced at her, surprise evident on his face. "What do you mean? We can't back off now. We're getting close."

"What makes you say that?"

"Why else would she target our computers?"

His words made sense, but they did little to loosen the knot of worry in her stomach. "I don't like this."

"I don't, either," he said. "But I've never been forced off a job before, and I'm not going to start now."

"You've also never gone up against Livia Colton," Felicity pointed out.

Dario studied her thoughtfully for a moment, as if reassessing his impression of her. "Are you really that scared of Livia?"

Felicity shrugged. How could she explain her emotions? People always thought that because she was a marine and had been in combat, she was fearless. But the opposite was true. War had taught her that life was precious and could be gone in the blink of an eye. She'd seen too many people cut down in their prime, all because they'd made a careless mistake. She'd learned to be cautious and to avoid taking unnecessary risks in both her professional and personal life.

"I'm not afraid of her," she said slowly. "I knew when I took this job I might face dangerous people and situations. That doesn't bother me. What does frighten me is the thought of Livia targeting innocent people as a way to get to me." She stood and paced, needing to burn off energy. "My family didn't sign up for this. I'd never forgive myself if something happened to them."

Dario stood and reached for her, but she evaded his touch. "Hey," he said calmly. She let him catch her as she walked past again. "Hey," he said again, his voice gentle. "That's not going to happen. Livia isn't going to hurt them."

"How can you be so sure?" She wanted to believe him, but she couldn't ignore the voice of doubt in her mind.

"Well, for starters, they're out of town. I doubt even

Livia has the reach to get to them while they're on their cruise."

"That's true," she admitted. "But she could always set some kind of booby trap in their home." She'd seen the results of such sabotage before; it was a common tactic insurgents had used in Afghanistan, with deadly results.

"I'm sure we can talk Sheriff Colton into stepping up patrols in your parents' neighborhood."

"Maybe." Then a terrible thought occurred to her, and Felicity froze as her blood ran cold.

Dario felt her stiffen in his arms. "What's wrong?" He drew back to look at her, his eyebrows drawn together in concern.

Felicity pulled his head down until his ear was close to her mouth. "What if she hacked the microphones on the computers? Do you think she's listening to us now?"

Dario leaned back and his eyes went wide as he considered the possibility. *Maybe*, he mouthed.

Felicity's stomach sank. If her parents weren't on Livia's list of targets before, they certainly were now. Had her careless talk put them in danger?

Dario released her and walked over to the laptops. He opened them both up and Felicity tensed, expecting to see the image of Livia and her hateful message again. But the screens were blessedly blank.

Dario pressed some keys, but the machines didn't respond. He held one of the laptops up to his ear, listening intently. Then he lowered it.

"They're not on," he said. "She may have been listening in before her stunt took effect, but she can't hear us now."

Felicity exhaled in relief. She smiled weakly at Dario, but he was still studying the laptop in his hand. "That's odd," he muttered.

"What?" Had he found something wrong with the exterior of the computer?

"I think there's something in the USB port," he said absently. He set the laptop on the table and dug a Swiss Army knife from his pocket. He extracted a small set of tweezers and began to pry at the port, clearly trying to remove something. "Gotcha!" He held up a small, dark piece, his eyes bright with triumph.

Felicity drew closer, trying to focus on the device. "What is that?"

He passed it to her and she got a good look at the tiny chip he'd pulled from the USB port. "That," he said excitedly, "is how Livia Colton hacked our computers."

Felicity glanced at her own laptop but Dario was already checking it. He carefully withdrew an identical chip from the port on her computer and placed it on the table. "I'm willing to bet these chips contain the malware that deleted all our files."

The pieces clicked into place. "That's why she broke into the office," Felicity said. "She had to plant the chips so she could sabotage our computers."

Dario nodded. "Exactly. Far easier than trying to hack through Adeline's security features."

Felicity's heartbeat picked up. "Does that mean the network is still intact?"

"Probably. We'll need to check to be sure, but I imagine only our computers were affected." He noticed her growing smile and tilted his head to the side. "I take it from your reaction this is good news?"

"Oh yes," Felicity said. "I backed up my laptop yesterday to our cloud-based storage system. If Livia's malware didn't affect that, then most of my files are still intact!"

"Excellent," he replied. "I did the same as well."

"Sounds like Livia's attempt to derail our investigation wasn't as successful as she'd hoped." The realization filled Felicity with a smug satisfaction. Livia thought she was in charge, but she had miscalculated.

There was a shout from the lobby, and she and Dario moved down the hall to find Knox Colton headed toward them, Emiliano hot on his heels. They must have arrived at the same time, and they both appeared eager to know what had happened. Felicity led them back to her office, her nerves quieting as she and Dario explained everything. Livia might have the element of surprise on her side, but Felicity had a team of dedicated people helping her. Together, they would bring Livia down.

Dario reached for a French fry and dipped it into the puddle of ketchup on his plate. "Feeling better?"

Felicity nodded. "Much. This was a good idea."

Dario smiled and took another bite. It had taken several hours for Knox Colton and the FBI to finish asking questions about what they had seen during the hack, and Emiliano and his team had taken their laptops and the chips he'd found for additional testing. By that time, Dario's stomach had been audibly growling, and given Felicity's increasingly short responses, he'd figured she was hungry, as well. So he'd suggested dinner at the burger joint down the street from the office, and to his surprise, she'd accepted.

"We need to come up with a plan," she continued. "We can't afford to let this setback derail the investigation. And the sooner we stop Livia Colton, the better I'll feel."

"I agree," he said. "Tomorrow morning, I'll connect my personal laptop to Adeline's network and make sure the hack didn't compromise the firm's digital storage. If everything looks good, you can download all your files to a new computer and we can move on."

She nodded, chewing thoughtfully. "I've got my fingers crossed. And hopefully by tomorrow the Realtor's boss will have decided to let us check their systems, as well. The more evidence we can hand over to your brother's team, the faster they can catch Livia."

"I have to say, I'll be glad to put this case behind me." He shook his head. "I've never worked on a project that went sideways so quickly."

A shadow crossed Felicity's face, but her expression cleared quickly. "No kidding," she said. Her voice sounded a little forced, but before he could ask if everything was okay, the waiter returned with the check.

Felicity wiped her mouth and reached for her purse. "It's been a long day," she said, pulling a few bills from her wallet.

Dario felt a surge of disappointment at the impending end of their dinner. He'd hoped to use this as an opportunity to reconnect with Felicity, to bring back some of the magic he'd felt when they'd shared that kiss. But Livia Colton had gotten in the way, and now he wondered if he'd get another chance. Felicity seemed pretty confident they would be able to wrap up the investigation soon, and once that happened, he wouldn't have a legitimate excuse to spend so much time with her.

"When this is over," he began, fumbling for the words, "maybe we can go to a real restaurant and have a celebratory dinner."

Felicity smiled, and he caught a spark of attraction in her eyes. "I'd like that."

They fell into step as they walked back to their cars. His shoulder brushed against hers and he decided to take a chance. Dario slung his arm around her shoulders, and he was rewarded by Felicity snuggling closer. She was warm and soft, and the floral scent of her shampoo filled his nose.

They drew to a stop in front of her car, and she turned to face him. The streetlight cast her face in a soft glow and her eyes shone, dark and liquid, as she stared up at him.

"I really appreciate all your help," she said softly. "I don't know how I would have made it through today alone."

He reached up to trace his fingertip down the curve of her cheekbone. "I'm glad I was here with you." He hated the thought of Felicity facing Livia's threats alone—he knew she could take care of herself, but he had a chivalrous streak that demanded he protect her from danger.

She sighed softly, her breath ghosting across his lips. His heart flip-flopped and he couldn't stop staring at her mouth. Would their second kiss be as good as the first? Was that even possible?

He couldn't wait any longer to find out. He dropped his head and pressed his mouth to hers, raising his hands to cup her face as he kissed her.

Felicity responded instantly, coming alive in his arms. She threaded her hands through his hair and stretched, pressing herself against his chest. The thin fabric of his shirt was no barrier to the warmth of her body, and a flash of heat burned through his limbs.

He tasted salt and a lingering sweetness from her soda. Her tongue stroked his, and the blood drained from his head and began to pool in his groin.

His response did not go unnoticed. Felicity made a satisfied sound in her throat that only heightened his arousal.

Suddenly, she pulled away. Dario struggled to catch his breath. "What's wrong?"

"Nothing," she said, her voice husky. "I just remembered we're in public."

"We don't have to be," he said. He mentally winced. *Smooth, Ortega. Real smooth.*

"My apartment isn't far from here."

He did a mental fist pump and nodded. "Okay. I'll follow you there." Only the knowledge that he would soon be holding her in private allowed him to let go of her and take a step back. "My car's a few spots over." He jerked his head to the left. "Just give me a minute."

She nodded and turned to her own vehicle. He made

it a few steps away before her voice stopped him in his tracks. "Dario!"

Her fear was almost palpable, and his arousal died suddenly, quenched by a swell of concern. "What's wrong?"

"My car."

He was by her side in a matter of seconds, instinctively stepping between her and the car. She grabbed his arm, leaning against him as they stared at the driver's-side door.

A crown was scrawled on the window in garish pink lipstick, the shape immediately recognizable even in the shadows of the parking lot. But it was the list of names written on the door in white paint that made Dario's blood freeze.

"My parents," she whispered. "Adeline."

"Livia," he said hoarsely. "She's got to be close." The realization made the hair on the back of his neck stand on end, and Dario could practically *feel* eyes on him. He grabbed Felicity's arm and pulled her toward his car, glancing around as he guided her into the passenger seat. He didn't see anyone lurking nearby, but that didn't mean they were safe. Livia or one of her goons could be yards away, watching them through the scope of a sniper rifle.

Would he even hear the crack of the gun before he felt the bullet slam into his chest? He kept his head low as he darted around the hood and jumped into the driver's seat.

"What are we doing?" Felicity said incredulously. "We can't just leave. We have to call the sheriff's department. My car is evidence."

Dario grabbed his phone and tossed it into her lap as he cranked the engine. "Call them if you want. But we're not staying here." He slammed the car into gear and stepped on the gas. There was a screech of protest from the tires and the pungent stench of burned rubber filled the air as they shot forward. But Dario was too worried to care about his vehicle right now.

He had to protect Felicity.

# *Chapter 9*

"What happens now?"

Felicity sat on the edge of the hotel bed and rubbed her arms, trying to warm herself. The graffiti on her car door and window had chilled her to the bone, and now she feared she might never feel warm again.

She closed her eyes and was immediately assaulted with the image of her parents' names scrawled in dripping white paint. The memory made her stomach cramp and she opened her eyes again, looking for a distraction.

Dario pulled the comforter off the second bed and draped it around her, then sat next to her. "We try to get some rest."

Felicity clutched the slightly scratchy fabric to keep it from sliding off her shoulders and laughed darkly. "Sure. That's going to happen."

"I could order room service?" he offered.

"I don't think I can handle eating anything right now," she said. She glanced around the hotel room, hoping to find a minibar she could raid for a stiff drink. But the room was disappointingly empty of alcohol.

"We could go down to the hotel bar," he suggested, as if he'd read her mind. "Maybe a drink will help take the edge off."

Felicity considered it for a second, but shook her head. She didn't want to be around people right now. She felt too brittle, as if the noise of the after-work crowd and the smooth jazz piped over the speakers might cause her to break.

"I don't think I'm up for that." She shivered and pulled the comforter tighter around her body.

Dario had driven them there while she'd spoken to Knox Colton. At first, she hadn't understood why he'd brought them to a hotel in nearby Austin, but he'd explained his worry about taking her home. "My name was on your door, too," he'd pointed out. "So I can't exactly take you back to my place." He was staying in one of the guest rooms at his parents' ranch, and Knox had assured Felicity he was sending officers to watch the Ortegas' home, along with her parents' house.

"Everyone on the list will get extra attention from my men," Knox had said. His declaration had made her feel a little better, but she was still a nervous wreck inside.

Dario's hand trailed down her back, a solid weight that pulled her out of her head. "It's going to be okay," he said. His voice was deep and calm, and Felicity wanted to wrap the sound around herself like a suit of armor. "Livia is just trying to frighten you."

"It's working," Felicity said.

"Try not to play into her hands," Dario said. "This is how she operates—she uses threats and intimidation to make people do what she wants. But she's not all-powerful. She won't be able to hurt the people you love. Especially now that Knox and his department are on high alert. And maybe we'll get lucky—it's possible she left behind some evidence that will help the deputies find her. They're checking over your car now, and hopefully they'll discover something useful."

Felicity shook her head. She wanted to believe Dario; she hoped with every fiber of her being he was right. But she couldn't turn off her worry like a spigot, not where her family and friends were concerned.

"I can't get the image of the car door out of my mind," she said. "Every time I close my eyes, I see it."

Dario draped his arm around her and pulled her close. She leaned against him, pressing her ear to his chest. His heart thumped reassuringly in a comforting rhythm, and she felt her muscles relax a bit.

"I'm sorry for what she did to your car," he said.

Felicity huffed in a poor excuse for a laugh. In truth, she hadn't even thought about the damage to her vehicle. "I'm glad you were there," she said quietly. If Dario hadn't been with her, she didn't know how she would have responded. She certainly wouldn't have had the presence of mind to go to a hotel instead of her apartment. Without Dario, she'd probably be sitting at home, an easy mark for Livia Colton.

She snuggled closer against him, seeking solace from his strength. The change in position left her half-draped across his lap, and Dario emitted a small, strangled sound.

"What's wrong?"

"Nothing," he said quickly. He shifted a bit, and she felt the bulge in his pants brush across her breasts as he sought to reposition himself.

His physical reaction struck a chord inside her, and Felicity was suddenly very aware of Dario's body. Warmth spread from every point of contact between them, suffusing her body until she felt like she must be glowing from within. She glanced at the skin of her arm, a little disappointed to find it looked normal. How was that possible, when she felt so alive inside?

"Dario," she said softly. She sat up slowly, deliberately grazing her breasts across the flat expanse of his chest as she moved. He sucked in a breath, and her nipples hardened, sending small zings of sensation to her core.

"Yes?" His voice was tight, and she could tell by the way he ground his jaw he was trying to rein in his arousal. In another time, she might have laughed at the idea of

Dario the playboy trying to resist a seduction attempt. But right now, she simply wanted Dario the man, the one she'd gotten to know over the past few days. The one she trusted.

The one who made her feel safe.

"Kiss me."

He squeezed his eyes shut and turned his head. "I don't think that's such a good idea right now," he said.

Felicity used her hand to gently turn his head until he faced her again. "I know what I'm asking you," she said.

His eyes popped open, the hazel depths bright with need. "Are you sure?"

"Yes." She nodded for extra measure. "I'm sure if you are."

The world spun suddenly, and she gasped as she found herself flat on her back. Dario rose over her, his deft fingers making quick work of the buttons on her shirt.

Cool air kissed her skin as he pulled the edges of her blouse apart. She shivered, but the chill didn't last long. Dario covered her with his hands, then lowered his head as he worked his way down her torso.

His breath was warm as it ghosted across her goose bumps, and she lifted her hips instinctively. Dario's large hands settled on her hips, and he pressed her down onto the mattress in silent instruction.

She was content to follow his lead, and her ready surrender surprised her a little. Felicity had always been take-charge in every aspect of her life, and the bedroom was no exception. But there was something about Dario that made her relax, made her want to cede a degree of control. For the first time in a long time, she felt safe with a man.

Her thoughts brushed against the memory of her last relationship. She and Ross had been high school sweethearts. Their fire had burned hot and bright, and every time Ross had looked at her she'd felt like the center of the universe. She'd thought they would last forever, but Ross hadn't been able to cope with her decision to join the Marines. His older brother had been a soldier in the army and had died in Iraq. When Felicity had told him about her enlistment, he'd been so afraid for her he'd actually cried. She'd tried to talk to him about it, but he hadn't listened. Unable to cope with her decision, he'd ended their relationship. He'd broken her heart, and while time had dulled the pain, she still had moments when she wondered what might have been if she hadn't put her country ahead of Ross's feelings.

"Hey." Dario's voice cut through her thoughts and brought her back to the present. "Where'd you go?"

She shook her head, feeling a little guilty at having drifted away from him. "Nowhere important. I'm sorry."

He ran his hand lightly down the side of her torso. "Don't apologize. There's a lot going on right now. We can put this on hold."

"No. I don't want to wait." She'd spent the last twelve years of her life putting her job before her personal desires. And while she didn't regret those choices, she was tired of being alone. Besides, she knew better than most that tomorrow was not guaranteed to anyone. With Livia Colton gunning for them both, Felicity wasn't going to take anything for granted.

She reached for Dario and pulled him down, capturing his mouth once more. His kiss was warm and sensual, and Felicity emptied her mind of all thoughts and distractions, focusing only on Dario and the way he made her feel in this moment. She opened her heart and her body to this man, reveling in the intensity of their connection. Some faint voice in her brain insisted she was feeling too much, too soon, but she dismissed the warning. Right now, she didn't want to think. She had surrendered to her baser instincts, and she craved the sensations that only Dario could provide.

He didn't disappoint.

\* \* \*

He'd never experienced anything like this before.

Dario had slept with other women, sure. And he enjoyed sex. Who didn't? But this experience with Felicity was like nothing he'd ever imagined. For the first time, Dario knew what it was to fully open his heart to a woman.

It was a revelation. Never before had Dario felt simultaneously vulnerable and protected. He was used to keeping a small part of himself reserved, locked safely away behind an impenetrable wall. He enjoyed relationships, and because he kept that piece of his soul protected, he never had to worry about feeling the kind of heartache and loss that affected other people. It was self-preservation, pure and simple, and until now, he'd never questioned his strategy.

But Felicity changed all that.

He still wasn't sure how it had happened. What was it about this woman that had affected him so deeply? And how had he not felt his protective barriers weakening? How had he missed the signs?

She was in his arms, and for the first time in his life, he was truly naked with a woman. It frightened him, this potent intimacy. His first instinct was to retreat, but his pride wouldn't let him shy away from this new experience.

Every touch, every brush of skin against skin—it was familiar and yet strangely novel. He took his time discovering Felicity's body, learning what made her sigh, what made her writhe, what made her moan. It was an exploration he never wanted to end. But all too soon she pushed him down on the bed and rose over him, a sensuous smile on her face as she whispered something about payback in his ear.

His brain took a back seat as Felicity set about licking and teasing and caressing every inch of his body. She was enthusiastic about giving him pleasure, a fact that surprised him a little. His past lovers had tended to assume that his satisfaction was a foregone conclusion. But not Felicity. She did everything in her power to heighten his arousal, to make him feel like the center of her world. It was a heady rush to know this strong, confident woman was so dedicated to his enjoyment, and he felt both awed and humbled to be the focus of her attention.

Dario placed his hands on Felicity's shoulders and pulled her back up his body. Her flushed cheeks and mussed hair were nearly enough to send him over the edge, but he bit the inside of his cheek to stay in control.

His chest was so tight with need he couldn't speak. Instead, he gently guided her onto her back and positioned himself between her knees. But just as he was about to enter her, he realized what was missing.

"Oh God," he whispered hoarsely.

"No condom," she said, apparently reading his mind. "I'm on the pill." She sounded a little hesitant, though, as if uncertain that would be enough.

Relief flooded through him. "I'm clean," he blurted out, seeking to reassure her. "I got tested after my last relationship, which ended six months ago. But I'll run downstairs and get condoms if it will make you feel safer."

Her eyes shone with an emotion he couldn't name and she smiled at him. "It's okay. I trust you."

Those three words knocked the breath from his chest, and Dario could swear he felt his heart actually swell with emotion. He moved slowly, joining their bodies together with care, determined to savor every aspect of the experience as their relationship changed forever.

Felicity gasped and moved with him, her hands tightening on his shoulders. Encouraged by her response, Dario increased his pace until soon, they were both clinging to each other, panting with exertion and emotion.

He felt her clench around him, heard her call his name through the pounding of blood in his ears. Only when he was certain she was truly satisfied did he slip the reins of his self-control and allow his own pleasure to lead him to release.

The moment seemed to go on forever, stretched between them and suspended in time. He gave himself fully to Felicity, body and heart. But instead of leaving him empty, he felt more complete than ever.

He lay next to her on the bed and gathered her boneless warmth in his arms. She snuggled against him, emitting a sigh of feminine contentment that settled over him like a soft blanket. Filled with a bone-deep sense of peace, Dario drifted to sleep.

When he woke in the morning, Felicity was gone.

## *Chapter 10*

Felicity stared at her computer screen, wondering why she'd even bothered to come to work. She wasn't focused on the case—no matter what she tried, she couldn't keep her thoughts organized enough to make any kind of progress.

She'd been distracted for the last three days, and it didn't take a rocket scientist to know why.

Sleeping with Dario had been a mistake, but she couldn't quite bring herself to regret it. The sex had been amazing, a mind-blowing experience like none she'd ever had before. But more than that, she'd felt deeply connected to Dario on an emotional level. She'd meant to keep things purely physical, to give in to hedonism, enjoy their chemistry and move on. But her heart hadn't been content to stay on the sidelines.

As soon as she'd opened her eyes the next day and seen his sleeping face, she'd known the truth. She was falling in love with Dario Ortega, and if she didn't extricate herself soon, she wouldn't be able to stop it.

He was the worst possible choice. After all, he was only in town until his brother's wedding. Then he would be leaving again, taking off for greener pastures and other beautiful women. Felicity knew that, and ignoring those facts was only going to end in heartache.

So she'd slipped out of his arms and left, hailing a cab

back to her apartment, where she showered alone, her tears mingling with the water.

She'd spent the past three days avoiding Dario, working from home or at a nearby café, ignoring his calls. It was the coward's way out, but the thought of explaining her reasons for leaving made her stomach cramp. He was so much more experienced at keeping things casual—if he heard she was having trouble keeping her heart under control, he'd probably run for the hills. The last thing he wanted was for a woman to try to tie him down.

Not that she would. Felicity still had her pride, after all.

"Can we talk?"

His voice cut through her thoughts and sent her heart pounding. Oh God, he was here! Standing in her office doorway holding two cups of coffee and wearing a friendly smile. Her first instinct was to run, but she couldn't very well shove him aside and race past. She took a deep breath and forced herself to calm down. She was an adult, and a professional, not to mention a marine. She could handle an awkward conversation.

"Of course." She gestured for him to come inside, and he approached her desk, setting one of the cups in front of her.

"Peace offering," he said quietly. Then he settled in the chair across from her desk.

When he didn't speak, Felicity decided to take charge. "Any new findings?"

He tilted his head to the side, and for a second, Felicity wondered if he was going to respond. "I checked over the network," he said, leaning back in his chair. "There's no evidence Livia's hack made it past our individual computers. Adeline's system integrity appears to be intact, so you don't have to worry that Livia is watching your every move."

Felicity nodded. "That's good." One less thing to worry about.

True to his word, Knox Colton had set up regular patrols of her parents' house. They had returned from their cruise late last night and had taken the news of Livia Colton's threats in stride. Felicity was still concerned for their safety, but she felt better knowing the police were keeping an eye on her folks.

"Why did you leave?"

She'd expected the question, but she hadn't thought he'd ask it so suddenly. "I— Ah, I had to get back to work," she fumbled.

Dario's hazel eyes pinned her. "That's crap," he said. "I've spent the past few days giving you some space, but after what we shared together you owe me an explanation. Why did you run out on me?"

Felicity's heart pounded in her chest and she ran her palms down her thighs to dry them. "What we did was a mistake," she said simply. "We never should have slept together. We should have kept things on a professional level and not brought sex into the equation."

"Is that all it was for you?" His eyes glittered with an emotion she couldn't name. "Just sex?"

"You're the one who likes to keep things simple," she fired back. "You tell me."

A muscle along the side of his jaw ticked and she knew her barb had struck a nerve. She considered apologizing, but decided against it. Better for him to walk away angry than to know how much she was coming to care for him.

"I hate to disappoint you," he said, his voice tight, "but that wasn't just another roll in the hay for me. And I don't think it was for you, either."

Felicity dropped her gaze but said nothing, not trusting herself to speak.

"I think you're scared," he continued. "And you know

what? I am, too. But unlike you, I'm not willing to walk away so quickly. I think we're good together, and I think we have a chance. I'm not going to pretend we don't simply to make you feel better about leaving me without even saying goodbye."

She felt her cheeks warm as shame rose in her chest. Dario was right—she should have at least left him a note. Sneaking out had been a low blow, and no matter how scared she was, Dario hadn't deserved that.

He stood abruptly and placed his hands on the edge of her desk, leaning forward slightly. "I'm not giving up on us yet, Felicity," he said quietly. "I don't know what's gotten you so spooked, but I'll be here when you decide you want to tell me."

Felicity watched him walk away, his back straight and head held high. Her heart ached to know she'd hurt him; that had never been her intention. She'd truly thought she was protecting herself and that he had seen their encounter as nothing more than a pleasant diversion. Part of her was thrilled to know her developing feelings weren't all one-sided and that Dario cared for her, too. But his words echoed in her mind, putting a damper on her emotional celebrations.

*I'll be here when you decide you want to tell me.*

"No," she whispered sadly. "You won't."

Dario parked in the gravel lot of Hill Country, Jade Colton's operation. He was there to talk to Jade about her bids on the neighboring property, in the hopes of getting more information that might shed light on the mysterious disappearance of her paperwork. He probably could have taken care of everything when he'd spoken to her over the phone, but given the tension between him and Felicity right now, he'd wanted to get out of the office, if only for a little while.

Damn stubborn woman! He'd seen the look in her eyes and known she had feelings for him. But why wouldn't she admit it? He'd practically bared his soul in her office, hoping that his confession would make her feel safe enough to express her feelings, too. But she'd remained silent, staring up at him with those big scared eyes that reminded him of a doe ready to bolt at the first sign of danger.

Well, he wasn't going to give her an excuse to run. Her disappearing act had stung, and he couldn't pretend it hadn't hurt to wake up and find her gone. But he wasn't going to hold it against her. He was feeling overwhelmed, too, and he knew they probably both needed time to process the changes in their relationship. Normally, he bailed at the first sign of trouble. But not this time. Felicity wasn't a fling— she was a woman he wanted in his life long-term, and he was going to do whatever it took to make her understand he truly cared for her.

He headed for the door of the main ranch house but a gust of wind carried the sound of a woman's voice. Redirecting, he followed the noise to find Jade in the pasture to the side of the ranch house, standing between two horses. She didn't see him; she was busy running her hands over her mount, checking the cinch of the saddle and the placement of the stirrups.

"Hello there," he said, careful to keep his voice calm and level so as not to spook the horses.

She glanced up. "Howdy," she replied.

The horses flicked their tails, their ears pricking forward at his appearance. Dario walked forward until he stood next to one of them, and the animal stuck its nose against his stomach, clearly searching for a treat.

"Sadie," Jade scolded affectionately. "You big flirt."

Dario ran his hand down the side of the mare's face, enjoying the feel of her velvet-soft coat. "Sorry, pretty girl," he said quietly. "I didn't think to bring any apples with me."

Sadie snorted, her breath warm and damp against his skin.

Jade turned her attention to the other animal, and Dario shifted to watch her work. "Did I come at a bad time?" he asked.

"Not at all," Jade replied. "I was hoping we could maybe take a quick ride while we talked. Are you up for that?"

"Ah, okay," he said, a bit taken aback by her suggestion. "But in the interest of full disclosure, you should know I haven't been on a horse in years."

Jade chuckled. "That's okay. I've got Sleepy saddled for you. She's a sweetheart, and she hasn't been above a trot in ages."

Dario eyed the brown mare with concern. She looked sturdy enough, but he wondered if she was too old to carry him. "Are you sure I won't hurt her?"

"I'm positive," Jade assured him. "Sleepy is fully capable of running—she just can't be bothered to do it."

"Sounds like a horse after my own heart," he quipped.

It didn't take long for Jade to finish her checks, and the two of them mounted and set off. It was a beautiful day for a ride, and as the sun warmed his back, Dario felt some of the tension leave his muscles.

The trail sloped gently as it meandered through a stretch of tall grass. They crossed a babbling brook and stopped to let the horses take a quick drink. Jade nodded to the land on the other side of the fence standing about fifty feet away. "That's the property I was hoping to purchase."

Dario nodded, taking in the green expanse, dotted with a few trees. "I'm sorry about your bids," he said.

Jade's shoulder jerked up in a shrug. "Not much to be done now," she said bitterly. "I just wish I knew what had happened."

"Do you have copies of the emails you sent to the Realtor?" Dario asked. "I can't make any promises, but if I can verify you sent the documents, and that the Realtor received them, you might be able to make a case that the land should have been yours."

"How can you do that?" she asked, frowning slightly. "The problems started because she had no record of receiving my bid paperwork. It disappeared."

"They were hacked," he said flatly. "I think by the same group responsible for hacking into the Colton, Incorporated, system. I've asked the real-estate company to let me access their network so I can look for evidence of the crime. If I can get your emails, I'll have a better chance of piecing together how they sabotaged your bid."

Jade nodded. "I'll send you what I have. I think there are copies of my emails in my sent folder."

"Perfect," Dario replied. "That should be enough to get me started."

They spurred the horses on, following the fence line for a few more miles. Dario was enjoying the ride, but he was also eager to get to work to solve the mystery of Jade's disappearing files. "Where are we headed?" he asked.

"There's a spot I want to check, just a bit farther," Jade replied. "Some of the hands have reported signs of what might be a squatter on the property, and I want to look around for myself."

A tingle of apprehension slid down Dario's spine. A squatter? That sounded a little ominous. His mind immediately conjured up the image of Livia Colton flashing on his computer screen, followed by the graffiti on Felicity's car. But he told himself to relax. Not everything was connected to the Colton, Inc., hacking case. A few teenagers had probably shared a bonfire, toasting marshmallows and sipping beer smuggled from their parents' refrigerators. Nothing to worry about. He and Emiliano had had their fair share of campouts as kids, and they hadn't always worried about whose property they were on when they'd pitched their tent.

A few minutes later, they came upon the evidence. Someone had taken the time to dig a small pit in the earth and to line the edges with rocks. A few charred logs sat atop a pile of ashes, and he caught the dull gleam of a dirty spoon, apparently forgotten after a meal.

Jade dismounted to poke around the site a bit. Dario glanced around and caught a glimpse of asphalt through the grass. "Is that a public road?"

"County service road," Jade replied absently. "Usually pretty deserted." She pulled a plastic bag from her pocket and deposited a few cigarette butts inside with a grimace. "Rude," she muttered, shaking her head.

"What do you think?" he asked as she mounted Sadie once more.

"Probably just teenagers," Jade said. "I'll have the guys dismantle the fire pit and post a few more no-trespassing signs. Hopefully that will take care of the problem." She reined Sadie around and Dario did the same with Sleepy. But as the horse turned, he saw a flash of pink in the grass a few yards away. He frowned, trying to find it again. But it was gone, obscured by the movement of the grass as it swayed in the breeze.

"You coming?" Jade called back.

"Yep." He nudged Sleepy, who obstinately refused to pick up the pace. Fortunately, Jade waited for them to catch up before setting off again.

"Everything all right?"

Dario debated telling her about what he'd seen, but decided against it. After all, there wasn't much to tell since he hadn't really gotten a good look. It was probably some kind of winter flower, or maybe a piece of trash left behind by the teens.

Definitely not one of Livia Colton's handkerchiefs.

The ride back passed quickly, and Jade turned down his offer to help unsaddle the horses. "I'll take care of it," she said, waving him off. "After I'm done I'll email you all the information I have on the bid. Let me know what you discover."

"Of course." He headed down the path, his thoughts still on the abandoned campsite and the flash of pink he'd glimpsed in the grass.

He heard the crunch of gravel before he saw the lot and drew up short as he spied a man by his car. "Can I help you?" he asked, striding forward.

The man jumped, apparently startled by the sound of Dario's voice. "Oh. No, I was just checking out your car. Is this the latest Mustang GT?"

Dario relaxed slightly. "Yes. I bought it a few months ago. Runs like a dream."

"I bet." The stranger ran his gaze along the car, nodding to himself. "Were the Shelby mods worth it?"

"Oh yeah." Dario grinned. "I've taken her out to the track a few times. Best money I've ever spent." He stuck out his hand. "Dario Ortega."

The man hesitated, then shook his hand. "Rodrigo Artero. I'm one of the ranch hands."

Dario nodded. "Artero," he repeated thoughtfully. "Where have I heard that name before?"

"My uncle was Fabrizio Artero. Jade's father."

"So that makes you her cousin."

Rodrigo frowned as if unhappy to be reminded of his relative. "Yes," he said shortly. "She is." He turned and began to walk away.

"Nice to meet you," Dario called after him. He climbed behind the wheel and shook his head, trying to make sense of the odd interaction. Jade hadn't mentioned hiring her cousin, but perhaps she didn't think it was news worth discussing with him. Still, there was something about the man's attitude that struck him as wrong, and Dario made a mental note to look into Rodrigo Artero's background.

He pulled onto the main road and, after a second's deliberation, took the first right that led onto the county service road he'd seen earlier. He'd just make one quick check of the site, reassure himself that he'd imagined the handkerchief and be on his way.

A few minutes later, he was bent at the waist, combing the grass in his own personal snipe hunt. "This is ridiculous," he muttered. "There's nothing here."

He heard a whisper of sound behind him, but before he could turn around, something cold pressed against his neck and a hard voice sounded in his ear.

"Don't move."

# *Chapter 11*

"**W**here is he?"

Felicity glanced at her watch for the third time in ten minutes. Adeline had called a meeting in twenty minutes, wanting an update on the Colton, Incorporated, hacking case now that she was back in town.

She reached for her phone and dialed Dario's number, but it went to voice mail. Again. She knew he was probably still upset with her after their conversation that morning, but she'd left him several messages explaining the meeting. It wasn't like him to go silent like this.

Was he off sulking? Or was something else going on? Her thoughts drifted back to her car and the sight of Dario's name scrawled on that horrible list. There had been no sign of Livia Colton since that night, but Felicity didn't think the other woman had disappeared. She was probably biding her time, waiting for the right moment to strike.

Her worry mounting, Felicity called Jade. She knew Dario had gone out to talk to the rancher about her sabotaged bids, and perhaps he was still there.

"No," Jade replied. "He left about an hour ago."

Felicity thanked her and ended the call, unable to ignore the alarm bells in her head. Where was he? And why wasn't he responding?

She glanced at her computer. There was one way she could find out, but it was a violation of his privacy. Still, given the threats Livia had made against him, Felicity decided she would risk Dario's anger. She had to make sure he was safe.

Feeling a bit like a stalker, she pulled up the GPS program that allowed her to track the location of a cell phone and entered Dario's number. As long as his phone was on, the software could pull his location using cell tower triangulation... It didn't take long for the software to pull up a map, and she leaned forward, studying the blinking red dot on the screen that indicated the location of Dario's cell phone.

"That's odd," she muttered. It looked like he was in a field, just off a county service road. She enlarged the area, looking for nearby cross streets. There was an intersection a few miles back, but the location appeared fairly remote. It definitely wasn't the kind of spot Dario would regularly frequent, and a chill skittered down her spine as her imagination went wild.

Felicity pushed to her feet, committing the map to memory. It was probably just some glitch in the system, but she was going to have to check it out or else she'd drive herself crazy coming up with ever more fantastical theories about Livia Colton and her hired goons. She scribbled a note for Adeline, then grabbed her keys and her phone, and after a quick debate, she reached into her desk drawer for the small revolver she'd taken to carrying as Livia's threats had escalated.

"I can't believe I'm doing this," she said to herself as she climbed behind the wheel of her rental car. Talk about a wild-goose chase! But she had to see for herself. No matter how much she had tried to keep him at arm's length, Dario had gotten under her skin and she truly cared about him. Even though they had no future together, she had to make sure he was safe. She'd never forgive herself if something happened to him, something she could have prevented.

"Here I come."

\* \* \*

Dario froze, his mind going blank as he realized he had a knife to his throat. His assailant took advantage of his shock and pulled his cell phone free of his pocket, tossing it away where it vanished in the tall grass. Then the knife was gone, and Dario spun around to see a petite, dark-haired woman glaring up at him.

"Livia." She was immediately recognizable, despite the dye job to disguise her signature blond hair. "I should have known."

She offered him a tight smile. "I believe you have me at a disadvantage," she said, her Southern-belle manners in full effect. "You are?"

"Dario Ortega. I'm the one who figured out you're behind the hacks on Colton, Incorporated. Do you still go by Livia, or should I call you Sulla?"

Recognition flared in her eyes and she laughed, a pretty, musical trill that seemed at odds coming from such a monster. "You say that like I should be impressed. I didn't exactly make it hard for you."

"Why'd you do it?"

She rolled her eyes. "Why do you think? To get revenge on my family! They betrayed me at every turn. It was only fair I punish them for it."

Dario shook his head, stunned by the raw hatred in her voice. He'd never imagined a mother could view her children with such scorn—it simply wasn't natural.

"How long have you been squatting on Jade's property?"

"Long enough," she said easily. "It's been the perfect place to hide in plain sight. No one thought I'd have the guts to come back here, after everything that happened."

"So what's your plan now?"

She jerked her chin at his car, parked about fifty yards away. "You and I are going to take a little ride."

"I don't think so," he replied. He had a good six inches and at least fifty pounds on the woman, and even though she had a knife, he liked his chances.

Livia lifted the hem of her shirt, revealing the butt of a gun that was tucked into her waistband. "Think again."

"Or what, you'll shoot me?" The sight of the gun unnerved him, but Dario knew if he cooperated with Livia, his odds of survival got considerably worse.

"Yes, that's exactly what I'll do. And then I'll go into town and pay a visit to that pretty little thing you've been spending time with. Do you think she'll see me coming?"

The bottom dropped out of Dario's stomach. He knew it wasn't an idle threat. His mind racing, he turned and began to slowly walk to his car. Livia fell into step a few paces behind him.

"How'd you do it?" he blurted. "That's the one thing I haven't been able to figure out. You're no master hacker. How did you manage to infiltrate the Colton, Inc., systems and the Realtor's computer?"

"I didn't," she said. "My associate did."

"Rodrigo Artero," he said, the pieces falling into place. No wonder the man had grown cold at the mention of Jade Colton. Had Livia poisoned him against his own cousin?

"That's right," she confirmed. "Good old Rodrigo. He's so gallant—excellent manners. His uncle was one of my former husbands, who died tragically." She tsked in false sympathy. "He's had it out for me ever since. When I told him my husband had been killed by that scheming bitch Livia Colton, he was only too happy to put his considerable technical skills to use to help me take my revenge on the family."

"He doesn't know who you are?" It was hard to believe. Livia's face had been plastered everywhere in the wake of her escape from prison. How had the man not recognized her?

"Rodrigo has only recently left Argentina," Livia said. "Jade hired him, thinking she was doing her cousin a favor. Little does she know he hates her and the rest of the family, and has been working to sabotage Colton, Incorporated, and Jade's business as well."

He must have helped hide her presence on the property as well, Dario realized. No wonder Jade hadn't known about the campsite until recently…

"And he never suspected your motives for the hacking?"

Livia shrugged. "He thinks I'm Jane Damian, a poor rancher's widow who lost everything, thanks to the Coltons." She sounded smug about her deception.

They were almost to the car and Dario slowed his pace, trying to stall. There had to be something he could do to stop Livia! But his fear for Felicity kept him from trying to act. He knew if he tussled with Livia and lost, she'd head directly to the office to kill Felicity. He wasn't naive—he figured as soon as Livia had disposed of him she'd focus on Felicity next, but if he could draw this out just a little bit longer, maybe Felicity would realize he was missing and could take steps to protect herself. It was a long shot, but he had to try.

He pictured Felicity's face, then planted his feet and turned.

And all hell broke loose.

# Chapter 12

Felicity crouched in the grass, waiting for the right moment to strike. She saw the bulge of the gun in the woman's waistband and knew if she gave away her position too early, the woman—Livia, she thought; who else would it be?—wouldn't hesitate to shoot Dario in the back.

Sweat ran down her cheeks but she ignored it. Her time in the Corps had taught her to block out physical distraction. It had also left her in excellent condition, which was how she'd been able to park her car a mile back and hike into the area without being detected.

She'd told herself she was overreacting a million times. But as soon as she'd rounded the bend and seen the two distant figures—one tall, one small—her doubts had vanished. Felicity had yielded to her training then, employing all the tactics she'd learned to creep up on the pair, her weapon at the ready.

What she wouldn't give for her service rifle right now! If she'd been holding her M16A4, this wouldn't even be a contest. She eyed the small .38 Special in her hand with some misgiving. It was a solid enough gun, but it was a close-range weapon. She'd get only one chance to do this right.

Dario and Livia approached his car, which was parked about fifteen yards to the west of her. Just a few more steps, and Livia's back would be to Felicity's position. If Felicity played her cards right, she could break from cover and have her gun between Livia's shoulder blades before the other woman even knew she was there.

*Come on*, she coaxed silently. *Just a little farther*...

Dario stopped a few feet away from the car and turned to face Livia. At this angle, they were both in profile to her, so she couldn't move without risking exposure. She cursed silently. *Keep moving!* she shouted in her mind.

In the event, it didn't matter. Just as Livia reached for her gun to threaten Dario, a man ran out from behind Dario's car. He let out a horrible cry and swung at Livia. Felicity heard the *thump* as the pipe he was carrying connected with Livia's head. Livia crumpled to the ground, and the man stood over her, screaming in Spanish.

Dario put out a hand and the man turned on him, clearly intending to hurt Dario next. Rage and fear propelled Felicity to her feet. "Stop!"

Her voice split the air and both men froze. Dario wore an expression of almost comical disbelief as he watched her approach, while the stranger gave her a quick once-over and turned his attention back to Livia. He lifted his arms again, ready to beat her with the pipe.

"I said stop," Felicity repeated. She was close enough now that the man heard the *click* of the hammer as she cocked the gun. He froze and shot her a look of such anger it made her stomach quaver.

"Drop the pipe," she instructed.

He did, but she still didn't trust him. "Step away from the woman."

"She is not a woman," he said, sneering. "She is a monster."

"I won't argue with you on that," Felicity said. "But she's down. Move away."

He took a reluctant step, and Felicity nodded at a patch of grass a few feet to the left. "Sit there."

"Felicity—"

She spared Dario a quick glance, enough to assure herself he was unharmed. "Do you have any rope?"

His face went blank. "Uh, I have jumper cables in my trunk."

She'd used worse before to restrain a man. "Get them. Tie him up."

Dario quickly obeyed her orders, and only when the stranger was secure did she relax. "Call the sheriff."

"I can't," Dario said apologetically. "Livia threw my phone into the grass. I have no idea where it is now."

She pulled her own free and tossed it to him. "Here you go."

It only took a moment for Dario to make the call. He hung up with a nod. "Knox and some deputies are on their way."

"Good." Felicity relaxed a bit more at the knowledge the authorities would soon be there. "Why don't you tell me what happened while we wait?"

Dario launched into his story, but after a few minutes, he turned to the other man. "This is where you come in. What were you doing out here?"

"I followed you," he said simply. "I didn't trust you after meeting you in the parking lot, and when I saw you take a right instead of leaving the ranch, I knew you must be headed here. So I grabbed a horse and raced out here."

Dario frowned and glanced around. "I don't see your mount."

The man nodded at a copse of trees on the other side of the road. "I left him there. I didn't want to alert you to my presence. I snuck back over, intending to help Jane." His face darkened, and he glared at Livia's limp form. "But then I heard her talking and realized who she really is." He spit in Livia's direction. "Evil witch. She lied to me, making me think she had suffered at the hands of the Coltons as I had. I trusted her, helped her in her quest for revenge against that horrible family. But I was wrong."

A swell of pity rose in Felicity's chest. Livia had obviously tricked him into hacking Colton, Incorporated, a decision he clearly regretted. "I'm sorry she hurt you," she said. Given his involvement with Livia, he probably wasn't of lily-white character, but since he'd saved Dario's life she was willing to cut him a little slack in that moment.

"What about you?" Dario asked, stepping closer. "How did you find me?"

Felicity glanced down, feeling suddenly shy about telling him. "I used GPS to track you," she confessed. Dario laughed, but a flash of movement caught her eye. She watched in horror as Livia raised her arm and pointed the gun at Dario's unsuspecting back.

Before she could scream a warning, Livia fired. Dario fell against Felicity with a grunt. A second shot rang out, and Rodrigo grunted in pain. Acting on instinct, Felicity dropped to the ground and took aim, squeezing off round after round at her target.

Livia's body jerked, and blood bloomed on her shirt. She fell to the ground, a frozen smile on her face as her eyes stared up at the sky. Felicity ran over and grabbed the woman's gun, tossing it far away from her body. Then she turned back to Dario, her heart already breaking at what she knew she would find.

She spared a glance at Rodrigo, who was clutching his leg, cursing a blue streak in rapid Spanish. She knew she should help him, but her priority was Dario.

He was lying on the ground, a stunned expression on his face. "My God," he gasped, reaching up to clutch his shoulder. "That hurts!"

Felicity dropped to her knees, hardly daring to believe her eyes. "Dario?" she whispered, running her hands across his chest. "Don't try to talk. Just stay quiet. The ambulance will be here soon." Her view went blurry and she realized she was crying. She moved his hand to press her own over his wound, trying to stop the bleeding. "It'll be okay."

"I know it will," he said. His voice was heavy with pain, but he was surprisingly lucid for a man who'd just been shot. "She hit my shoulder. It hurts like you wouldn't believe, but it's not going to kill me."

It took a moment for his words to sink in. She blinked away her tears and realized he was right. His bleeding was slowing down, and the wound seemed to be centered in the fleshy part of his shoulder, just below his collarbone.

"Now I'll have a scar to match my brother's," he said, trying to smile.

Felicity stared down at him, unimpressed by his attempt at levity. "You could have been killed!"

He winced, and she realized she'd shrieked at him. But her emotions were all over the place, and she couldn't control the volume of her voice. "I thought you were dead," she said, choking back a sob. "I thought I was going to have to watch you die. And you think this is funny?"

"No, I—"

She shook her head and buried her face in her hands. "I killed her, Dario. I took her life because I thought she had taken yours."

"You did the right thing," he said.

The wail of approaching sirens saved her from having to make a reply. Not that she knew what to say. Even though she had been to war and seen combat, Felicity had never killed anyone before.

In a matter of seconds, Knox and his deputies swarmed the area. Paramedics clustered around Dario and Rodrigo, while Knox pulled Felicity away to talk. She told him everything she knew, but her gaze kept straying to Dario, still on the ground as the EMTs worked above him. Would he really be okay?

She wanted to go to him, but Knox and his men were insistent she stay and talk to them. So she could only watch as the paramedics rolled Dario into the back of the ambulance and took off, sirens blaring as they drove away with a piece of her heart.

*Two weeks later...*

Adeline threw open the door and reached for Felicity. "I'm so glad you could make it!" she exclaimed.

Felicity smiled as she returned her friend's embrace. "Thanks for inviting me. But I think I must be really early." She glanced back at the empty drive and frowned. "Where's everyone else?"

"Oh, they'll be along," Adeline said breezily. "Jeremy is upstairs getting Jamie dressed. Thorne and Knox both called to tell me they were running late due to kid challenges. Leonor and her husband are stuck in traffic, and Jade said she had a horse go into labor, so she might not make it at all. Claudia has apparently never been on time to anything in her life, and I asked River and Edith to stop at the store to pick up ice." Adeline smiled brightly.

"It was nice of you to throw a party for everyone," Felicity said.

Adeline shrugged. "It's my pleasure. We're all so happy to put this case behind us, it seemed like a good reason to celebrate."

Felicity smiled, but the reminder of just how the case had ended sent her into a spiral of doubt. "Are you sure this is a good idea? I know there was no love lost between Livia and her children, but I can't imagine they'll all be happy to see me after I killed their mother."

Adeline grabbed her by the shoulders and gave her a

little shake. "How many times do we have to go over this? You fired in self-defense. You did not murder her in cold blood. Although," she said thoughtfully, "if anyone deserved that fate, it was Livia Colton."

"I still feel bad," Felicity began, but Adeline cut her off.

"No. None of that. Not today. This is why I wanted you to come—so you could see the Coltons don't blame you for what you did." She guided Felicity into the expansive kitchen. "Now, grab a glass of lemonade and head outside. I need to finish putting some hors d'oeuvres together, and I don't want you moping around while I do. Get some fresh air and try to relax."

Recognizing a dismissal when she heard it, Felicity did as she was instructed. She walked through the sliding glass doors and onto the patio, then stepped onto the path that led to the garden. It was an unseasonably warm day, and even though there would be no flowers blooming, the walk would do her good.

Her mind drifted back to that afternoon, the image of Dario lying bloody in the dirt bringing tears to her eyes. He was recovering nicely, or so she'd heard. But that split second of terror when she thought she'd lost him forever had broken her heart.

*I can't do this.*

The memory of her words echoed in her ears, blocking out the birdsong in the yard. Dario had stared up at her from his hospital bed, his brows drawn together in puzzlement.

"What do you mean?" he'd asked.

"I can't keep seeing you. It's too hard for me."

Dario had tried to reach for her hand, but she'd moved away, knowing that if he touched her, her resolve would crumble.

"What about me? What about what I want?"

Felicity had forced herself to smile. "I'm giving you

what you want—the freedom to move on to the next pretty face. The way you always do."

Dario had flinched at her words. "I see," he'd said, his voice dull.

"It's better this way," she'd said. She couldn't let him know that she was falling for him. Even though it hurt, she'd rather end things now than have him dump her in a few months once he realized they had different goals.

Felicity wanted a husband and a family of her own someday. Dario had made it clear from the beginning he wasn't the marrying kind. But she didn't hold it against him—her heart had simply ignored that fact, and now she was paying the price.

Even though she knew they couldn't be together, she drew comfort from the fact he was still alive. The world was a richer place with him in it, and the memory of his laugh eased the ache in her chest.

And then suddenly, he was there before her.

She blinked, expecting him to vanish as quickly as he'd appeared. But he remained, solid and whole on the path in front of her.

"Dario?"

He smiled, and in that moment, Felicity decided that if this was a hallucination, she didn't want it to end. He extended his hand and she took it, allowing him to lead her into the small garden patio.

The scent hit her first. Roses. Their fragrance perfumed the air, bringing a breath of spring to this midwinter's day. She glanced around, amazed at the sheer number of bouquets on display. Red, white, pink flowers. Pale peach. Vibrant yellow. Every shade imaginable was present, the blooms surrounding her with their beauty.

"I don't understand," she whispered.

Dario gestured to a small table set in the middle of the

patio. As she approached, she saw he'd used rose petals to write a message.

Will you date me?

She turned to look at him, her happiness at his sudden appearance draining from her. "How can you ask me that?" she said, her voice quavering. "After what I said to you in the hospital."

"I've been doing a lot of thinking about you and me, and I figured out you're scared because of my playboy reputation. But that's not the life for me anymore. It's time for me to settle down. Adeline has offered me a job with the firm, right here in Shadow Creek. I'm going to start putting down roots, and I want you to be a part of that. Unless I've completely misjudged everything and you don't want that." A flicker of doubt crossed his face, and Felicity realized he truly didn't know how she felt about him.

She'd done such a good job of guarding her heart, she hadn't let the one man she cared about know how much he meant to her. And yet despite his uncertainty, he was still willing to take a chance on her.

On them.

"No," she said firmly. "I want that, too. I want you in my life, now and in the future. I need you to stay, if it will truly make you happy."

She saw relief wash over him and she felt an answering lightness in her heart. "You make me happy," he said softly. He reached for her, and she pressed herself against his chest with a contented sigh.

"This means we'll be working together, you know," he said in her ear. "And I seem to remember you saying something about how we shouldn't mix work and sex."

"That was a mistake," she said. "Forget I ever said it."

He chuckled, his chest vibrating against hers. "I'm so

glad to hear you recant your statement." He trailed one hand down her back and rested it on her bottom. "Because I have plans for us."

Felicity moved against him, reveling in the feel of his strong, broad chest against her curves. "Don't you need to rest and recover?"

"My doctor said exercise is good for me." He nipped gently at the top of her ear and she shivered.

"You're really going to stay?"

He drew back and looked down at her, his hazel eyes filled with warmth. "Do you really want me to?"

"Yes," she whispered, reaching up to cup his face. "I do."

He grinned. "Then it sounds like we have a deal."

She laughed. "Should we shake on it?"

Dario shook his head. "I have a better idea," he murmured. He lowered his mouth to hers, and Felicity lost herself in the promise of his kiss.

\* \* \* \* \*

# BACHELOR UNDONE

**BRENDA JACKSON**

To the love of my life, Gerald Jackson, Sr.

To all the family, friends and dedicated readers.
This one is for you.

For God hath not given us the spirit of fear; but
of power, and of love, and of a sound mind.
—II Timothy 1:7

# *PROLOGUE*

SPENDING HER VACATION in New York during the month of December was not on Darcelle Owens's list of things to do, which was why she was in a cab headed for JFK International Airport. She loved living in the Big Apple, but when forecasters had predicted the city's coldest winter ever, she was glad she had plans to get the hell out of Dodge.

*Jamaica, here I come,* she thought relaxing back in her seat. While her coworkers would be battling the snow, she planned to be lying half-naked on the beach under the heat of the Jamaican sun. And then at night, she'd become a sophisticated hooch and let her hair down, party and even do a little man-hunting. She deserved it after working her tail off the past two years.

She had the whole month of December off and would have loved to spend the entire time in Jamaica. But her parents expected her to come home for Christmas, as usual. She got a chill in her bones just thinking of returning to Minneapolis for even a little while.

She'd always hated cold weather and would have headed south to attend college if her parents hadn't convinced her of how much money they could save not having to pay out-of-state tuition. When she talked to her mother just that morning, it was twenty below zero. *Brrrr.*

And then her best friend Ellie Lassiter expected her to spend a few days with her at her lake house in North Carolina before Ellie and her husband Uriel's New Year's Eve bash.

Darcy planned to keep her family and Ellie happy, but first she intended to relax in the warm weather for at least three weeks.

Darcy cringed when she heard the chime of a text message on her cell phone. How dare her younger brother Prescott teach their mother how to text! Darcy bet between her, Prescott and her older brother Jonas that their mother, Joan Owens, sent out over one hundred text messages a day. Okay, maybe she was exaggerating a tad bit, but it would seem about that number.

Checking her phone, Darcy smiled when she saw the message hadn't come from her mother after all. It was from Ellie.

Behave yourself in J. Have fun. E

Darcy chuckled and quickly texted back. Can't behave myself and have fun, too. LOL.

Got Bruce with you? the responding text asked.

Darcy's smile widened. Bruce was the name she'd given her little sex toy. Nope. Left Bruce behind this time. I hope to get lucky and find someone who's looking to have some fun. Looking forward to relaxing, reading and replacing Bruce with the real thing.

She wasn't surprised when within seconds of sending that message her cell phone rang. Of course it was Ellie. "Yes, El?"

"And just what do you mean by that?" her best friend asked.

Darcy threw her head back and laughed. "Just what I said. It's time Bruce goes into retirement. He's earned it."

"Girl, you're awful."

"No, I'm not. If I was awful, I wouldn't have gone without being in a relationship for two years. If it hadn't been for Bruce and my romance novels, I don't know what I would have done to keep sane."

And that was so true. She had moved from Minneapolis after taking a job as a city planner for New York City. Over the past two years, she had been working day and night trying to prove the city hadn't made a mistake by hiring an outsider.

She had worked hard and hadn't taken any time off other than the recognized holidays, which was why she had accumulated so much vacation time. And now she intended to enjoy it. It was the end of the year, and her boss had warned her to "use it or lose it." The only thing she planned to lose was two years of abstinence.

"Chill, El," she said when there was silence on the other end. "I'm taking plenty of condoms with me if that makes you happy."

She glanced up and saw the elderly cabdriver looking at her in the rearview mirror. *Oops.* She couldn't do anything but smile. She lowered her head and whispered into the phone. "Look, you're going to get me in trouble, El. The cabbie heard my remark about condoms and is looking at me funny. Like he thinks I'm a loose woman or something."

"Nobody's fault but your own for saying what you did."

"It's the truth."

"Whatever. Go and have your fun, but be careful,

stay safe and you better have a lot to tell me when you get back."

Darcy felt giddy all the way to her toes. "Trust me, I will. I intend to become one of the heroines in those romance novels I enjoy reading so much. And I got this hot pink bikini with the word *seduction* written all over it."

Darcy then clicked off the phone and glanced out the cab's window. It had started snowing. She drew in a deep breath thinking she couldn't get to Jamaica fast enough.

YORK ELLIS, FORMER NYPD officer and present-day security expert, felt adrenaline flow through his veins. It was always that way at the start of a new case, and from the sound of things, this one would be a challenge. As far as he was concerned, anything would top the last case he had protecting the horse who'd won the Kentucky Derby when rumors of a horse-napping had begun circulating.

He glanced across his desk at Malcolm Overstreet, renowned director and screenwriter. Malcolm was there to represent a group of New York filmmakers whose movies were getting put on the black market before they got the chance to be released to theaters. This was causing the filmmakers enormous loss of profits and almost forcing them into bankruptcy. In this case, the actual movie footage was being sold while the production was still in process. Certain scenes were even appearing on the internet.

On top of that, idle threats had been made against the making of a controversial movie. Malcolm wanted

York's firm to find out who was behind the bootlegging as well as handle the security for the movie.

York had enough people working for him to do the latter, and as far as finding out who was involved in advance footage being released to the public, he figured with the right plan in place that should be easy enough.

"Have you ever considered the possibility this might be an inside job?" he asked Malcolm. He could tell from the man's expression that he hadn't.

"We have good people working for our production company," Malcolm said. "If we lose money, they lose money."

*Not necessarily,* York thought. "When does the movie continue shooting?" he asked.

"Next week in Jamaica," Malcolm responded.

York nodded as he jotted down a few notes. He knew the film was a controversial biography on the life of Marcus Garvey, the black civil rights activist from Jamaica. And he knew it would depict a side of Garvey that some didn't want told—which was the reason for the heightened security while they were on the island. "Has any current cast or crew member worked on your last couple of movies?"

"Yes, we usually hire the same crew for all our productions. Some of them have been with us for years, and it's hard to imagine them being a part of anything illegal."

"What about your cast?"

"Johnny Rush is my leading man as Garvey, and Danielle Simone is my leading lady as his love interest. But you can scratch them off the list," Malcolm said confidently.

York lifted a brow. "Why are you so sure?"

"Their egos. Both are too vain to want their work anywhere other than the big screen, trust me. They think having their work out on the black market is an insult to their talent. In fact, the only way they would agree to work with Spirit Head Productions again is if we assured them their work will not be undermined and hit the streets before a premier date."

"What about Damien Felder?" York asked, glancing down at the papers on his desk. "I've noticed his name has shown up on probably every production you've done."

Malcolm nodded. "You can mark Damien's name off the list as well. He's my line producer, and a cut in our profits slashes into his bank account as well. He has nothing to gain from our movies appearing on the black market. If another one of our movies gets bootlegged, we'll be filing for bankruptcy."

Malcolm then leaned forward. "I believe whoever is behind things will try and get the footage sometime while my cast and crew are shooting the final scenes in Jamaica. And I want you to make sure that doesn't happen, York. My partners and I are sick and tired of losing money that way. It's not fair not only to us but to every person who has a stake in the production."

The man paused and then added, "And then there's this threat on Rush. Some think he fabricated things for publicity, but we can't take any chances."

York closed his notepad. Malcolm and his group were heavy hitters who could open the doors to even more business for York's security firm. But more importantly, it was the principle of the thing. Someone was breaking the law and cutting into the profits—actually outright stealing them—and they were profits they didn't deserve.

He knew one of the main reasons Malcolm had come to him was because Malcolm was a friend of his father's. Malcolm had also attended Morehouse College as a young man along with York's father and five godfathers before getting a graduate degree from Columbia University Film School. "I understand, and I intend to fly to Jamaica immediately and find out who is behind things."

Malcolm lifted a brow. "Will it be that easy?"

York met the man's gaze with an intense look. "No, but once I establish my cover, I'll be a regular on set and I can keep an eye on what's going on. And the six men and three women working for me are the best of the best. Rest assured, whoever is behind this has messed with one of your productions for the last time."

# CHAPTER ONE

DARCY STOOD ON the balcony and glanced out at the beach. It was hard to believe this was her third day in Jamaica and she was just getting out of her hotel room today for the first time. She, who rarely got sick, had gotten a stomach virus her first day and had stayed in her hotel room in bed. What a bummer of a way to start off her vacation.

The good thing was that today she was feeling like her old self again, and she intended to spend as much time outside as she possibly could. She had lost two valuable days, but from here on out it was full steam ahead.

When she had checked in, the hotel clerk had given her a list of the hotel's activities for the week, and tonight they would be hosting a classy beach party. Her health had improved just in time. A party was the last thing she wanted to miss.

She turned away from the window and crossed the room to glance at herself in the full-length mirror. She had purchased the wide-brimmed straw hat from a gift shop at the airport, and the sundress she was wearing had caught her eye the moment she'd seen it at Macy's over the summer. At the time, a trip to Jamaica had been just a fancy, and in a way, it was hard to believe she was actually here.

Instead of donning a bikini and lying on the beach today, she thought she would take a tour of the island and get some sightseeing in. She had purchased a new digital camera and intended to put it to good use. And she definitely intended to do some shopping. When she had visited Jamaica a few years ago—a college graduation present from her parents—she had purchased several pieces of jewelry that had been handcrafted by an island woman. Darcy intended to see if the small shop near the pier was still there. There were several more pieces she would love to add to her collection.

She glanced around the room. Since she would be here for three weeks she'd decided to get one of the residential suites, and she loved it. It was huge and spacious, and although it was costing her a pretty penny, it was worth it. Besides, she deserved it.

The furniture in the sitting area was elegant and the decor colors of cream, yellow, mint green and plum perfectly reflected an island theme. Floor-to-ceiling windows lined one wall and provided a balcony view of the water.

French doors led from the sitting room directly into the bedroom, which had its own balcony. There was nothing like waking up to the beauty of the Caribbean Sea. But it was the bathroom that she'd found simply breathtaking. It had a dressing room area and a closet large enough to camp out in if the need arose. Then there was the humongous Jacuzzi tub that could hold several couples if you were inclined to get that kinky... which she wasn't. She wasn't into sharing of any kind when it came to relationships.

Grabbing her purse off the table, she headed for the door. It was a beautiful day, and she planned to spend

as much of it as she could outside. Then she would return and take a shower and a nap before getting ready
for the party tonight.

York walked along the pier. It hadn't taken any time to
get his game plan in place and head toward the island.
Jamaica was beautiful, but unlike all the other times he
came to the island, he was here for business.

Regardless of what Malcolm thought, every member
of the cast and crew was a suspect. His team had divided
the list, and every single person was being checked out.
He was hoping it wouldn't take long to expose the cul-
prit since he planned to spend the holidays back in the
States. His parents had moved to Seattle a few years
ago and luckily didn't expect everyone to show up on
their doorsteps for the holidays. In fact, as long as he
could remember, once he and his siblings began having lives of their own, his parents would spend the holidays in Toronto, visiting friends they had there. Usually
York would spend a quiet Christmas at home, and those
times he wanted company, he had five sets of godparents he could visit.

Most people knew the story as to how six guys who'd
met and become best friends while attending Morehouse had on graduation day made a pact to stay in
touch by becoming godfathers to each of their children and that the firstborn sons' names would carry
the letters of the alphabet from U to Z. And that was
how Uriel Lassiter, Virgil Bougard, Winston Coltrane,
Xavier Kane, York Ellis and Zion Blackstone had come
into existence. He was close to his godparents and god-

brothers and couldn't imagine them not being a part of his life.

He checked his watch. A couple of his men had checked in already with their reports, and it was obvious Malcolm didn't know some of his people as well as he thought he did. However, there was nothing to indicate any of them could be suspected of anything other than engaging in a number of illicit affairs.

York glanced around and saw he was the object of several women's attention. He didn't mind, and if he'd had the time, he would even indulge their fantasies. He was well aware that a number of women came to the island alone to get their groove on. They were man-hunters who were only looking for a good time.

He kept walking. He was on assignment, and there wasn't a woman he'd met yet who could make him take his mind off work.

DARCY SQUINTED AGAINST the brightness of the sun while moving from shop to shop in Montego Bay. Reggae music seemed to be playing just about everywhere. Pausing, she pulled out her sunglasses to shield her eyes from the sun. It was hard to believe how bright it shone here when, according to weather reports, it was still snowing in New York.

She stopped at a fruit stand, admiring the basket of strawberries, all plump and ripe, when something out of the corner of her eye caught her attention.

A man.

And boy, what a man he was. She could only see his profile, but even from almost fifteen feet away she could tell he was a fine specimen of the opposite sex. He was in a squatting position, going through a rack of T-shirts that some peddler was trying to sell him.

Darcy tilted the sunglasses a little off her eyes to get a better view, deciding she didn't want to miss anything—especially the way the denim of his jeans managed to stretch tight across his thighs. And the way his shoulders filled the shirt he was wearing.

He stood up a little and his tush—OMG, it was definitely the kind a woman would drool over. She bet they were perfect masculine cheeks, firm and fine.

Her mind began working, and she immediately began seeing him as a hero from one of the romance novels she read. *But which one?* she asked herself, thumping her finger against her chin.

She immediately thought of Jansen Trumble, the bad boy from the spicy novel *Mine Until Morning.* That had been one hot book, and even after reading it at least four or five times, she would give just about anything to have a rumble with Trumble. She settled her sunglasses back on her eyes thinking if she couldn't have the fictional Trumble then a look-alike would have to suffice.

"Miss, would you like to try some of my strawberries? I just rinsed this batch off. I bet you'd like them."

Her attention was pulled momentarily away from the gorgeous hunk when an island woman offered her a tray of fresh strawberries, sill wet from a recent rinsing. "Thanks, I'd love to try one."

She popped a strawberry in her mouth, immediately enjoying the taste when the sweet flavor burst on her tongue. It was wet, juicy and so delicious. That made her glance back over at the man. Now he was standing to his full height as he continued to consider the T-shirts. He was tall, and she could see just how well built he was.

She tilted her head, thinking there was something about him that was oddly familiar, although she had yet to see his features. Like her, he was wearing sunglasses. His were aviators. And even from a distance she could tell he was an American. He had chocolate-colored skin, and his dark hair was cut close to his head.

"Delicious, miss?"

She glanced back at the woman and smiled, remembering they were talking about the strawberries and not the man. "Yes, definitely delicious."

"Would you like another?"

Darcy chuckled. She hadn't intended on being greedy but since the woman asked… "Yes, I'd love another."

She put another strawberry into her mouth, and when she glanced back over at the man, she saw he was staring over at her. Facing him, she immediately recognized him and almost choked on the strawberry in her mouth.

York Ellis!

Even wearing sunglasses she would know him anywhere. The shape of his mouth and his chiseled jaw would give him away each time. What the heck was he doing here?

She felt irritation invade her entire body. Staring into his handsome face did nothing to calm her rising anger. Her best friend was married to one of his godbrothers, so they were usually invited to the same family functions.

She and York always managed to rub each other the wrong way whenever they would run into each other. Things had been that way between them since the time they'd met at Ellie and Uriel's wedding two years ago. During that time, her ex-husband Harold had tried threatening her to take him back. York had tried coming on to her at the reception. She had been in a bad mood at the time and had rebuffed his advances. Evidently he hadn't taken rejection well.

He removed his sunglasses and stood staring across the way at her, evidently as surprised to see her as she was to see him. She felt her body get hot under his intense stare but forced her emotions to stay in check. She certainly couldn't be that hard up for a man that she would be attracted to him.

And this wasn't just any man. It was York Ellis. He was arrogant. Cocky. Too damn sure of himself at times to suit her. So why was she having such a hard time dragging her gaze from him? Why instead was she allowing her eyes to roam all over him, taking in how well he fit his jeans, his shirt? And then, there was his looks…

So, okay, he had a nice-looking mouth, one that was shaped just for kissing and those other scandalous things mouths could do. And his eyes were dark, so compelling and so magnetic. And at the moment, those dark eyes were intent on staring her down.

His half smile told her he knew she was checking him out and evidently found it amusing, considering their history. Anyone who'd ever hung around them knew they had one. He rubbed her the wrong way, and it seemed she always managed to rub him the wrong way as well.

He continued to smile, and she tried to ignore the fact that doing so made the angular plane of his face more pronounced, made dimples slash deep in his cheeks.

This was the first time she ever noticed them. But then this was the first time he'd smiled at her.

But she quickly reminded herself he wasn't smiling at her now. He was smirking at having caught her sizing him up. Good grief! With his arrogance, he'd probably assumed she was interested in him sexually—not on her life and not even if he was the last man on this earth.

But then she couldn't help noticing that he was checking her out as well. His gaze was scanning up and down her body, and in response she could feel the nipples of her breasts press hard against the material of her sundress. She broke eye contact to reach for another strawberry. She needed it.

"All the others are for sale, miss," the woman told her gently.

Darcy couldn't help but chuckle at the woman's game and conceded it had worked. The woman had offered her two free strawberries to taste, knowing she would like them enough to buy the rest. And she was right.

"All right then, I want the entire basket. They are delicious."

The woman's face beamed. "Thank you. Would you like to try any other fruit?"

Darcy figured she might as well—anything to get her mind off the man across the street. Ellie liked York and couldn't figure out why her best friend and one of her husband's godbrothers could not get along. She had constantly told Ellie not to lose any sleep over it. Life wasn't intended for every single person to live together in harmony.

She glanced back at York and saw he was still staring over at her. Data rushed through her brain as to how much she knew about him. He was thirty-four, had gotten a criminology degree from a university in Florida and had been a cop with the NYPD for a few years before going into business for himself as a security expert. Both of his parents were living, and he had a younger sister and brother.

She also knew that he and his six godbrothers had formed the Bachelors in Demand club, with each one vowing to remain single. Now it was down to only four since two had married. Uriel Lassiter had married Ellie and Xavier Kane had married a woman by the name of Farrah earlier in the year.

"Here are your purchases," the woman said, handing her a huge brown paper bag containing the strawberries, mangoes and guineps. Darcy figured her next destination would be the hotel. Seeing York had practically ruined her day. She needed to revamp and get prepared for her night on the beach.

"Here, let me help you with that."

Darcy turned her head at the deep, husky male voice who'd spoken close to her ear at the same time her bag was smoothly taken from her hand. She frowned when she glanced up at a face that was too handsome for his own good. "York, what are you doing here in Jamaica?" She all but snapped the question out at him.

He smiled, and she had to force her gaze from the curve of his mouth when he said, "Funny, I was about to ask you the same thing. Are you sure New York can handle things without you?"

"It will be a struggle, but they'll manage," she responded smartly. They both lived in New York but made it a point not to have their paths cross, which had always been fine with her—definitely preferable. "What about with you? Is the security of the city being tested with you gone?"

"Not at all," he said smoothly. "And you never answered my question as to what you're doing here in Jamaica."

She glared up at him. "Not that it's any of your business but I'm here vacationing for three weeks. I've earned the time off and intend to enjoy myself. And why are you here?"

"Vacationing as well. Funny we picked the same place to unwind and seek out relaxation."

Darcy didn't see anything amusing about it. Being on the same island with him was definitely not how she wanted things to be. It was bad enough that they lived in the same city. "Well, enjoy your vacation, and I can carry my own bag, thank you." She tried tugging her bag from his grip and he held tight.

"Excuse me, but will you let go of my bag?"

Instead of doing so, he asked, "Where are you on your way to?"

She let out a deep, frustrated sigh. "My hotel."

"Which one?"

"The Ritz-Carlton," she said, without thinking.

His smile widened. "Now isn't that a coincidence? So am I."

He had to be joking, she thought. There was no way he could be staying at her hotel. As if he'd read her thoughts, he chuckled and said, "I guess this isn't your lucky day, huh?"

She snatched her bag from him. "You're right, it's not."

She turned and thanked the woman for her purchase and moved to walk away. Why wasn't she surprised when York fell in step beside her? She stopped and turned to him. "And just where do you think you're going?"

"Back to the hotel. Since we're headed the same way, I figure we might as well keep each other company."

"Has it ever occurred to you that I might not want your company?"

His answer was simple. "No, that thought has never occurred to me."

"Like the time you rushed over to my place thinking I was a helpless female in distress?"

He laughed. "Hey, that was Ellie's idea, not mine."

He was right. It had been Ellie's idea. She and Ellie had been talking on the phone late one night when Darcy had heard a noise downstairs. She put Ellie on hold to investigate, not knowing Ellie had panicked and called York, who lived less than a mile away. Ellie had asked him to go to Darcy's house to make sure everything was okay.

It turned out there had been a burglar. Some guy had broken into her house, and she had caught him rummaging through her kitchen drawers. By the time York had gotten there, the guy had discovered just how well she could defend herself when she'd demonstrated the karate skills she'd acquired growing up and taking classes with her brothers.

York, who had arrived before the police, had gotten extremely angry with her, saying she had no business taking on the likes of a burglar. Of course, she had disagreed with him.

"Okay, your showing up at my place might have been El's idea, but you had no right to scold me in front of those police officers."

"You took your life in your hands when you should have called the police," he said, and she could tell from the tone of his voice her actions that night last year was still a sore spot with him.

"Had I waited for the police, the man would have gotten away just to break into someone else's home. I had no intentions of letting him do that."

York frowned. "Does it matter that you could have gotten killed?" Anger laced his every word.

"Could have but I didn't. I had sized up the situation and knew it was one I could handle. Not every woman needs a man for protection, York."

"And evidently you're one of those kinds."

She wasn't sure what he meant by that, but hell yes, she was one of those kinds. She didn't need a man around to protect her. Her first husband had learned that the hard way when he began showing abusive tendencies. "I guess I am," she finally said, smiling as if she was proud of that fact.

She began walking again, convinced he would decide he wouldn't want her company after all. He proved her wrong when he picked up his pace and began walking beside her again. She decided to ignore him. The good thing was that the hotel was less than a block away.

YORK WALKED BESIDE Darcy and tried not to keep glancing over at her. She looked cute in her wide-brimmed straw hat and sundress. He had noticed her checking him out, and when she'd removed her sunglasses and he'd seen it was Darcy, he hadn't known whether to be amused or annoyed. She certainly hadn't known who he was at first, just like he hadn't recognized her.

But once she had known it was him, he could immediately see her guard go up. She had intended to put distance between them. At any other time he would let her but not this time. He wasn't sure why, but all he knew was that was how it would be.

"Would the lady like to look at my bracelets?" a peddler asked.

She stopped and so did York. He observed her when she conversed with the man who had several bangle bracelets for her to see.

York continued to watch as the man ardently pitched his goods and was impressed with the way Darcy handled the anxious merchant by not giving in to his outrageous prices. He inwardly chuckled, thinking she definitely had no intentions of paying an exorbitant amount.

She seemed pretty sharp for a twenty-eight-year-old, and he figured she rarely missed anything. It would be hard, if not next to impossible, for a man to run a game on her.

He could vividly recall the first time he'd seen her rushing into the church for Uriel's wedding rehearsal. She'd been late since her plane had had mechanical problems.

Like all the other men, he had simply stared at her— the woman with all that dark brown hair flowing around her shoulders, hazel eyes, striking cocoa-colored features and a body to die for. The last thing he'd expected when he'd tried coming on to her later was to be told she wasn't interested. He would admit it had been a blow to his ego. That incident had been almost two years ago, and if the way she'd been sizing him up moments ago was anything to go by, it seemed she was pretty interested now.

He knew he should let go and move on, but so far he hadn't been able to do that. And whenever he saw her they had a tendency to get on each other's last nerves. If the truth be told, he had a mind to pay her back for rebuffing his advances that day. He could seduce her, make love to her and then walk away and not look back. Yes, that would serve her right.

"Well, that's that," she said, reclaiming his attention. He saw the way her lips quirked in amusement as well as the gleam of triumph shining in her eyes. He gathered she'd made a purchase she was pleased with.

They continued walking again, side by side, and he wondered how long she would continue to ignore him. He decided to stir conversation and asked, "When was the last time you talked to Ellie?" He eased the bag containing her fruit from her hand once again.

Darcy glanced over at York and decided that she would allow him to carry that bag since he seemed hell-bent on doing so anyway. She would keep the bag with the four bracelets she'd purchased from the peddler at a good price. "We're best friends, so I talk to El practically every day," she said. "But she hasn't called since I arrived here. She's going to be busy this week."

"Doing what?"

She wondered if he thought everything was his business. "She's hosting several holiday parties."

"Oh."

"It is the holiday season, you know," she reminded him.

"Yes, I know."

She didn't say anything and for a moment regretted bringing up any mention of the holidays. She'd heard from El that a woman York had been dating and had begun caring deeply about, and who'd been a fellow officer when he'd been a cop with the NYPD, had gotten gunned down on Christmas Day while investigating a robbery. That had been over six years ago. After that, he'd sworn never to get seriously involved with a woman again, especially one in a dangerous profession. She knew all about the Bachelors in Demand club, one he formed along with his bachelor godbrothers who were all intent on staying single men forever. She had met all six of the godbrothers and got along with each of them...except for York.

"So how are your parents?" she asked, deciding to change the subject. She had first met the Ellises at Ellie and Uriel's wedding and had run into them again when another one of Uriel and York's godbrothers, Xavier Kane, had gotten married earlier in the year.

"They're doing fine. I visited with them a couple of months ago." He glanced back over at her. "So what do you plan on doing later?"

She glanced up at him from under the wide-brimmed hat. "I'm resting up for the big beach party the hotel is hosting tonight. I hear it's a real classy black-tie affair. You are going, aren't you?"

"Hadn't planned on it."

"Oh, well." She should have felt relieved that he wouldn't be there, but for some reason she felt a pang of disappointment in her chest. Why was that?

"Behave yourself tonight, Darcy."

She lifted a brow. If he was being cute, she wasn't appreciating it. "Let me assure you, Mr. Ellis, that you don't need to tell me how to behave. And just for the record, I don't plan on taking your advice. The reason

I'm here is to have a good time, and a good time is what I will have—even if it means misbehaving."

He stopped walking and stared at her, and she could see anger lurking in the dark depths of his eyes. She knew it was probably bothering him that she was standing there, facing him and looking nonplussed. Her two brothers were dominating males, so York's personality type was not foreign to her. But that didn't mean she had to tolerate it or him.

She glanced around. They were now standing in the plush lobby of the hotel. "I guess this is where we need to part ways, and hopefully we won't run into each other again anytime soon. You didn't say how long you intend to visit here."

He smiled at her. "No, I didn't say."

And when she saw that he had no intention of doing so either, she released a sigh, took her bag from him and said, "Goodbye, York." She then turned and headed for the bank of elevators.

Darcy drew in a deep breath with every step she took, tempted to glance over her shoulder. But she had a feeling he was still standing there, staring at her, and she didn't want to give him the impression that she'd given him another thought…although she was doing so.

A few moments later, she stepped on the elevator and turned. She'd been right. He was still standing there. And while others joined her on the elevator their gazes held. At that moment, she felt a pang of regret that the two of them had never gotten along. Too bad. She was too set in her ways to make any changes now. Besides, she didn't want to make any changes. For some reason, she much preferred that she and York keep their distance. The man was temptation personified. She could deal with temptation but not when it included an extreme amount of arrogance.

The elevator doors swooshed shut, breaking their eye connection. She released a deep breath, only realizing at that moment she'd been holding it. He was staying in another section of the hotel. It was a humongous place, but their paths might cross again and she would be ready and prepared. She had no intentions of letting York Ellis catch her off guard again.

# *CHAPTER TWO*

DAMN, THE WOMAN was too beautiful for her own good, York thought, watching the elevator door close behind Darcy Owens. Beautiful with a smart mouth, a delectable-looking mouth. More than once he'd been tempted to kiss it shut and to demonstrate just what he could do when his tongue connected with hers.

But then he had to remember that Darcy was too brash and outspoken to suit him. He didn't want a "yes" woman by any means, but he didn't want a woman who would dissect his every word looking for some hidden meaning. For some reason, she couldn't take things at face value when it came to him, and he couldn't understand why.

If he had the time, he would put it at the top of his list to seduce the smart-mouthed Darcy Owens just for the hell of it. If she wanted to misbehave, he could certainly show her what misbehaving was all about. But he had to remember she was the best friend of his godbrother's wife, and Ellie probably wouldn't take too kindly if he seduced her best friend just for the hell of paying her back.

He was about to head over to his side of the hotel when his cell phone rang. He pulled it off his belt and saw it was Wesley Carr, one of the retired police officers that he used as part of his investigative team. It had been his father's idea.

Jerome Ellis had retired a few years ago as a circuit judge. He was a firm believer that retired police officers could better serve as more than just bailiffs at the courthouses. Most had sharp minds and loved the challenge of working on a case. York had taken his father's advice and hired three such men at his firm and never regretted doing so.

"Yes, Wesley, what you got for me?" York asked.

"First of all, are you taking those vitamin supplements I told you about?" Wesley asked.

York shook his head. One of the pitfalls of hiring the men was that they liked to run his life by making sure he got the proper rest, ate healthy and didn't overdo it when it came to women. They claimed all three things would eventually take a toll on a man.

"Yes, I'm taking them, so what do you have?"

"I think Damien Felder might be your man," Wesley said with certainty.

"Why?"

"He has a ton of gambling debts."

York rubbed his chin thoughtfully. "He's a gambler?"

"Of the worst kind. Although he's tried covering his tracks, I was able to trace his ties to the Medina family."

"Damn." The Medina family had their hands into anything illegal they could touch. York hadn't gotten wind of them involved in movie piracy before now, though. Mainly it'd been drugs, prostitution and the transportation of illegal immigrants.

And Roswell Medina's name had been linked to the homicide investigation involving Rhona, the only woman York had ever considered marrying. Like him she had been a police officer and had gotten struck down by a bullet when she had investigated a robbery. The authorities believed the rash of burglaries in Harlem had been organized by Medina but could never prove it.

"I can see them getting interested, if they had the right person on the inside to help them. It's evidently a profitable business," York added.

"Apparently."

He inhaled a deep sigh. He knew Damien Felder would be the one to watch for a while. "I want all the information you can get me on Felder's association with any of the Medinas." He would just love to nail any member of that crime family for something, even if it was for jaywalking.

As he headed back toward his side of the hotel he thought about Darcy and doubted the two of them would be running into each other again any time soon.

Hell, he hoped not.

A TWENTY-PIECE orchestra on the beach.

The hotel had thought of everything, Darcy concluded as she stepped outside. Everyone had been told that tonight's affair was all glitz and glamour, and everyone had dressed to the nines. Men were in tuxes and women were in beautiful gowns. She had decided to wear the short white lace dress and silver sandals she had purchased a few months ago when she had joined Ellie on a shopping spree when she'd visited her best friend in Charlotte.

With a glass of champagne in her hand, Darcy made her way down the white stone steps with towering balustrades on both sides. She could see the beach and see how the water was shimmering beneath the glow of the moon. To her right, tables of food had been set up, and shrimp, lobsters and oysters were being steamed on an open fire.

For those not wanting to get sand in their shoes, a huge wooden deck had been placed on the ground, and several light fixtures provided just the right amount of light to the affair.

She was about to grab another flute of champagne from a passing waiter when she happened to glance across the way and saw a man looking at her. He looked American and she placed his age in his late thirties. And she had to give it to him—he looked like a million bucks in his black tux.

But compared to York there was something lacking. He was handsome, although he wasn't of the jaw-dropping kind like York Ellis. And she would have to be the first to concede that even with all the stranger's handsomeness, she couldn't even conjure up what hero he could represent from those tons of romance novels she had read. She'd had no such problem with York.

She bit down on her lip wondering why she'd just made the comparison. Why had York even crossed her mind? The stranger smiled over at her, and she smiled back before another partier walked up to him and claimed his attention. At least it hadn't been a woman. As she sipped her champagne, she saw him glance over her way, as if assuring himself she was still there—still unattached, possibly still interested.

Deciding not to appear too interested, she began mingling, enjoying the sights and sounds. Moments later, she was leaning against a balustrade watching a group of the island dancers perform. Their movements were so romantic and breathtaking beneath the stars.

"I can tell you are enjoying yourself," a deep, husky male voice said.

The first thought that flashed through her mind was that it wasn't as deep as York's, and it wasn't making her skin feel like it was being caressed. Pushing that observation to the back of her mind, she looked up at the stranger she'd seen earlier and asked, "And just how can you tell?"

"You have that look. And whatever the cause of it, do you mind sharing it because I'm simply bored."

She fought from shaking her head. She had heard that pickup line so many other times, surely the man could have thought of something else. But she could go along with it for now. "Then I guess I need to make sure you enjoy yourself as much as I do."

He smiled, flashing her perfect white teeth. "I would definitely appreciate it." He then held his hand out to her. "I'm Damien Felder, by the way."

She returned his smile. "And I'm Darcy Owens."

"Please to meet you, Darcy. And is that a Midwestern accent I hear?"

"Yes, it is," she replied. "And yours is part southern and part western."

Instead of saying whether her assumption was correct, he took a step closer to her. "Are you staying at this hotel?"

She didn't have to wonder why he was asking. The man was a fast mover, and she had no problem with that if her vibes had been in sync with his. They weren't for some reason. "Yes, I'm at this hotel. What about you?"

"No, my hotel is a few miles from here. I was invited tonight by a friend. But an emergency came up, and he had to leave the island. He encouraged me to come anyway. He thought I would enjoy myself. I hadn't been until I saw you."

She smiled. "Thank you."

"You're welcome. And why would a beautiful woman travel to this island alone?"

She took a sip of her champagne and smiled as she looked up at him. "What makes you think I'm alone?"

A gleam appeared in the depths of his brown eyes. "Because no man with a lick of sense would let you out of his sight for long."

Darcy smiled. The man was full of compliments, although she'd heard most of them before. "I needed a little vacation." And before he could ask her anything else, she decided to ask him a question. "So what brings you to the island?"

"I'm associated with a movie that will be filmed on the island starting tomorrow."

She lifted a brow. "A movie?"

He chuckled. "Yes, one from Spirit Head Productions."

She nodded. She had heard of them. In fact, their main headquarters were in New York. "Let me guess," she said, smiling. "You're the leading man."

From his expression, she could tell he enjoyed getting compliments as much as he enjoyed giving them. "No, I hold an administrative position. I'm a line producer."

"Sounds exciting."

He met her gaze. "It is. How would you like me to give you a tour of the set tomorrow?"

She thought his offer was certainly generous, and she could tell from the way he was looking at her he thought so, too, and expected her to jump at it. So she did, all but clapping her hands in fake excitement. "Oh, that would be wonderful. I'd love to."

"Well then, it's settled. Now how about if I come up to your room tonight so I'll know where to come get you tomorrow."

"I prefer that we meet in the lobby."

She could see the disappointment flash in his eyes. She all but shrugged at the thought. He might eventually share her bed before she left the island, but he would work hard for the privilege. So far she didn't feel a connection to him but was hoping it was just her and not him. For some reason when she looked at him, visions of York entered her mind. And that wasn't good.

"Would you like to take a walk on the beach?"

She smiled. "No. In fact, it's been a tiring day for me. I think I'll call it an early night and go back up to my room now," she said.

"Alone?" he asked.

"Yes, alone. I'm recovering from a flu bug and don't want to overdo it."

"I understand, and I wouldn't want you to overdo it either." He reached into his jacket and pulled out a card. "Here's my business card. Call me when you get up in the morning. Maybe we can share breakfast."

"Thanks, and I will give you a call," she said, taking the card.

"Are you sure you don't need me to walk you back to your room?"

"Thanks for the offer but I'm positive. Good night. I'll see you tomorrow, Damien."

And then she walked off, knowing he was still watching her. She knew he thought he had her within his scope, but he would soon discover that she was the one who had him in hers.

YORK STOOD IN the shadows, behind the orchestra stand, and sipped his wine. He watched the man he'd identified earlier that day as Damien Felder, hitting on Darcy Owens of all people. And from the way the man was still looking at Darcy as she disappeared among the other partiers, he was definitely interested in her. That York could understand. Not only did she have striking features but the dress she was wearing showed a pair of gorgeous legs and a very curvy body.

"Damn." He drew in a deep breath. The man's interest in Darcy was the last thing York needed. Based on the report Wesley had given him earlier, Felder was the last person she should even be talking to. Even Malcolm and his group didn't know half the stuff Damien Felder was involved in, but York didn't plan on sharing any of it with them until he had concrete proof to back it up.

But first he needed to make sure Darcy stayed out of the picture. He had seen the moment Felder had slid his business card into the palm of her hand. Since York could read lips—something he taught himself to do after his sister was born deaf—he knew that Felder had invited her on set tomorrow. He wasn't sure what her response had been since Felder had been the one facing him, while Darcy's back had been to him.

The man had also tried inviting himself up to Darcy's room, which she apparently turned down since she had left the party alone. At least York was grateful for that. He felt a deep pull in his stomach and tried convincing himself that the only reason he was grateful was because he was looking out for her. After all, she was Ellie's best friend, so that was the least he could do. Wanting to keep her out of the picture had nothing to do with the jealousy he'd felt when he'd seen Felder approach her. He assured himself that it hadn't been jealousy, just concern. Besides, too much was at stake with this case, and the last thing he needed was Darcy screwing things up.

He was about to leave when he noticed Felder giving the nod to another woman at the party. He recognized her immediately—Danielle Simone, the leading lady in the movie they were filming. Malcolm was pretty convinced that Danielle was not in any way a part of the black market ring. Now York wasn't so sure when he watched as she walked toward the beach with Felder following her, keeping a careful distance.

Interesting. He couldn't help wonder what that was about. Were the two having a secret affair? His cell phone rang, and he picked it up. It was one of his men who was attending the party undercover. "Yes, Mark, I picked up on the two. Follow them from here, and let me know where they go and what they do."

He clicked off the phone, satisfied his man was on it and wouldn't let the couple out of his sight. York then turned toward the part of the hotel where Darcy's room was located.

DARCY HAD SHOWERED and slipped into the hotel's complimentary bathrobe when she heard a knock on her hotel room door. She frowned, wondering who it could be. It was way past midnight, although she was sure a number of people were still at the party having a good time.

She crossed the room to look out the peephole in the door, and a frown settled around her mouth. *York Ellis.* Why on earth would he visit her room, and most importantly, how did he know her room number? She knew for certain that she had not given it to him.

Knowing he was the only person who could answer that question, she tightened the belt around her robe before taking off the lock and snatching open the door. "York, what on earth are you doing here, and how do you know my room number?"

"We need to talk."

"What?" she asked as she nearly drowned in the dark eyes staring down at her. She'd always thought they were such a gorgeous pair—although she would never admit such a thing to him or anyone else for that matter. She wouldn't even confess it to Ellie. Nor would she ever mention how heat would course through her body whenever he stood this close to her. She'd noticed it that first time they'd met, which was why she had deliberately avoided him. The last thing she had needed at the time was to be attracted to a man after what she'd gone through with her ex-husband.

"I said we need to talk, Darcy."

She stiffened her spine and glared at him. "Why? And you haven't answered my question. How did you get my room number?"

He leaned in the doorway, and her gaze watched his every movement at the same time her nostrils inhaled his manly scent. Her heart skipped a beat when her gaze roamed over him. He looked good in a tux. Had he attended the party when he'd said earlier that day that he wouldn't be doing so?

"I have ways of finding out anything I want to know, Darcy."

The deep huskiness of his voice had her gaze returning back to his. Even leaning in the doorway, he was towering over her. For some reason, her gaze shifted to his hands. This wasn't the first time she had noticed just how large they were. Heat spread throughout her body when she recalled the theory about the size of a man's hands and feet in comparison to another part of his anatomy. Automatically her gaze shifted to his feet.

"Looking for anything in particular?"

She snatched her gaze up to him. He had caught her checking him out again. "No, I was just thinking." That wasn't a total lie. He didn't have to know what she was thinking about. "And as far as you having ways of finding out whatever you want to know…well, that's probably true, but you won't hold a single conversation with me unless you tell me what it's about."

He rubbed his hand down his face as if annoyed with her. "It's about Damien Felder. You were flirting with him at the party tonight."

They were flirting with each other, but his impression of how things had been meant nothing to her. "I thought you weren't going to the party."

"I changed my mind."

"And you know Damien?"

He shook his head. "No, but I know *of* Damien, which is what I want to talk to you about."

There was no denying that York had her curious. "Very well, come in."

She took a step back, and he entered her hotel room and closed the door behind him. He glanced around the room, and when his gaze returned to her, it seemed the intensity in the depths of his eyes was pinning her in place.

She drew in a deep breath, refusing to get caught like a deer in the headlights where he was concerned. So she tightened the sash of her robe around her even more and broke eye contact with him and beckoned him to the sofa. "Have a seat and let's talk."

She watched him move to the sofa while heat spread throughout her body. He looked too darn comfortable for her liking. There was something about the way he was sitting, with his arms spread across the back of the sofa, that made her want to slide down on the sofa with him, ease the tux jacket off his shoulders and run her hands across the broad width of his chest.

Where on earth had those thoughts come from? This was York Ellis, the one man she didn't get along with, the one man who seemed to enjoy rubbing her the wrong way whenever their paths crossed. "What about Damien?" she spoke up and asked, reminding herself the only reason he was sitting on her sofa was because she was interested in what he had to say.

For some reason, the mention of Damien made him lean closer, cause something akin to anger to flash across his features. "You met him tonight."

She heard the censure in his tone and wondered the reason for it. "Yes, and why do you care?"

Evidently her question stumped him. The irritation in his face was replaced by a slow smile, one that didn't quite reach his eyes. "Personally, I don't other than the fact that you're screwing things up for me and my investigation."

She bit down on her lips as she struggled to keep a civil tongue. "What investigation?"

As he sat back, York drew in a deep breath, trying to calm the anger that was flowing through him. And it was anger he could not explain. What she did and who she did it with was her business. He shouldn't care one bit, and he had tried convincing himself that he didn't. But the truth of the matter was that he did. There was no way he would allow her to blindly walk into a dangerous situation.

"I wasn't absolutely up front with you earlier today when I gave my reason for being here on the island."

"You weren't?"

"No. I'm here on a job. My company was hired by a group of moviemakers for security detail on a movie being filmed, the same one Felder is associated with. And while my outfit is doing that, I'm working behind the scenes to protect their interest. Someone is slipping the movies to the black market before their theatrical release."

She lifted a brow. "And what does that have to do with Damien Felder?"

It was hard to explain why a part of him wanted to kiss her and strangle her at the same time. What was there about her that could drive him to such extremes? "I have reason to believe Felder might be involved in some way."

"Do you have any proof?"

"No."

"Then it's merely speculation on your part."

"For now. But he is being watched, and if he is guilty, I would hate for your name to be linked to his."

She glared at him. "And what if your suspicions are wrong? Do you expect me not to enjoy the company of a man because you think he might be involved in some case you're investigating?"

"I was hoping that you would. And as far as me suspecting him, I'm almost sure he's my man. I wouldn't have come to you if I didn't."

Darcy wondered just why he had. They weren't friends, so his concern about her had nothing to do with it. He must have been truthful earlier when he'd said she had the potential of screwing things up for him.

She stood. "Okay, you've warned me. I'll walk you to the door."

He remained sitting. "And what the hell does that mean?" he asked.

The anger in his tone made her lift her chin. "It means just what I said, York. You've warned me. Now you can leave."

"But you will take my advice."

To Darcy, it sounded more like a direct order than a question. "No, I don't plan to take your advice. Unless you have something more concrete than assumptions, I see no reason not to see Damien again. In fact, we've made plans for later today."

He held her gaze, and she could see the fire in his eyes. He was so angry with her that he was almost baring his teeth. He slowly leaned forward in his seat, and in a tone of voice tinged with a growl, he asked, "Why are you being difficult?"

She curved her lips into a smile only because she knew it would get on his last nerve. "Because I want to."

She knew she was being childish. Pretty darn petty, in fact, when for whatever his reason, he had come to warn her about Damien. She had no intentions of telling him that the warning was not needed since she wasn't attracted to Damien and didn't plan on seeing him again after their date that day. And the only reason she was keeping her date with him was because she'd always wanted to check out a movie set, nothing more. Even with Damien's handsome looks, he hadn't done anything for her.

And definitely not in the way the man sitting on her sofa was doing. Even now she was struggling, trying hard to fight the attraction, the magnetic pull, especially since it was an attraction she didn't want or need. And it was an attraction she didn't intend to go anywhere.

"You like rattling me, don't you, Darcy?"

His words pulled her attention back to the present. She figured there was no need to lie. "Yes, I guess I do."

Darcy didn't think there could be anything sexy about a man who merely stood up from sitting on a sofa. But with York, watching his body in movement was enough to cause heat to flare in her center and the juncture of her thighs.

And when he slowly walked toward her, advancing on her like he was the hunter and she his prey, she merely stood her ground. She refused to back up or retreat. And it seemed he had no intentions of halting his approach until he came to a stop in front of her.

"I've heard of stubborn women before, but you have to be the stubbornest."

She glared up at him. "I'll take that as a compliment, York. Now if you don't mind, it's late and you need to leave."

York thought some women had to be born for trouble, and this one standing in front of him was one of them. Against his better judgment, he had come here tonight to give her fair warning and he had done so. If she didn't want to heed to his warnings, there was nothing he could do about it.

He tried to push the thought from his mind that while he'd been sitting on the sofa, whether she knew it or not, he had been fighting desire for her that had all but seeped into his bones. Why on earth would he be attracted to her of all women?

Before he'd come up to her room tonight, he'd been approached by a couple of women who'd all but invited him to their hotel room. One had brazenly offered to give him a blow job right there on the elevator. But he hadn't wanted any of them. He wanted this one. This haughty-looking female, who had blood firing through his veins, who was staring him down and standing in front of him looking as sexy as any woman had a right to look in a bathrobe.

He glared down at her when the room got too quiet for his taste. "Don't say I didn't warn you."

"I won't. Now goodbye, York."

At that moment, something inside of him snapped. She was glaring at him, yet earlier tonight she'd been smiling at Damien Felder. Not only had she been smiling but she'd also flirted with the man. "You like pushing my buttons, don't you, Darcy?"

"Yes," she said, smiling. "Gives me great pleasure."

"No, this is pleasure." And then he reached out, pulled her to him and captured her mouth with his.

# CHAPTER THREE

HE WAS RIGHT, Darcy thought, when York began kissing her with a hunger that surprised her. This was pleasure. And it began overwhelming her as sensations tore through her. When she felt those big hands she'd checked out earlier tighten their hold on her, she became wrapped in his heat with every languorous stroke of his tongue. That was all it took for desire to start coiling deep in her body, thickening the blood rushing through her veins. And when she released a surprised gasp, he slid his tongue deeper inside her mouth.

He shifted, and his body pressed hard against her and she felt him—his aroused thickness. His hardness. It was poking her in the belly. A part of her wanted to push him away. But another part wanted to draw him even closer. She knew what part won when a moan flowed from deep within her throat. Instinctively, she eased up on tiptoes to return the kiss with the same demand and hunger he was putting into it. And when her tongue tried battling his for control, his arms tightened even more around her, almost crushing her body to his. Easing upward shifted his aroused part from her belly right to the juncture of her thighs, and immediately she could feel her panties get wet.

York's heart was hammering hard in his chest. He didn't understand why he was kissing Darcy this way, a woman he'd convinced himself that he didn't even like. Evidently his personal feelings toward her had nothing to do with lust, and he was convinced that was what was filling his mind at that moment. That was what had him eating away at her mouth as if it was the last meal he would have. And she was kissing him back with just as much intensity. It seemed as if a floodgate had burst open, and they didn't know how to stop the lusty water from rushing through.

*They didn't know or they didn't* want *to know?*

At that moment, it didn't matter to him, and he had a feeling it didn't matter to her either. He wanted her, and from the way she was kissing him back, she wanted him as well. And if she didn't let up on his tongue he was certain he was going to lose his mind. He hadn't made love to a woman in a while, and he couldn't recall one being this passionate, this aggressive, this damn hot. He had initiated the kiss, but there was a big question as to who was being seduced.

Suddenly, he pulled back, reached out and ripped the bathrobe off her body. Just as he thought, she was completely naked underneath.

"What do you think you're doing?" she asked, inhaling a deep breath of air.

He glanced over at her while tearing off his own clothes, not believing she had to ask. But just in case she had any intentions of suddenly deciding she didn't want this as much as he did, he stopped short of removing his slacks. Instead he reached out, pulled her to him and captured her mouth once more.

Darcy couldn't help the moan that eased from deep in her throat. Had it really been two years since she'd felt sensations like this? Sure, there'd been Bruce, but York was showing her that when it came to hot sex between a man and woman, there was nothing like the real thing. A sex toy couldn't compare.

She felt everything. The hardness of his erection was pressed against her center, the material of his tux was rubbing against her thigh causing all kinds of sensations to erupt within her. And when she felt those large hands of his stroke the soft skin of her backside, molding her cheeks closer to him, she couldn't do anything but surrender. He had blazed a fire that was consuming them both.

Knowing she was capitulating didn't sit too well with her, but every stroke of his tongue in her mouth was making her appreciate the benefits. The man didn't intend to hold anything back, and she decided at that moment, neither would she.

She'd had all intentions of having an island fling, so there was no stopping her now. Besides, this would be a one-night stand. She would merely use him to take the two-year edge off, since he seemed to know just what he was doing.

He broke off the kiss, and his gaze burned into hers as he kicked off his shoes before easing his pants and briefs down his legs all at once. Her breath got caught in her throat when her gaze lowered. Maybe that saying about the size of feet and hands in comparison to other parts of a man's body wasn't just a theory at all. It was a truth.

Her gaze moved back to his face, and she wasn't sure who made the first move—nor did she care. All she cared about was that she was in his arms again while

he kissed her with a madness she felt to her toes. And
she was convinced what they were doing was sheer
madness. A thought entered her mind that maybe they
should slow down and talk about it. Then she decided
there was no need to waste time talking.

He tore his mouth from hers, and the look she saw
in his eyes indicated his agreement. "I want to get inside you, Darcy."

He couldn't have said it any plainer than that, she
thought. She went to him and then spread her hands
out across his stomach. His skin felt hot beneath her
fingers, and that same heat spread through her when
she moved her hands lower. When her hand pressed
against the thickness of his muscular thighs, she felt
a stirring in the pit of her stomach. The intensity of it
was almost frightening.

She was convinced the desire taking over her mind
and her body had nothing to do with York per se but
with the fact that he was a man. But not just any man.
He was a red-hot, good-looking man who had the ability
to shoot adrenaline up her spine in very high dosages.

And she couldn't discount the fact that she hadn't
slept with a man in almost two years, not since moving
to New York. Before then, thanks to her ex-husband,
she had washed her hands of men. She found there was
too much drama where they were concerned. Bruce had
been given to her as a prank gift and she—who'd never
considered using a sex toy before—had discovered in
time of need he could be her best friend.

But now York was reminding her in a very explosive
way that there was nothing like a flesh-and-blood male.
Nothing like a real man breathing down your neck,

kissing you, touching you, letting you touch him. And at that moment, it didn't matter one iota that the man causing her so much sumptuous turbulence was the one man she thought she didn't even like.

She might have regrets for her actions in the morning, but at that very moment, she wanted him, too. She wanted him inside of her.

Her breaths were coming out in tortured moans when she lowered her hand and touched his erection. Ignoring his masculine growl, she cupped him, loving the feel of his hardness in her hand, loving the heat of it. It was rock hard. Solid. Big. And when she began running her thumb over the shaft's head, wanting to feel the protruding veins beneath her fingertips, she felt him shudder in her hand.

She imagined in the deep recesses of her mind this same solid flesh sliding all the way inside of her and how her muscles would clench it, possess it, milk it for everything it was worth and then some. It had been a long time for her, way too long. She was greedy and wanted it all.

She glanced up at him, met his gaze through desire-glazed eyes and saw the state of his arousal in the dark eyes staring right back at her.

"Condom?" she asked him almost in a moan. When he nodded and made a move to step back, she had to release him and immediately felt the loss.

And then he took time to remove his socks before retrieving a condom packet from his wallet. As if having a woman watch him don a condom was the most natural thing, he proceeded to put on protection.

She was suddenly engulfed in strong arms when York swept her off her feet to carry her to the bedroom.

YORK COULD NOT recall when he'd wanted a woman this much. And why did that woman have to be Darcy Owens? He should find the very thought unsettling, but at the moment too much desire was running through his body to be concerned with emotions he wasn't used to.

He figured there had to be a full moon out tonight, or maybe there was something to that passion fruit he'd had at lunch. Regardless, tomorrow and the days that followed he was certain he would be back on track—revert to his right mind and be ruled by logic and less by lust. He shouldn't have any problems keeping his distance from Darcy during his remaining time on the island.

But at this very moment his thoughts, his actions were ruled by a yearning that had taken over his entire body. Deep down, he knew it was almost two years in the works. He had wanted her the first time he'd seen her at Ellie and Uriel's wedding. He had even warned his other godbrothers to keep their distance. And when she had snubbed him, told him in no uncertain words that she wasn't interested, his attraction had turned to outright dislike. He hadn't taken her rejection well.

That's why one of the most satisfying things for him right now was to know she was as much of a goner as he was. She definitely wasn't rejecting him now. The thought made him smile as he placed her on the bed and then took a step back. Seeing her naked body in the middle of the king-size bed made him more aroused, especially when the mass of dark brown hair looked in total disarray around her shoulders. She looked sexy. She looked hot. She looked as if she was ready for anything he had to give her. And tonight he had plenty.

But she intended to play the vixen. He figured as

much when she deliberately stretched to make her breasts lift at an angle that made them appear ready for his mouth. And her legs slowly opened, showing how ripe, wet and ready she was. A fierce need ripped through him, and he moved back toward the bed. He was well aware of the rules he would be breaking about never losing control when it came to a woman.

He chuckled. It was too late. He'd already lost it. And he would make sure that her payback for driving him over the edge was a night she wouldn't forget. He knew for certain that he wouldn't.

York moved toward the bed, and his main thought was to reconnect his mouth to hers. He pulled her toward him and captured her mouth. There was something about her taste that had him wanting more. But she seemed just as ravenous as he and was returning his stroke lick for lick.

He broke off the kiss and lowered his gaze from her wet lips down her breasts, and he saw how her nipples were hardening to stiff buds right before his eyes. He felt all his senses begin to flash and his tongue all but thicken in his mouth with thoughts of just what he wanted to do with those nipples.

"You want to taste them, York? If so, don't let me stop you."

Her words had him glancing up. She must have seen the intensity in his gaze when he'd been staring at her breasts. He found a woman who spoke her mind in the bedroom pretty refreshing. But then he wasn't surprised that was the tactic an outspoken woman like Darcy would use.

His gaze lowered back to her nipples. Yes, he wanted to taste them. He was getting harder just thinking about all the things he'd liked doing to them with his mouth. But he wouldn't stop at her breasts. He intended to taste every inch of her and felt he should at least warn her.

"Your breasts aren't the only thing I want to taste, Darcy." He didn't feel he had to go into specifics. And just the thought rocked his senses.

York immediately drew a turgid nipple into his mouth and began devouring it with a greed he knew she'd feel all the way to her toes but especially at her center. And speaking of her center...

His hand found its target at the juncture of her thighs, and sensations sizzled through him, making him ache. His fingers spread her apart first, then delved into her heated wetness, and he felt his erection throb in response.

She moaned when he allowed his mouth to pay homage to the other nipple, letting his tongue lap at it a few times before easing it between his lips. He sucked on it while a lusty rush filled him, obliterated his senses and sent a fierce need rushing through his bloodstream.

And when he couldn't hold back any longer, he pulled away from her breasts and went straight to the source of her heat. Lifting her hips, he lowered his mouth to her, intent on licking every inch of her and lapping up her dewy wetness, tasting her until he got his fill. He wanted every lusty cell in his body to be satisfied.

Darcy began trembling the exact moment she felt the heat of York's tongue ease inside of her, and it became nearly impossible to breathe. All she could do was whimper in pleasure. So she did. He knew what he was doing by using his tongue to stroke her. He was so skilled that it had her shaking from head to toe. He felt her shudders and was lapping up every single shiver.

She needed to grab hold of something, and the bedspread just wouldn't do. So she reached for his head instead. She held him steady, kept him in place, but the feel of his tongue moving inside of her was too much. Her fingers clenched the side of his head the moment her world exploded in a orgasm that detonated every part of her body.

And she heard herself call his name. It was a blazing rush from her lips, a satisfying ache that she felt when his tongue delved deeper, lapped harder. She was transformed into a mass of lusty mush, and it had to be the most exquisite feeling she'd ever encountered. This single act was worth the two years she'd gone without.

When she felt him release her and pull out his tongue, she almost screamed her regret. Watching through passion-glazed eyes, she saw him straddle her, felt the hardness of him replace his tongue to ease inside of her, stretching her to the point where she wondered if they would fit and knowing he would die trying.

As if her body was made just for him, her insides expanded, got wetter, felt slicker. He continued to push his way inside, and she gazed up at him, saw the beads of perspiration on his brow. He lifted her hips, intent on her taking him, receiving him and welcoming him.

When he had reached her hilt, he began moving, stroking her with a rhythm that had every cell in her body, every single molecule responding. The heat of his skin rubbed against her thighs as he thrust back and forth, going deeper and deeper with every stroke. Her clit was on fire, and he wasn't trying to put out the flames. Instead, he was taking the flames higher, sparking every single ember inside of her.

And she clenched him, refusing to let him take without giving. She began milking him and felt her muscles tighten then pull to get the full benefit, maximize the sensual effect of what he was doing to her. The bed was shaking in its frame as he rode her in a way she'd never been ridden before. And his shaft seemed to get bigger and harder inside of her.

Just when she thought she couldn't take any more, she was pushed over the edge, and her body erupted in a colossal explosion. Her fingers dug into the muscles of his shoulders, and the lower part of her lifted off the bed with the massive blast. He growled when he pressed harder into her body, spreading her thighs apart even more.

York was replacing two years of pent-up, half filled, half measured pleasure. Before now what she'd assumed was satisfaction had only been appeasement. This was better than anything she could have imagined from any man or toy. It was beyond her wildest dream—and over the years she'd had plenty of wild dreams. But none could compare to this reality.

He continued to ride her, continued to pound into her, intent on getting in the last stroke, gratifying her every pulsation as well as his own.

"York…"

She heard the sound of his name from her lips as she continued to come, but she couldn't make herself stop as pleasure continued to hold her in its grip. She knew if she never made love to another man again she would have memories of tonight stored away in the back of her mind.

"Darcy…"

The rough and deep sound of his voice rushed over her, made her body respond the way it had never responded to a man before. She looked up into his dark gaze. He had slowed down but not stopped. And then he slowly began easing from her body when all of a sudden he thrust right back in all the way to the hilt. He lowered his head and whispered in her ear in a deep, primitive growl. "I want more."

And in response, she wrapped her legs around him as she felt need coupled with desire rush through her veins, overtake her senses. Tonight she would give him more because giving him more meant she was taking just as much for herself.

DAYBREAK WAS PEEKING through the window blinds when York glanced over his shoulder at Darcy. He slowly eased from the bed, determined not to wake her. Drawing in a deep breath, he tried to regain control of his senses while piecing together everything that had happened last night in this room. He should feel vindicated at having seduced her, but instead he was wondering who had seduced whom.

He'd known before last night there was sexual attraction between them, which was the cause of a lot of their bickering. But he hadn't known until last night just how much he'd wanted her—not just to prove a point or to right what he'd considered a wrong. He refused to think making love to her had anything to do with revenge or getting back at her. And he refused to consider the pleasure had been one-sided. She hadn't shown resistance to anything they'd done in that bed.

And hell, they had done a lot. He hadn't known a woman's skin could taste so luscious or that hazel eyes could turn so many different shades while in the throes of heated passion. Nor had he known that a woman could ride just as hard as a man.

Even when he had fought to keep himself in check and to regain control, he'd found his efforts wasted. Darcy had given him the kind of pleasure he hadn't shared with any woman before her. That said a lot, considering his reputation.

Before leaving her bedroom, he glanced over his shoulder. She was still sleeping, and he understood why. They had made love almost nonstop through the night. One orgasm was followed by another. The pleasure had been too intense to even think about stopping, and she hadn't complained. In fact, she had kept up with him all the way. At that very moment, he didn't see Darcy Owens as a woman with a smart mouth but as a woman who definitely knew how to use that mouth.

She was lying on top of the covers, and he couldn't stop his gaze from roaming over her naked body. Passion marks were visible on her thighs, stomach and around her breasts, and he could immediately recall the exact moment he'd placed each of them there. He shook his head and glanced down at himself. He had a number of passion marks on his body as well. Darcy definitely believed in equal play.

York glanced back at her and felt his body grow hard all over again. He drew in a deep breath and forced his gaze from her or else he'd be tempted to crawl back in bed with her, hold her in his arms and patiently wait until she awakened. Then he would make love to her all over again.

Damn. He was losing control again, becoming undone. Okay, he had enjoyed the Darcy experience, but he needed to regroup and remember the reason he was in Jamaica. And it wasn't to spend his time in Darcy Owens's bed.

But still, he wasn't sure if they understood each other where Damien Felder was concerned. She had started out defying him, and in the end, she still hadn't yielded to his way of thinking. He hoped what they shared last night gave her other ideas on the matter. He truly couldn't see how it couldn't.

And there was another thing he had to consider. He had gotten so into making love to her that he'd done something else he usually didn't do. He had taken risks by not putting on a new condom at the start of each lovemaking session. Although he wanted to believe it was a long shot, what if she was pregnant at this very moment?

*Hell, York, don't even go there, man,* a part of his mind screamed. *She's probably on the Pill, which means that although you got sloppy this one time, she managed to save the day...or in this case, the night.*

When she shifted her position in the bed he took a step back, feeling the need to put distance between them and knowing it would be best if he wasn't there when she woke up. There was no telling what frame of mind she would be in, and he didn't want her making it seem as though making love was all his idea. Nor did he want to hear that she regretted anything about their time together—especially when he had no regrets.

Once in her living room, he quickly picked up his clothes off the floor and put them on. He glanced at the clock on one of the tables and saw the time was six in the morning. Chances were he would be getting a lot of strange looks when he made his way from one part of the hotel to the other still wearing a tux. But then chances were anyone who saw him would figure out why. Liaisons were a way of life.

He crossed the room to glance into the bedroom once again before leaving. She was still sleeping like a baby, and as much as he wished otherwise, a part of him regretted that he wouldn't be there when she woke up.

# CHAPTER FOUR

DARCY STIRRED AWAKE when the sun spilled in through the window to hit her right in the face. But she refused to open her eyes just yet. She expected at any moment to feel York's warm breath on her neck or have his aroused body part—one that she'd gotten to know up close and personal—cuddle close to her backside, right smack against her bare cheeks. And she wouldn't mind it at all if he threw one of his legs over her. Nor would she care if he were to run his fingers through her hair.

But as she continued to lie there all she heard was silence and felt no human contact. Moments ticked by, and she flipped onto her back and glanced over at the empty spot beside her. Had York gotten up to use the bathroom?

Easing out of bed, she went into the bathroom and found it empty. She then strolled to the living room and found it vacant as well. Her bathrobe was tossed across the sofa, and his clothes that had littered the floor last night were gone. That meant he was wearing them.

Disappointment settled in her chest, and for a moment she wondered just what she had expected. York had handled last night for what it had been—a one-night stand. Why had she assumed he would think of it as anything more? Why did she care that he hadn't? And why was she taking it as a personal affront?

Both men and women had meaningless sexual liaisons all the time. She had even caught the plane from New York with plans to have a fling, had even joked with Ellie about it. But that was when she would have been in total control, and the man was to have been a stranger. Someone who wouldn't leave any lingering affects or someone she wouldn't miss once the moments passed. In other words, she hadn't expected York Ellis to be so overpowering, so overwhelming, so doggone good between the sheets that her body still throbbed between her legs.

She slid into her robe as she recalled her actions and behavior of the night. Red-hot embarrassment reddened her cheeks. She had gotten wild and outrageous. She guessed two years of celibacy could do that to you. And she didn't need to look at her body to know there were probably passion marks all over every inch of her skin. And she was certain he was sporting his fair share of the marks as well.

She ran her hands through her hair, frustrated. No matter how good the sex had been, she could literally kick herself for tumbling into bed with York. They didn't even like each other, although it was apparent they'd gotten along pretty well between the sheets. He had made her feel things she hadn't ever felt.

And after each lovemaking session, before they would start all over again, he would hold her tenderly in his arms. She certainly hadn't expected that. There had been something so calming and relaxing to lie there in his arms. And when she had dozed off to sleep that last time, weary after rounds and rounds of lovemaking, she had assumed he would be there whenever she woke up.

Wrong. He had skipped out like a thief in the night. It was hard to explain why she felt so annoyed about it but she was. His actions were probably his M.O. when it came to a woman. Why had she assumed things would be different with her?

Fine, he could continue to handle his business that same way. It meant nothing to her. In fact, now that they'd gotten what they'd undoubtedly wanted from each other, she hoped she didn't run into him again while she was here. He wouldn't be the first man she'd written off.

Her marriage to Harold Calhoun had started out like a storybook romance. They had met in college and had married soon after graduation. But within a year after living under the same roof, she had discovered things about her husband she hadn't known—like the fact that he had a tendency to get abusive at times. The verbal abuse was bad enough, but the first time he'd tried getting physically abusive with her, it had been his last time. He had found out, much to his detriment, that his wife could defend herself so well, he'd been the one hovering in a corner pleading for mercy by the time the authorities had arrived.

She drew in a deep breath and turned toward her bedroom. She then recalled York's words to her about Damien Felder. As far as she was concerned, a man was innocent of any crime until proven guilty. Besides, she doubted had it been Damien who'd slept with her last night he would have left the way York had done, without even a wham, bam, thank you ma'am.

And speaking of Damien…

It was probably too late to join him for breakfast, but she would keep her date with him to let him show her around the movie set. She was a big girl who could handle herself, regardless of what York thought. And frankly, what he thought didn't matter to her.

She would arrange to meet Damien just as she'd planned. She had gotten what she wanted from York, and she was confident he'd gotten what he wanted from her. They were even. Now things could go back to how they'd always been between them.

YORK GLANCED AROUND the movie set. Today the location was a cottage on the beach where the scene would be shot. The crew and equipment were in place, and the cast was in their individual trailers getting the attention of the hair and makeup artists.

He had been introduced earlier and was told his job was to provide backup security to the production team since they would be filming in several parts of the island, some less than desirable.

Several members of his security group would keep that focus while others worked undercover to identify who was crippling the production in another way. So far Damien Felder hadn't shown up on set, and York hadn't missed the whispered jokes of several crew members as to why. A number were wondering whose bed he'd spent the night in. Evidently, Felder was a known playboy. So far, no one had linked Felder's name with that of the leading lady, and York found that slightly odd since very few secrets survived on a movie set. Someone was working extremely hard to keep their affair a secret. He definitely found that interesting.

"Um, looks like Damien has been busy," someone whispered behind York, and he glanced up to see Damien walk in with Darcy at his side. At that moment,

York discovered firsthand what it meant to see bloodred. What the hell was she doing here with him? Hadn't she listened to anything he'd told her about Felder last night?

And he could tell from the whispers behind him that many assumed she had been Felder's sleeping partner last night. He was tempted to turn around and tell them how wrong they were since she had been his. But just the thought that she was getting whispered about, by those who didn't even know her and who assumed false things about her, pissed him off to the point where he was fighting intense anger within him.

He continued to pretend to peruse documents on a clipboard while watching Felder show Darcy around. It was obvious he was trying to impress her, probably was working real hard to get into her bed tonight or to get her in his. The thought of either happening set York on edge, made him madder.

"Ellis, I need to introduce you to Felder," Bob Crowder, the production manager, said.

York glanced up. "Fine. Let's do it," he said, placing the clipboard aside and trying to keep the hardness from his tone.

They crossed the room to where Felder stood with Darcy by his side near a tray of coffee and donuts. He smelled her before he got within ten feet of her. Aside from the cologne she was wearing, she had a unique feminine scent that could probably drive men wild. He wondered if he was the only man who detected it and quickly realized he had reason to know it so well. Her aroma had gotten absorbed into his nostrils pretty damn good last night.

"Damien, I need to introduce you to the guy who

owns the company we're using for security now," Crowder said, snagging Felder's attention.

Felder turned and gave York a once-over before asking, "What happened to the other company that was hired?"

"Evidently, they didn't work out," York responded before Crowder could. Felder really was in no position to ask questions.

"And you think your outfit will be able to do a better job?" Felder asked.

York smiled, well aware that Darcy was staring at him, listening attentively. At least she hadn't let on that they knew each other, and he was grateful for that. "I *know* we'll do a better job." He figured his response sounded pretty damn confident, overly cocky to an extreme, but that sort of attitude was probably one Felder could relate to.

Felder proved him right when his lips curved into a smile. "Hey, York Ellis. I like you."

It was on the tip of York's tongue to respond that the feeling wasn't mutual. Instead, he said, "My job is not to get you to like me, Felder, but to make sure you and everyone else who're part of this production are safe."

York knew his statement was establishing his persona as a no-nonsense sort of guy. That's what he wanted. He'd heard Felder had a tendency to try and cozy up to those in charge so when he decided to break rules they would look the other way. It was good to let the man know up front he wouldn't allow it and not to waste his time trying to earn brownie points.

He then shifted his gaze from Felder to Darcy. "And you are?"

York knew Felder assumed he was asking for security reasons. Darcy opened her mouth to respond, but Felder beat her to the punch. "She's with me, Ellis, and her name is Darcy Owens. She's my guest."

York nodded as he glanced down at the clipboard in his hand. "Her name isn't on the list, Felder." He could tell from Felder's expression that the man didn't appreciate being called out on breaking one of the production rules about bringing visitors on set.

"I made her an exception," Felder said, smiling.

"There are no exceptions around here," York said, not returning the smile. "In the future, make sure all exceptions are cleared by me first."

He glanced over at Darcy and saw her glaring at him, actually saw a spark of fire in her eyes. He then turned to Crowder. "I need to check on a few other things around here."

"All right, come on," Crowder said, before leading him away. York didn't say anything else to the couple, just merely nodded before walking off.

"HE's NOT GOING to last around here long," Darcy heard Damien mutter as they watched York leave.

"Why do you say that?" she asked, curious to know. She felt York's annoyance at seeing her as well as his immediate dislike of Damien. It was funny how well she could read him.

"He's trying to throw his weight around much too soon. I'd heard the bigwigs were sending in some new guy to handle security, but I can tell he's not going to work out. I don't like the fact that he questioned anything about you when you were with me."

She shrugged. "I'm sure he was just doing his job."

It wasn't that she was taking up for York's brash behavior but she didn't want to do anything to blow whatever cover he had, although she still wasn't convinced Damien was someone he should be watching. York had his reasons for being here on the island and she had hers. She intended to have a good time and enjoy herself.

Damien gave her a tour of the set while telling her bits and pieces of what scenes they would be shooting. Every once in a while she would glance over to where York was standing and find him staring hard at her. She would stare back. It seemed things were back to normal with them.

At least they were to a degree. Since sharing a bed with him she felt an intimate connection that she didn't want to feel. She could no longer look at his large hands and wonder. Now she knew. She couldn't look at his mouth without remembering all the naughty things his lips and tongue could do. Even from across the room he was emitting a heat that could sear her. Knowing that was the last thing she wanted, she let out a deep sigh.

"What's wrong? Am I boring you?"

She glanced up and forced a smile at Damien. "No, in fact I'm a little overwhelmed by it all. The next time I go to a movie I'm going to appreciate all the behind-the-scenes things it took to bring the movie to the big screen."

"Now you know." He glanced at his watch. "How would you like to have lunch with me? And then I can take you back to your hotel, let you rest up a bit and then we can go out tonight. I heard there's a club that's a hot spot on the island. I would love to take you dancing."

His suggestion sounded good, and there was no reason she shouldn't have lunch with him or go dancing at the club. Her smile widened and she said, "That sounds wonderful. I'd love to."

OUT OF THE corner of his eye, York watched Darcy leave with Felder, and his heart banged against his chest causing a deep, hard thump. What the hell was wrong with him? He had gone above and beyond by warning her about the man, yet she still was with him today. It was as if she'd deliberately ignored what he'd said about Damien Felder.

"Looks like Damien's got another looker."

York turned around slowly to face the production's leading man, Johnny Rush. He'd officially met the man yesterday. "Yeah, looks that way," he said dryly, as if the thought of who Felder was with didn't interest him in the least.

He knew that Malcolm was convinced Rush and Danielle Simone were in no way involved in the bootlegging activity, but as far as York was concerned, there was still a possibility. At least he was suspicious of Simone since she and Felder had met up somewhere last night.

"I wonder where they met."

He studied the man's features. "Is there any reason you want to know?"

Johnny shook his head and chuckled. "No, in fact I'm happy for him. Maybe now he'll leave Danielle alone."

York couldn't help wondering why Rush felt the need to drop that information. Since he wasn't sure, he decided to play it out as much as he could. "I didn't know he and Ms. Simone had something going on."

He saw the frown settle on Johnny's face. "They

don't. Damien thinks he's someone important with this outfit and has been trying to box her into an affair. But she's not interested in him."

York nodded and decided not to say that wasn't the way he'd seen things last night. "And that bothers you?"

The man met his gaze and held it. "Yes, I want Danielle for myself."

The man couldn't get any plainer than that. Again, York wondered what purpose Johnny had for revealing that…unless the man assumed York would develop a roving eye where Danielle Simone was concerned. He decided to quickly squash that idea. "Good luck. I know how it feels when a man truly wants a woman."

Johnny lifted a brow. "Do you?"

"Yes. There's a woman I'm all into back in New York. She's the only woman for me." He said the lie so Johnny wouldn't think he was a threat.

"You engaged?" Johnny asked.

"Not yet. I'm thinking of popping the question around the holidays," York lied further. What he'd just told Johnny was a whopper. There was no way he was thinking about proposing to any woman around the holidays.

"Hey, man, congratulations. I'm thinking about asking Danielle myself around the holidays."

York lifted a brow. "Things are *that* serious between you two?"

Johnny beamed. "Not yet but they will be. I'm working on it now that my divorce is final. She is destined to become the next Mrs. Johnny Rush."

York held his tongue from saying that would probably come as a surprise to Danielle. One of his men had followed Danielle and Felder to their lovers' hideaway on the beach last night. And from the man's report, he had seen enough to let him know the two were involved, and it wasn't all Felder's doing as Johnny assumed.

"Where is Ms. Simone anyway?" York asked, glancing around.

"She overslept. She had a bad migraine yesterday and went to bed early last night."

Like hell she did, York almost said.

"She gets to sleep in because her scene isn't getting filmed today," Johnny added.

York didn't say anything; he just nodded. He'd heard of romantic entanglements on movie sets but he figured the one between the leading man, the leading lady and Damien Felder was a bit outrageous.

"ARE YOU SURE you don't need me to walk you to your room?"

Darcy glanced up at Damien as they stood in the lobby of her hotel. He'd spent most of the day with her, as well as the evening, going to dinner and a club, but now it was late, close to midnight. She had enjoyed herself but if walking her up to her room meant he assumed he would be staying the night then she rather he didn't. "I'm positive."

"All right then. Can I see you again tomorrow?"

She figured she shouldn't let him dominate her vacation, but she'd had a good time with him. He hadn't tried coming on to her and actually seemed to enjoy her company, as well. "I've made plans to have a day of beauty tomorrow. Most of my time will be spent at the spa and then later the hotel is throwing another party. You can come as my guest if you'd like."

He shook his head. "No, I need to fly to Miami tomorrow night for a couple of days since we won't be filming over the weekend. Can I contact you when I return?"

She saw no reason why he couldn't. "Sure, just call the hotel and ask for me. They will connect you to my room."

"All right, no problem."

If he was bothered about her not giving him her contact information, he wasn't showing it. "And thanks for the tote bag," she said. "I've been doing a lot of shopping, and I intend to fill it up with all sorts of goodies."

He smiled. "No problem. I thought you'd like it since it promotes the movie and will be a memento of your day spent on the set."

"Yes, it will be. Good night, Damien, and thanks again for a wonderful day and evening."

"You're welcome." He then leaned over and placed a kiss on her cheek. "I hope to see you when I return. Not that you need one, but do enjoy your day of beauty tomorrow."

"Thanks for the compliment, and I will."

She turned to head toward the bank of elevators when she felt heat in her midsection. She wasn't surprised when she glanced to her right and saw York sitting at one of the restaurant's tables that gave him a good view of the lobby. Their gazes met, and the penetrating dark eyes staring at her made her increase her pace as she moved toward the elevator. Why did his look have such a mesmerizing effect on her? Even before last night, his stare could get next to her, and after last night, the effect was even worse.

She couldn't help noticing he was frowning, and the frown was so deep she could see the fierce lines of displeasure slashing between the darkness of his eyes. Darcy set her jaw, not caring one iota that he was probably pissed with her for not staying away from Damien.

She stepped on the elevator, and when she turned around, she saw he'd left the restaurant and was heading toward the revolving doors, the same ones Damien had left through moments ago. As she watched him cross the lobby, she couldn't help but think that York Ellis was undoubtedly six feet plus of heart-stopping masculinity. She thought he was an awesome sight last night in a tux, but tonight in a pair of jeans and a pull-over shirt, he looked hot.

The elevator door closed, and she backed up against the wall to give others room. There was no use wishing last night had never happened, because it had, and as much as she wished otherwise, she had no regrets.

Subconsciously, she took her tongue and ran it across her bottom lip when she remembered the searing kiss they'd shared. She wasn't surprised that York was a good kisser and was convinced she could still taste him on her tongue.

*You have it bad, girl. You shouldn't go two years without sex again.* She couldn't help laughing out loud at that thought. She quickly wiped the amusement off her face when others in the elevator turned to stare at her as if she had a few screws loose.

Hell, maybe she did, because at that moment she knew if given the chance, she would definitely do York again.

# CHAPTER FIVE

DARCY HADN'T EXPECTED to go all out when she'd arrived at the spa that morning, but a few hours later, she was walking out of the place feeling like a brand-new woman. She was definitely more at peace with herself for the time being. In addition to the body massage, she had waded in the serenity fountains, spent time walking through the private herbal gardens and indulged in a mineral bath. It had been a peaceful interlude, an emotional escape and a chance to let her mind just relax and unwind.

She had needed the peaceful diversion since she had spent the majority of the night tossing between the sheets while memories of what she'd shared with York the previous night racked her body. It was one of those times that Bruce would have probably come in handy. But after York, she was convinced she was putting Bruce in permanent retirement.

She hadn't gotten much sleep as memories washed through her, making her body tense, irritable and in a need that could get satisfied only one way and with only one man. She was totally convinced that no other man would be able to make her body hum the way York had.

She glanced at her watch as she entered her hotel room. More than half of the day had passed by already. She felt another presence the moment she entered her hotel room. She glanced around and nearly dropped the shopping bag filled with items she'd purchased at the spa. York was sitting on her sofa as if he had every right to be there waiting on her return.

She closed the door and glared at him. "How did you get in here?"

He smiled. "I have my ways."

She placed her bags on the table. "Breaking and entering now, York?"

"A man has to do what a man has to do."

She crossed her arms over her chest. "Meaning?"

"I came to check on you."

She watched as he rose to his feet, appreciating the way his entire body moved with charismatic precision, fluidity and an agility that not only held her attention but was dousing her with an arousing effect of sensations. He was wearing a pair of khakis and an island shirt. He looked laid-back, too sinfully sexy for his good—as well as for hers.

Knowing she needed to keep their conversation on a straight and narrow path, she asked, "Why would you need to check on me? You saw Damien return me to the hotel last night. And I saw you follow him, so don't pretend that you didn't."

He shrugged as he placed his hands in his pockets. "Why would I pretend? I told you my reason for being here in Jamaica."

Yes, he had. "But why are you inside my hotel room? Why couldn't you call or sit in the lobby and wait for me there?"

He shrugged. "I don't have your phone number, and why sit in a lobby when I can have a comfortable spot in here?"

Her frown deepened. "You could have contacted me through the hotel's operator."

"I did. I called your room several times, but you didn't answer."

"I spent most of the day at the spa. And you've got a lot of nerve being here. What if I'd brought someone back with me?"

She saw a tick in his jaw when he responded. "Then I guess it would not have been his lucky day."

She felt swamped with varying emotions at the subtle threat she'd heard in his voice. She fought them off by refusing to believe her having a fling with another man meant anything to him other than the typical male possession. They make love to you and thought they owned you. But she knew of York's reputation with women. He probably wouldn't know how to be possessive of one.

"I'm going to ask you one more time, York. Why are you in my hotel room?"

"I told you," he said, sinking back down on the sofa. "I wanted to make sure you were okay. Evidently you didn't take my warning about Felder at face value. Why are you still seeing him?"

She crossed her arms over her chest. "Because I want to. He hasn't done anything to me, and I enjoy his company."

She then rubbed a frustrated hand down her face. "Look, York, I understand you have a job to do, which is why I didn't give anything away yesterday while we were on set. I pretended we didn't already know each other. You placed me in an awkward position."

"No, I didn't. You placed yourself in an awkward position by being with Felder in the first place."

Darcy felt a headache coming on and decided she

needed for York to leave. They weren't getting anywhere. "No need to rehash anything, York. We don't
think the same way about things."

"We seemed to be in accord the other night."

She glared at him. "A real gentleman wouldn't bring
that up."

He chuckled, but she could tell the amusement on his
face was forced. "And who said I was a gentleman?"

Her chin firmed. "Sorry, my mistake."

She licked her lips to keep her teeth from grinding.
She just didn't get it. He was right. In bed, they were
of one mind, their dislike of each other tossed to the
wayside as they concentrated on something else entirely. Something hot and simmering. Pleasure of the
most intense kind. However, out of bed they were constantly at each other's throats, bickering, biting each
other's heads off.

"Don't you think we should consider a truce?" he
asked.

"Why?"

"So we could try and get along."

"We get along as much as we need to," she said, waving off his words. "What I think we should do while
we're in Jamaica is put distance between us. This island
is big enough for the both of us so our paths shouldn't
cross too much."

"Distance won't work now. Problem with that, Darcy,
is that I've made love to you."

She looked at him confused. "What does that have
to do with anything? I'm sure you've made love to a lot
of women over the years."

"But I particularly enjoyed making love to you."

She didn't want to admit that she had definitely enjoyed making love with him as well. But she didn't intend to lose any sleep over it. She drew in a deep breath. Who was she fooling? She had lost sleep over it. Last night she had lain awake in a bad way. She had needed him. She had yearned to be touched the same way and in the same places he had touched her the night before.

"I'm glad you enjoyed our romp between the sheets, York, but we need to move past that. When I left New York to come here, you weren't even on my mind. And I'm sure I wasn't on yours. People have flings all the time with no lasting effects."

"That might be true, but I refuse to believe I'm not on your mind right now or that you don't want me again."

She was so taken back by his direct assertion that she was left momentarily stunned. He was right on both accounts, but she would never admit to it. "You're wrong."

She then watched him ease off the sofa. Seeing him do so was a total turn-on once again. She was so filled with sexual awareness of him that she knew he had to know it. He began walking toward her, and her gaze tracked his every movement. No matter what kind of clothes he wore he was striking, and he had the ability to stir emotions deep inside of her. She considered backing up, running for cover, but decided to hold her ground.

"I can prove that I'm right and you know it," he said when he came to a stop in front of her. "You want me to prove it?"

No, she didn't want him to prove it because he would prove her wrong. She figured the best thing to do was to stay on a topic that would keep them at odds with each other. "You don't like Damien," she said.

If the change of subject seemed odd, he didn't let

on. "No, I don't like him," he said easily in a hard-ened voice.

"Why, York? Because he's showing interest in me?"

York drew in a deep breath while tossing Darcy's question around in his head. In a way, she was right but then in a way she was wrong. He decided to be honest with her. "I had reason to suspect Felder of wrongdoing even before seeing the two of you together. But then I will admit that I don't like the interest he's showing in you or the interest you're returning, especially after our time together the other night."

"It was a one-night stand, York. Don't try to make it into more than it was because jealousy doesn't be-come you."

He had news for her. It was already more than that, and evidently jealousy *did* become him, although he wished otherwise. And he couldn't understand why it mattered to him. He of all people had never been possessive where lovers were concerned. He enjoyed women and had no problem moving on when boredom set in. But he had a feeling Darcy was a woman a man wouldn't get bored with easily.

He hadn't been able to sleep last night for thinking of her, wanting her. And it hadn't helped matters that he'd followed Felder after he'd left her only to see him meet up with Danielle Simone. York was still trying to figure out that angle. If Felder was so into the lead-ing lady then why was he spending as much time as he could with Darcy? And if Rush was so into Danielle, why hadn't he figured out that something more was going on between her and Felder?

After the accusation Darcy had just thrown at him—that he disliked Felder because he was jealous—she wouldn't believe him if he told her the man was probably just using her as a decoy for some unscrupulous purpose. He might as well keep his mouth shut on the subject until he could prove his theory.

In the meantime, there was a subject he wanted to bring up and decided just to come out and ask. "Are you on the Pill or any other type of birth control?" He knew it was crazy but he had lowered his voice, as if there was someone else in the room besides them.

York could tell from her expression that she was surprised not only with the swift change in subject but also with what he'd asked. "Why do you want to know?"

"Because of the other night." The memories were etched in his mind and with her standing there in a cute sundress that showed what a gorgeous pair of legs she had, he could recall the feel of those same legs wrapped around him.

His gaze raked over her, and he couldn't help but appreciate her feminine curves, small waist and firm and full breasts. The fact that she was a looker wasn't helping matters—or the fact that he'd seen her naked.

Seeing the way he was checking her out made her gaze drill into his. "And if I remember correctly…and I do…you wore a condom each time. I hope you're not about to break the news to me that they were defective or something."

He shook his head. "No, that's not it."

"Then what is it, York?"

He wished she wouldn't ask so many questions. It would really help matters if she just told him what he wanted to know. "I wasn't as careful as I usually am with the condoms," he finally said.

She tilted her head at an angle that pinned him to

the spot. "Yes, I happened to notice, but I was enjoying myself too much to call it to your attention."

He laughed. The woman never ceased to amaze him. She said just what she thought or felt.

"I'm glad you find me amusing, York."

"Only when you say whatever the hell you feel like saying," he said.

She shrugged. "And that's all the time. I do the professional thing at work but when I'm out among friends—or those who might not be friends—I am the real me. What you see is what you get. Now to answer your question…yes, I'm on some sort of birth control but it's not the Pill. So you're safe this time, and I want to think you're also healthy because I am."

"Yes, I am."

"Good, then there's nothing you need to worry about. I came to Jamaica to relax, read and romp. Since sex was on the list, I definitely came prepared."

She then glanced at her watch. "Don't you have somewhere to go?"

"No. So what about that truce?" he asked her, taking a step closer.

Darcy tried not to notice his fascinatingly sexy mouth, a mouth that had nearly driven her insane two nights ago. She wished she didn't have to think about that now but found she couldn't help herself. "You think a truce will work with us?"

A slow smile touched his lips. "It wouldn't hurt."

She wasn't too convinced of that. When she'd left New York, she'd made plans, had such big ideas of how she wanted her three weeks of vacation to start and end. She'd intended to kick up her legs and have some fun. Well, she'd certainly kicked up her legs, right his way.

And he hadn't wasted any time getting between them. "I wouldn't want you to get any ideas."

He chuckled. "About what?"

"What a truce between us means. I didn't come here to have an affair with you."

He flashed her another smile, one that made her body shiver inside. "But you came here intending to have an affair with somebody, right?"

"Yes."

"Then it might as well be me since we've already gotten off to a good start where sex is concerned." He held out his hand. "So, can we agree on a truce? Even if we decide to take sex off the table and never sleep together again?"

She looked at his outstretched hand and asked, "Will you stop accusing Damien of things you're not certain that he's done?"

He frowned. "Why do you keep defending him?"

"And why are you so convinced he's guilty?"

He didn't reply for a moment and then said, "May I suggest we leave Damien out of this for now? This is between me and you."

She narrowed her gaze. "Fine. For now," she said, finally taking his hand. The moment she did so she knew it had been a mistake to agree to a truce with him. Stealing a look at him from beneath her lashes, she saw the smoldering look in his gaze.

She knew she should heed the warning bells that suddenly went off in her head, but she didn't have the strength to do so. The man had the ability to blur the line between reason and desire. She pulled her hand from his when it seemed he was in no hurry to release it.

"Have dinner with me tonight, Darcy."

She lifted a brow. "Dinner? What if we're seen together? Would you want that?"

York responded to Darcy's question with a shake of his head. No, he shouldn't want it but he did. And she had openly admitted she'd come to Jamaica for relaxation, reading and sex. Was Felder someone she'd placed on her to-do list? If that was the case then she could scratch him off. He intended to be the only man she made love to while on the island. A part of him knew that sounded crazy. They'd made love that one time, and it didn't give him any right to possess her. But he couldn't help it for some reason.

He was satisfied with the fact that Felder had caught a plane off the island for a few days, and coincidentally, Danielle Simone had left the island as well. He had men tailing them both, and he wouldn't be surprised to receive a call saying they were together somewhere. He couldn't help wonder where that left good old Johnny-boy. What lie had Danielle told him so he wouldn't suspect anything? And why was Darcy being pulled into their little game? What role did they intend for her to play?

"Since filming has stopped for the weekend the majority of the cast and crew have scattered with plans to return on Monday," he said. "But even if they were here, it wouldn't matter to me if we were seen together. But if it makes you feel better, I know just the place to ensure our privacy."

She shrugged beautiful shoulders. "Doesn't matter to me."

He stared at her. Today her skin appeared smoother than before, and the scent emitting from her skin was different from those other times. The fragrance was just as seductive but reminded him of a flower garden. "You sure? There's still that chance that no matter where we go, we might still be seen by someone. So, if you're so into Felder that it would matter if he finds out we were seen together, then say so. I know some women get all excited by those Hollywood types."

He could tell by the tightening of her lips and the flash that appeared in her eyes that she hadn't liked what he'd said. "I'm not one of them. I only spent yesterday with him, and he seems to be a nice guy. I think you're wrong about him, York."

He rolled his eyes. "Just remember there are a lot of nice guys sitting in jail right now, Darcy."

He checked his watch. "What about if I come back around six?"

For a moment, he thought she wouldn't agree, and then she said, "That's fine. I'll be ready."

"And wear something with an accent on having fun. I plan to take you for a walk on the beach later," he said, dragging in a deep breath as he headed for the door. He needed to get out of there now. It wouldn't take much to pull her into his arms for a repeat of what they'd shared two nights ago.

They would make love again. He was certain of it. That night she had been simply amazing, had met him on every level and then in a surprising move, she had ridden him, given him an orgasm that still made his body tremble just thinking about it. Afterward he had been weak, wrung out and exhausted. And then she had proceeded to arouse him all over again.

When he reached her door, he turned unexpectedly, and the guilty look on her face let him know she had been checking him out from behind. The gaze now looking at him was hot. He could easily change their plans and stay in—order room service, then spend a night between the sheets. They could take turns riding each other like they'd done the other night.

A predatory and primitive urge eased up his spine. He felt great satisfaction in knowing she wanted him as much as he wanted her. "I'll see you at six."

Then he opened the door and walked out.

# CHAPTER SIX

THEY WERE JUST going to dinner and taking a walk on the beach later, Darcy said, looking at herself in the bathroom's full-length mirror. No biggie. It meant nothing.

First of all, York wasn't her type. But she would have to admit he had been the best lover she'd ever had. With him, there were no limitations. He was willing to try just about anything, and she'd had a lot of ideas. When you read as many romance novels as she had over the years, you were bound to have a few unique positions stored up in your brain.

She left her bedroom and entered the living room area. York had said he would return at six, and it was a few minutes to that time. She was dressed, so with nothing else to do, she began pacing the floor, feeling hot and restless.

Another first when it came to York. She would have to give him credit as being the first man she'd dated that not only made her aware of her power as a woman but encouraged her to flaunt it, to wrap herself up in her femininity in a way she'd never done before.

Harold had been a total jerk, she could see that now. In the early days, all she'd wanted to do was to please him, both in and out of the bedroom. But he was never satisfied.

When his job began going bad, he wanted to blame his problems on her since she was happy at her job.

Then after he'd gotten laid off he resented that she was working. That was when the abuse began and when the love and respect she'd thought she had for him went plummeting down the toilet. It was then she'd vowed never to be ruled by another man. They were just heart-break waiting to happen, and she'd learned her lesson. From what she'd heard, York was just as commitment phobic as she was—smart man.

But the one thing she couldn't forget, although she'd tried, was that they'd made love. He wasn't the first man she'd made love to since her divorce, but she had even put affairs on the back burner. In fact, she'd begun to wonder why she'd even bothered getting those injections for birth control when there hadn't been any real action going down in that neck of the woods. But York had reminded her of why it was always important to be prepared for the unexpected.

She hadn't expected to make love to him that night. Nor had she expected him to get so carried away he would get careless. The thought of having some man's child would cross her mind every so often, but she would push it way to the back. She loved kids and wanted some of her own one day. But she knew since she didn't plan to ever marry again that she would venture into the life of a single mother.

The knock on the door made her breath catch in her throat knowing York was standing on the other side. Not surprisingly, he was right on time. She looked down at herself. He'd suggested she wear something for fun; she felt the short tropical-print dress did the trick. It was one she'd purchased on one of her infamous shopping sprees. This was her first time wearing it, and she couldn't wait to see York's reaction to it.

Her insides were churning when she opened the door and saw him standing there. The way his gaze roamed over her from head to toe made her smile at the look of male appreciation in the dark depths of his eyes. She had gotten the reaction she'd wanted and had hoped for.

"Hello, York, you're right on time. It will only take me a second to grab my purse."

She walked over to the table knowing his gaze was following her every step. Usually she didn't wear her dresses this short, but when she'd seen it on a mannequin while shopping with Ellie one day during her best friend's New York visit, El had convinced her it would look even better on her. And from the way York kept looking at her she had a feeling it did. She heard the door close behind him and knew he'd stepped over the threshold to come into the hotel room.

She turned and saw the deep frown on his face. "Is anything wrong?"

He placed his hands in the pockets of his slacks. "I suggested you wear something for fun. Not something to keep me aroused the rest of the evening."

She tossed her head, sending a mass of hair around her shoulders. She couldn't help the smile that touched her lips. "Poor baby. You'll survive. In fact, I'll make sure that you do." She liked the fact that he spoke his mind just like she spoke hers.

She placed the straps of her purse on her shoulder. "I'm ready."

She'd made the statement, but neither of them made an attempt to move. They just stood there staring at each other. Then he spoke. "Don't think that I don't know what you're up to, Darcy."

She threw him an innocent look. "I have no idea what you're talking about." She then smiled smugly. "But then, maybe I do."

He took his hands out of his pockets and placed them across his chest. "You play with fire, and you're liable to get burned."

She gave him a thoughtful look. She'd already encountered his fire and knew how hot he was capable of getting things. And as long as he was the one doing the burning she wouldn't back down. "Fire doesn't scare me, York."

He shook his head and chuckled. "Maybe it should. Come on, let's get out of here."

She led the way out of the hotel room, figuring he was still enjoying the backside view. "So where are you taking me?" she asked when they reached the elevator.

He smiled down at her. "You'll see."

YORK WAS GLAD there were others on the elevator with them or else he would have been tempted to take her right then and there. Every single cell in his body had to be aroused right now, thanks to the sexiest minidress a woman could wear. And she definitely had the body for it. He could just imagine other men checking her out in this outfit and felt pressure at the top of his head just thinking about it. Now he was glad he'd made the decision to take her to a place where it would be just the two of them.

His lips thinned when he recalled that he had run into Johnny Rush on the way up to Darcy's room. He knew for a fact the man was staying at a hotel a few miles away, so who had he been visiting here at this hotel? If he'd expected to drop in on Danielle Simone, then he'd discovered she was long gone, since Danielle and Felder were together in Miami.

"You've gotten quiet on me, York."

He glanced down at Darcy as he led her through the hotel's glass doors. Just as he'd figured, they'd gotten plenty of attention walking across the lobby. Men had literally stopped what they were doing to stare at her. And he had seen the look of envy in their eyes when they'd gazed at him walking by her side.

"Um, I'm thinking about all the heat you and I seem to stir whenever we're together."

Instead of making a comment, she arched her brows. There was no need for him to elaborate. He was certain that she understood what he was talking about. Even now he was convinced he could still taste the most recent kiss they'd shared.

He studied her underneath his lashes and thought now the same thing he'd thought when he first saw her that day two years ago. She was a whirlwind and could probably have a man falling for her without much effort on her part. You couldn't help but be drawn to her. And now he wanted to get to know the real Darcy Owens— uncensored, up close and personal. He knew she figured since they had slept together that should be the end of it, and maybe under normal circumstances that would be. But as far as he was concerned, the circumstances weren't normal. They shared the same close friends, yet there was a lot about her that he didn't know. He wanted to get to know her better. He *intended* to get to know her better.

It didn't take long for the valet to bring his rental

car to him. Watching her get in the car and ease down on the leather seats in that dress was worth the last few sleepless nights he'd endured thinking about her. She definitely had nice thighs, shapely and perfect for her legs. He wanted her. He had been convinced that a strong-willed woman turned him off, but the one sitting in the car beside him in that short dress turned him on big time.

"Penny for your thoughts," she said when they had driven away from the hotel.

He hadn't said anything for a while, trying to get his thoughts and his libido under control. He glanced over at her and decided to be honest. "I was thinking about making love to you again. I want you."

He did no more than steal a quick glance at her expression before turning his gaze back to the road. He'd seen what he had wanted to see. A mirror image of the desire he felt was reflected in her shocked gaze. He was beginning to understand just how to handle Darcy. She didn't need a man who sugarcoated anything but a man who could dish it out just like she could. She spoke her mind and appreciated a man who did the same.

She was different from the women he usually dated, those who preferred being told what they wanted to hear. And he had no trouble obliging them if he got what he wanted in the end. With Darcy, there was no need to play games or talk in circles. He liked that.

When he braked the car to a stop at the traffic light, on impulse he reached over and traced his fingertips along her thigh, liking the way her skin felt there— soft and smooth. He couldn't help but remember how it felt riding those same thighs and how those thighs had also ridden him.

He glanced over at her and saw fire flaring in the depths of her eyes. It was fire he'd generated, fire he intended to stir into a huge flame, fire he intended to extinguish in his own special way. He returned his hand back to the steering wheel when the traffic light changed.

"What's your sign, York?"

He chuckled. Now she was going to try and figure him out. He really wasn't a complicated sort of guy. He was just a horny one at the moment, thanks to her. He answered merely to amuse her. "Scorpio."

Now it was her turn to chuckle before saying, "I figured as much."

He wasn't into that astrology stuff but was curious as to how she'd figured it. "You need to expound on that."

"No problem." And then she said, "Scorpios are very passionate beings. They crave physical contact. In other words, they love sex."

He wouldn't go so far as to say he loved sex, but he certainly enjoyed it. "And how would you know that?"

"Because I'm a Scorpio."

If her words were meant to make him get hard, they succeeded. The erection already there got even harder, bigger. The thought that she liked sex made him throb. He should have figured that much from when they'd made love. There had been something else about that night that stayed with him. He could tell that it had been a long time since she'd made love to a man. Her body was tight. And if that hadn't been enough to give something away, he couldn't forget that several times in the course of their lovemaking she'd let it slip that it had been a long time for her, which was why she thought she was being so greedy. If she loved sex so much, why had she gone without?

He decided to ask her. "Then why did you go without it for a long time?"

She looked at him as if wondering how he'd known and he said, "That night, you let it slip that it had been a long time for you."

How much time passed before she answered he wasn't sure, but he was certain he'd been holding his breath for her response. Finally she said, "I hadn't meant to tell you that, but I guess I sort of got caught up in the moment."

He smiled remembering. "You did. So did I," he said, not ashamed to admit it.

He could feel the constant thump of his heart in his chest when she said, "Yes, it had been a long time for me."

"Why?"

He thought she would tell him it wasn't any of his business. She certainly had every right to do so. Instead she surprised him by saying, "I decided to take a two-year hiatus. I was starting a new job and needed to stay focused on something other than male body parts. Besides, I had gotten out of one hell of a marriage and refused to even consider getting into a serious relationship."

He brought the car to another stop. He'd heard from Uriel that her ex-husband had been a jerk. "If you like sex so much, how did you survive going without it?"

She shrugged delicate-looking shoulders beneath her spaghetti straps. "I had my ways of keeping myself entertained."

He quickly caught on to what she'd meant. What a

pity. A woman with profound needs should not have had to settle for a substitute.

"We might as well clear things up about something else while we're in a talkative mood, York."

He glanced over at her. "About what?"

"That day we met at Uriel and Ellie's wedding and you tried coming on to me and I was a smart-ass and all but told you to go screw yourself."

He could clearly recall that day, and that's not all she'd said. "Yes? What about it?"

"I was in a bad mood. I had just received a call from my ex that he intended to make my life miserable by moving to New York just to aggravate the hell out of me."

"So you took it out on me?"

"I would have taken it out on anyone with a penis, and you just happened to be the first man who approached me after that phone call."

He remembered she had left the wedding rehearsal for a short while, and when she'd returned he had hightailed it over to her to see if she wanted to go out with him later that night. Her words had set his face on fire, and he'd walked off intending to never have anything to do with her again.

"I took it out on you, and I apologize."

Her apology was two years in coming, but there was no need for either of them to hold a grudge forever. But still… "Why are you apologizing now, Darcy?"

"Because I think I should. Okay, I admit I should have done so long ago, but every time I ran into you at one of Ellie's functions, you would avoid me like I had a disease or something and it sort of pissed me off."

He frowned as he stared over at her. "And after what

you said to me, you really expected me not to avoid you? You threatened to all but castrate me if I got in your face again."

"Okay, I remember all that, and I'm sorry. Do you accept my apology?"

He drew in a deep breath. It would be silly if he didn't, especially since he knew for a fact she wouldn't harm that particular body part. She'd held it in her hand, had taken it in her mouth. The memory of her doing both was increasing his arousal. "Yes, I accept your apology. It's in the past, so let's leave it there. We've moved beyond that now, haven't we?"

"Yes. Ellie will be glad to hear we're no longer enemies. That bothered her," she said.

He decided not to say that their less than friendly attitude never bothered Uriel. It had taken a while for Darcy to grow on him, as well. It had something to do with a prank Darcy had gotten Ellie to play on Uriel when the two women were in their teens. It had taken Uriel a long time to get over it.

"You and Ellie been best friends a long time?" he asked her.

"Almost forever. She's the sister I never had, and since she was an only child, I got to go a lot of places with her, like to Cavanaugh Lake for the summers."

Since he was godbrother to Uriel, whose parents also owned a place at Cavanaugh Lake, he spent a lot of his summers there as well. He could remember Ellie and her annoying little friend but hadn't known until Ellie and Uriel's wedding that Darcy had been that annoying friend. She had grown into a beautiful woman—not that she'd been an ugly kid or anything but just one not all that noticeable. Besides, she'd been five years younger, and he'd never paid her much attention. Now he did.

"So you're not telling me where we're going?" she asked, glancing over at him.

He smiled. "Not yet. We'll be there in a minute. Just relax. You have nothing to worry about."

DARCY WASN'T TOO sure of that. Just sharing a car with York was pure torture. The man was too virile. When he made such blatant statements as he'd done earlier, he made her remember everything about the night they'd made love.

Being coy was not a part of her makeup, and it seemed it wasn't a part of his either. She liked that, and she hated to admit it—since they had avoided each other for so long—that she kind of liked him, too. He was a Scorpio; so was she. According to their signs when it came to compatibility, a Scorpio and Scorpio match was rated high, the same when it came to sex between a Scorpio and a Scorpio. So it seemed they had that in the bag. After the other night, she had no reason not to believe it. But the ratings weren't so high when it came to communication between two Scorpios. She wondered why. She enjoyed discussing things with York, at least when they stayed away from controversial subjects like Damien Felder. York had his own opinions about the man, and she had hers.

She was glad she'd apologized for her behavior two years ago. Ellie had kept telling her that she should, and like she'd told him, she had tried. But he hadn't given her the opportunity. Even that night when he'd shown up at her place because Ellie had convinced him to come, he had come arguing about it, which set her off again.

"How do you like your job as a city planner?"

She looked over at him. "I like it on those days politics aren't involved." On the days it was, she wanted to quit and do something else. But her job paid her well even with the headaches. And she did enjoy living in New York, especially when the weather was nice. There were so many things to see and do.

"So, did your ex follow you to New York?" he asked her.

"Yes, and he tried making my life a living hell for a couple of months. I ended up getting a restraining order on him. That's the reason Ellie had you rush over to my place that night. She was convinced my intruder was Harold."

Over the next few minutes she engaged in conversation with him and found herself telling him the reason she had gotten a divorce.

She also told him about her job and that she hadn't taken a lot of time off for the two years she'd worked as a city planner and that in addition to much needed R & R, she'd also wanted to escape the cold weather in New York for a while.

And just the opposite, he told her how much he enjoyed New York winters and that he was missing the snowstorm passing through even now. As they talked, it dawned on her just how laid-back he was once you got to know him. She was enjoying the conversation. He was arrogant, true enough, but there was something about his arrogance that she found a total turn-on at times.

And she couldn't dismiss the fact that being with him did something to her, gave her an adrenaline rush like she'd never experienced before. Especially when he was so up front and candid about certain things. She had a feeling how he intended the evening to end. He'd all but spelled it out to her. The thought that he pretty much had sexual ideas that included her didn't bother her in the least. In fact, if truth be told, she was still in awe of their lovemaking the other night. Although at the time she'd figured it was one and done, it still had lingering effects on her.

She couldn't look at her naked body in the mirror without remembering how he'd licked every single inch of it. And her nipples would strain against her top when she recalled how he had sucked the dark pebbles into his mouth and feasted on them. Even now, the memory of his head between her legs had heat rushing all through her.

"What are your plans for the holidays, Darcy?"

She glanced over at him, wondering why he'd want to know and then quickly figured he'd asked for conversational purposes only. "When I leave here, instead of flying back to New York, I'm headed to Minnesota to spend Christmas with my parents and brothers. I've timed it to be with them Christmas Eve and Christmas Day. That's the most I can take of the harsh, cold Minnesota weather. Then on the day after Christmas I'm heading to Cavanaugh Lake to help Ellie with her New Year's Eve bash. She's planning a masquerade party this year."

"That should be interesting and a lot of fun."

She thought so as well and looked forward to the event.

As the car continued to move through the streets of Jamaica, she glanced out the window to take in the sights they passed. They were on the grander side of the island, where the wealthy resided, which was evident by the spacious homes they passed. She knew the houses were owned by wealthy Americans and Europeans who wanted to get away to the tropical island whenever they could. Cheyenne Steele Westmoreland and Vanessa Steele Cody, along with their husbands, owned beautiful homes in this part of the island as well. The two women were first cousins to Donovan Steele, a close friend of Uriel's. She had met most of the Steele family through Ellie at family functions and gatherings.

It had turned dark, and the lights that lined the streets seemed to shimmer across the water. When York turned off the main road and onto a street lined with palm trees on both sides, she studied the homes they passed. *Huge, magnificent* and *beautiful* were just a few words she could use to describe them. And when he pulled into the driveway of one such home, she turned and glanced over at him questioningly.

He smiled. "This is where we'll be spending the evening. I plan to treat you to my own brand of an island feast."

She glanced back at the house and then back at him. "And the owner has no problem with you doing that?" she asked, trying to downplay her excitement at the thought that he wanted to prepare a meal for her.

He chuckled. "Trust me, he won't mind since I know him well."

"Do you?"

"Yes. I own the place. And I want to welcome you, Darcy Owens, to my summer home in Jamaica."

# *CHAPTER SEVEN*

YORK LEANED BACK against the closed door and watched as Darcy moved around his living room. It was as if she was fascinated by each and every thing she saw, whether it was the furniture, the paintings on the wall or the large potted plants he had strategically arranged to get the optimum amount of sun. Then there was the sea view from every window.

He had bought the home when it had been in foreclosure and never regretted doing so. It was his haven, his escape when he'd found himself working too hard and needing playtime. He liked spending time on the water and owned a Jet Ski that he enjoyed taking out every chance he got.

"This place is beautiful, York, and the view of the ocean is simply breathtaking."

"Thanks." He smiled, pleased with her assessment of his home. He was a man who really never cared what others thought of his possessions, but knowing she liked this place filled him with something he'd never felt before. It was then that he realized he had never brought a woman here. Usually his time spent at this place was what he considered as "me" time—his time alone to unwind and enjoy the beach that was literally in his backyard.

He studied her as she continued to look out one of his

floor-to-ceiling windows and thought she was breathtaking, as well. That short dress had practically undone
him the moment he'd seen her in it. She was the only
woman that could get him wound up to this point, where
he was filled with a simmering need that was hard to
keep in check. And it didn't help matters to know he'd
already sampled her, already knew her taste and scent.
Knew how it felt to ride her.

She turned and caught him staring but didn't seem
surprised. He had a feeling she was aware of every move
he made. He wondered if she was privy to his thoughts
as well. If she was, then she knew those thoughts were
salacious, indecent at best, highly X-rated. Even now
he was wondering what was or wasn't under her dress.

He drew in a long breath when their gazes held, and
the silence between them was becoming noticeably
long. It wouldn't take much to cross the room, lift that
short dress and take her just where she stood.

It was she who finally broke the silence by asking,
"How long have you owned the house?"

"A few years. I always wanted a place on the island,
and when I heard about it I couldn't pass up the chance
to get it. It's my escape from reality. I've been a beach
bum here a time or two."

"Why are you staying at the hotel when you have
this place?"

He moved away from the door. "I'm on the island
working, and I need to be in the thick of things."

"Oh."

He knew his words reminded her of his allegations
about Felder. She tilted back her head, stared at him
and asked, "Why are you so hell-bent on Damien Felder
being guilty?"

"And why are you so hell-bent that he's innocent?"

He could feel a confrontation coming on, and he could deal with that. A verbal sparring with her was always refreshing. But what he didn't like was the thought that they would be arguing about another man—a man who when he wasn't with her was sleeping with another woman. And it was a woman who another man wanted or assumed he had. If that wasn't a mixed-up affair, he didn't know what was. He didn't want Darcy to be a part of such foolishness.

"I like giving people the benefit of the doubt, York."

He rolled his shoulders in a shrug. "That's a nice gesture, but people aren't always what they seem to be."

"I know that," she all but snapped and he had a feeling she wanted to smack him.

"Did Felder make that much of an impression on you, or do you just want to refute what I say just for the hell of it?" he asked, regarding her intently.

She smiled, and he thought back to the first time he had seen her smile…although the smile had not been directed at him. It had been at Uriel and Ellie's wedding, and she'd smiled a lot, genuinely happy for her best friend. And her hazel eyes had sparkled a lot that night, too.

"You shouldn't be so quick to jump to conclusions about people, York," she said, interrupting his thoughts.

"And you think that's what I'm doing?" he asked.

"Don't you?"

"No. And for you to assume I would consider a man guilty of wrongdoing just because he's shown an interest in you is unfair to me."

He knew his comment had given her food for thought when she hung her head to study the grain of the wood on his floor. She lifted her head. "You're right, and I owe you another apology."

"Yes, you do."

She frowned. "You don't have to rub it in."

He began slowly walking toward her, and the frown on her face showed no signs of disappearing. In fact, it deepened, and he thought she looked pretty darn sexy when angry. He came to a stop in front of her and said, "I didn't bring you here to argue with you, Darcy."

She tilted her head at an angle to meet his direct gaze. "And why *did* you bring me here?"

He smiled. "To feed you, for starters. You can have a seat here in the living room and enjoy a view of the water, or you can join me in the kitchen to see what else I can do besides nab the bad guys."

He could tell by the light that lit her eyes that the latter suggestion caught her interest. He was proven right when she said, "I'll join you in the kitchen."

DARCY SAT ON a stool at the breakfast bar and sipped a glass of wine as she watched York in action. She was paying attention to how well he handled himself in the kitchen as he went about chopping vegetables to go with the chicken he'd put in the oven to bake.

But her attention went beyond that. For such a tall, well-built guy, he was quick on his feet as he moved around the huge kitchen. It was obvious that he knew his way around the room, which meant he spent a lot of time in it. A man with decent cooking skills was hard to come by these days. And she liked how he could carry on a conversation with her while preparing their food. He liked giving her pointers about how to keep the chicken moist and the easiest way to chop the vegetables so they could retain their nutritional value under heat.

However, what she enjoyed the most was just sitting there and watching him while memories of their one night together continued to consume her. The man was handsome and well built. And his ruggedly handsome features were definitely a plus in her book. He looked good in jeans, and any woman would appreciate the way his muscle shirt covered his broad shoulders. He was definitely eye candy.

She was fairly certain that with his looks and build York could have his pick of women and probably did. Although he'd never brought one to any of the functions Ellie gave, she knew he dated a lot. She'd heard that right after his lover's death he had quit the NYPD and traveled abroad for a year with another one of his godbrothers by the name of Zion Blackstone. Zion had continued living abroad but York had returned to the States and instead of returning to work as a police officer, he had opened his own security firm with money his grandmother had left for him when she'd died. That had been over five years ago, and now his security business was a successful one, and he had nine employees working for him.

"Tell me about some of the cases your company has handled."

He glanced up at her and smiled. "Why? You thinking about changing professions?"

She chuckled. "Um, you never know. Right now, anything would be more appealing than having to deal with the politics of getting things done. Everyone loves New York, but my job is to make sure they continue to love it. Budget cuts haven't helped things."

"I'm sure they haven't." He then began telling her about one of his cases that involved protecting a well-known celebrity from an overzealous fan. "The woman was eventually arrested," he said.

Darcy nodded. She had her favorite celebrities but couldn't for the life of her imagine herself stalking any of them.

"Everything is almost ready. I can give you a tour of the place while we're waiting for the chicken to finish baking."

"Thanks. I'd like that."

YORK THOUGHT THAT the only thing better than a woman who looked good was one who smelled good as well. And Darcy smelled good. He wasn't sure of what cologne she was wearing tonight, but it was one that made everything inside of him feel primitive and male each time he sniffed it.

She walked beside him as he took her from room to room. It was a big place, but it was cozy enough for him and he made use of every available space. But then he didn't believe in overcrowding. He had hired a private decorator and had been pleased with the results.

As soon as he entered his bedroom and saw his huge bed, he immediately thought of Darcy sharing it with him. And he had a feeling before the night was over, she would. He'd told her on the way here that he wanted her. Nothing had changed. And he'd been aware of how she had been watching him while he'd prepared dinner. Knowing that her eyes had been on him, studying his every move, had made him want her even more.

When they returned to the living room, she sat down on the leather sofa; he sat opposite her on the matching love seat. He watched her cross her legs and clasp her hands together in her lap. The simple gestures turned him on. She had that much of an impact on him without even trying.

And then he watched as she took a sip from her wine glass and remembered just how well she could use that mouth of hers. Suddenly he envisioned Darcy in his bed riding him while he kissed her senseless. He imagined them flipping positions so he could ride her. And just like before, he would ride her hard.

He sat there and listened while she talked, telling him more about her job and then about some of the escapades she and Ellie had gotten into as children. When he asked her about the prank they had once played on Uriel, she told him how she had talked a six-teen-year-old Ellie into kissing Uriel on a dare. Uriel had been in college at the time and hadn't liked it one bit. In fact, it had taken him a while to get over it and his anger had been with Darcy just as much as it had been with Ellie. He could tell by the sparkle in her eyes and the laughter in her voice while she retold the story that she still thought what happened that day had been funny, especially when a furious twenty-one-year-old Uriel had found out he'd been set up by two teenage girls.

York checked his watch before glancing up in time to see her take her last sip of wine. He liked the way the liquid trickled down her throat and remembered how his tongue had licked that part of her. He stood. "Let's get dinner out of the way so we can take a walk on the beach."

She stood as well and returned his smile. "I'm definitely looking forward to that."

MEN, DARCY THOUGHT, glancing across the table at York, could be unpredictable creatures at times. On the drive over, York had all but hinted he would jump her bones the first chance he got. Yet, she had been here for a couple of hours and he had yet to make a move on her. She wondered if he really did have plans for them to take a walk on the beach.

"You've gotten quiet on me, Darcy."

She chuckled, deciding she wouldn't share what she'd been thinking. "Dinner was delicious," she said, slightly pushing away from the table. And she meant it. He had done an outstanding job.

"Ready to spend some time on the beach?"

So he had been serious. "Sure."

He glanced down at her shoes. "Go ahead and take them off. You're going to love the feel of the sand beneath your feet."

"All right."

She kicked off her sandals and watched as he did the same for his own. She noticed he grabbed a blanket off a shelf before leading her out of his back door. It was dark, and she could hear the sound of the sea roaring through her ears, while the scent of salt water filled her nostrils. He took her hand and they began walking to the beach, which was right in his backyard.

When she'd had thoughts of spending three weeks in Jamaica, her plans included meeting a man with whom she would share a walk on the beach. At the time, she hadn't thought the man would be York.

He'd been right. She liked the feel of the sand beneath her feet, and that, combined with the scent of the beach and the knowledge that she had a virile man walking beside her, one whose fingers were entwined with hers, was reminding her of just how much of a woman she was.

It also reminded her of what had happened once already between them and what she looked forward to happening again. Before this trip, she had gone without sex long enough, so wanting to make up for lost time was a strong and healthy urge. Making love to York that night had been like a welcome back to life. She felt good and knew without any doubt that she wanted York again.

"This is a good spot."

They stopped walking, and he released her hand to spread the blanket on the sand. It was dark, but the brightly lit lantern on his back porch provided enough light to see their surroundings. And then there were the stars that dotted the sky overhead and the full moon right in front of them that cast a romantic glow upon where they were. It was like a scene straight out of one of her romance novels. There was nothing better than a romantic night and an ultra-handsome man. A woman couldn't ask for much more.

"That's that," York said, interrupting her thoughts. She saw he had finished spreading the blanket out and had turned toward her. He was standing about five feet away, yet she was able to feel the moment their gazes connected. Desire immediately began oozing through her bloodstream. Her lips suddenly felt dry, and she automatically ran the tip of her tongue over her bottom lip and was well aware his gaze had followed the movement.

She wanted him. He wanted her. It was all about lust. He knew it, and she knew it, as well. The man had haunted her thoughts since making love to her two nights ago. She had tried convincing herself the reason she'd gotten so into him the way she had was because he had been her first in two years. But now she knew that excuse wouldn't fly. It was deeper than that. As a lover, he had not only satisfied her yearning but he had also captivated her mind. No other man had been able to do the latter, not even Harold.

She tilted her head as an intense yearning continued to fill her. Refusing to be denied what she wanted, she sauntered toward York, deciding she had no problem making the first move if things called for that. There was a slight breeze in the air that carried moisture to dampen her skin, and the night air seemed to carry the sound of her footsteps in the sand.

There was something about being out on the beach tonight with York and the way he was standing there not moving, watching her and waiting for her to come to him. Her inner thighs clenched with every step she took, and she breathed in deeply when she came to a stop in front of him.

Later, she would wonder why they were opposites capable of becoming magnets that could attract each other in such a volatile way—and why the need to make love to him on the beach was a *must do* on her list.

He didn't say anything for a long moment. He just stood there and stared at her, letting his gaze roam up and down her as if he could see through her clothes. And then, when she thought she could not take any more of his blatant perusal or the intense yearning filling her to capacity, he reached out and pulled her to him. He pressed her body close to his, letting her feel just how hard and erect he was for her. Her breasts, pressed hard against his chest, began to throb, and she breathed in his scent at the same time she felt a tingling sensation between her thighs.

"I could make love to you out here all night, Darcy."

His words, spoken in a deep, desire-laced voice, inflamed her mind and she nearly released a groan when she felt the erection pressed against her get even larger. The feel of it sent heat rushing through her, and her breathing became labored. Making love on the beach under the stars with a man had always been a fantasy of hers after reading such a scene in a romance novel. Now here she was with York and a burst of desire, the magnitude of which she'd only ever experienced with him, was taking over her senses.

She studied the gaze staring back at her, saw the need that was as deep as her own. She reached out and pressed her hand to his chest and felt the hard, thumping beat of his heart beneath her palm. How could she feel this immediate desire for him and not for Damien?

She wasn't sure just how much time had elapsed while they stood there, with intense desire building between them by the second. Then, not able to handle the anticipation any longer or the forceful longing, she rose up on her tiptoes, leaned in and took that same tip of her tongue she'd used to moisten her lip earlier and ran it along his jaw. She heard the sound of his heavy breathing in her ear. She heard his moan. She felt the hardness of him swell even more against her belly.

"Will your neighbors see us out here?" she whispered as she continued to use the tip of her tongue to lick underneath his ear. She liked the taste of his skin, hot against her tongue.

"No," he said huskily. "They can't see a thing. The

homes on this beach were built to provide ultimate privacy."

"Are you sure?"

"Positive."

Taking his word, she stepped back and began removing her dress. To be honest, even if his neighbors could see anything she was beyond stopping at this point. Modesty was the last thing on her mind. Him getting inside of her and stroking her to a powerful orgasm headed the list right now. The prospect of that happening consumed her thoughts. The breeze whispering in off the water did nothing to cool her heat. It merely intensified it.

She eased her dress up to her waist, and it didn't take long to whip the garment over her head. She hadn't worn a bra, and her thong slid down her legs easily. As the breeze flitted across her naked skin, she knew what this night held for her, and she couldn't downplay her body's excitement or the urges that were taking over her mind and making her want him even more. She was filled with the need for him with every catch of her breath.

York had stood there and watched Darcy strip, and now seeing her without clothes did something to him. He quickly unzipped his jeans and removed them. Then came his briefs and shirt. When he stood before her completely naked, he took the time to sheath a condom over his engorged shaft. His hand nearly trembled with the need for her.

Never had he known a woman quite like her, and in a way, he'd known she would be the one to send his mind in a topsy-turvy. He had hit on her that first time, and when she had rejected his interest, he should have been grateful for her sparing his sanity. Instead he had been resentful. Now he knew it hadn't been meant for them to connect then. But now the field was wide open, and there was no stopping them. It had taken two years for him to accept the intensity of his desire for her, even when he hadn't wanted to crave her to such a degree.

He reached out for her. Instead of lowering her on the blanket, he swept her into his arms and began heading toward the water.

"Where are you taking me, York?"

He glanced down at her and smiled. "You'll see."

And moments later he lowered her naked body into one of those heavyweight vinyl floaters. The inflatable floor cushioned her backside, and he shifted her position to where her legs were spread open. The raft was large enough for more than one person, and he joined her, bracing himself against the side to stare down at her, taking note of the position he'd placed her in, all spread open for him to see. He then took his hand and traced a path up her inner thigh. Then his fingers began inching inside of her, and he studied the emotions that crossed her face when they did.

"You're hot," he said in a deep, husky tone. "You're still tight, and I plan to loosen you up a bit."

"Is that a promise?" she asked, in a whimpering tone.

"Definitely a promise."

And then he shifted positions to straddle her while simultaneously sliding his hands beneath her hips to lift her backside to receive him. His entry inside her was swift, and his heart began thumping hard in his chest when his thrust went to the hilt as he spread her legs farther apart, making them hang off the sides of the raft.

He used his hands to push the raft into the water,

and as soon as they were afloat, he began moving in and out of her. This was crazy, but he wanted her this way. He wanted her here. Making love to a woman on a raft in the water had always been a fantasy of his and now he was doing it here with Darcy—only with Darcy.

It was a new float, one he had purchased recently, one that hadn't ever been in the water. Now he was using it for the first time, officially christening it with her. With the water flapping beneath them, every stroke inside of her made his want that much more intense. The low ache in his belly was being appeased with every thrust.

He wanted to make her his.

Why such a thought had even crossed his mind, had lurked its way into his thoughts, he wasn't sure. All he knew at that moment was that he intended to be the only man to ever make love to her in a raft, on the beach or any place else. There would be no Damien Felder in her future. Anyone who knew York was well aware that once he staked a claim about anything that was that. With every lunge into her body, he was doing more than staking a claim; he was declaring possession.

DARCY MOANED DEEP within her throat when York's thrust became ever more powerful. She had fantasized about making love on the beach, but doing so in a raft in the water hadn't crossed her mind. And with each breath she was taking, York was driving into her, pushing her over the edge. His thrusts were hard and so intense she figured they would tumble out of the raft and into the water, never to be heard from again. But he managed to handle both her and the raft. He might be keeping the watercraft afloat, but her mind and body were drowning in waters so sensual that she had to pull in deep breaths to survive what he was doing.

What if they ended up in one of his neighbors' back-yards or right smack in the middle of the sea? She could see the headlines now. "Man and woman found naked on a raft—bodies can't be pried apart."

That scenario should concern her, but instead she pushed it to the back of her mind. It couldn't compete with the sensations tearing through her. And when York shifted his body slightly and touched an inner part of her that had never been touched before, she screamed. Then an orgasm rammed through her and shook her to the core. The feelings were so intense that he had to grip down on her to keep her body from pushing them both out of the raft and into the water.

He was stroking her into sweet oblivion, and she closed her eyes and threw her head back when she burst into a second orgasm. She moaned his name, and when his mouth captured her to silence the sound, she felt his body buck above her just seconds before he drove even deeper into her.

He released her mouth, and she bit down on her bottom lip to keep from screaming out again. The motion of the water beneath them sent waves pleasure through her. She opened her eyes and saw he was staring down at her and the sound emitting from between his clenched lips could be considered a growl.

"You're mine, Darcy."

The strong tread of York's voice floated through her mind. She heard his words but couldn't fathom why he'd said them or what he meant by them. She quickly figured he had gotten caught up in the moment and to-morrow he wouldn't even remember them.

As he continued to push her into another orgasm, she knew his virility was unlimited, his desire was primitive and his ability to bring her pleasure was unprecedented. Her breathing got shallow as sensual bliss took over her mind and body. Her heart raced so fast she thought she might faint.

Several pleasure-filled moments later, her body calmed, and when she felt him lift off her she felt an intense sense of loss. She was too afraid to look around, too nervous about where they might have drifted.

"You okay, baby?"

His question made her glance up at him, and she saw the stars were still dotting the sky overhead. At least it was still nighttime. She hadn't been sure how much time had passed. When you were in the throes of extreme sexual pleasure, you were destined to forget about time.

She shifted and moved her legs. If they were out in the middle of the sea, she didn't want her legs hanging over the sides. Sharks could be hungry creatures, and she didn't want to be one's meal.

"Where are we?" she asked him.

He smiled. "Out in the water."

She couldn't help returning his smile. "Please tell me we're not near a cruise ship and that you can still see land."

He chuckled, and it was then that she realized just how large the raft was. "No cruise ship on the horizon and yes, we can still see land. I'll have us back to shore in no time."

She felt both relief and excitement upon hearing that. "You sure?"

"Positive."

Believing him, she sat up and let out a deep sigh of

relief when she saw they were probably no more than fifty feet from land. He pulled oars—that she noticed for the first time—from the sides of the raft and began using them.

"Need help?" she asked him.

He smiled over at her, his pupils glimmered with sensuality. "No. I got us out here, and I'll get us back. No problem. Besides, I want you to keep all your energy for later."

She took his words as an indication of what was yet to come. He wasn't through with her yet, and she didn't have a problem with any plans his mind was conjuring up. No small surprise there. He could create an intense yearning within her, a hunger, with just a look. She'd thought it before and still thought it now. She'd never met a man quite like York.

As they got closer and closer to land, she could feel the quickened beat of her heart, and as she watched him handle the oars, she saw as well as felt his strength. His broad chest, belly and hips tightened with every push and pull of the oars, and he was still hard and fully erected. She was entranced with the sight before her. His naked body was a total turn-on and knowing what that body had done to her was unforgettable.

She could tell from the way he was looking at her that he was fully aware of just how much he had satisfied her. No doubt even in the moonlight her face was basking with a heated glow that only the pleasures of lovemaking could cause.

She blinked when the raft hit land and then he was out of it to secure it. Then he was reaching for her, carrying her into his arms toward the blanket. Moments later, he was lowering her onto it. By the time she felt the material against her back, York had spread her thighs and was settling between them. He looked down at her and their gazes held. When he entered her, stretching her again, she knew tonight would be one she would remember for a long time.

## *CHAPTER EIGHT*

HE WAS A bachelor undone, York decided as he eased out of bed the next morning. And the woman who had slept beside him all night was responsible. He glanced over at her as he made his way to the bathroom. After making love to her on the blanket several times under the moonlight, he had carried her inside and they had showered together, washing sand from their bodies. Eventually they made love again.

They had tumbled into bed too exhausted to make love in the place where most normal people did, but just like she had christened his raft he had plans for that bed. He figured she would be sleeping awhile and after washing his face, brushing his teeth and slipping into a pair of jeans he padded barefoot and bare chested out the room and down the stairs.

He checked his phone and saw he'd missed several calls. One was from Rich, the man he had tailing Felder, and the other two were from Uriel. He quickly called Rich back, and a few moments later the man had brought him up to date. Felder and Danielle Simone were still together, and another interesting fact was that the couple had gotten a visit from someone else, a man not yet identified. But that man was now, too, being tailed as well.

When York ended the call with Rich he called Uriel.

"You called?" he asked the moment he heard his god-brother's voice.

"Where the hell are you, Y?"

"I'm in Jamaica working on a case."

"Oh." Then Uriel said, "You probably couldn't care less, but Ellie mentioned that Darcy went to Jamaica on vacation."

"You don't say," he murmured, smiling.

"I do say, so don't be surprised if you run into her."

Evidently Darcy hadn't mentioned to Ellie that she'd seen him on the island, so he wouldn't give anything away. "Thanks for the warning."

"No problem. I called to give you some news."

"What?"

"I got a call from Donovan."

York nodded. Donovan Steele was one of Uriel's closest friends from college. "Yes?"

"He told me that Eli's getting married."

York almost dropped the phone. Eli Steele was one of Donovan's cousins who lived in Phoenix. York and the rest of his godbrothers had gotten to know Eli and his five brothers when they'd traveled as a group to the NASCAR races to support Bronson Scott, Donovan's best friend who was also a mutual friend to everyone.

"He's getting married?" York asked. Eli was the second of the Phoenix Steeles to marry in a year's time. What was surprising was that those Steeles were die-hard bachelors who'd vowed never to marry.

"Yes, he's marrying on Christmas Day. Can you believe that?"

York was finding it hard to believe. Earlier that year, Eli's brother Galen had gotten hitched to some woman he'd known less than a month. It wouldn't be such a shocker if Eli and Galen, along with their other brothers, hadn't been known womanizers. For them to settle down with one woman was more than a surprise. It was a downright shock.

He talked to Uriel a few more moments before finally ending the call. He then called his parents and another one of his men who was following Johnny Rush. He discovered Rush had spent the night at a bar, probably drowning in grief since he didn't know the whereabouts of Danielle Simone.

York placed his phone back on the table and headed for the kitchen, deciding Darcy deserved breakfast in bed.

A POLICE SIREN sounded in the distance and woke Darcy. She opened her eyes to the glare of the bright sunlight shining into the bedroom window and glanced around, immediately remembering where she was and whose bed she was in.

She shifted and immediately felt the tenderness between her legs, which was a blatant reminder of all the lovemaking she'd participated in the night before. Had she really made love on a raft in the sea? And on the beach? Jeez.

And she couldn't forget how they'd come inside later to shower together and ended up doing that and a whole lot more. She recalled how they'd slept during the night with his body spooning hers.

She lay on her side to glance out the window, and all she could see was the beautiful blue-green water. Waking up to such a sight was simply awesome.

She heard movement downstairs and immediately felt the quickened beats of her heart. What had brought her and York to this? Why even now she had to admit that he had to be the most generous of lovers…and the most skilled. The man didn't miss a beat when it came to pleasuring a woman. He had mastered the skills. It was certainly an ingrained talent that some men never gained. After making love with him she doubted she could ever turn to the likes of Bruce again for anything.

And now that she'd apologized for her behavior of two years ago, they were getting along. At least they were when neither of them mentioned Damien Felder. She knew York suspected the man of wrongdoing, but she was of the mind that a man was innocent until proven guilty. All it took was to remember what had happened to her father years ago when Darcy had been in her early teens.

Her father was a high school teacher, and one of his female students had accused him of inappropriate behavior toward her. Matlock Owens was about to lose his job as well as the respect of the community before the young girl tearfully admitted she had lied just to get attention from her parents. The girl and her family, totally embarrassed by what they'd done, had eventually moved away, but it had taken years before the Owens family had gotten over what had been done to them. Darcy, who'd always been a "daddy's girl," had seen firsthand what the false accusations had done to her father and didn't want the same thing to happen to Damien.

She knew York assumed she was defensive of Damien because she was interested in him, but that was not the case. And in a way she shouldn't really care what York thought. But for some reason she did.

"You're awake."

She turned to the sound of York's voice. He was

standing in the doorway with a breakfast tray in his hand. She couldn't help but smile. No man had ever treated her to breakfast in bed before. She pulled up into a sitting position, realizing she was completely naked under the covers. Where were her clothes? She recalled racing into the house naked last night, then remembered they'd left their clothes in a heap near the blanket. They'd probably gotten washed away by now.

As if reading her thoughts, York came into the room and placed the tray on the nightstand. "I got our clothes. I just shook the sand from your dress because I didn't know if it was washable. But everything else I tossed into the washing machine."

She nodded. The thought of him handling her underthings sent flutters all through her. "Thanks."

He then glanced down at the tray. "I wasn't sure what you liked, so I brought you a little bit of everything."

He was right. It was loaded with pancakes, sausage, bacon, scrambled eggs, a bowl of fresh fruit and toast. She felt she gained five pounds just looking at all the food he'd prepared. "Thanks, and I hope you know there's no way I can eat this all by myself. You are planning to join me, right?"

He chuckled. "Right. But I need to go back for the coffee."

It was only after York had left the room that Darcy was able to breathe normally. He needed a shave but that *I-could-use-a-shave* look made him appear even sexier and more rugged. She shook her head. Ellie would never believe that she and York had called a truce long enough to toss between the sheets.

"I'm back."

Darcy glanced over at him as he entered the room.

He was wearing a pair of jeans that rode low on his hips, and he was bare chested. She recalled licking every inch of that broad chest last night. She also remembered licking other parts of him as well. The scorching sensuality of her actions, as well as her risqué behavior, almost entrapped her into a deep-rooted desire that could overtake her if she wasn't careful.

She watched as he placed two cups of coffee beside the breakfast tray. He then proceeded to remove his jeans before crawling back into bed with her. She quickly scooted over and made room for him. But he didn't let her go too far before pulling her close for a kiss.

Dang. No man should be able to kiss that good in the mornings. Such a thing should be outlawed. It was a kiss so arousing that her body tingled.

She was the one who finally pulled back from the kiss knowing if she didn't she would be spread eagle beneath him in no time. And as much as she didn't want to admit it, being with York could be habit-forming, and she'd never wanted to find herself addicted to any man. She was deeply attracted to him; that in itself could make her vulnerable, and she didn't want that.

"I think you need to feed me," she said, lifting a finger to his jaw and rubbing the stubble there as she gazed at his mouth. He had such a beautiful pair of lips, and he definitely knew how to use them to his advantage. She would always have to be a few steps ahead of him, otherwise she would risk getting in too deep. This was a man who—if she wasn't careful and on her toes—would make her want the one thing she swore she would never want with a man again. An exclusive relationship.

He reached for the coffee and handed her a cup. "Be careful, it's hot," he said.

*And so are you,* she wanted to counter and decided to keep that thought to herself.

He then placed the tray of food between them and began eating off of it. Several times he actually fed pieces of bacon to her. And when he leaned in to nibble a piece of bacon off her lip she thought she would come in a full-blown orgasm then and there.

There was something she needed to ask him about, something that still bothered her although it shouldn't. "York?"

"Yes?"

"That morning after we made love in my hotel room. You left before I woke up. Why?"

He held her gaze. "Had I not left then, Darcy, I might not have left. You had a tendency to make me forget I was on the island for a reason. I had a job to do. My team needed me in place, although I wanted more than anything to stay right in your bed."

She inwardly smiled and didn't want to think how his words had her floating on a cloud of contentment. He *had* wanted to stay with her.

"Any more questions, Darcy?"

She shook her head. "No, not right now."

"Good. What do you want to do today?" he then asked her.

She took a sip of her coffee, surprised by his question. She had assumed he would be taking her back to the hotel after breakfast. She'd figured taking up his time was not an option.

"What do you suggest?" she asked him.

That I-can-think-of-a-number-of-things smile tempted

her to lean over and kiss it off his lips, but she decided to refrain from doing so. "We can go back rafting today," he suggested, reminding her of what they'd done last night. "Or we can stay in, naked, and watch movies," he added.

She chuckled as she took another sip of her coffee. "Sounds interesting."

"Trust me, I can make it as interesting as you want."

She could believe that. "Don't you have work to do today? Need I remind you that you're working on a case?"

He grinned. "Need I remind you that it's the weekend? No filming today and the cast and crew have scattered. I have several men assisting me, and they are keeping tabs on those I need to keep up with."

She couldn't help but wonder if Damien was one of those. She couldn't imagine having her privacy invaded in such a way and pushed the thought to the back of her mind. Otherwise, she would speak her mind and she and York would end up arguing again. "Watching movies sounds good, but I'm not doing so in the nude. The first thing I plan on doing is washing my dress."

"You're a spoilsport, Darcy Owens," he said, chuckling, a pretend pout on his lips.

They continued to eat breakfast, and he mentioned the call he'd gotten from Uriel with the news about Eli Steele. She knew Eli and his brothers through her association with Ellie and Uriel. She glanced over at York after taking another sip of her coffee. "Did you mention to Uriel that we were together?"

He met her gaze and shook his head. "No. I didn't feel it was my place, especially since he didn't mention it, which to me meant you hadn't said anything to Ellie."

She paused in chewing a piece of sausage. "I haven't

talked to Ellie since arriving. I'm due to give her a call, but I prefer not saying anything about us being together. At least not yet. El gets carried away with certain things," she said. *Especially when it's about me and a man.*

"No problem. We will handle our involvement whatever way you prefer."

*Our involvement.* Were they actually involved? Did their actions on two separate occasions account for an involvement? She couldn't help wondering if an involvement and a fling were basically the same thing. She considered a fling as short term and an involvement as something a little longer.

She continued to eat wondering just how he really saw their affair.

YORK SIPPED ON his coffee in thoughtful silence. He couldn't get the vision out of his mind of him making love to Darcy last night—first on a raft and then later on the blanket he'd spread on the sand. Both times had been simply incredible. And he couldn't forget that night in her hotel room.

While he'd been downstairs preparing breakfast, he had found himself watching the clock, anticipating the moment she would awake. He had never felt possessive when it came to a woman, but he did so with her. He could even recall the exact moment he felt he had made her his.

He wondered how he was going to break the news to her. He'd told her at the time, while they'd been making love, but he doubted she remembered.

He had a gut feeling that Darcy was a woman that didn't want to belong to anyone. But he wanted to prove her wrong. York shook his head thinking something was wrong with him. Here he was on the island and working an important case, and the only thing he wanted to think about was making love to Darcy again. He'd thought that calling for a truce had been a good idea. He hadn't known doing so would entice him to build a relationship with a woman who had built a wall around herself. What he'd told her earlier was true. They were involved, and it was an involvement that he intended to explore to the fullest.

"This is delicious, York."

"Thanks. I enjoy being in the kitchen when I have the time. Usually I don't."

"You travel a lot?"

He glanced over at her and nodded. "Not as much as I used to when I was getting the business off the ground. Now I have people who travel for me. This case was different, though, and I wanted to be in the thick of things. One of the men who invested a lot of money into the movie production is a close friend of my father's. He's been losing a lot of money lately."

When he told her just how much, her eyes widened as if she'd found it hard to believe. "That's a lot of money for anyone to lose on a business deal," she said.

"Yes, it is, and it bothers me to think that it's an inside job."

Darcy didn't say anything, and York knew she was thinking of Felder and whether his accusations about the man could be true. She wouldn't bring him up and neither would he. The man was a touchy subject between them, and it was best his name remained out of their conversation.

And speaking of conversation, he decided to switch things. "Have you ever ridden a Jet Ski?"

She shook her head. "No."

He smiled. "Then that's what we'll do today. I'll teach you how it's done."

"You own one?"

"Yes."

She nodded. "Sounds like fun." She then leaned over and softly kissed his lips. "Thanks for last night, York. It was wonderful."

Yes, what they'd shared had been wonderful, and he intended to spend more of such wonderful times with her.

DARCY COULDN'T HELP but smile as she watched York give her a demonstration on the proper way to use the Jet Ski. It was a beautiful piece of equipment, but then the person showing her how to use it was a beautiful man.

After breakfast they had dressed and he had taken her back to the hotel where she had packed an overnight bag and returned here. They had gone swimming for a while and now he was showing her how to use a Jet Ski, and she was having a great time watching him.

They were still wearing their swimsuits. She was wearing a fuchsia bikini, which he seemed quite taken with when she'd put it on. In fact, he'd seemed quite taken with taking it off her as well. He had stripped her naked, tossed the bikini on shore while they went skinny-dipping.

She smiled remembering that time as she studied him. His swimming trunks showed just what a fine physique he had—tight muscles, firm stomach, and thick muscular thighs. His skin was glistening from the water, and her tongue tingled, tempted to lick him dry.

"Any questions?"

She smiled upon realizing that he had asked her a question. "About what?"

He laughed and shook his head. "About anything I just went over with you."

The only thing she could remember—and rather vividly—was listing parts of his body she found fascinating. But not to give anything away, she said, "No, I don't have any questions."

"So you're ready to try it?"

She wouldn't say that. "Only if we can do it together."

That statement made him grin, and she immediately understood why. They had been practically doing it together most of the morning. Ever since she had let the cat out of the bag that she'd gone without sex for almost two years, he had definitely made himself available without any trouble, and she had readily taken him up on his offers.

After breakfast they'd made love, and when they had gotten to her hotel room after she'd thrown items into her overnight bag, they'd made love again. There was just something about him that pushed thoughts of sex to the forefront of her mind. Their lovemaking sessions were always wild and out of control, unrestrained and uncontrollable. He seemed to enjoy it that way, and so did she.

"What I meant," she decided to clarify, "is to ask if we can ride the Jet Ski together."

"We sure can. It can hold up to three people," he said, smiling over at her.

Darcy nodded. She was about to tell him how

nice the brightly colored Jet Ski was when her cell phone rang.

She recognized the number and felt a deep thump in her chest. She glanced over at York and knew she didn't have to tell him who was calling. She probably had a guilty look on her face, although there was no reason for her to be guilty about anything. She had come to the island to enjoy herself and have fun. York didn't mean any more to her than Damien did.

She knew it was a lie as soon as the thought left her brain. She considered ignoring the call and then decided to go ahead and answer it, knowing full well that York would be listening to her every word. "Yes, Damien?"

"I'll be back on the island Monday night, and I was wondering when I can see you again."

# CHAPTER NINE

A FROWN SETTLED around York's lips. Part of his brain tried convincing him that he didn't care, that whatever Darcy did and with whom was her business and that it didn't concern him. But that was a bald-faced lie. It did concern him, not just personally but physically.

He continued to wipe down his Jet Ski while trying to ignore her conversation with Felder. The man was with Danielle Simone, so why was he calling Darcy? He fought to keep his teeth from clenching and had to suck in a deep breath when he was struck by an intense urge to take the phone from her and ask him. The very thought was insane, but the one thing he wasn't feeling at the moment was sane.

*Keep your cool, Ellis. Just because you and Darcy have been mating like rabbits every chance you get is no reason to get all possessive and territorial. But then again, maybe you have every right since you did claim her and decided she was yours.*

He crouched down to wipe off a lower part of the Jet Ski while thinking he could bet all the tea in China that Darcy wouldn't agree with that assessment. She would probably box his ears if she even knew he had such thoughts and was making such assumptions.

He pretended not to notice when she ended the call. He tried ignoring the moment of awkward silence that followed and figured he should say something but decided considering how he felt it was best to keep his mouth shut. He was encountering emotions he'd never felt before, and he wasn't quite sure how to handle them. No woman had ever made him feel this way, and quite honestly, he didn't like it.

"That was Damien."

He glanced over at her without stopping what he was doing. "I gathered."

She didn't say anything for a moment and neither did he. A part of him wished he could concentrate on something else. For the last hour or so, he had been admiring how she looked in the bikini, appreciating her curvy figure and long legs. Now all he could see was the color red flash across his eyes.

He knew his attitude wasn't helping matters, but at the moment, he truly didn't give a damn. Standing less than five feet away was the woman he had made love with most of the night—the woman who had somehow gotten underneath his skin. He broke eye contact with her and continued his work.

"You have no right to be this way, you know."

Her words did something to him, snapped off the last of his patience. He rose to his feet and faced her. Instead of saying anything, he stepped around her and went inside through the back door. She was watching him curiously, and he knew eventually she would follow.

Once inside his kitchen, he turned the moment she swept in behind him. Before she could open her mouth, he was on her, kissing her. Every part of him was throbbing in both anger and arousal. She evidently didn't know anything about rights when it came to him. And he intended to teach her a few things.

God, he wanted her again. He wanted to wipe Damien Felder's name from her memory. He wanted to feel the way their bodies connected when they made love, feel her fingers digging deep in his shoulder blades while he rode her hard, hear her scream his name when she came. Hell, they didn't just have sex together; they had something a lot more remarkable and astonishing.

Instead of pushing him away, she gripped his shoulders and pressed her mouth even closer to him, and he took it with fierce intensity, using his tongue to seduce her to a moan.

And it seemed that she needed the kiss as much as he did when she proceeded to feast hungrily on his mouth. He lifted her up slightly, and she instinctively wrapped her legs around him. Without breaking the kiss, he began walking toward the living room. It was hot outside, but nothing could compare to the temperature he was feeling inside.

York was determined by the time things were over she would know what rights he did have.

This was madness. When he kissed her, Darcy couldn't form a coherent thought. All she knew was that if she continued to get wrapped up in York she could get hurt, because he was awakening emotions she preferred not feeling.

Darcy felt the back of her legs touch the sofa, but instead of lowering her to the sofa, York scooped her into his arms, headed over to the desk and placed her on it. He kissed her again greedily, and she returned the kiss with the same intensity, urgency and hunger.

Moments later when York broke off the kiss to look at her, all she could do was stare into his eyes, just moments before moving her gaze to his wet lips. Then her gaze moved lower, past his bare chest to the swimming trunks. They were no longer wet, probably from all the heat being generated in that area. He was hard and enlarged, and she couldn't stop herself from reaching out and sliding her fingers inside his swimming trunks.

His erection felt hot to the touch, and she cupped him in her hand and could feel the huge veins along the head of him throbbing. She couldn't stop running her fingers along the side of his thickness, thinking he was getting even larger with each stroke.

He reached down and covered her hand with his and asked huskily, "Do you want this?"

His question was definitely a no-brainer. Yes, she wanted it. Since he asked, he evidently wanted to hear her say it and she had no problem doing so. She said, "Yes, I want it." And then because she wanted to hear his admission as well, she asked, "Do you want me?"

He released her hand and slid his own inside her bikini bottom, and then his fingers began exploring her like they had every right to do so. Instinctively, the moment he touched her feminine mound she spread her legs to give him better access. And when he touched her clit, she moaned deep in her throat.

"Oh, yeah, I want you," he whispered close to her lips and leaned over while his fingers continued to stroke her inside. Her heart pounded fiercely in her chest as sensations began overtaking her.

Every nerve inside her body began tingling. And then he leaned forward and used his teeth to lower her bikini top and bared her breasts. Before she could release a gasp of surprise, his mouth latched onto a nipple and began sucking.

Darcy tossed her head back when she felt unbearably hungry for him. Her body was craving him with an intensity that shocked her.

Suddenly he released her to take a step back, and she was forced to let go of him as well. She drew in a deep breath when he eased his swimming trunks down his legs after removing a condom packet from the pocket. She loved a man who believed in being prepared. She then watched as he sheathed his erection, forcing herself to swallow during the process.

He returned to her, and she assumed he would take her off the desk. Instead, he lifted her hips and proceeded to remove her bikini, tossing both somewhere behind him. "You like undressing me, don't you?" she asked in a trembling voice. They had made love several times before, but with York, she never knew what to expect. There was never a dull moment with him when it came to making love—in or out of the bedroom.

"Yes," was his husky response, and before she could say anything else, he lowered his head to her breasts again.

She moaned and lifted her hand to stroke the side of his face, close to his mouth, and she could feel how hard he was sucking her breasts. It caused a myriad of sensations to invade the area between her legs. He had a way of making her feel desired and wanted.

And then he released her nipple, and before she could move, he lifted her hips just seconds before lowering his head between her legs. The second his tongue touched her clit, sensations rammed through her, and she let out a deep moan. He began tonguing her as if she would be his last meal, as if he was intent on exploring every single inch of her satiny flesh.

"York!"

Instead of answering her, he pulled her body closer to his mouth, and his tongue delved even deeper. She'd never felt this aroused in her entire life. He was doing something with his tongue, drawing little circles inside of her, especially on her G-spot.

She felt an orgasm coming on and tried pushing him away, but just as he'd done the last time he had performed oral sex on her, he remained unmovable, unstoppable. Sensations exploded inside of her, and her entire body shook in extreme pleasure. His mouth closed deeper on her and his tongue continued to lave her clit, and her orgasm seemed endless. A rush of heat infused her, and she couldn't help screaming out his name when more and more explosions shattered her body.

"Damn, you taste good," he said moments later when he raised his head and smiled at her. Before she could give him a response, he had grabbed her by the hips and eased her toward his waiting erection. It felt hot when it brushed against her thigh and when he was easing it inside of her. Immediately, her inner muscles clamped down on his pulsating erection. He went deep and deeper, until she could feel his testicles resting against her flesh. He filled her so completely, so totally, she didn't think he had room to move inside.

He proved her wrong when he began stroking her, easing out and going back in, making sensations rush through her veins and pour into her bloodstream. She was convinced she felt him all the way to her womb, and she knew for certain that her body could feel every hard inch of him.

His strokes seemed urgent, and her inner muscles

began milking him, needing to keep him inside her for as long as she could. The more he pounded into her, the deeper he seemed to go and the more she wanted him. He lifted her hips, held them tight and steady to receive each and every one of his hard thrusts.

"Tell me, Darcy," she heard him say. "Tell me this gives me the right. Tell me."

She bit down on her mouth, not wanting to say the words he wanted to hear. She had made love to other men and would have thrown such a request back in their face. But she knew he was right. No other man had made love to her like York did or could. No other man could make her womanhood contract with such intense pleasure.

But should that alone give him the right to anything when it came to her? Oh, hell, she thought, when he increased his pace and began pounding into her with an intensity that almost left her speechless. To get this type of pleasure she would give him whatever rights he thought he wanted.

"York!"

She screamed his name and felt her entire body tremble when an orgasm tore into her. And she knew at that moment what else she wanted, what else she wanted to feel. If he was demanding rights from her then she wanted what she considered as the ultimate in pleasure.

When he pushed hard inside of her and then retreated to thrust back into her, she shifted her body to ease away slightly. Before he realized what she was doing, she reached out and tugged the condom off his erection and tossed it to the floor. She looked at him and said, "With rights come sacrifices. I want you to let go inside of me. I want to feel your semen."

DARCY DIDN'T HAVE to ask twice. Before she could draw in her next breath, York was back inside of her, skin to skin, and he felt the difference all the way to his toes. Hell, he wanted her to feel his semen as well.

There was something about her that had his erection throbbing mercilessly inside of her. That had pressure building up inside him just for the purpose of exploding inside of her. He began stroking her again, almost nonstop.

"Oh, baby, I'm coming." He leaned forward to claim her mouth the moment his body exploded, blasting hot semen inside of her and rocking his entire body from head to toe. This was lovemaking as it should be, lovemaking as it was for him and Darcy. They had made a deal, and both had delivered. At least he had given her what she wanted, and he intended to get what he wanted—rights with her.

He broke off the kiss and threw his head back when he kept coming. Rocking his hips against her to go deeper, he knew he was branding her in a way that he had never branded a woman before. He knew the first time they'd made love there had been a chance some of his semen might have escaped inside of her, but this time he knew for certain.

He had intentionally flooded her with his seed, not for a baby but because she had asked for it. And he knew at that moment he would just about give Darcy Owens anything she wanted. And when she screamed out her orgasm it triggered another one within him, and he shot off inside of her again.

At that moment he knew that no matter how she felt about it, he would not give Damien Felder the chance to ever touch her this way or any other way.

# CHAPTER TEN

DARCY CAME AWAKE and glanced out the window. It was still light outside, which meant it was still the same day. She inhaled the scent of sex. She glanced around the room and saw she was in York's bed, and all she had to do was close her eyes to remember when he had brought her in here.

It had been right after he'd made love to her on the desk. He had gathered her naked body into his arms and taken her into his bedroom where he had placed her in the bed. He had joined her there, stroked her body all over with the pads of his fingers to bring her to another aroused state before straddling her to make love to her again.

His arms tightened around her, and she knew he was awake as well and then he was tugging her closer to him, shifting her on her back and taking possession of her mouth. Only York could kiss her this way and make her want to demand things from a man she'd never demanded before—like his semen.

He released her mouth and stared down at her. "While you were asleep, I've been thinking," he said. His gaze was intense.

She lifted a brow. "About what?"

"Why Damien is so determined to keep you within his reach."

She released a frustrated breath. A part of her wanted to clobber him for bringing up the other man at a time like this, and a part of her wanted to reach up and wrap her arms around his neck to kiss the other man's name from his lips.

"Why are you bringing him up? I gave you rights while we're together on the island. I won't be seeing him or talking to him. Isn't that what you wanted?"

He nodded slowly. "Yes, but there are still unanswered questions in my mind."

"What kind of unanswered questions, York?"

He released a deep sigh and rubbed his hand down his face before sitting up. "My men and I have been keeping close tabs on Felder, and I haven't told you everything."

She lifted a confused brow. "Everything like what?"

"Like the fact that as soon as he parts company with you, he seeks out Danielle Simone or vice versa. Something is going on with those two."

She shrugged. "If you think you were sparing my feelings by not telling me, you were wrong. The thought that he was hitting on her or any other woman for that matter doesn't bother me. He and I never slept together. We didn't as much as share a kiss. In my book, I was doing something that could be considered worse. I was talking to him and making love to you, a man who was having him investigated."

"That might be true, but I still think he sought you out for another reason."

She rolled her eyes. "And what reason is that?"

"To use you as a decoy to get something off this island. Has he given you anything to keep for him?"

"No. I wouldn't take anything from him."

He nodded slowly. "And you're sure he hasn't slipped anything into your purse without your knowledge?"

"No, I keep my purse on me at all times, so he wouldn't have gotten the chance." A frown then marred her forehead when she remembered something. "However, Damien did give me one of those tote bags that promoted the movie before we left the set that day. But it was empty."

"You sure of that?"

"Yes." And then she shook her head and pulled herself up in bed. "At least it felt empty. I didn't look inside of it."

"Where is it now?"

"Back at the hotel."

He was easing out of bed. "Do you mind if I take a look at it?"

Darcy shook her head, not wanting to believe he was starting back up on his mistrust of Damien all over again. "I'm going to ask you one more time, York. Why is it you want to nail everything on Damien? Why are you so convinced he's guilty of anything?"

He didn't answer immediately. Instead, he walked over to the window and glanced out. Moments later, he turned around and said, "A woman who meant a lot to me was killed when she accidentally stumbled into a robbery. Recently I found out one of the men Felder is associated with is someone the authorities believed set things up that night. There was not enough proof to arrest him. If that's true, I might be able to solve two cases, and one is deeply personal."

Darcy didn't say anything for a moment as she absorbed everything he said. She recalled everything Ellie had told her about the woman he was to marry and how she'd gotten killed.

"So what about you?" he asked. "Why are you so hell-bent on believing Felder is innocent?"

She drew in a deep breath. "I believe a person is innocent until proven guilty."

She then told him what had happened with her father while she was growing up. "So you see, York, my father was accused of something he didn't do, and I saw what it did to him. I don't want any part of doing something similar to another human being."

He nodded slowly. "I understand, Darcy, and would love to tell you I might be wrong about Felder but I don't think that I am. He has too many ties to unsavory individuals."

He glanced at his watch. "I want to check out that bag he gave you."

Darcy eased out of bed, met his unwavering gaze and sighed. "Fine. Give me a few minutes to shower and get dressed and then we can leave. But don't be surprised if you discover you're just wasting your time."

IT DIDN'T TAKE any time getting back to the hotel. York was well aware that Darcy thought he was wasting his time and that might very well be the case, but he refused to leave any stone unturned. Someone was sneaking footage off the set some way, and he intended to find out if his hunch was right.

York slid his hands into the pockets of his jeans after they entered Darcy's hotel room, and he closed the door behind them. His gaze drifted over her as she moved in the sunlight coming in through the windows. She was wearing a short denim skirt and a cute zebra-print midriff blouse that showed a lot of skin. He could vividly recall how his hands had moved over every inch of her body, touching her, caressing her, igniting heat wherever he touched and eliciting her whimpers and moans.

He had liked the sound of her calling his name. He had liked it even more when she'd reciprocated and touched him all over, making his body quiver beneath the contact of her hands to his flesh.

Since he'd told her what he thought Felder was up to, she had a no-nonsense air about her. At least he now understood why she'd always come to the man's defense. After what had happened to her dad he could understand her trying to defend anyone she felt was being falsely accused. But he hadn't told her everything about Felder. The man had all the reasons for wanting to make a little bit of extra money on the side, even if it was at York's client's expense.

It took him a moment to realize Darcy had said something. "Sorry, could you repeat that?" he asked.

A frown appeared between her neatly arched eyebrows. "I said the tote bag is in the bedroom. I had already packed it up with my stuff since I wouldn't be using it. I'll go and get it."

He thought about following her in that bedroom and decided that wouldn't be a good idea. He might be tempted to toss her on that bed and make love to her, which was definitely something he enjoyed doing. Being around her was pure torture. If her touch didn't get to him then her scent definitely did.

He moved away from the door and crossed the room to the sliding glass doors to look out. If his theory was right then Darcy wasn't in any real danger; however, the thought that anyone, especially Felder, was using her made his teeth clench again.

There was something about her that brought out not only his protective instincts but his possessive instincts as well. A part of him just didn't know what to make of it when he'd never acted this way around other women. He needed to be in better control of his emotions since for the first time ever they seemed to be getting the best of him.

"Here's the bag, and just like I assumed, York, it's empty."

He slowly turned from the window. He tried to focus on the canvas tote bag she was holding in her hand but instead he concentrated on her hands, and he recalled just where those hands had touched him, all the things those hands had done to him.

His gaze roamed over her, and he thought today the same thing he thought every time he saw Darcy. She was a beautiful woman—beautiful and striking. The sunlight highlighted her creamy brown skin and the luster of her dark hair.

He took the tote bag to check for himself. Carrying the bag over to a table, he heard her sigh of frustration when she followed him.

"I hope you don't plan to rip my bag apart trying to find something that's probably not there, York," she said with a degree of agitation in her tone.

He merely glanced over at her and smiled. "If I have to, I'll make sure you get another one." Although he knew he was petty and childish, he didn't like the thought of her stressing out over a bag Felder had given her.

He knew she had gotten really upset with him when

she left his side and sat down on the sofa. He glanced over at her and met her gaze and saw the fire in her eyes. She'd gotten uptight again, and when they got back to his place, he would look forward to loosening her up a bit.

From his pocket he pulled out what to a layman looked like an ink pen. The tip of the pen had a scanning light, and he slowly skimmed it across the bag. He smiled when the tip began blinking. He turned to Darcy and said, "According to this scanner, Darcy, this bag isn't empty."

She was off the sofa in a flash. "That's not possible," she said adamantly as she came to stand beside him, giving him more than a whiff of her luscious scent.

"We'll see," he said as he glanced back down at the tote bag. It looked empty and it felt empty, as well. Evidently there was a secret compartment somewhere in the bag. He flipped it inside out and didn't see anything suspicious. He then began feeling around and still didn't detect anything. Whatever was being hidden was a small object.

Using the scanning pen again, he skimmed it over the bag, and when the light turned red over a certain area York smiled again. Bingo. He glanced back over at her. "Like I said earlier, I'll get you another bag."

With that said, he reached into his back pocket to retrieve a pocketknife and sliced through the seam. "What do we have here?" he asked when two memory cards slid out.

Darcy inched closer, and he noted the surprised expression on her face. Her eyes had widened, and her mouth had fallen open. "I don't believe it," she said in both disbelief and anger.

"Seeing is believing, baby. Now if we had a video camera we could see just what's on here, although I have an idea."

"I have a video camera." With that said, she rushed off toward the bedroom.

He held up the memory cards in his hand to study them. Filming had just begun, so he couldn't imagine anyone collecting too much footage yet.

He looked up when Darcy reentered the room carrying her video camera. "Nice camera," he said, when she handed it over to him.

"Thanks. It was a birthday present from my oldest brother."

He slipped in the memory card, and they watched the screen flare to life. "Whoa!"

Flashed before them was footage of the scenes being shot for Spirit Head Productions. "I don't believe this!" Darcy gasped in anger. "Felder is ripping off the company."

York clicked off the camera. "Looks that way," he said, barely able to contain his anger. "Do you know what would have happened to you if these were found in your possession by anyone?"

He could tell by her expression that she knew the seriousness of the predicament Felder had placed her in. And he could also tell that the more she thought about it the angrier she was becoming.

"I can't wait to see him, and when I do I'll—"

"Say nothing," he said with a dark scowl. "I tried to warn you about him, but you wouldn't take heed to my warning."

She lifted her chin. "I know that, York, and I regret

not doing so, but not saying anything to him is not an option."

"It has to be," he said. "Calm down and think for a minute. Felder believes that you're clueless that he's using you as a decoy to get these back into the States. Now I'm curious as to who is supposed to get these. I'm sure it's probably not anyone you know, so when was he going to get the bag from you? Who is it going to? And who—"

"And you think I give a royal flip about any of that?" she asked, fuming. "If I would have gotten arrested returning from vacation carrying those memory cards I might as well have kissed my job goodbye. I can imagine the article that would have appeared in the papers, the embarrassment it would have caused my family."

"But you would have been innocent."

"Yes, just like my dad had been innocent—but the humiliation almost killed him," she said furiously.

York knew she was taking in the blunt reality of what could have happened and he understood. Now it was imperative that he make her understand something as well. "But you've been spared all of that, Darcy. Think of the next person he might use. Think about how Felder and his accomplices are getting away with it."

He knew his words had gotten to her when she lowered her head to study the floor. Her breathing indicated she was still upset and angry. But at least he had gotten her to start thinking. "Just think about it, Darcy. I'll have a chance to nail this guy and his associates for good."

She lifted her head and met his gaze head-on. "Correction, York. *We'll* have a chance to nail them. I'm the one he's set up to take the fall if anything went wrong."

She didn't say anything for a moment and then added, "But he's counting on nothing going wrong. Now I'm just as curious as you as to who is supposed to take this bag off me. I wouldn't just meekly turn it over to anyone."

York's expression was mixed with wariness and caution. "What do you mean 'we'?"

"Just what I said. In order for you to find out who this bag was meant for and how they plan to get it, I'll need to be a player in all this."

He crossed his arms over his chest and stared down at her. "No, you don't. Now that you know the truth about Felder, I want you to bow out of the picture."

Darcy shook her head. "No, I won't do that. I'm keeping that bag."

"And risk going to jail?"

"Then I guess it will be up to you to make sure I don't," she replied as she brought her face close to his.

That wasn't the only thing close. Her breasts were now pushed up to his chest. Desire as thick as it could get suddenly rushed through his veins. All sorts of scenarios entered his mind of what could go wrong if he went along with what she was proposing. But at that moment, he couldn't think. Lust was taking over, and logical thoughts couldn't compete.

He leaned forward, and he growled close to her lips before he took her mouth with all the hunger he felt.

DARCY KNEW SHE wasn't thinking sensibly. But she hadn't thought sensibly since she'd planned this trip. She had wanted action and a man, and by golly she was getting them both in the form of York Ellis. And the way he was kissing her was making her realize she was one lucky woman.

No man could kiss the way he did. No other male had his taste. And she was totally convinced that no man's tongue could do all the things that his could. He'd told her at breakfast that he thought her mouth was made for kissing. Well, she thought his was, too.

He was kissing her with a sexual tempo, a seductive rhythm that had her moving her body even closer to his. They didn't just fit together, she thought. They fit together perfectly. She could feel the hard tips of her nipples press against the T-shirt he was wearing.

And that wasn't all she was feeling. She knew the moment his hands cupped her backside to make them an even more perfect fit. She liked the way his huge and hard erection was nestled at the juncture of her thighs and the way his breathing sounded while he was kissing her.

Heat rushed through her bloodstream. She wasn't surprised when he lifted up the hem of her jeans skirt and with eager fingers explored underneath.

She moaned deep in her throat when those same fingers came in contact with her thong and moved beyond them to her satiny folds. He dipped his fingers in her wetness, and she gripped his shoulders to keep from tumbling in desire.

She pulled her mouth from his and moaned out his name. "York."

"I want to take you into that bedroom, strip you naked and lick you all over."

His words had her mind, her senses and her entire body spinning. She met the heated gaze. "If you get to do it to me then I get to do it to you. Is that a deal?"

He smiled. "Hell, yeah." He then swept her off her feet and carried her into the bedroom.

DARCY'S HEART POUNDED hard in her chest. She had never made love in this position. She was straddling York's face and he was straddling hers, and the moment his tongue slid inside of her she nearly lost it. Every nerve in her body responded, and when he began feasting on her clit, she moaned deep in her throat.

And that's when she knew she needed to taste him the same way he was tasting her. Her fingers gripped his erection and brought it to her mouth. She began devouring him the same way he was devouring her. She could feel the strength of him throb in her throat, expand in her mouth, thicken around her tongue.

She loved the taste of him, and she loved what he was doing to her, how he was making her feel. Some type of movement that he did with his tongue made her moan out loud. What was he doing to her? To retaliate, she deepened her hold on him, and he rocked his hips against her mouth when she rocked hers against his.

She felt sensations burst to life inside her belly and knew what was about to happen. She sank her mouth deeper on him when her body exploded about the same time that his did. And she applied even more pressure on him to absorb the very essence of him like he was doing with her.

It seemed as if this orgasm for the both of them was endless and they rode it out, satisfying their taste buds as he filled her the way she was filling him.

Moments later, he rolled away from her, and she was forced to let him go. He faced her, then straddled her again and slid into her still wet warmth.

"York."

"Darcy."

And then he began thrusting inside of her. Hard. Penetrating. Deep. With every hard stab, every delicious pounding, she groaned. He was filling her, going deeper and deeper, and her greedy inner muscles were gripping him, clenching him, demanding he give her now what he'd shot into her mouth moments ago.

He lifted his head to stare down at her while the lower part of his body continued to ride her. "Like it?"

"Love it."

He smiled, and that smile coming from York sent pleasure reeling all through her. "You're mine, Darcy."

She heard his words, and for the moment she couldn't argue with him. At that moment, she and every part of her being were his. He was giving her insurmountable pleasure and she felt it from the top of her head to the soles of her feet, and when another explosion took its toll on her, she knew one thing was for certain. She knew she would never play around with a sex toy again. Not when she could have the real thing from York Ellis.

# CHAPTER ELEVEN

"York, you are definitely a bad boy."

York smiled as he shifted to his side to gaze down at her. She sounded out of breath, like she could barely get the words out, like she had gotten worn out. He was filled with male pride that he was the reason.

"A bad boy?" he asked, holding her gaze.

"Oh, yes, definitely bad. I've never done anything like that before. In fact, I've never done half the stuff I've done with you. Who makes love on the beach or in a raft for heaven's sake?"

He chuckled. "A man hard up for the woman he's with."

She smiled as if pleased with his answer. "And were you hard up for me?"

"Baby, I'm hard up for you now." He knew there was no way she could not believe what he'd said with the strength of his erection resting against her thigh, throbbing like it hadn't come a few times already.

"Now to get back to the subject we were discussing earlier," she said softly.

He shook his head. "I don't recall us discussing anything."

She gently punched him in his arm. "Liar. If I have to, I will refresh your memory. And speaking of memory, it was about those memory cards."

York didn't say anything for a moment. He had hoped she had somehow forgotten about that but should have known better. He reached down and swept a lock of hair off her forehead and said softly, "Let me handle it, Darcy."

She held his gaze. "I appreciate you wanting to, but I'm the one Felder figured to use. I owe him."

York pulled in a deep breath. He'd heard about a woman scorned, but he had a feeling a woman a man had set out to use would be just as resentful and spiteful. She would also be revengeful, and that's what he didn't have time for. He didn't need her or anyone else getting in the way of him bringing down Felder and whoever he was working for and with. "Darcy, I want you to let me handle it. Let it go."

"I can't."

He heard the seriousness in her voice and realized at that moment she truly couldn't. Then he again remembered what she'd told him about her father. She was a woman wronged, and she intended—come hell or high water—to get even. At that moment, he truly felt sorry for Felder.

But still, York decided to try to appeal on her logical side, to get her to back away from the unknown. He had some names of those Felder might be in cahoots with and expected there might be others. The bootlegged films would bring in a lot of money and would possibly bankrupt the production company. It wasn't fair that many people would lose their jobs due to shameless greed.

"You have got to let me do this, York."

Her words regained his attention, and he glanced down at her, saw the determination in her eyes. "This is not a game, Darcy. It's serious business. You don't know the type of men we're dealing with. You could get hurt." He came short of saying she could lose her life. He thought about Rhonda, how her life had ended and she had been trained to take down the bad guys. But a bullet had stopped her, anyway.

"Yes, but think about it for a moment. They'd singled me out as their fall guy. Supposedly, without my knowledge, they have given me something to pass on to someone. But who? How is the contact supposed to be made? Why was I singled out? All we know is someone is supposed to get those memory cards. But when? I think I should go along pretending that business is usual and see how this plays out. I'm just as capable as any female employee you might bring in. Have you forgotten I can defend myself?"

No, he hadn't forgotten. He knew she was trained in martial arts. And from what he'd heard she was pretty good. But still, karate couldn't stand a chance against a gun aimed at you with a bullet destined to kill you.

He rubbed his hand down his face and then said, "Let me think about this."

She nodded, but again he saw the determined look in her eyes. Regardless of what his decision might be, she'd already made hers. "Did Felder say when he'll be back?" he asked her.

"Yes. He said he was returning Monday and wanted to see me again."

He thought for a second and then said, "That tote bag isn't something you would automatically bring with you, and he knows you'll probably get suspicious if you were asked about it. He plans to get it some other way. And I don't think it will be on this island. I believe he plans for someone to get it from you when you get back to Miami. I think he just wants to keep up with you while you're here on the island. Those videos are worth a lot of money, and he'll want to keep tabs on them."

"Let him."

"Did you ever mention to him how long you'll be on the island?" he asked.

"Yes, that night he took me to dinner and dancing. He also knows that I have a few hours layover in Miami before flying on to Minnesota."

York nodded slowly. "Come on, let's get up, get dressed and go back to my place. We can think some more there."

But it wasn't thinking that he wanted to do. He wanted nothing more than to make love to her again. And more than anything, he wanted to keep her safe from men like Felder. But he knew she wouldn't appreciate his protection. She would see it as a weakness on her part.

He eased his naked body out of bed and glanced around the room for his jeans. "Can I ask you something, York?" he heard her say.

He turned his attention to her. "Yes."

"How do you manage to stay hard for so long? Even when you don't have sex on your mind?"

Of all the things he had expected her to ask, that wasn't it and he couldn't help his quick laugh. But then he really shouldn't be surprised. Darcy did have the tendency to speak her mind. "And what makes you think I don't have sex on my mind?" he countered.

She shrugged beautiful naked shoulders. "I just figured you didn't."

He smiled. "You're lying in bed naked and you think

I don't have sex on my mind? Less than an hour after I got to perform one of my fantasy positions?"

A smile curved her lips. "That was your fantasy position?"

"Yes, but I have several."

She pushed the bedcovers aside exposing her nakedness. "Show me another one. I'm game."

The pulse at the base of his throat was fluttering erratically as he raked his gaze over her. He thought she was simply beautiful whether she was in clothes or out of them. Lying there naked in bed, looking more gorgeous than any woman had a right to look, made him get harder and thicker. He wasn't surprised she noticed that as well.

"You're getting even more aroused, York. There's no need letting a good, hard erection go to waste, is there?"

He truly liked the way she thought. "No, there's not," he said and headed back to the bed.

THEY HAD BEEN back at York's beach house less than ten minutes when Darcy's cell phone rang. York had gone outside to put away the Jet Ski and set up the grill. She smiled when she saw her caller was Ellie. She was glad her friend was not there to see the deep blush that suddenly appeared on her features. If Ellie knew what she'd been doing for the past few days and with whom, she wouldn't believe her.

"Hello."

"Hey, girl, just thought I'd give you a warning. Uriel mentioned at dinner that York is also on the island."

Darcy smiled. Everyone in their inner circles knew of her and York's dislike of each other and would probably be shocked and surprised as hell to discover they liked each other after all. In fact, she would go so far to say they liked each other a lot.

Their last escapade in her hotel room had turned into a sex game for them, one she had enjoyed. She hadn't known there were so many naughty ways to have fun with one's lover.

*Lover.*

Yes, he was definitely her lover…at least while she was here on the island. She knew once they returned to New York that it would be business as usual, although she doubted she could draw enough energy not to like him again. She liked him way too much now. What woman wouldn't like a man who could make her head spin, her knees go weak and her toes curl? A man who had the ability to dish out multiple orgasms?

"Darcy?"

"Yes?"

"Why aren't you saying anything? I expected you to have sent out a few colorful curse words by now, especially since you and York can't get along."

And under any normal circumstances when it came to York, she would have. But that was before she had discovered a lot more about him, including some things not connected to the bedroom. Over the past couple of days, they had talked a lot over dinner, breakfast and when they weren't busy blowing each other's minds in the bedroom. She believed he was a great brother, as great as her two, and a girl couldn't ask for more than that.

She also believed he was a natural-born protector. That was evident in the way he was still trying to talk her out of any involvement with those memory cards.

And she would even go so far as to admit that once

you got to know him, he was a likable person, a lot of
fun to be around and wonderful company. He was well
versed on a lot of things. She liked the fact that they
shared the same political party, held strong in their be-
lief there was a God and thought no matter how old he
got, Prince was the bomb.

"Darcy!"

She snapped to attention. "What?"

"What's the matter with you?" Then in a low voice,
Ellie asked, "Did I catch you at a bad time?"

Darcy smiled. "If you're asking if you caught me
with my panties off and in bed with a man, then the
answer is no. But had you called an hour or so earlier
the answer would be a resounding yes!"

"You are protecting yourself, right?"

She swallowed deeply. "Yes, I am protecting myself."

She knew why Ellie was asking. Ellie was the only
person who knew how much she enjoyed the feel of a
man's release erupting inside of her. That had always
been a deep, dark fantasy of hers—one she could never
indulge in with a man. It had been okay with her and
Harold when they were married, but after her divorce
she could never trust any man to go that far with her.

But she trusted York. She believed he was in good
health like he believed she was. He had told her he didn't
make it a point to make love to a woman without a condom, regardless of whether she was on any type of birth
control or not. Too many women out there were looking
for some man to become their baby's daddy, and he did
not want that status. However, he didn't mind letting go
inside of her. In fact, she would probably be safe to say
he enjoyed giving it as much as she enjoyed getting it.

"So you've met a man…"

Ellie's statement reclaimed her attention. She decided to be honest. "Yes, I've met a man."

"Is he someone from the islands?" Ellie asked.

"No."

"American?"

"Yes."

"I don't have to ask if he's nice looking," Ellie tacked on.

Darcy smiled. "No, you don't have to ask. And don't bother asking if he's good in bed because he is. And yes, he was well worth my two years of abstinence."

There was a pause on the other end, and then Ellie asked quietly, "Is he someone you can see yourself falling in love with, Darcy?"

At that moment, Darcy's heart sank from her chest right into the pit of her stomach. Ellie's question hit her like a ton of bricks and made her realize something she had tried not to think about. She had come to the island for fun and sex but not love. *Love* had been a word that had gotten torn from the pages of her memory the day she'd divorced Harold. Love was an emotion she hadn't thought about since the day she had refused to take any more of her ex's foolishness, and had come to the realization that she could do bad all by herself and that he wasn't worth the heartache.

But now thanks to Ellie that one word was back, and all the emotions that came with it were staring her right smack in the face. And the sad thing was that she knew the answer to her best friend's question. Yes, York was someone she could see herself falling in love with, and heaven help her, she was almost there. It wouldn't take much to push her over the edge and get her heart screwed up all over again.

She rubbed her hand down her face. How could she have let it happen? When did it happen? Was it too late to pull back and run in the opposite direction?

"You've taken too long to answer, Dar. Should I include another place setting at the New Year's Eve dinner party?"

She closed her eyes, trying to force her body, her mind, her thoughts into denial. York was just her island lover. When they returned to New York, things would go back to how they were before. Her mind could agree with that reasoning but her heart was playing hardball.

Darcy drew in a deep breath, knowing why. She would want to continue to play all those naughty and fun games with him. She couldn't imagine being in the same room with him and not being able to plan their next sexual escapade. And she refused not to be able to kiss him, tangle her tongue with his, suck on it as if she had every right.

*Rights.*

He wanted rights when it came to her, and hadn't she given them to him to some degree? Did he expect those rights to extend beyond Jamaica? Would it truly bother her if he did expect it? She shook her head knowing it would probably bother her if he didn't.

"Maybe I need to call you back later. Sounds like I've given you a lot to think about," Ellie said, once again interrupting Darcy's thoughts.

"Yes, you have."

"And when you call me back you will let me know if I should add another name to my guest list, right?" Ellie said.

Darcy forced a chuckle. She was one hundred percent certain her lover's name was already on the guest list. But she wasn't ready to tell Ellie that yet. "Yes, I'll let you know then."

Moments later, she hung up the phone. Ellie was right. She had been given a lot to think about.

## CHAPTER TWELVE

"IT'S A GOOD THING you discovered those memory cards on Ms. Owens, York," Wesley Carr was saying. "There's a chance she would have cleared security like Felder counted on her doing. But what if she hadn't?"

York leaned against the shed in his backyard and rubbed a hand down his face as he talked to Wesley on his cell phone. That scenario Wesley had just mentioned was one he really and truly didn't want to think about. It would have been hard for her to convince anyone that those memory cards had been planted on her and that she knew nothing about having them.

"I know, Wesley. And she's determined to let Felder think he's using her and has her just where he wants her. I'm just curious to know how he intends to get that tote bag from her."

York released a deep breath. Unknowns were what had his gut twisting when several scenarios flashed across his mind. He didn't like a single one of them since all of them placed Darcy in some sort of danger. And all he had to do was think of what had happened to Rhonda to know he had no intention of letting that happen.

"Where is the tote bag now?" Wesley asked.

"We brought it back from the hotel, and it's here at my place."

"So what's your plan, son?"

York couldn't help but smile. Wesley personified the saying "Once a cop always a cop." "Don't know. But what I do know is that I don't want Darcy Owens placed in any danger."

"And we will work hard to make sure that doesn't happen. You got good men and women working for you."

York knew that to be true. But still…

There had to be that *but* in there somewhere, and he didn't like it. And of course Darcy was trying to make things complicated. She should have taken his advice from the jump and not become involved with Felder. But the stubborn woman refused to do so, and now she had the nerve to want to help him nail the guy. Well, he had news for her. Things would not go down that way. He couldn't take the chance.

"York, you still there?"

It was then that York remembered he had Wesley on the phone. "Yes, Wesley, I'm still here. I'll check in with Marlon to see how things are going with Johnny Rush. He seemed put out that Danielle Simone is missing."

"I guess he would be when it appears that she and Felder have a thing going on right under the man's nose. In my day, a man found the woman he wanted and settled down with her. Nowadays you young people shy away from commitment. Why is that, York?"

York knew he couldn't speak for others, only for himself. "Marriage isn't easy to deal with anymore, Wesley." He then thought about Rhonda. He had planned to ask her to marry him Christmas night. Her untimely death had shown him you couldn't take much for granted. It had also made him vow never to fall for another woman who didn't mind putting herself in a dangerous position.

So why was he falling for Darcy?

And he would admit that he was falling for her big time. It wasn't just the sex, although he would be the first to admit any time he was inside of her was off the chain. But there was a side of her he hadn't gotten to know until recently when he'd begun spending time with her. Besides being sexy, she was witty and fun to be around.

"I'll check in with the others. As you know, Felder and Simone aren't the only ones I'm keeping a close eye on. I have a feeling there are others in this game of deceit. And I think it's time we need to move to plan B. And fast."

A few moments later, York had ended his conversation with Wesley and was about to go back inside his house when he got another call. This one was from his godbrother Zion to say he would be returning to the States for the holidays since Ellie insisted he attend her New Year's party.

They talked a little while, and Zion brought him up to date on how the jewelry business was doing. His handmade jewelry was now on every woman's wish list, after the president had purchased a few pieces for the first lady. Moments later, he hung up the phone thinking he had left Darcy to her own devices way too long. It was time for him to go check on her. And time to come up with a game plan to get any ideas out of her mind of working with him to bring Felder down.

"So what's our game plan, York?"

York glanced up from his breakfast and looked

across the table at Darcy. Yesterday they had gone swimming and later he had treated her to grilled trout, a salad, roasted corn on the cob and ice-cold lemonade. As before, she had sat at the kitchen counter and watched him work. She had volunteered to pitch in to help, but he'd convinced her his kitchen was a one-man show and that he preferred she just sit and watch him in action. She had a way of undressing him with her gaze. Usually thinking that any woman found him that interesting would annoy him, but not with Darcy—mainly because he was just as interested in her as she seemed to be in him.

And he'd proven just how much at bedtime. Memories of making love to her were still vibrant in his mind. She had surprised him upon waking up this morning. She had treated him to breakfast…only after treating him to something else. He'd never enjoyed early morning lovemaking so much.

He met her gaze. "Would it matter very much if I said we don't have one?" he responded while twirling his wineglass between his fingers. He had taken her up on her suggestion of swapping orange juice for wine, and he rather enjoyed it.

She gave him a sweet smile, one that didn't fool him for a minute. He'd figured it was only a matter of time for her to recall they still had a bone to pick. "Of course it would matter, York. I thought we agreed that I would be included."

He didn't want to argue with her, but he decided to try once again to make her understand why he couldn't—wouldn't—let her become involved. "We didn't agree to anything." He took a sip of his wine and then said, "I don't want anything to happen to you."

Evidently it was how he'd said it more than what he'd said that gave her pause. For the longest moment, she just stared across the table at him, and he was able to feel the intensity of her gaze. Exactly how had he said it? Then he realized it was with more emotion than he had intended.

Too late he also realized the show of emotions couldn't be helped. Darcelle Owens had literally gotten under his skin in a way no other woman had since Rhonda and in a way he'd vowed that no other woman ever would.

"Tell me about her, York."

He took another sip of his wine and played ignorant. "Tell you about who?"

"The woman you lost that meant so much to you."

There was no reason to ask how she'd heard about Rhonda. Darcy and Ellie were best friends, and somewhere along the way, Ellie had probably heard the story from Uriel, who had shared it with her…at least the parts Uriel knew. But there was so much more that none of his godbrothers knew—like the fact that not only had York lost the woman he had planned to marry but he'd also lost his unborn child. Rhonda had told him a week or so earlier that she was pregnant.

He liked her a lot, but he wasn't sure he had been in love with her—at least not to the extent he figured his godbrothers Uriel and Xavier were with their wives. And he had taken extreme caution each and every time they'd made love. When she'd decided to begin using the Pill, he had thought things were safe enough for him to stop using a condom. She had gotten pregnant when the antibiotics she had been taking for the flu had counteracted her birth control pills.

He had been more than willing to step up to the plate and do the right thing and marry her. However, he was certain he wouldn't have thought of marriage without the pregnancy.

"Why do you want to know anything about Rhonda?" he finally asked, placing his wineglass next to his plate after deciding he needed to be in full control of his senses when engaging in such a conversation with Darcy.

"I just do."

He held her gaze for several long moments—so long that he would not have been surprised if she withdrew her request. Of course she didn't. A part of him was tempted to tell her that her reasoning wasn't good enough, but he decided not to even bother. She had asked a question and expected a response, regardless of whether he wanted to give her one or not. York wondered if it would always be that way with them. Would there ever be a time when they would be on an even keel?

He leaned back in his chair. "Rhonda and I met about seven years ago when she joined the NYPD. I had gotten out of rookie training, and she was just beginning it. We dated off and on for a while, then decided to date exclusively. We'd been at it almost eight months when she was killed."

"And you were about to ask her to marry you?"

"Yes."

She nodded slowly as if she understood everything and then she added, "You loved her that much."

He wasn't sure just what "that much" entailed, but for some reason he felt the need to set the record straight. Why he was doing it with her when he hadn't with anyone else, he wasn't sure. A slow, yet serious smile spread across his lips. Then he simply said, "No."

The room lapsed into a moment of dead silence, and he was certain he didn't hear anything. Not the sound of the waves beating against the shoreline, nor the sound of the clock on the wall ticking and not even the sound of her breathing. The look she gave him beneath silky long lashes would have him squirming in his seat had he not gotten immune to that look by now.

York watched the frown settle around her lips, and he thought that once again she looked annoyed—but not too annoyed not to ask, "And why were you planning to marry her, then?"

The answer was simple. "She was having my baby."

# CHAPTER THIRTEEN

DARCY SAT UP straight in her chair, pulled her bathrobe together when it gaped open, probably the same way her mouth did. His girlfriend had been pregnant when she'd gotten killed? Why hadn't Ellie told her that?

Evidently, that question was etched across her face because York said, "The reason Ellie didn't tell you is because she doesn't know. I've never told Uriel. No one knows. In the six years since Rhonda's death, you're the only person I've told."

Darcy wondered how she got so lucky and decided to ask. "Why tell me?"

"Because you asked."

Darcy wondered when she would learn to mind her own business. But then she recalled there was a reason for this line of conversation, and it had to do with him not wanting her to participate in exposing Felder. "I assumed the reason you didn't want me to be a part of exposing Damien is because you'd somehow feel responsible if something happened to me. Do you feel responsible for what happened to the mother of your child?"

He shook his head. "No. What she did for a living didn't bother me. I was a cop as well. I had no reason to feel responsible. We had parted that morning with plans to get together for dinner later that night. I had it all planned, a nice cozy dinner around the fireplace where I would ask her to marry me."

"But you didn't love her?"

He took another sip of his wine. "Evidently, there are several degrees of love. At the time I was in my twenties and thought I was in love but since then after hanging around Uriel and Xavier, I realized I didn't have the intense emotions toward Rhonda as they have toward their wives. If Rhonda hadn't gotten pregnant, there's no telling if the thought of marrying her would have entered my mind."

Darcy nodded. He was being honest with her, and she could appreciate that. She knew all about being in your twenties and thinking love ruled your heart and then finding out you didn't know the difference between lust and love. It had been a rude awakening for her and a period of time from which she thought she would never recover. Sometimes she wondered if she would truly ever fully recover.

"And had she lived?" Darcy heard herself prompting.

He held her gaze. "We would have married and I would have tried to be a good husband and father. But I have reason to believe we would not have made it past the five-year mark. When it came to me, she was too easy, too dead set on letting me have things my way. We rarely argued about anything because she would give in too quickly."

Darcy took a sip of her wine thinking it was just the opposite for them. Was that the reason he was attracted to her? Then what was the reason she was attracted to him besides the obvious—looks, body, his skill in the bedroom or any place you wanted to enjoy sex?

Deciding she needed to make sure he understood

her position about Damien Felder, she said, "I won't be changing my mind about helping out, York."

"You'd only get in the way. Become a distraction."

She lifted both her chin and her brow. "A distraction to who?"

"Me."

She narrowed her gaze. "That sounds like a personal problem."

"It is," he agreed. "But since I can't do anything about it, I have to handle it the best way I can." He leaned closer toward her at the table. "I suggest you agree to do things my way, Darcy."

She leaned closer toward him as well. "And I suggest you do things my way, York."

He didn't as much as blink when he said, "It seems that we have a problem."

She smiled. "Like I said, it's your problem and not mine."

There was something in the way he was looking at her, holding her gaze within his dark, sharp depths, that made her heart rate increase. If his eyes could talk, she knew just what they would be saying. It was evident that he was not pleased with the way things were going. She was not a "yes" girl, and he didn't very much like it. Well, that was too bad. She had no intentions of backing down.

"You know there is a simple solution to this, don't you?" he asked, still holding her gaze.

"Is there?"

"Yes, I can make sure you're out of the picture by holding you here against your will."

She smiled at the thought of that. "You don't look the type who would easily break the law."

"Then I suggest you look again."

She did. What she detected in his body language made her uneasy. "You wouldn't dare."

"You want to bet?"

No, she didn't want to bet. She wanted to leave. Standing slowly, she said, "I want to return to the hotel now."

He remained seated in his chair. His gaze was now speculative. Amused. "Running off so soon?"

She figured it was now or never. He had this way about him that attracted her way too much. Even now she felt her thighs trembling, her panties getting wet. The urge to mate with him was too intense for her comfort. If he thought he could divert her attention with something like sex…well, he was probably right. But she would stand firm and not let him.

"I'm going to get dressed. Are you taking me back or do I get a cab?"

"Neither."

He was serious. "I'm going to start screaming," she warned.

He chuckled. "Baby, you've been screaming a lot since you've been here, anyway."

That was true, but he didn't have to remind her or call her out on it. Her attention was drawn back to him when she heard his chair scraping against the floor, and she backed up when he stood. "Let's stop playing games, York."

"I'm not playing games, Darcy. By now, Damien has gotten word that you happened to meet an overzealous Johnny Rush fan who talked you out of your tote bag. That woman, Patricia Palmer, is an ex-cop and happens to work for me. She left the island with the tote bag in her possession this morning, headed home via a connection in Miami. My men are posted all over the Miami International Airport, along with Miami police, just waiting to see how things are going to go down."

Darcy stared at him, and when she saw he wasn't kidding and that he was dead serious, anger took over her body. "And just how did she get my tote bag?"

He crossed his arms over his chest, looking smug. "I gave it to her last night. She dropped by while you were asleep."

And because he knew how her mind worked, York added, "And no, I did not make love to you to the point of exhaustion for that reason, Darcy. Making love with that much intensity and vigor is normal for us."

She slowly rounded the table and crossed the room to him. "You had no right to give what was mine to someone else," she said, seething between clenched teeth.

"Would you rather I let you keep it and turn it over to the authorities and let you explain what the hell you were doing with it? This was not a game to be played out your way, Darcy. Lives were at risk. These men will kill anyone who gets in the way of what they consider a million-dollar business. I could not take a chance on your life. I had warned you about Felder, but you wouldn't listen."

She lifted her chin and glared at him. "I could have handled him."

Did she not hear a single thing he said? Was she *that* stubborn? At that moment, something inside him snapped. Did she think she was indestructible? A damn superwoman? Someone with nine lives or something?

She had the nerve to step closer, get in his face. "You used me."

He rolled his eyes. "If that's what you want to think, go right ahead. But when you calm down you'll realize what I did was keep you alive."

"I don't see it that way."

"One day you will."

And before she could utter another word, he captured her mouth with his, went at it with a hunger that even surprised him. He knew she was mad, and it would probably take a long time for her to get over things. He'd heard that she could hold a grudge like nobody's business. But he'd had to take his chances. At least she was alive and wasn't in any danger.

Her heart was beating just as fast and intense as his, and he released her mouth long enough to draw in air that was drenched with her scent—an indication that she wanted him as much as he wanted her. Their gazes connected. At that moment, heat surged between them, so strong it nearly singed his insides.

He was definitely undone.

Without any type of control, he reached out and his hands ripped the silk gown off her body. He tossed the shreds of torn fabric to the floor. He was about to take her like she'd probably never been taken before. She was in his blood, in his mind. And heaven help him, the woman had somehow wiggled her way into his heart. And she had the nerve to assume that he would let her walk blindly into a dangerous situation?

He opened his mouth to say something and couldn't. What could he say? An admission of love probably wouldn't ring true to her ears right now anyway. So he would speak in a way that they communicated so well, with their bodies. Whenever they were inside each other they were of one mind, like two peas in a pod.

And Lord knew he needed to get all inside that luscious pod of hers.

Time passed that was measured by the beats of their hearts, a thrumming sound that enlarged his erection with every single tick of the clock. And then he growled, a primitive sound that rented the air, as he lowered his gaze to her naked body and saw everything he wanted, everything he needed, every single thing he loved and desired.

He unzipped his jeans and quickly stepped out of them, flung them aside. He reached out and drew her into his arms and hungrily captured her mouth once again and began mating with it in a frenzy that he felt down to his gut.

He felt the moment tension flowed from her shoulders, the moment she forgot all about her anger for the time being to concentrate on their kiss. It was just as fiery and passionate as all the others. He sank his fingers in her hair, felt her scalp and he deepened the kiss. It was as if he couldn't get enough of her, and the more he got, the more he wanted.

It seemed her hunger was just as intense as his was for her. She had taken him in her hand, was stroking his head and he felt his erection get larger beneath her fingers. She broke the kiss to breathe against his moist lips. "Hurry, York. I want you now!"

He heard the hunger in her voice. She might still be mad at him, but at the moment she would put her anger aside for this. So would he. There would be a lot to talk about later. And they would talk. Their future depended on an in-depth discussion and whether she wanted to accept it or believe it, they had a future. He now knew how it felt to love a woman to the point where you felt it in every bone in your body, and the need to become one with her was as vital as breathing.

She twisted out of his arms. "You're taking too long."

The moment her feet touched the floor she fell to her knees and took him into her mouth. And he let out a groan that nearly pierced the back of his throat. Immense heat surged in his testicles, and he felt them about to burst. He knew what she was doing. She wanted as much juice from him as his body could produce, and she was making sure there would be plenty by drawing out the lust in him.

If only she knew. There was no longer lust—only love.

When he felt his body almost explode in her mouth, he held back. And then without warning he dropped down on his knees and turned her around so that her back was pressed against his chest, her backside snug against his erection. And then his fingers felt around for her, felt the moist heat of her feminine mound, and like radar, the head of his erection found her and he eagerly thrust inside her.

"Hold on, baby. I'm going to ride you good," he whispered hotly, close to her ear, and she threw her head back and moaned with every single thrust into her body. He cradled her hips tight into the breadth of his thighs while he pounded into her and she begged for more.

He reached around her and let his fingers caress the tips of her breasts, cupped them in his hands and kneaded them to his heart's content. Her nipples were firm, erect, like pebbles in his hands. And he knew at that moment he would never, ever get enough of her and that Darcy Owens would be a permanent fixture in his life.

DARCY FELT YORK in every part of her body each time he pounded into her and then withdrew only to thrust back. He had her thighs spread wide, and she could feel the heat of his chest on hers. He was riding her in a way she'd never been ridden before, driving her insane with pleasure. And when she was to the point of detonating he would slowly ease out of her and in one hard thrust, find his way back in. Over and over again.

He was literally breaking her down with a need she only knew about since meeting him. She was desperate to have him, to feel him come inside of her, drench her with his release. Intense pleasure was thrumming, bursting to life in her feminine core, making her whimper, moan, and she knew soon he would have her screaming.

He thrust deeper inside of her, and she wondered how that was possible. It was as if his shaft had grown in length to accommodate her needs and desires. And then she felt her body buck into an explosion, detonate in rapture and she screamed. It seemed her scream torched something within him, and he rammed into her even deeper, just seconds before exploding.

"Yes! Yes! Yes!" She felt the essence of him spill into her, flood her in a thick, heated bath of release. It did something to her, and she sucked in a deep breath; with it came the scent of mingled bodies, tantalizing sex. This was pleasure beyond anything they had ever shared, and she knew that as much as she enjoyed it that this would be it for them. The end. He had deliberately kept her with him last night for a reason. It had nothing to do with wanting her but all to do with solving his case.

But she was convinced that now, at this moment, he

needed her. And she hoped he realized that when she left and would refuse to see him again. This was more than a parting gift. This would fuel his thoughts of what he would never have again.

She pushed the thoughts out of her mind when he kept going for another round and her body was in full agreement when another orgasm swept through her the same time it did him. She gloried in the feel of his hardness exploding into her once again, and she knew at that moment that she loved him. She loved every part of him, but because of what he'd done, her love would not be enough to consider forgiving him.

YORK WASN'T SURE what woke him up, but he opened his eyes and glanced at the clock on his nightstand. It was almost two in the afternoon. He closed his eyes wanting to remember every detail of what had happened between him and Darcy after breakfast. He smiled as he recalled every luscious detail of them making love— doggy style—on his kitchen floor, showering together afterward before falling into his bed and making love again.

He opened his eyes knowing the time had come for them to talk. He needed to explain why he could not have let her take part in exposing Felder. She meant too much to him, and there was no way he could have put her at any risk. He loved her.

His phone rang, and he quickly eased out of bed and glanced over his shoulder. The place where Darcy had lain was empty. He figured she had probably gotten hungry and had gone downstairs to grab something to eat. After all, it was way past lunchtime.

He grabbed for the phone and recognized the number. "Yes, Wesley?"

"Mission accomplished."

He smiled knowing what that meant. Once again, his men had done an outstanding job. He had wanted to be there, right in the thick of things, but he had been needed here to keep his woman out of trouble, out of harm's way. "I need full details. Give me a minute to get downstairs to my office, and I'll call you right back."

He hung up the phone and glanced around and immediately knew something was wrong. Darcy's overnight bag, the one that had been sitting next to his dresser, was gone. He quickly went into the bathroom and found his vanity cleaned of her belongings. It was as if she'd never been there.

Grabbing a robe, like a madman he tore out of the room and rushed down the stairs. But the house was empty. He moved back to the kitchen and saw the note she had scribbled and left on the front of his refrigerator. She had written the message with red lipstick.

*You got what you wanted. Now stay away from me!*

Fuming, he snatched the paper off his refrigerator and crushed it in his hands before tossing it in a nearby trash can. He growled deep in his throat. "Like hell I will."

# CHAPTER FOURTEEN

"IF YOU THINK finally getting around to admitting you had an affair with York in Jamaica will exonerate you from spending New Year's with me then you are wrong, Darcelle Owens."

Darcy rolled her eyes as she stood at the window in her New York house. It was two days after Christmas. If her parents had been surprised that she had shown up on their doorstep a few days earlier than planned, they didn't let on. And she knew her brothers had been itching to ask why her eyes were so swollen and her nose was red. Instead, they did what they usually did when she was a kid and would fly into the house crying from a boo-boo. They would cuddle her and try to kiss her hurt away.

And for a while she was able to get York Ellis out of her mind but not out of her heart. Instead of leaving her parents' home the day after Christmas as planned to head to Cavanaugh Lake, she had returned home to New York, determined to spend New Year's alone. She was not surprised that Ellie wasn't happy with that decision. Even after confessing and telling her friend everything, she wasn't budging.

"Did you hear everything I said, El?"

"Yes, I heard you. I saw York on Christmas Day in

Phoenix when everyone flew in for Eli Steele's wedding. He didn't give anything away."

That meant out of sight, out of mind. She hadn't expected anything other than that anyway. She wouldn't be surprised if Ellie mentioned he had brought someone. She wouldn't ask for fear of finding out something she didn't want to know, something that would break her heart even more.

"Besides, Darcy," Ellie broke into her thoughts and said, "I heard on the news about that case his company busted. From what I understand it was pretty dangerous, so I'm glad he kept you from getting involved."

Darcy frowned. "I could have handled my own."

"Are you listening to me? Those men would not have hesitated to hurt you if you tried to disrupt their plan."

But still…

"He used me," she said, determined for her best friend to see her point. She needed some sympathy here.

"And I'm sure you used him as well, so get over it, Dar, and catch a plane here."

She nibbled on her bottom lip. "I'm not ready to see him, and chances are he'll be there."

"Yes, he will be. But that shouldn't stop you from coming as well. It will be business as usual since you and York have always avoided each other anyway." There was a pause, then Ellie said, "Unless there is more to it than what you're telling me."

Darcy continued nibbling on her lip. "More like what?"

"Your true feelings for him. You sound more like a woman in love than a woman upset for not getting her way."

Darcy frowned. "I'm not in love with York!" Maybe

if she said it enough times she would be able to convince herself of that.

"Um, if you say so. Look, I need to get out of here and go to the grocery store, but I'll call you later. The weather around the lake is beautiful. You don't know what you're missing."

Darcy wiped a tear that had just fallen from her eye. "Yes, I do." *I won't be seeing York again anytime soon.*

"Is there a message you want me to give York when I see him?" Ellie asked.

"Of course not. He means nothing to me. I just don't like being played."

"Well, it sounds to me you're getting played confused with protected. I'll talk to you later, Darcy."

She heard the phone click in her ear and shook her head. What did Ellie know? She loved a man who loved her back. Some women had all the luck. Not ready to start her day yet, she tightened her robe around her and headed toward the kitchen to grab something for breakfast.

Since she'd planned to be away for the holidays, she hadn't put up a tree this year. But she had decorated the fireplace with garland and had even hung out the stocking her secretary's eight-year-old daughter had made for her last Christmas.

With a cup of hot chocolate and small plate of crescent rolls, she went back to the living room to enjoy her breakfast alone. Turning on the television, she saw that more arrests had been made in the case York and his people had cracked, including members of the Medina family. She even caught a quick glimpse of a handcuffed Damien being led away by authorities. Feeling even more depressed she turned off the television and finished her breakfast.

An hour or so later after cleaning up the kitchen, watering her plants and rearranging items in her cabinets, she decided she would take a nap. She might as well since she still had her nightgown on underneath her robe. She would treat this as a lazy day. She was headed toward her bedroom when her doorbell sounded. She figured it was her neighbor who'd been kind enough to collect her mail while she was gone.

Darcy glanced out the peephole and caught her breath. York!

Mixed emotions flooded her. On one hand, she was tempted to pinch herself to make sure what she was seeing was real. On the other hand, she wanted to open the door just to slam it in his face. It had been over a week since that morning when she had slipped out of bed to flee the island, needing to put as much distance between them as she possibly could.

Over a week.

And she hadn't heard from him. But she had to admit she had warned him to stay away from her. However, when did men like York do what they were told? And why was he here now? And why was a part of her glad that he was?

He rang the doorbell again, and she drew in a deep breath. "I can handle this," she muttered under her breath as she slowly removed the chain off the door. "And I can handle him," she added to assure herself as she slowly turned the knob.

The moment she flung the door wide and his gaze connected with his, she knew she'd assumed wrong. She couldn't handle him. He was standing there, leaning in her doorway. Her nose inhaled his cologne that mingled was the scent of primitive man. He was dressed in a pair of snug-fitting jeans and a blue pullover sweater, looking like the man he was, the man who'd captured her heart.

The man she loved.

"DARCY."

York studied the woman standing in front of him. Had it really been eight days since he'd seen her, eight days since he'd made loved to her, heard her scream? Even with that little annoying frown forming around her mouth, she looked beautiful. She looked as if she'd raked her fingers instead of a comb through her hair. It was tossed in disarray around her shoulders, and the early morning sun gave it a sun-kissed luster.

"Why are you here, York?"

That question was simple enough. "I came for you."

She looked surprised. "For me?"

"Yes."

She crossed her arms over her chest, and the gesture uplifted her breasts. Her cleavage looked good, and he bet her nipples looked even better. His tongue seemed to thicken at the thought of being wrapped around one.

"Didn't you get my note? The one I left on your refrigerator?"

He shrugged. "Yes, I got it."

"And?"

"And I figured you were mad when you wrote it."

An angry tint suddenly appeared on her cheeks, and she just stared at him. York suspected that she was probably wondering what would be the best way to throttle him.

"Yes, I was mad when I wrote it and I'm still mad."

He held her gaze. "Then I suggest you get over it." And before she could pick up her mouth that had nearly dropped to the floor, he took the opportunity to walk past her into her house.

"Wait a minute. I didn't invite you in, York."

He glanced over his shoulder. "You didn't have to."

She slammed the door with enough force to make the room shake. "Now, you listen here."

He turned around. "No, you listen here," he said back at her. "I've given you eight days, and I refuse to give you any more."

"Y-you g-gave me," she stuttered in anger.

"Yes. I would have come after you right away but I figured you needed to cool off and think things through. That gave me time to wrap up the case and attend Eli's wedding since I knew you'd already made plans to spend the holidays with your own family. But I talked to Uriel last night, and he mentioned you had changed your mind about coming to the lake."

"Not that it's any of your business, but I have," she said, lifting her chin.

"Then you need to rethink that decision." He knew if she had something handy to throw at him, she would.

She crossed the room, and he could see flames bursting in her eyes. "Just who the hell do you think you are?"

He couldn't help the smile that touched his lips. "York Celtic Ellis," he said, moving to cover the distance separating them. "The last man you slept with. The only man you'll be sleeping with from here on out." When he came to a stop in front of her, he said in an even huskier voice, "I'm also the man who loves you more than life itself."

She nearly stumbled backward. "No."

He advanced forward. "Hell, yes. You might not ask for my love, probably don't even want it, but you got it, lock, stock and barrel."

"No."

"Why are you in denial, Darcy? There was no way in hell I would let you go into danger of any kind. Now I understand what true love is. I know what it truly is to love a woman."

DARCY STARED AT HIM, nearly frozen in shock at his words. She had to take a few moments to inhale and slowly exhale to fight the emotions that tried overtaking her. Did he know what he was saying? Did he understand the full impact?

She studied his features and saw the intensity in the dark eyes staring back at her. Yes, he knew and understood. She felt the sincerity of his gaze all the way to her bones when he lowered his voice to say, "I hadn't planned on loving any woman this much. I honestly didn't think that I could. You proved me wrong, Darcy."

His words propelled her to move, take a step closer to him. "How wrong?"

"Very wrong. But in my heart I know I did the right thing keeping you out of that mess with Felder."

In her heart, she knew the same thing. She could finally admit that. Not only had he and the people who worked for him exposed the persons behind the black marketing of those movies but they were able to establish a strong connection between the death of York's former girlfriend and the Medinas.

For a moment she couldn't say anything. She just stood there and stared at him, and she knew Ellie had been right. Her stubbornness wouldn't let her see what was quite obvious. He hadn't played her but had protected her.

She inched a little closer to him and heard his sharp intake of breath when a hardened nipple protruding through her silk robe came into contact with his chest. Electric energy flared between them and sent a jolt to the juncture of her thighs. She could feel every beat of his heart. If her move surprised him, he didn't let on. Instead, he was watching her with those dark eyes as if waiting to see what she would do next.

Darcy didn't give him long to wait. She wrapped her arms around his neck and then leaned in closer to bring her lips just a breath away from his sensual mouth. "And I love you, too, York. So very much," she whispered.

By the way his brow arched, she could tell that he was surprised by that, and from the immediate curve of his lips she knew her admission had pleased him.

"But don't think for one minute that I'm a pushover," she warned.

"Such a thing never crossed my mind," he responded, wrapping his arms around her waist.

And then he leaned in to kiss her, and she didn't hesitate in kissing him back. The hunger was immediate, the desire apparent. She needed to be his woman, the one to whom he'd declared his love. She relayed it in her kiss with a relentless attack on his mouth. When he lifted her up into his arms and wrapped her legs around him, she knew it was just the beginning.

He broke off their kiss and stared at her. "Marry me."

She smiled. It wasn't a request. Instead, it sounded

more like a demand. Would he never learn? "I'll think about it."

She let out a sharp gasp when he jousted her up and all but tossed her across his shoulders like a sack of potatoes. "York, put me down!"

"Soon enough."

It was a short walk from her kitchen to her living room, where he gently placed her down on the sofa and joined her. She couldn't help but laugh as she stared up into his love-filled eyes. And just to think she had fled New York three weeks ago because of the cold, and now she was back in the city surrounded by intense heat.

"There's nothing to think about, baby. I refuse to spend any more time without you, so plan a wedding."

She knew he was dead serious and deciding they needed to spend their time doing things other than arguing. She asked, "Would a Valentine's Day wedding be soon enough?"

"Yes, if I have to wait that long."

She smiled up at him as she reached up to entwine her arms around his neck. "I'll just have to make sure it's a pleasurable wait."

And then she pulled his mouth down to hers.

# EPILOGUE

York SMILED DOWN at his beautiful bride thinking she had kept her word and it had been a pleasurable wait. But as of an hour ago, the waiting had come to an end. Darcelle Owens was now Darcelle Ellis and he couldn't be happier. However, a quick glance across the room at his remaining three single godbrothers showed they were just the opposite.

He inwardly smiled thinking sooner or later they would get over it. But then again, in a way he knew just how they felt. If anyone would have told him months ago he was headed for the altar he would not have believed them.

"Do you mind if I have a dance with my daughter-in-law?"

York chuckled as he glanced over at his father. His parents, like everyone else, had been shocked at his wedding announcement. "Sure, Dad. That will give me some time to go over and smooth three of your godsons' ruffled feathers."

His father laughed. "Good luck."

York placed a kiss on Darcy's lips. "I'll be back in a minute, sweetheart."

"I'll be waiting," she said, grinning up at him.

He couldn't help the smile that touched his lips. Darcy had been a beautiful bride and he would never forget how she'd looked walking down the aisle on her father's arms in her beautiful wedding gown. He was convinced the memory would remain in his heart forever.

York came to a stop in front of Winston, Zion and Virgil. He was glad to see all three of them, as well as Uriel and Xavier who were on the dance floor with their wives.

"So the traitor has decided to say a few words, has he?" Winston Coltrane asked in a clipped voice.

York nodded, smiling. He couldn't help it. He was definitely a happy man. "Don't hate, guys. Appreciate."

"Appreciate what?" Virgil asked, frowning. "The fact that another member of the Bachelors in Demand club has defected? I see no reason to jump for joy at that. I hope you know what you've done."

York glanced over his shoulder at his wife and couldn't help the way his gaze lingered on her awhile as she danced with his father. He then turned back to his three godbrothers. "Yes, I know what I've done, and honestly, I don't expect the three of you to understand things yet. But I have a feeling you will one day. Trust me when I say I have no regrets in getting married."

"But you and Darcy never got along," Winston reminded him.

"Yes, but we definitely get along now," York replied.

"I guess you're out of the club," Zion said, shaking his head smiling. "And to think you were the president."

Yes, he'd been the president, and a staunch supporter of bachelorhood. "Sorry, guys, but I got a feeling one of you will be next. Probably in less than a year from now," York said grinning.

Virgil frowned. "Marriage has turned you into a fortune teller, Y?"

"No, just a happy man who wants to spread the cheer.
I'll see you guys around…after my honeymoon."

Moments later he returned to Darcy and pulled her
into his arms. She tilted her head back and glanced up at
her husband. "They still don't look too happy with you."

He brushed a kiss across her lips. "I've been where
they are before. In fact, I'm the one who delivered the
news to Uriel at his wedding that he was no longer in
the club. Not that he cared."

York sighed and added, "Winston, Virgil and Zion
see the club's members dwindling and can't help wondering what the hell is going on. That's three of us
that have taken the plunge and three still remaining as
bachelors."

She nodded. "What do you think they'll do?"

He tightened his arms around her waist. "Fight love
like hell when it comes knocking on their doors. But in
the end they will be what I had become."

"And what is that?"

"A bachelor undone by a gorgeous woman destined
to be my soul mate. You can't fight love. And I can't
wait to see when they find that out."

Darcy glanced over at the three men, and thought she
couldn't wait to see as well. That would definitely be
interesting. She then glanced back at the man she had
married just hours ago. York was her hero and the man
who would always have her heart. Forever.

\* \* \* \* \*

# LET'S TALK

## *Romance*

For exclusive extracts, competitions
and special offers, find us online:

- facebook.com/millsandboon
- @MillsandBoon
- @MillsandBoonUK

**Get in touch on 01413 063232**

For all the latest titles coming soon, visit
**millsandboon.co.uk/nextmonth**

# MILLS & BOON

## MODERN

# Power and Passion

Prepare to be swept off your feet by sophisticated, sexy and seductive heroes, in some of the world's most glamourous and romantic locations, where power and passion collide.

# MILLS & BOON
## True Love
## Romance from the Heart

Celebrate true love with tender stories of
heartfelt romance, from the rush of falling in
love to the joy a new baby can bring, and a
focus on the emotional heart of a relationship.